SOMETHING SLAMMED INTO
THE BACK OF HIS HEAD ...

Kreiger couldn't move, couldn't breathe, couldn't talk. He was lying on his back on the kitchen floor, his arms behind him.

Somebody had slapped him as he entered the kitchen, he realized, then tied him up. Tight!

He heard something . . . a slight noise above. Somebody was here with him.

Terror struck him and made his eyes bulge. His chest heaved, his heels hammered. Very cold liquid—gasoline!—splashed over his body.

When he opened his eyes he saw something dark mushroom above him. An umbrella! And then light, impossibly bright, and exquisite pain.

The scream echoing inside his skull carried him like a dark bird into death.

The Torcher backed from the kitchen. As always there would be no fingerprints. The flames were high. Though the sprinkler system sprayed water, Kreiger lay under the umbrella, burning steadily.

Everything was as planned.

The Torcher took the elevator downstairs, walked slowly through the lobby, and went out.

Into the dark. Alone. Smiling.

<u>BOOK YOUR PLACE ON OUR WEBSITE</u>
AND MAKE THE
<u>READING CONNECTION!</u>

We've created a customized website just for our very special readers, where you can get the inside scoop on everything that's going on with Zebra, Pinnacle and Kensington books.

When you come online, you'll have the exciting opportunity to:

- View covers of upcoming books
- Read sample chapters
- Learn about our future publishing schedule (listed by publication month *and author*)
- Find out when your favorite authors will be visiting a city near you
- Search for and order backlist books from our online catalog
- Check out author bios and background information
- Send e-mail to your favorite authors
- Meet the Kensington staff online
- Join us in weekly chats with authors, readers and other guests
- Get writing guidelines
- AND MUCH MORE!

Visit our website at
http://www.kensingtonbooks.com

THE NIGHT WATCHER

JOHN LUTZ

PINNACLE BOOKS
Kensington Publishing Corp.
http://www.kensingtonbooks.com

For
Bob Murray

When you walk through the fire you will not be burned,
The flames will not set you ablaze.
—Isaiah 43.2

> Yet from these flames
> No light, but rather darkness visible.
> —Milton, Paradise Lost

ONE

January 2002

It had been gusty as well as bitterly cold most of the day in New York, but by nightfall the wind no longer blustered and danced through the canyons of Manhattan. The cold remained.

Hugh Danner had decided to stay in tonight. He'd stopped at the deli down the street from his apartment in the Ardmont Arms and bought a dozen eggs. He'd hard-boil a couple of them to eat with some cut vegetables he already had in his refrigerator. That, along with some dietary yogurt dip, would be his dinner. Danner was determined to lose a few pounds so his suits fit better.

Halfway to the Ardmont, he stopped walking and ducked into a doorway, where he removed a straight-stemmed meerschaum pipe from a pocket and stuffed its bowl with tobacco. He tamped the tobacco firmly with his thumb, added a bit more, and repeated the process. Smoking a pipe wasn't all that pleasurable to Danner, who'd quit smoking cigarettes two years ago, but he was trying to get used to it as a career move. Most of the senior partners at Frenzel, Waite and Conners smoked pipes in the firm's air-purified conference room, while associates and lesser employees had to elevator to the lobby and huddle outside the building if they wanted to smoke. Danner much preferred the conference room and concluded a pipe might be a valuable aid to promotion and access.

He decided he liked this latest brand of tobacco, which burned with a somewhat sweet taste. He was already enjoying the necessary constant tinkering with a pipe. It brought him attention and could be used to good advantage in a courtroom—provided the pipe was never lit.

He struck a match and stared hypnotized into the flame as it flared and sank, flared and sank, while he held it over the bowl and sucked on the pipe stem. Best not to make too many wheezing, lip-smacking sounds, like old Vickers. An art, Danner decided. There was definitely an art to pipe smoking, and he would master it.

Finally the tobacco was burning well, and he flicked away the paper match and stepped from the shelter of the doorway. Though it was cold, he'd stroll around the block and finish this smoke before going home. He was tightly bundled against the weather, liked to walk, and there was something comforting about the pipe's glowing bowl nestled between his thumb and forefinger, a tiny, tamed, and fiery force he possessed almost as if it were a pet.

After returning to his apartment fifteen minutes later, Danner hung up his coat with the dead pipe in its right side pocket. He'd just started the eggs on the stove when there was a slight sound behind him. Like a sudden intake of breath.

He didn't have time to turn around before an explosion of pain behind his right ear made him bunch his shoulders and bend forward at the waist, almost as if he were taking a bow. When he attempted to straighten up, everything around him suddenly started whirling with dizzying speed. He was vaguely aware of his left leg buckling.

He knew nothing more until he regained consciousness.

Danner lay quietly with his eyes closed, disoriented rather than afraid, trying to put the pieces together. *Did I have a stroke? A cerebral hemorrhage like my father?*

He couldn't be sure. He did know he couldn't move his body. It felt as if he was tightly bound. His arms were twisted around behind him, and with one exploring fingertip he could feel rough grout and the sharp edge of a kitchen floor tile. And he was wet. His clothes, his entire body. Why was he wet?

He knew he wasn't thinking clearly but could do nothing about it.

Cautious here . . . be cautious . . . Do nothing sudden. . . .

Slowly he opened his eyes, and immediately a stinging sensation made him clench them shut. As he did so, his vision registered movement nearby, and he knew he wasn't alone. He realized also that he *was* bound, tied up and lying on his kitchen floor.

And now he *was* afraid.

Don't panic! Oh, God, don't panic!

He forced his eyes open narrowly, trying to make out what was happening, trying to make some sense of this. His eyes still stung, bringing tears. Something must have splashed into them. He could see, but barely, blearily.

There was dark movement and a soft sound close above him, like the single unfolding rush of vast wings spreading wide. Against the looming darkness appeared a pinpoint of light. The light grew in size and intensity, then became brilliant.

It was so sudden. Light, pain, time, all converged in and around Danner. Someone was screaming. Einstein was right: time was relative. It could even stop. Time and pain were unending. The dark thing had carried Danner to an unimaginable height and dropped him into the sun.

He was burning on the surface of the sun and it would never end!

TWO

She thought about how large and strong his hands were, and gentle. He even punched the elevator button with a kind of softness, as if he knew his strength and didn't want to harm the mechanism.

Rica Lopez removed her gloves and stuffed them in the pockets of her wool coat, then stamped her feet. It was below freezing in New York City, and what was left of the snow had turned to hardened clumps of gray slush. The two police cruisers parked outside were splattered with grime, as was the unmarked Ford Victoria that Rica and Ben Stack had arrived in. A knot of people, probably residents of the building who were still uneasy about going back inside, stood off near one of the radio cars. They were huddled together as if for warmth and staring curiously at Stack and Rica, like a small herd of sheep wary of what might be wolves.

It took only seconds for a chime to sound in the high-speed elevator and the doors to slide open onto the thirty-first floor of the Ardmont Arms. Stack waited as he always did for Rica to leave the elevator first. He was that way with doors and turnstiles and every other known kind of egress and ingress, Rica thought with a smile. Ladies first. An old-fashioned kind of gent was Ben Stack, for an NYPD homicide detective.

It was easy enough to find the right co-op unit. There were three uniforms lounging outside its door, keeping an eye on the hall and elevators, waiting for further instructions from Stack or Rica, maybe trying to keep away from what was inside the apartment. As Stack and Rica walked along the hall's plush blue carpet, past gilded white apartment doors identical but for identifying brass numbers and letters, Rica began to smell the faint burnt scent wafting from the luxury co-op unit with the open door. Mingled with the burnt smell was the scent of something sweet, a distinctive odor Rica had experienced only once before, when a truck driver had been trapped in his burning cab after an accident on the Veranzano Bridge. The scent had clung to her clothes, her flesh, her dreams, for weeks. It still clung to her memory. Now here it was again. Seared human flesh.

The three cops in the hall knew Stack. Everyone on the force seemed to know Stack and admire him, the cop who could instantly calm a panicked child with his touch and smile, and who had taken down three Gambino family members in a Brooklyn restaurant, two with his service revolver, one with his fists.

"We got a homicide, sir," the youngest of the uniforms said. He had brown eyes, long lashes, hair so black it looked dyed. *Too pretty to be a cop,* Rica thought. *Maybe prettier than I am.*

"Bill and I got the call half an hour ago. Then Ray, here." He nodded toward one of the other three cops, a tall, laconic-looking man with a bushy gray mustache. "We handled traffic for the FDNY."

Stack looked at Rica, who shrugged.

"We didn't see any fire department downstairs," Stack said. "Just your cars, and some of the residents standing around looking confused."

"The FDNY already left," the uniform said. "The fire was out when they got here. They knew right where to go. I mean, which unit. This building's got a sophisticated alarm system tells 'em all that up front when they get the alarm forwarded. The door was unlocked so they barreled ass on in here. When they saw the body, they got out and turned everything over to us."

"Anyone been in since?"

"No, sir. Scene's clean except for some big footprints on the carpet from the fire department's boots."

"So what makes this a homicide?" Rica asked.

"All I know is, the fire department said it looked fishy. I mean, maybe it's not a homicide. Ray and me, we only gave it a look. Guy on the kitchen floor, cooked. That don't happen a lot."

"Not according to the Gallup Poll," Stack said.

Jesus! Rica thought, as even *here* Stack politely stepped aside and let her enter the apartment first. Miss Manners would approve, Rica thought. *When at a homicide scene, the gentleman always . . .*

"Looks like the kitchen's this way," Stack said, stepping in front of Rica now to take the lead. *The gentleman should always be first to look at a dead body.*

As they approached the short hall to the kitchen, their soles began making squishy sounds on the soggy gray carpet. The apartment's sprinkler system was unitized, as in many expensive co-ops where priceless art or furniture might be a room away from a simple kitchen or wastebasket fire; no need to saturate the entire unit and cause unnecessary water damage.

Stack broke stride as he entered the kitchen, as if what he'd seen gave him pause. Not like him, Rica thought.

She went in and edged around him so she could see better.

Great kitchen. The kind she would kill for. White European cabinetry, marble sink, stainless steel refrigerator, large window with a view of the park. It struck her that while this was a fairly expensive co-op (and what co-op wasn't in Manhattan?), it was the apartment's furnishings that made it seem so luxurious. Like the glass-fronted wine cooler with divided sections set at different temperatures for red and white wines; the glass and wrought-iron table; the array of expensive copper cookware suspended on hooks above a cooking island and breakfast bar.

She heard her own involuntary gasp as she gazed beyond Stack at what was left of the man on the floor. His body was blackened and curled, reminding Rica of nothing so much as overdone bacon. Most of his legs were burned away; she knew that could happen, a human being's fat could catch on fire and blaze like meat in a frying pan.

Stack and Rica put on their rubber gloves. Rica hadn't seen the results of a serious kitchen fire before, but that was what this looked like. A cooking accident, maybe a heart attack while the deceased had been holding a match, lighting a cigarette. Or maybe burning grease had leaped from a pan to his clothes that were particularly combustible. She glanced at the stove. No frying pan. But there was a pot without a lid, centered on a lighted gas burner; he had been preparing something to eat. She peered into the pot and saw a couple of eggs dancing around in boiling water. She didn't turn off the burner. It could wait for the techs.

She turned her attention back to what was on the floor.

"Ever seen anything like this?" Stack asked in a calm voice.

"Only in training films." Rica swallowed. "There's hardly anything left of him—or her."

"I'd guess him," Stack said, "by the size and what's left of the shape."

The corpse's hair had been completely burned away, leaving an odor much like that created when Rica used a too-hot curling iron. She felt her stomach kick.

"You gonna be okay with this?" Stack asked.

"Yeah!" she almost shouted at him. *Don't ever think I can't keep up with you, big boy.*

He glanced over at her and smiled, reading her mind. "So what do you think?"

"So far, it looks like an ordinary cooking accident. The sprinkler system did its job and put out the fire. Everything in this room and the hall is soaked."

"So why wasn't the body soaked before it burned to that condition?"

That was a good question. Rica moved beyond Stack and started looking around the kitchen, being careful where she stepped. Stack didn't move, looking almost straight up.

"There's a sprinkler head right over the body," he said. "The victim might as well have burned to death in his shower as lying where he is."

"He looks plenty wet now," Rica said, "but obviously he took his shower too late."

"That could explain it," Stack said.

Rica looked where he was pointing, then stood motionless, realizing what he meant.

Propped in the corner where the stove met the wall was a partially folded black umbrella. It was wet, like just about everything else in the kitchen, and it reminded Rica of a huge bat that had roosted there.

"It's been three days since we've had any snow or rain," Stack said.

Rica had been thinking the same thing. She understood why the sprinkler system hadn't extinguished the burning man before it was too late. Someone had stood over him, holding the umbrella so he'd burn bright and long. *"Madre de dios,"* she said. "Why would anyone do such a thing?"

"You've been a cop too long to ask that question," Stack said. "You know there's no answer that won't drive you crazy."

"One answer we have," Rica said, "is why the FDNY figured we had a homicide here. They must have seen the umbrella."

"Or something else," Stack said. "Look at that." He took her arm and gently led her closer to the body, as if escorting her onto a dance floor. He pointed. "See that blackened piece of cloth near what's left of the legs?"

He stepped carefully around the body, keeping his distance, as she followed.

"I doubt if he died in that position naturally," he said. "Or if he had a choice, with his arms behind his back."

"His arms and legs were bound," Rica said. "After he was tied up, then probably soaked with something flammable, he was set on fire."

"And whoever did it stood holding an umbrella over him, shielding him from the water from the sprinkler system, watching to make sure he burned to death and then some."

Rica tried to push away the vision of someone seemingly politely holding an umbrella over a fellow human being who was on fire. Her stomach lurched again. It was the smell, mainly. She went over to the window and was relieved to see it was the kind that could be cranked open. She worked the metal handle, leaned forward, and breathed in some high, fresh air.

"Ain't we just in a hell of a business?" she said, when she finally felt steadier and straightened up.

But Stack had already gone down to the street to use the detectives' band radio in their unmarked to call for the techs and the medical examiner, leaving her with the burned man and the questions that hung in the air like smoke.

THREE

The week after the Ardmont Arms fire, Stack walked into Mobile Response, located in the Eight-oh Precinct, with Rica on his heels. The Mobile Response Squad had been formed to conduct investigations the regular detective division couldn't adequately handle because of case overload. It was authorized to operate in all five boroughs and had come to be regarded as a crack outfit.

Stack enjoyed the special status, though he knew for a fact that case overload wasn't the only reason for the squad's existence. It sometimes served as a kind of pressure valve; the higher-ups stepped aside and let sensitive, potentially damaging cases find their way to the MR Squad in order to minimize any political or PR damage. It was a situation Stack could live with. Departmental politics had worn him down at the edges. But only at the edges.

Though he wasn't the ranking officer, the mood of the place was subtly altered by his arrival. Detectives at their desks seemed to bend to their work. Those standing and talking or drinking coffee sidled back to their desks or the swing gate to the booking area and either busied themselves or left. Stack took the work seriously, and when he was present, so did everyone else.

He was a big man, six-feet-two and 230 pounds. Now

in his forty-seventh year, he was beginning to thicken around the waist, but his shoulders were broad and his big hands made fists like rocks. Even without NYPD politics, he might have climbed through the ranks on ability or looks alone. His head was large, his forehead wide. His dark hair was parted on the side, cut short around the ears and beginning to gray. Level gray eyes studied everything calmly from beneath thick dark brows. His cheekbones were prominent and his jaw was firm with a cleft chin. If it weren't for a slightly crooked nose that hadn't been set right after one of the bad guys broke it with a beer bottle, he would have been merely handsome instead of interesting and . . . well, scary. To civilian employees and probationary patrolmen he was Detective Stack. To his fellow officers who had been through the wars with him, he was simply "Stack."

Sergeant Redd at the booking desk had told Stack that acting MR Squad Commander Jack O'Reilly wanted to see him. The regular commander, Lieutenant Vandervoort, was hospitalized after major surgery for colon cancer and would be gone for at least a month. If chemotherapy was required, Vandervoort would be gone longer.

"Still working on that hot one, Stack?" a detective-second-grade named Mathers, whose nickname, of course, was Beave, asked with a grin.

"You must mean me," Stack heard Rica say behind him. Mathers and several other officers laughed.

"Try to be more professional," Stack said, when he and Rica were out of the squad room and in the short hall, lined with file cabinets, that led to the commander's office.

"They don't take me seriously," Rica said.

"*I* take you seriously." Stack immediately wished he'd

phrased it differently. He was aware of how Rica felt about him, and he didn't want her misplaced affection to become obvious to the others in the department.

Rica, trundling along beside him, didn't answer. But he could *feel* her smiling.

She'd gotten more blatant about her fondness for Stack as his divorce from Laura progressed. Stack knew what Rica was thinking: Laura had finally had enough of being a cop's wife—which was true. And Rica, being a cop herself, was exactly what Stack needed. Not true, thought Stack. It wasn't that Rica was unattractive—she was petite, with dark hair and eyes, and with a firm and compact physique that prompted locker room speculation when she wasn't around. Not that she wasn't respected for her abilities. It was, in fact, Rica Lopez's remarkable talents as a homicide detective that kept Stack from having her transferred to break up their partnership.

Stack had never made any remarks about Rica when some of the other cops, male and female, were commenting on her looks. What worried him now was that, since word of his impending divorce had gotten around, he'd stopped hearing raunchy remarks about Rica. Apparently no one wanted to comment on her when he was present.

"You want me to go in with you, Stack?" Rica asked beside him as they approached the partly opened door to the commander's office.

"Sure" he said. "Maybe O'Reilly wants to chew some ass."

Stack opened the door all the way, then stood aside so Rica could enter first. As she moved around him he caught a whiff of her perfume. Lilacs or some such. When the hell had she had time to put that on? Cops weren't supposed to smell like lilacs.

The office was the only one in the precinct house that was carpeted—a thickly napped beige surface that ran wall to wall and stopped at a wooden baseboard that over the years had been painted countless times in the same bureaucratic pale green. The walls had wainscoting that disappeared behind a row of gray file cabinets. Two deep, brown leather chairs sat facing the large and ancient mahogany desk. All in all, a place where you might enjoy brandy and a good cigar while trying to avoid prison.

The wall behind the desk was paneled in oak. On it hung framed color photos of the New York police commissioner and the chief of police. Around the photos were mounted Vandervoort's plaques, medals, and framed commendations, along with photographs of Vandervoort shaking hands with pols and assorted department VIPs. Somehow a photo of O'Reilly shaking hands with the chief of police at an awards ceremony had found its way onto the wall. There was a lot of bright winter light streaming through the window and glancing off all the award plaques and photographs. It made O'Reilly's right cheek appear especially pockmarked. Old acne scars, Stack figured.

O'Reilly stood up behind the desk, a tall man with a lean waist, wearing a white shirt, blue suspenders, and dark, chalk-striped suit pants. The coat that matched the pants was on a wooden hanger looped over one of the hooks on a coatrack near a five-borough map pinned to the wall. Despite the acne scars—or maybe partly because of them—he had a face like a mature, perverted cherub's, with wary, rapacious blue eyes and receding ginger-colored hair, a lock of which was somehow always curled over the middle of his forehead. Stack had long ago pegged O'Reilly as a smart-ass with ambition, an eye for opportunity, and a blind spot the size of Soho. The assessment had proved accurate.

Obviously relishing his acting commander's role, O'Reilly nodded to them solemnly and motioned for them to sit in the leather chairs facing the desk. Then he sat down himself, folded his hands before him, and smiled faintly, as if posing for a photograph. Took the *acting* part of his title seriously, Stack thought. He glanced at Rica, who had looked over at him, and knew she was aware of his thoughts. Not the first time. Damned, intuitive little—

"So fill me in on the Ardmont Arms fire," O'Reilly said to Stack.

"The victim was Hugh Danner, forty-nine, single, a corporate tax attorney. He lived alone at the Ardmont for eight years. Well liked at Frenzel, Waite and Conners, his law firm. No known enemies so far. He'd been seeing a woman named Helen Sampson—"

"Seeing her?"

"Screwing her, by all accounts."

"Okay, just so we're clear."

Stack heard Rica sigh, then pressed on. "The Sampson woman owns a little bookshop in the Village. She's broken up, says she and the victim had been getting along well. That they'd always gotten along well."

"And I guess she told you two how much everybody loved Danner."

"More or less," Rica confirmed.

"Well, don't we know how people have different ways of showing love?" O'Reilly said, staring down at his desk.

A rhetorical question if ever Stack heard one.

He found himself also looking at the desk. It was uncluttered, barren of work in progress. Not at all like when the incredibly sloppy and overworked Vandervoort sat behind it.

"The ME said cause of death was shock and asphyxiation," Stack said.

O'Reilly looked up at him. "Asphyxiation? Like smoke inhalation?"

"He breathed in flame when his shirt was on fire. It burned away his lungs."

O'Reilly looked disgusted. "Mother of Christ! What a way to die!"

"The lab said the fire was started with, and helped along by, an accelerant. A combination of ordinary gasoline mixed with household cleaning fluid that makes it thicker. A detergent. That way it sticks to the body and won't go out as long as there's an oxygen source, sort of like napalm."

"The lab's trying to figure out the brand name of the cleaning fluid," Rica said.

O'Reilly didn't look at her. "And this Hugh Danner was tied up before he was set on fire?"

Stack nodded. "With strips of cloth, apparently. Most of it burned away, but not in time to help Danner."

"So the guy was an attorney, solid citizen, all that crap," O'Reilly said. "And it's a dangerous thing, a fire in a high-rise building. Whoever used Danner as kindling put a lot of other tenants in peril. I'd like this one cleared from the books as soon as possible."

Before Vandervoort gets back, Stack thought. He said, "We're canvassing the building, and we'll talk some more to the doorman, but so far nobody's been much help. A search of the apartment didn't turn up anything that seemed relevant. No drugs, no names of known felons in Danner's address book. The techs say there was nothing unusual on his computer: some business correspondence; some downloaded soft-core porn; a stock and bond portfolio worth about a quarter of a million."

"Soft-core porn?"

"Nothing that'd move you, unless you like to watch bare-breasted women operating jackhammers." Stack was pretty sure he heard Rica roll her eyes. "There were no messages on his answering machine. Gold cuff links and a gold chain in a dresser drawer in the bedroom, and Danner was wearing a Rolex when he burned. It doesn't appear the apartment was burglarized, but since we don't know exactly what Danner might have had in there, we can't be sure. His lady love, Helen Sampson, is going to look around the place with us today, take an inventory, and see if anything might be missing."

"Good," O'Reilly said. "You two keep me posted." He stood up, signaling the end of the conversation.

"Will do, sir," Stack told him. He and Rica stood also.

As they stepped into the hall, Stack closed the door behind them.

"What the hell was all that about?" Rica asked beside Stack, as they were walking back toward the squad room. "Does he think we're just wandering around with our thumbs up our asses?"

"He might," Stack said, "but what I think it was really about was O'Reilly wishing he were Vandervoort."

And where, Rica wondered, *is that going to take us?*

FOUR

June 1997

Vernel Jefferson had screwed his neighbor's ten-year-old daughter. He'd been arrested twice before for child molestation, never for anything violent done against an adult. Sweating like Niagara there in the dark tenement hall, Rica didn't think she'd need her gun. Her partner Wily Stanford was at the other end of the hall, knocking on Jefferson's apartment door so he could arrest him. Jefferson figured to cave like most child molesters and come along quietly, especially since he was in his sixties and only slightly over five feet tall. Rica the rookie cop was breathing hard, nervous, but she figured this was nothing she couldn't handle.

The tenement hall smelled like a blend of every cooking spice known to man, with an underlying stench of stale urine. There was a single dim overhead lightbulb halfway down the narrow hall. Stanford, at the distant end of the hall, was a barely visible figure despite his six-foot frame.

Rica heard him knock on the door again, louder. "Mr. Jefferson, open up! This is the police!"

There was no way out of the fifth-floor apartment except through Stanford or down the fire escape. Another uniformed cop was waiting down at street level if Jefferson decided to bolt that way. Rica was insurance in the unlikely event the little pervert would somehow manage to get past Stanford.

Another apartment door opened near the middle of the corridor. A dark woman with cornrow hair stuck her head out and peered up and down the hall. When she looked Rica's way, Rica silently motioned for her to get back inside. The woman nodded, drew back out of sight, and the door closed. Stanford pounded on Jefferson's door now, impatient. It was damn near the end of the shift.

Rica tightened her perspiring grip on her baton as she watched Stanford hoist his huge foot with its size-twelve shoe and prepare to kick in the door.

At first she thought the explosion was the sound of Stanford's foot shattering the door, incredibly loud. When she saw Stanford hurled back against the wall, she thought she might have heard a shot. Then she realized the sound she'd heard was the apartment door shattering, but not because Stanford had kicked it in.

Someone inside had kicked it out, and with great force.

"Look out, Rica!" Stanford shouted.

The form that broke from the apartment was massive and moving fast. The guy wasn't built like Vernel Jefferson. He should have been an NFL linebacker. He came toward Rica head down, legs and arms pumping. She gulped and moved to stand in the center of the hall, wielding her baton, holding her ground.

The man rushing toward her grinned as he flashed beneath the dim lightbulb.

The hell with this, Rica thought, and drew her 9mm handgun from its holster.

"Halt! Police! Halt!" Rica's command sounded feeble even to her.

But miraculously he did halt. He skidded to a stop about ten feet from her, his face stiff, his bulging eyes fixed on the gun.

Then his grin returned.

"Sheeeeit!" he said. He was wearing a sleeveless gray undershirt to show off his muscles and baggy pants. His chest was heaving and he blew breath like a cornered bull as he shot a glance back at Stanford, who was just now getting to his feet, then back at Rica. His smile broadened and he began strolling toward her with a deliberate, casual gait. She couldn't help thinking he was a handsome guy. Great smile. She smelled his sweat and fear as he got closer. "You gon' be a good lil' pussy," he said softly. "I jus' know it."

And he did know it. Rica was frozen. She could only stare at him as he approached her, then gingerly removed the 9mm from her hand. Then oddly, for he was on fleeing fugitive time, he reached out and squeezed her left tit. Not hard, and his fingers danced in a quick massaging motion as he withdrew his hand.

The man sensed greater danger from behind and turned to aim and fire at Stanford, who was running toward him, still moving unsteadily after being struck by the exploding door.

That was when Rica's paralysis passed. She used the baton in her left hand to strike the man hard on the side of his head. Then she switched hands and clubbed him on his right collarbone. The crack of the bone was something she still dreamed about.

The gun dropped to the floor.

He didn't attempt to pick it up. Instead he turned slowly

toward her. He looked betrayed, and damned if she didn't feel as if she *had* somehow betrayed him.

"Nigger bitch!" he said, kind of surprised, and reached for her.

Training took over. She used the baton as a jabbing weapon, driving its tip deep into the man's stomach just beneath the sternum. Warm breath that carried the stench of bourbon whooshed out of him as he doubled over. She brought the club down twice on his head, driving him to the floor, knocking him into a daze if not unconsciousness. As she bent over him in the dim hall to wrestle his wrists behind him and click on the handcuffs, she picked up her gun and slid it back in its holster.

"That's good fucking work!" Stanford said, as he reached the fallen suspect and got down on one knee to make sure she didn't need help.

"I dunno," Rica said, breathing hard. "This can't be Jefferson."

Stanford laughed. "Whoever he is, he didn't want any part of the law. Maybe he's Jefferson's brother."

In fact, he turned out to be Jefferson's cousin and dealer, who'd just finished administering a beating to Jefferson for molesting his girlfriend's young daughter and for not paying money owed on a drug delivery. Vernel Jefferson was unconscious inside the apartment. Cousin Jamal Jefferson hadn't found Vernel's stash, which earned Vernel a possession charge to go along with the child molestation. There were three active warrants on Jamal the dealer, one of them for a homicide in Queens.

It turned out to be a productive night's work.

If Stanford had seen what happened with Rica's gun, he never mentioned it, at least to her. Maybe the hall was too dim. Maybe he'd been woozy from getting cracked with the door and knocked back against the wall. Definitely he might have been shot and killed that night, and it would have been Rica's fault. Jamal the dealer didn't mention the gun during his trial two months later, possibly out of embarrassment at being brought down by a five-foot-two female cop.

Rica knew she'd somehow gotten a second chance.

At Blender's Lounge the night after the shooting, where some of the cops from the Eight-oh went to drink when off duty, they toasted Rica. The place was noisy and crowded, warm with so many bodies.

Ed Kaline, still in uniform, raised a mug of beer high and whistled shrilly for silence. "To Rica Lopez!" he shouted. "A small cop with a big blue heart!"

Everyone applauded and shouted. Rica felt great, but at the same time wondered if she should have said something about the gun. It didn't figure anyone would ever find out. Even if Jamal Jefferson mentioned it at his trial, who would believe him? Anyway, it wouldn't be mentioned in court. How he was captured had no bearing on his case.

Rica forced her concerns aside, grinned, and drank.

She'd probably drunk a bit too much when a tall, handsome plainclothes detective came up to her and patted her on the back. She'd heard about him, seen him around, knew his name was Stack. Even then, the other cops seemed to think he was something special, though she didn't know why.

"Congratulations on a fine collar," he said with a smile that suggested he meant it.

Rica thanked him and he introduced himself.

"I was lucky," she said.

"No," he told her.

"I was scared," she admitted.

He nodded and looked closely at her. There was something about his calm gray eyes that held her. He rested a big hand gently on her shoulder and his voice was soft and only for her. "Everybody, especially when they're new, gets scared, does something wrong. The best of them make it right. I think you'll be among the best of them."

That's when she realized he knew about the gun, and that he wasn't the only one who knew. There were few secrets in the badged and blue, mostly male world she had entered and had now become a part of, peopled by fellow professionals who understood in ways only other cops could comprehend.

That was the night Rica became a better cop. The night the blood coursing through her veins turned blue.

Looking back on it, she realized it was also the night she fell in love with Ben Stack.

FIVE

The sweet, burnt smell remained in Hugh Danner's co-op unit. Rica wondered if it would ever leave completely.

Helen Sampson said, "I don't want to go into the kitchen."

"You don't have to," Rica assured her. "We only want you to look around, see if anything might be missing or out of place."

"Not in the kitchen."

Rica exchanged glances with Stack. "Of course not."

Helen Sampson was wearing a simple black dress and black flat-heeled pumps. Her straight blond hair was lank and looked greasy, and it had dark streaks, though Rica was sure she was a natural blonde. She was a gaunt, attractive woman with pale blue eyes, but she looked almost unbearably weary. Her grief was dragging her down. She glanced around her, then began walking slowly about in the living room, now and then running a finger lightly over things as if checking for dust, or maybe making sure she was among real objects and not in a bad dream.

"Approximately how many times have you been here?" Stack asked her.

She paused and looked at him as if he'd awoken her. "I'm not sure . . . a dozen, maybe more."

He smiled at her and made a palms-up motion with his hands held low, gently urging her to continue.

She resumed her seemingly aimless slow roaming, her haunted eyes constantly moving.

"Do the wall hangings look the same?" he asked.

She nodded but said nothing.

"Nothing missing? I mean, did Mr. Danner have any valuable art?"

"He didn't like art," she said. "A decorator did the apartment a few years ago, and Hugh just left things the way they were."

She left the living room and went down the hall to the main bedroom, moving along the wall as far away from the kitchen door as she could, actually holding her hand up to her eyes to block her view into the kitchen in case she might accidentally glance in that direction.

In the bedroom she went immediately to the bed and ran her hand over the wooden footboard, then touched the mattress softly with her fingertips. She clenched her hands together as if squeezing something between them and turned in a slow circle.

"It all looks the same," she said. She walked to the bureau, where there was a framed photograph of her and Danner standing before what looked like a lake with boats in the distance. There were no leaves on the trees, and both of them wore jackets and were smiling, huddled tightly together. Danner had his arm around her waist and she was clutching his wrist with both her hands, as if she didn't want him ever to release her.

"May I take this?" she asked, floating out a hand and touching the frame.

"We'll let you know when," Rica told her, "and we'll make sure that you get it."

"Hugh didn't have any family he cared about other than his ten-year-old daughter in Oregon. I know he had a sister in Philadelphia, but they never saw each other and hardly even spoke except on birthdays. She wouldn't want a photo like that. No one else would want it."

"I wouldn't think so," Rica said.

"I think we were going to be married."

"Had he asked you?"

"No, but I'm sure he was going to."

"Miss Sampson—" Stack began.

"Helen."

"Of course. Helen. You're an attractive young woman. Might there be somebody in your life who was jealous of Danner's involvement with you? Who might have resented it and turned to violence?"

She seemed to take the question seriously, chewing her lower lip for a moment as she searched her memory, then shook her head no. "In the relationship I was in before I met Hugh," she said, *"he* left me."

"What about Danner's former wife?" Stack asked.

"That was long over. They weren't even good friends. Would never have had anything to do with each other except for their daughter."

"There's a woman's dress and some blouses and slacks in the closet," Rica said.

"Mine," Helen Sampson said.

Rica smiled. "I thought so. They looked like your size."

Helen Sampson went to a modern, glass-topped dresser

in a corner and opened and closed a few drawers. Then she surprised them by gripping the dresser with both hands and shoving it to the side. It was on rollers and moving it had taken little effort even for so slight a woman. "Did you know that was there?' she asked, pointing at something low on the wall.

Stack walked over and looked. A small safe with a combination lock was set in the wall about a foot above floor level and had been concealed by the dresser. "No," he said. "Do you know what Danner kept in it?"

Helen Sampson shrugged. "I think just papers and such. He was an attorney, you know."

"Yes, we did know about him being an attorney."

"He had to put up with all those cruel lawyer jokes. So unfair."

"Would you happen to know the combination?" Rica asked.

"I'm sorry, I don't."

"That's okay," Rica said. "We'll have a locksmith open it."

They went into the smaller bedroom Danner had used as a home office. There was a wooden desk and chair, a bookshelf containing mostly reference books, a black metal file cabinet, and over in the corner a treadmill that looked brand-new. A stack of *Money* magazines was in another corner, and near it a pair of New Balance running shoes and a wadded pair of socks. The carpet was spotted with what appeared to be coffee stains. Stack's carpet had similar stains; they were from pacing with a coffee cup while the mind was elsewhere. A large *Far Side* calendar was tacked to the wall behind the desk. Apparently the decorator hadn't made it into this room.

"It was always like this," Helen Sampson said, as if in apology.

She glanced into the gleaming tile bathroom. "The same as usual," she said.

On the way back to the living room, Stack made it a point to stay between her and the kitchen doorway.

"I guess I wasn't much help to you," she said.

"We know now that nothing's been moved around or stolen, and that there's a safe," Stack told her. "I'd say you helped us a lot, dear. We're grateful to you."

She managed a kind of half smile that faded fast. "I guess I won't be coming back here."

"You don't have to," Rica said.

"I mean, I'll probably never see the place again. I don't even know if I'll want to. It's so damned unbelievable about Hugh . . . so fucking unfair!"

Rica hoped she wasn't going to start sobbing.

Stack moved to Helen Sampson and rested a hand softly on her shoulder. "Are you going to be okay?"

She nodded and swiped at an eye with a knuckle, then drew a deep breath.

"Want us to go downstairs with you?" Stack asked.

"No, no, I'm fine now, really. . . ."

He opened the door to the hall for her, giving her a comforting smile, a final pat as he withdrew his big hand from her shoulder. "You sure?"

"Sure."

"If you're not going to be okay, or if you think of anything you might want us to know, you call us, you promise?"

"Of course I will."

"Thank you, Helen."

Rica watched Helen Sampson go, admiring the way Stack had handled her. The thing was, he did feel compassion for the woman. The other cops at the Eight-oh thought he simply had a knack for schmoozing along witnesses and victims, but Rica knew better.

"Let's get somebody here to dust that safe for prints, then get it open," he told her.

But she was already moving toward the phone.

They'd had time to eat lunch at a diner around the corner before the techs finished dusting the safe and the locksmith arrived to open it.

Back in Danner's apartment, Rica could still taste pastrami. It didn't go well with the lingering scent of Hugh Danner.

The locksmith pronounced the safe one of high quality, then used a carbide-bit drill to open it within minutes while Stack and Rica stood watching.

When the man was finished, he gathered his tools and bustled from the apartment, leaving it to one of them to open the safe door more than the few inches he'd eased it out to make sure the lock was destroyed.

Stack waited until Rica was out of the way, then stood to the side himself and slowly pulled the small, thick steel door the rest of the way open; you never knew about spring guns or explosives that might be triggered to foil safecrackers.

But there was only one item in the safe—a roll of bills held tight by a rubber band.

"Isn't *this* suspicious?" Stack said.

Rica didn't know if he was doing some kind of TV cop act, putting her on.

He withdrew the money, then sat on the edge of the bed and counted the bills, mostly hundreds and twenties.

"Twenty thousand dollars even," he said, looking up at Rica. "The bills have all been in circulation awhile and appear unmarked."

Rica shrugged. "He was an attorney, you know." Being unfair. Like life.

Stack dreamed of Laura that night. They were making love frantically, joyfully, rolling in a bed of soft green money. Then the money was on fire, the flames sweeping toward them. Stack didn't want to part from Laura. They didn't want to release each other but they had to in order to survive. If they stayed together, they would burn alive.

It was wrong! Stack thought, sobbing in his sleep. It wasn't fair!

They would burn alive!

He awoke as if breaking the surface of a lake, finding himself alone in his cold bed.

SIX

Myra Raven sat on the one piece of furniture in the co-op unit, a cheap imitation French provincial chair, and waited for them. Ordinarily she would have assigned one of her agents to show the unit, especially considering its modest price, but she'd liked the Markses immediately when they'd come into the office. Both of them. The woman, Amy—girl, really—was pretty and very pregnant. Her husband, Ed, a gawky kind of young guy with a shy smile, interested Myra right away when she saw his plain black shoes, the curved mark on his forehead just below his hairline. She recognized cop's regulation shoes, and the semipermanent crease left by a cop's blue six-pointed garrison cap. Her first husband, the cop, the only man she'd really loved, had been struck and killed by a passing car when he was helping a woman change her tire on the highway shoulder.

Years ago, Myra thought. Worlds ago.

She got up and paced to make herself feel better. Then she wandered into the tiny bathroom and looked at herself in the mirror. The light was harsh but she still looked okay. Her cosmetic surgeon, Dr. Preller, had removed exactly the right amount of fat from the fleshy part between her eyebrows and eyes, giving her a wider-eyed, younger look. Not only that, for insurance purposes the doctor had classified the process as necessary rather than elective, a procedure to restore her peripheral vision.

This latest improvement made Myra, who at fifty-four was still rather attractive, appear somewhat less predatory. Still there was the angular bone structure, the smooth, taut flesh from too many visits with Dr. Preller, and the prominent chin (an insert) and perfectly straight nose. Her skinned-back blond hairdo was perfect, as it should have been at the price paid to her hair stylist, and her makeup was thick to hide faint surgery scars. She'd heard her looks described as brittle, herself described as a bitch. The remarks hurt her deeply, but at least she knew she was a successful bitch. In business, anyway. Her personal life, her interior life, was mostly pain. The more youthful image in the mirror didn't mean she was actually younger, or that she could live over the years of tragic luck and wrong decisions. Still, it was a younger Myra who looked back at her; she would have to settle for the illusion.

The cosmetic surgery was another reason she'd taken the appointment with the Markses. She'd been sitting around the office, still wearing dark glasses while her eyes healed completely and the bruises faded, and she was going crazy needing something to do.

The Markses were something to do. The husband reminded her of her early marriage days. The young wife with her slight underbite (less severe than Myra's, before she had it repaired years ago) reminded Myra somewhat of herself when she was in her twenties. When she heard Amy, the wife, remark that she was expecting twin girls within a month, Myra had made up her mind. One of Myra's early regrets in life was that she hadn't borne children. She didn't like them, in fact. Told herself over and over that she didn't like them or want them, until finally the regret went away. Children were like—

The doorbell chimed.

Myra, who owned and managed the most successful real estate agency in Manhattan, hurried into the living room like an eager rookie salesperson and pressed the intercom button.

"Ed and Amy Marks," the husband's voice declared, made faint and hollow by the intercom.

Myra buzzed them up.

She was smiling, as she trained all her agents to do, when she opened the door.

The Markses weren't smiling. They looked apprehensive. And appropriately so, since they were considering embarking on the largest investment of their young lives.

"So wonderful to see you again!" Myra said. She stepped back and waved an arm in an encompassing sweep. "This is it!" she said of the 800-square-foot unit. It was the smallest in the building, but she knew it had what the Markses wanted and needed: a separate, second bedroom for the twins.

"It doesn't look very big," Ed Marks said.

"Two bedrooms, though, darling." Amy coming through for Myra.

"And it boasts a wonderful eat-in kitchen!" Myra said. "These units have quality cabinetry, and the refrigerator is brand-new. The stove's electric, so you can warm those baby bottles to exactly the right degree."

"Great view," Ed Marks said. He'd wandered over to the wide window.

"Look," Myra said, "I wouldn't try to kid you, this is a gorgeous unit, but it's smaller than what you probably had in mind. Still, like Amy said, it has separate bedrooms. The kitchen and bath are terrific, and if the payment is a stretch, you don't have to buy all your furniture right away. The girls will need room to crawl." Myra threw up her hands and laughed. "Don't believe me, look around and the place will either sell itself or it won't."

Amy assessed her calmly and after a while nodded. Maybe there was something operating inside that pretty young head. Potential, such as Myra had at that age. She hoped Amy would see it in herself and do something more with it than simply raise offspring.

Myra knew when not to talk. She stayed in the living room and admired the view from the window while Amy and Ed took a walk around the place. She could hear them talking in the main bedroom. Couldn't understand what they were saying but knew by their tone that Ed was sold and was now trying to talk Amy into it.

"What about price?" Ed asked, when they came back into the living room. Amy, tired from lugging around her pregnancy, sat down in the one chair. A good sign; she was prepared to settle in and negotiate.

"There's wriggle room," Myra said in a confidential tone.

She listened carefully while Ed Marks made the offer and Amy watched with her somber brown eyes.

"It might be doable," Myra said. "What about down payment?"

"No problem there," Ed said. "My father died last year

and I have a small inheritance. That's the only reason we might be able to afford this place on a cop's salary."

A cop only a year out of the academy, Myra thought. Ed had mentioned that and the inheritance before and apparently forgotten.

"You are offering twenty percent off the asking price," Myra pointed out.

"If the owner's as eager to sell as Myra thinks," Amy said from behind her pregnant bulk in the tiny chair, "he should make a counter offer."

Myra grinned at her. "That's exactly the way it works, dear."

A cricketlike chirping erupted from her Coach handbag on the floor near the chair where Amy sat. Myra excused herself and drew her cell phone from the purse, then carried it into the short hall to the bedrooms. She wasn't surprised by the interruption. Louella at the office had been told to call her at this time.

Myra asked Louella what was happening at the office, listened carefully, then gave her instructions.

As Myra walked back into the living room, slipping the phone back into her purse, she said, "Believe it or not, that was the owner. I made your offer. You have your counter offer."

Ed stared at her. Amy squirmed and sat back in her chair. They both looked scared.

"You're lucky if you want to be," Myra said, and quoted him a price ten percent below asking.

Amy wanted to speak but instead looked up at Ed, who was staring at the carpet.

"I'll go into the next room," Myra said, "and let you two discuss this privately."

"There isn't any need," Ed said. Man of the house, already looking around in a proprietary way. "We'll take it at that price."

Myra looked at Amy. "Are you sure?"

Amy grinned and nodded yes. She began to cry. Ed leaned over and kissed her. Myra had had about enough of it. But the deal was good; she knew the owner, who was pressed by time before moving out of the country, would gladly accept the offer.

"What happens next?" Amy asked.

"One of the things that happens," Ed spoke up, "is that the co-op board has to approve us."

"He's right," Myra said, "but believe me, you two won't have any problems there. Unless Ed is secretly the city's crime czar."

"Not yet," Ed said with a grin.

Myra laughed. "If you two have the time, we can go back to the office now and write up the contract."

Again Amy looked to Ed.

"We'll make the time," he said.

"This place," Amy said when they were leaving, "This day! Everything's absolutely perfect!"

"Days like that are so rare," Myra said, thinking hormones, young love, pregnancy. It was all so much more complicated than contracts, title searches, and closing statements. She decided she was glad to be where she was in life, and glad for Amy, where she was.

Myra smiled most of the way down in the elevator. The world seemed to be in order. Young Ed Marks had his castle in the air. Mrs. Marks had her family and home. Myra had her tubal ligation and her deal. And would never change a diaper.

SEVEN

January 2002

Eden Wilson was at Rollie's Restaurant celebrating her sixth birthday. The clown who blew up balloons and twisted them and put them on everyone's nose like funny red noses had just left. Eden's school friends, Letty and Carmelle and Vincent, were at the table with her. Everyone had ice cream and cake and it was wonderful. Mommy and Daddy were at the next table, but they were leaving the kids alone unless someone acted bad. Colored hats, presents, things if you pulled on a string they went pop and shot little red pieces of paper . . . They scared you at first, but only at first. Eden's favorite present was the doll with the blond hair that her mommy said looked so much like her.

Nothing had ever been this much fun.

At the next table, Eden's parents forgot about their half-eaten pieces of chocolate cake and watched their daughter enjoy herself. Her golden laugh was marvelous. If only she could laugh like that from time to time all through her life.

If only her future could be as wonderful as her sixth birthday party.

* * *

Stack watched Rica perch on the edge of his desk, arching her back and trying to look seductive. Succeeding. He pretended not to notice. Mathers, walking past the desk, glanced over and smiled. Stack decided Rica was getting to be a real embarrassment.

He mused again on the idea of transferring her out of Homicide, save himself the trouble that was sure to happen. On the other hand, she *was* undeniably sexy, and he was in the process of getting a divorce. What would it hurt if they had a bit of fun? Other than destroy their working relationship, threaten the terms of his divorce settlement, ruin both their careers, and take from him the thing he loved most in what he knew was a perverse way—the Job.

". . . no prints other than Danner's on the safe," she was saying.

Stack hadn't thought there would be. Whoever killed Danner probably didn't know the wall safe was there. And nothing in the apartment seemed to have been stolen or even rearranged.

"Any trace on the bills?" he asked.

Rica shook her head no, causing the light to change in her dark eyes, to soften them. He knew she was only half Hispanic, on her father's side. Her mother had been a Swede working as a maid on Park Avenue, and had died five years ago from ovarian cancer. Rica was short for Erica. He didn't think she'd told anyone else at the Eight-oh about that; he seemed to be the only one who knew.

"No record on the serial numbers," she said. "The bills appear to be clean. Danner himself appears to be clean. Upstanding attorney, or seems to have been. Kept up on his child support payments to the ex-wife in Oregon, served on the board of his co-op, gave regularly to charity as well as political contributions."

"To which party?" Stack had been absently tapping a pencil point on the desk. Rica was almost imperceptibly pumping a shapely, crossed leg to the rhythm. He stopped with the pencil.

"Both parties," she said. "Danner was a man who hedged his bets. Everybody seemed to like him at least okay. And you saw how broken up his girlfriend was."

"Yeah. So he was a Mr. Nice Guy."

"Well, yes and no. A few people described him as distant, kind of arrogant and standoffish."

"A Jekyll and Hyde?"

"Nothing like that. A Mr. Nice Enough Guy."

"And he had twenty thou in cash in a wall safe when he died."

Thou. Rica wondered if anyone other than Stack had said *thou* since Frank Sinatra died. "When you think about it, it isn't *that* much money, Stack."

"I guess not, to a man like Danner. But nobody at his law firm or who knew him socially seems to know where he might have obtained it."

"Might have sold some stock."

"No record of it with his broker."

"Bet on a horse and won."

"Possible."

"Or collected a fee from a client without the knowledge of his law firm."

"More possible. The sort of thing I'd like to believe, since it'd provide a motive."

"Hm . . . the partners in an established law firm get together and decide to murder one of their own who screwed them out of twenty thousand dollars. Sounds real reasonable, Stack."

He wished she'd take her sarcasm and—

Rica shifted position on the desk, flashing some thigh and jumbling his thoughts. "I don't think whoever killed Danner did it for the money, Stack. If that had been the motive, the apartment would have been tossed, and there was no sign of a search."

"What had he been working on?" Stack asked. "As a lawyer."

"Most recent court case, he defended one Raymond Masters on a drug possession charge. Pro bono."

"Mr. Nice Enough Guy again," Stack said.

"Not necessarily. Danner's field was corporate law. He had the Masters case because a certain amount of pro bono work is required at his law firm."

"That's . . ." Stack glanced at his notes ". . . Frenzel, Waite and Conners. Anybody talk with them?"

"Them?"

"The three partners."

"The last one died in nineteen-forty. That's the kind of law firm it is, very traditional. Everybody's in a contest to see who has the rattiest briefcase. Most of the younger lawyers probably don't think that way, but they pretend."

"You seem to know a lot about lawyers."

"My divorce," Rica said. "You'll learn."

"How long have you been divorced?"

"Thirteen years. I was young and dumb, but I wised up fast. Lawyers haven't changed."

Stack thought about his own divorce attorney, Gideon

Fine. He wasn't anything like Rica had described. Or was he? . . .

"We should talk to Raymond Masters," Stack said. "Where's he being held?"

"He's not. He beat the rap. And it would have been his third conviction, the first two for beating the hell out of his wife. Illegal search. Danner did a good job defending him."

"We'll locate Masters and talk to him," Stack said. "See if we can find out what kind of confidences passed between attorney and client."

"You smell motive?"

"Maybe. A lawyer like Danner might know an embezzler or two, but Masters would probably be his only acquaintance in the even less desirable corner of crime where violence is a regular occurrence."

"Speaking of desirable," Rica said.

"Get off my desk," Stack told her, "before you char it."

Rica didn't bother playing dumb.

Rica knew this: Early in her life she'd let circumstances control her, push her around. She'd settled for whatever came her way and tried to make the best of it. That hadn't worked. That had, in fact, become hell.

Not anymore, she'd decided just before becoming a cop. It didn't matter what the other female cops said, or the men. She'd determine what she wanted, be at the mercy of what she longed for, and go after all of it hard, be it Stack or anything else.

There had been some tough times in the years after the divorce, in the department. Jagged emotional debris to sort through. But Rica ran Rica's life. Rica would play the game hard because she'd learned she had to be hard.

Rica was afraid to play it any other way, of where it might lead.

Even lighting a cigarette, Chips had to stare at the lighter flame longer than was necessary. More and more often he thought a lot about fire, the way it warmed and destroyed, gave light and death, comfort and pain, protected and imperiled. It was a friend but it was dangerous. You couldn't trust it even when you got to know it well.

Tonight, when there was no reason to stay and every reason to leave, he had to stand and watch how it danced and devoured. It fascinated, the way it licked at the fringe on the bottom of the sofa, writhed along the carpet, and flicked out a tongue of flame at the drapes, liked the taste, and began to devour the material, curled smoking black at the ceiling, testing, testing bare plaster, *nothing there,* across the valance to the matching drape, twisting and curling like a woman who couldn't get enough—

"What the hell are you doing?"

He turned and saw the man standing in the doorway. A big man with bull shoulders, eyes wide and bright with the flames, face a mask of rage writhing like the fire. His fists were clenched, his bulky body tight for the charge.

The man did charge, but in a measured, ominous way, body hunched, fists balled tight and held at chin level. Maybe he'd been a fighter, a pro. He was so methodical. Maybe he could kill with a bare-fisted punch.

Christ! Fear took over. Nothing to do but show the gun, scare him. Stop him, for God's sake!

The gun made the big man pause, then shrug. Something about his eyes and the way he cocked his head, as if he'd been drinking. "You really think that fuckin' peashooter's gonna stop me from tearin' meat from your bones?" He kept coming. Faster.

The first shot merely made him grunt and brush his stomach with his hand where the bullet had entered, as if he might flick away the wound.

The second made him stagger.

The third dropped him to his knees.

Don't get up! Please, don't get up!

But he did get up. Slowly swaying in the hot wind. The only sound was that of the flames crackling. The fire was like the searing, rancid breath of a beast now, a dragon closing in like the man only from another direction.

The fourth shot brought the man down again but didn't kill him. He was on his stomach, trying to raise himself with his arms, looking confused and scared for the first time. "Legs don't goddamn work! Can't . . ."

The heat was getting unbearable. Reflections of flame in the man's saucer eyes. Terrified now. Bewildered. He began thrashing around, his arms and upper body, even his head. Everything but his legs. His left arm was bleeding where a bullet had caught it, bone or sinew showing glistening white. He tried again to raise his upper body and drag himself along with his arms, but the left arm bent at an unnatural angle and he flopped back down. "Help me! Help me stand up, damn you! . . ."

He was going to burn if he didn't get help. He was going to die in flames.

Nothing to do now but run.

Christ!

"Help me! Can't get up . . ."

Help us all! You're the one that wanted trouble, asshole! Your fault! Why couldn't you have just let me finish here and leave?

"Please! . . ."

Your fault, not mine!

Christ!

EIGHT

May 2000

Sitting in her luxuriously appointed office with its grand view of Central Park, Myra Raven thought about when she had been Myra Ravinski. Her gaze fixed on a horse-drawn carriage wending its way through the park, but its image didn't really register on her mind. She was trying to conjure up the face of her first husband, the cop like Ed Marks and about Ed Marks's age when he died.

But she found that she couldn't. Not with any precision. That was the real tragedy, not that we remembered the faces of the dead, but that with time we forgot them. Only now and then, unbidden, did they appear out of time and with memory like pain.

A different life for Myra Ravinski so long ago, a young woman nominally educated, not particularly attractive, and—thank God!—not pregnant. Newly widowed, she'd returned to college at NYU, then left when her money ran out.

She'd thought her life was finally straightening out when she met and married Irwin Seltzer, a man in his fifties but still handsome and vigorous. But there were two problems: she was still in love with her dead husband, and Irwin couldn't stop ending their increasingly frequent arguments by using his hands on her. Not his fists, which would leave bruises, but his palms, slapping so the red marks and occasional welts would fade quickly. It turned out that Myra was his second wife; the first had accused him of physical abuse and left him. Myra, no fool, left Irwin in the position of searching for piñata number three.

That's when she learned why Irwin had gently insisted they sign a prenuptial agreement. The money she walked away with after the divorce lasted about six months.

No way to return to school now, and no desire. Myra had studied for her sales license and gone to work at a real estate agency in New Rochelle. Here was something she could do well, concentrating on the woman, if she were selling to a couple; letting the property seemingly sell itself; sometimes deftly steering the conversation so she could sense what the potential buyers *really* wanted, what they *needed,* rather than what they said were their wants and needs. Seeing into them. It was the gift everyone working in sales thought they possessed, or they belonged in other occupations. Myra didn't only *think* she had the gift—she had it, and converted it into fat commissions.

But the commissions were even fatter in Manhattan, in the high-end residential property in the Upper East Side, Sutton Place, and areas of the Upper West Side, as well as potentially trendy neighborhoods. Myra had a nose for money, and it led her to a position with an agency in Tribeca just when the neighborhood was getting hot.

The track was faster in Manhattan real estate, and she became faster. Myra was cunning, which is better than smart, and she was ruthless, which is better than cunning. Whatever the cost to take a step forward, she paid it. Whatever sacrifice it took to get out ahead of the pack, she made it. Whatever was required to close a sale, she somehow came up with it.

Within two years she'd opened her own agency, and within three more the Myra Raven Group (which sounded so much better than "Ravinski") was the most successful apartment sales and rental agency in New York City.

Five years, three severe diets, three rounds of cosmetic surgery, and three men later, she was the present and complete Myra Raven, molded by survival of the fittest to persevere and to thrive. Lean and attractive in a way striking if brittle, she was single and independent, knew personally the city's wealthy and influential, and was successful and rich. And contented as a shark in a stocked pond.

Meeting the Markses had stirred old memories in Myra. Ed the shiny new cop. Amy the naive and love-struck wife, and with an obvious devotion and loyalty Myra recognized. And pregnant with twins. How might that last have been if it had happened long ago to Myra Ravinski? Young Myra would have shown the same determined happiness and burgeoning love that glowed in young Amy.

What a different life Myra Ravinski would have led if things had been only slightly different. How careful she'd been not to become pregnant! How she'd wished, at least for a while after her young husband's death, that she *were* pregnant.

Only later did she realize what a pregnancy at that time would have meant. What a millstone and a hardship.

Well, Amy Marks's husband was alive, and she *was* pregnant. Not only that, the young couple had a windfall and could afford a nice place to live and bring up twin daughters.

Myra would see to it that the co-op contract would go through; she was a genius at putting together deals, at settling differences and arranging financing, at fitting customer to co-op or condo. An absolute genius, or so had said the *Times* last year in a feature article they did on her.

Smiling, she watched the horse-drawn carriage with its white canopy disappear in the darkening park below. She had it in her power to help the Markses buy some happiness, and she would help them. There was no need to closely examine her motives. It did occur to her that maybe she was trying to prove to herself she wasn't quite the hard, venal bitch she knew some people said she was. She had overheard that assessment of her more than once, in a restaurant where she used to dine, even in the elevator in her building. It didn't concern her. Usually.

The hell with that kind of thinking! She was simply doing a good deed and that was the end and all of it. There was no need to question herself. She wasn't some rich bitch trying to squeeze through the eye of a needle and enter heaven.

Then why would it have occurred to her that she was?

"Fuck it!" she said softly to the lowering night. If there really was a heaven, it was right here on earth, and you made it for yourself and by yourself.

The streetlights had winked on in the park, graceful patterns of curved illumination, like stars in a galaxy with pattern and purpose. She turned away from the window and lit a cigarette with a silver lighter. Then she sipped from the glass of single malt scotch she'd set aside on a marble-topped table, glanced at her Patek Philippe watch, and picked up her cell phone to place a call before it got too late.

Worked on a deal.

NINE

January 2002

Raymond Masters was easy enough to find. He lived in his mother's house in a run-down neighborhood in Astoria.

Rica stood to the side on the wooden porch while Stack knocked on the door. She thought this was better than the neighborhood where she'd grown up, and wondered what it would have been like to have a room of her own in a house like this, have girlfriends who lived on the block, maybe walked to school without worrying about—

"Rica?"

She started at the sound of Stack softly calling her name. This wasn't the time to be daydreaming. What seemed routine could any second turn deadly. Cops who forgot that part of their training could die suddenly or cause it to happen to others.

Without thinking about it, she moved her hand closer to the 9mm in its shoulder holster beneath her coat.

"Yes?" a woman was saying warily.

Judging from what they could see of her deeply etched features, and her one visible faded eye as she peered from behind a door open only a few inches, she was hardly the lover of a desperado. Probably Masters's mother.

"We'd like to talk to Raymond," Stack said amiably. They might have been old friends of her son.

"Who should I say is calling?" Formal and wary.

"We're with the police," Stack said, "but please don't be alarmed. I assure you we're not here because Raymond's in any trouble."

Yet, Rica thought.

"We only want to talk to him for a few minutes, to reaffirm some things he told us earlier."

Mom—if she was Mom—wasn't that dumb. She put on a smile. "When he gets home, I'll sure tell him you were here."

Stack tuned to her wavelength; now they were older and worldly types, the sort of people who might say *thou*. "Between us . . . Mrs. Masters, is it?"

She nodded. Nothing in the faded eye changed.

"We both know we're going to talk to your son one way or the other. I do pledge to you that there are no active warrants on him, nothing left over from his last problem. When we leave here, he'll stay. Talk is all we want to do. And since we both know that conversation is going to take place sooner or later, why not now, in your own comfortable home, instead of the more unfriendly atmosphere of a Manhattan precinct house?"

"If he was here, I'd tell—"

"You don't believe or trust me," Stack said. He sounded crushed. "Well, I guess I can understand that. But ask yourself, dear, did what I just tell you make sense?"

Still no change in the bleary eye. But the door closed, the rattle of a chain lock being taken off sounded from inside; then the door opened and Mrs. Masters stepped back to admit them.

She was probably only in her fifties but might have passed for seventy, wearing a stained blue robe and huge fuzzy slippers though it was past noon. The place was a mess, with newspapers and magazines spread around, half a sandwich on the coffee table next to a bottle of bargain beer that was leaving a ring on the wood, a couple of roaches feeding on crumbs scattered over the cushions of the worn sofa. Stack and Rica remained standing.

Stack was still being reasonable. "Would you come with us to make the introductions? So as not to scare the boy unnecessarily."

Raymond's mother stared at him, still thrown off balance by this strange combination of officialness and kindliness, then shrugged. "It's this way." She preceded them to a hall leading past the door to the kitchen, then on toward the rear of the house. She must have been cooking. The scent of frying onions was in the air, almost strong enough to make Rica's eyes water.

There was no sound as they walked down the hall. Rica's gut told her something was wrong. Raymond might be scrambling out a window about now. Or loading the clip of a gun. Too damned quiet. Or maybe it was those fuzzy slippers the size of sheep.

Mrs. Masters waved a hand for them to stop, then walked ahead and knocked on a closed door. After a few seconds, she opened it and looked inside. "Raymond? *Raymond!*" She turned to stare at Stack, her eyes wide now and glittering with fear. "I think there's something wrong with him!"

Stack pushed forward and moved the woman out of the way. *Be careful!* Rica almost shouted.

And he was careful. As Rica nudged the woman farther

out of possible trouble, then removed her 9mm from its holster, Stack shoved the door all the way open with his foot and peered around the door frame over the barrel of his Police Special, keeping most of his body out of sight and a slight target.

Then he lowered the gun and stepped through the doorway.

Rica followed.

The air in the bedroom was stale and suffocating. A gaunt blond man wearing only stained Jockey shorts was curled in the fetal position on the bed. His scrawny arms were tucked in close to his body, encompassing drug paraphernalia as if he had gathered it near him because it might save instead of kill him.

Mrs. Masters screamed, *"Raymond!"* Once. It might have been heard all over the neighborhood. Then she bolted from the scene, which seemed an odd thing for a mother to do.

As Rica hurried to the phone in the living room, putting on a show for the woman even though her son was obviously dead, she caught a glimpse of Mrs. Masters in the kitchen, pouring gin from a bottle into a glass with trembling hands.

"The deal is," said Stack to acting MR Squad Commander O'Reilly, "we've pretty much come to the wall on this case."

O'Reilly, who was standing with his hands clasped behind his back and pretending to gaze out his office window, shook his head in denial and turned around. "Doesn't sound right to me, Stack. We got Mr. Prominent Citizen burned like a log in his kitchen, and we're gonna let it slide?"

"If we've got no choice," Stack said. "We have no logical suspect and we're out of moves. Raymond Masters might have helped us, or even been involved, but he's dead and not talking."

Rica, standing off to the side and behind Stack, thought she'd better come to his rescue before he got into it heavy with O'Reilly. "We've followed all the leads, sir," she said in a reasonable tone. "Danner's friends, coworkers, girlfriend, neighbors . . . Nobody has a clue or can give us a clue as to why he was murdered."

"And the truth is," Stack said, "Danner wasn't that much of a prominent citizen. A well-paid attorney with a middlin'-size midtown firm."

"What about the twenty thou you found in his safe?"

"It isn't *that* much money."

"But has it been explained?"

Rica thought she could imagine a thou explanations.

"No" Stack admitted.

"Maybe he bet a winner at the track," Rica suggested. Stack glared at her.

O'Reilly seemed not to have heard her. He was back at the window, posing and gazing at some imagined horizon. "The girlfriend," he said, then turned around and slid down into his desk chair—Vandervoort's chair. He looked up at them as if he'd said something profound. "Helen whazzername."

"Sampson," Rica said.

"Stay on the girlfriend," O'Reilly said. "You tie up some poor bastard and light him on fire, then stand over him with an umbrella so he don't go out, I'd say that's a crime of passion. Check the girlfriend, see if she's going out with some other guy now and was maybe two-timing Danner."

"The way we read the relationship," Stack said, "it was between two people who'd been around and wouldn't get their underwear all twisted up if one or the other happened to see someone else. Maybe they'd argue and split, but hardly set each other on fire."

"Who told you about the relationship?"

"Helen Sampson," Rica chimed in, not wanting Stack to have to say it.

O'Reilly smiled broadly, his pockmarked face creasing in the morning light. "So stay on the girlfriend." He motioned with a sweeping motion of his arm at his cluttered desk. "Now I got goddamn paperwork, if you'll excuse me. I don't know how the hell Vandervoort kept up with this shit."

"Part of the job, I guess," Stack said noncommittally. But it seemed to aggravate O'Reilly.

"Stay on the girlfriend," he said again, as Stack and Rica left the office, "even if it takes weeks."

"The girlfriend," Rica said, when they were out in the hall.

Stack didn't answer her. She knew he was pissed off, and it amused her.

She knew it shouldn't, but it did.

TEN

Where the hell was Sharon?

She'd gone out over an hour ago to get a pedicure in Shear Ecstasy, the salon just off the lobby of the Bennick Tower, where the Lucettes lived in a fortieth-floor apartment. She should have been back before now, even waddling in her open sandals, balls of cotton tucked between her toes to keep them from rubbing together and smearing wet nail polish.

The heat was running behind today, and the luxury apartment was uncomfortably cool. For some reason sound was penetrating more than usual, the blasting of car and truck horns, the occasional roar of a bus at the stop near the corner. A police or fire department siren was screaming shrilly nearby, as if the vehicle was unable to move and protesting vociferously, adding to Dr. Ronald Lucette's aggravation, and his anger. Had Sharon opened a window and forgotten to close it? It had happened before.

But the doctor wasn't really upset with his wife Sharon. The object of his anger was one of his patients, Lillian Tuchman. So the woman's navel was a few centimeters off to the left. What did she expect, after he'd performed liposuction and a tummy tuck on a 250-pound woman? It wasn't as if he'd messed up Gwyneth Paltrow. What were Lillian Tuchman's postoperation plans, anyway, to enter a bikini contest?

But he knew what her postoperation plans were: she was suing Dr. Lucette and New Beginnings Cosmetic Surgery Center for two million dollars. New Beginnings had a law firm on retainer, but as Dr. Lucette's partners pointed out, the new, almost slim Lillian Tuchman was a woman not in a mood to compromise. She had already refused a nuisance settlement offer of $100,000, and her lawyers were hinting that there were intimations of sexual misconduct while she was under anesthetic.

Thinking about that last absurd charge made Dr. Lucette more than simply angry—he was outraged. Never had he touched a patient improperly under any circumstances, much less in a brightly lighted OR full of assistants. The charge would never stick!

But he knew better than to be so certain of such matters. Any charge might stick in court. Juries were more and more unpredictable, and if you were rich, as Dr. Lucette had to admit he was, jurors considered you fair game, one of the enemy caught in the sights of the common man. The jurors would be much like Lillian Tuchman herself, rather than Dr. Lucette. In the minds of people like Lillian Tuchman, the rich existed only to be envied, cursed, and plucked—unless of course they could be joined.

Dr. Lucette got up from where he was sitting in his soft green leather armchair and went into the bathroom. He stood at the basin and washed his hands in a way so practiced that he thought little about his actions as he studied his haggard face in the mirror. He was sixty-two now and looked fifty, meaning he was almost ready for another eye operation and forehead lift. There wasn't much more he could do about his thinning gray hair. Growth stimulants didn't seem to work for him, and within another few years he'd be one of those men who plastered strands of hair sideways over the tops of their skulls so they looked like lines drawn with a felt-tip pen. Well, perhaps there would be advances in the field of toupees.

He suddenly realized several minutes had passed and he was still soaping and scrubbing his hands. He'd been doing too much of that kind of thing lately. Nerves? Or a developing compulsive disorder? Obsessive compulsion ran in the Lucette family on his mother's side. He'd had a cousin, Herbie, who had actually scrubbed all the hair from the backs of his hands with a coarse brush.

He grimaced and turned off the water, then dried his hands roughly on a nearby towel. Not obsessive compulsion! he assured himself. Nerves! He sure as hell had plenty to be nervous about. His daughter, Minerva, about to flunk out of Wellesley. His son, Bob, probably hooked on cocaine.

And now goddamn Lillian Tuchman and her off-center navel. It would be hilarious if it wasn't so potentially costly!

The doctor went back into the living room and sank again into the leather armchair. Always he warned patients not to expect too much from cosmetic surgery. If done correctly, once the healing was complete they would look much as their usual selves, only younger or well rested. But for some of them that wasn't enough; they wanted to look like someone else because they wanted to *be* someone else. He sighed. They were seeing the wrong kind of doctor, he felt like telling them. They should—

He heard the apartment door open and close. Sharon—finally! Already he felt better. They could talk things over. She would sympathize with him. Then, after her toenails dried, they could go out and get some dinner at a nice restaurant. Maybe that new place on Amsterdam that served a tasty Caesar salad and genuinely medium-rare steak with garlic potatoes—comfort food. A drink, a good meal, another drink, and the world might seem habitable again.

Dr. Lucette waited, but Sharon didn't emerge from the entry hall. Maybe she was waddling carefully, not wanting to get any nail polish on the carpet fibers.

She was taking her damned time, feeding his irritation.

At last he noticed a slight change of light and sensed her presence behind him and off to the side. He turned to look up and greet her but instead gasped.

Someone was standing silently staring down at him, but it wasn't Sharon.

ELEVEN

Outside the window, a cruel winter wind blew icy rain almost horizontally along the narrow avenue. The small patch of sky visible between the buildings across the street was gray as a bullet. Who was it who said weather needn't affect mood?

Myra sat at her wide, custom-built cherry-wood desk in her Myra Raven Group office and tried to reason on the phone with Web Thomas without sounding desperate. "I managed to rearrange schedules here at the office so I could be away for the weekend, Web." Making him feel guilty.

Not Web. He probably couldn't even spell *guilty.* "I wish we could make it, Myra. I talked to somebody on the phone this afternoon, and the place is snowed in tight. She said it's still snowing upstate."

What did this guy want? Did he forget that he was the one who worked to talk her into this? They'd had three dates and he'd pushed her for three days—and nights—at what he called his "cottage" in upstate New York. Then suddenly, like so many before him, he'd changed his mind. Maybe because of something she'd done or said, some way she'd glanced at him. Whatever the reason, she knew he'd come to see her differently. Even through the phone connection she could feel him pushing her away.

Myra had been very much looking forward to this weekend. She knew that to somebody as rich as Web, a cottage could be somebody else's idea of a mansion. She also knew from a conversation she'd overheard that he'd recently bought a new all-wheel-drive BMW that could probably cut through snow like an Olympic skier.

So maybe he didn't want to risk a new car on icy country roads. "Our company car is a Lexus SUV," she told him.

"That would be great except for the bridge."

"Bridge?"

"Yeah, you have to drive across an old covered bridge to get to the cottage, and the weight of the snow caused the thing to collapse."

He hadn't missed a beat; maybe his excuse was genuine. Maybe he was going to suggest someplace other than his cottage. Dinner, a show, a hotel here in town. Or her place, her bed. She was ready to offer her bed if he hinted.

But he didn't suggest something else. "Maybe it's just as well, Myra. I've got a load of reports to go over, anyway."

That was a laugh. If anyone had a make-work job, it was Web. Worthless Web.

"Maybe if—" She stopped herself. She had pride— maybe too much of it.

"Myra? You still there?"

"Not anymore," she said, with more bitterness than she'd intended.

He laughed. "You're taking this a bit too seriously."

She didn't like his laughter, or his remark. Because she *was* beginning to take him seriously.

"Here's an idea, Myra. Why don't we just meet at the Royalton about eight, have something to drink, then go on up to a room? The snow is all upstate, not here where we can still get together."

Too late. And not even dinner and a show. "A weekend at the Royalton?"

"Not a weekend. Just tonight. I wouldn't try to talk you into an entire weekend."

"No, thanks, Web." *I don't want to be your casual fuck.*

"It isn't as if we don't know each other well enough, Myra."

She didn't like that last remark, either.

He didn't misinterpret her silence. "Why don't you think about it and call back in an hour or so?" he asked in a forced conciliatory tone.

"No need for that, Web. I already have my weekend appointments set up, including this evening and tomorrow morning."

"I thought you rearranged your schedule."

"I was going to," she snapped.

"C'mon. You're a group, Myra—all your advertising says so. You have salespeople to do that sort of work."

"I have salespeople because I've got a successful agency. And I have a successful agency because I still do myself what I ask my people to do."

"*Your* people. Jesus, Myra! The world won't stop spinning if you take a weekend off and enjoy yourself. Your people should be able to get along for a short while without you, maybe even sell a few condos and co-ops."

She knew he wouldn't understand. He'd been born to money, gone to excellent schools, then gone to work in the family business—yacht parts or something—and that was the extent of his experience and the limits of his horizons. He hadn't come from where she came from. Hadn't even visited. They were good together in bed, but not in the rest of the world. "If you don't understand," she said, "I'm sorry."

"Now you're pissed at me."

"No, I'm just frustrating you and you're misinterpreting it as my being pissed. That's because you're used to getting what you want."

"My, my . . . coldhearted bitch." He said it as a joke, but it had steel in it.

What did he expect? Of course she was angry. Fighting mad, in fact. He had left her no escape route from her embarrassment at being stood up, no way to save face, to maintain her facade. So she became combative. Even a sparrow would fight to the death when cornered. He didn't think of her as a sparrow. She lowered her voice. "I thought you liked it that way, Web."

"Myra, play above the belt. This kind of confrontation makes no sense. Why don't you think things over, then call me back in about an hour and give me a definite answer?"

"I've got a better idea, Web. Why don't *you* call *me* back—when you have a piece of property to sell?"

She hung up crisply but without banging the receiver.

She knew he'd call back. If not today, tomorrow. Or maybe he'd find somebody else for his hotel tryst tonight, start another surface relationship. Myra didn't care.

Couldn't care.

Standing up behind her desk, she smoothed the wrinkles in the slacks of her business suit, then walked from her office to the sales cubicles where her agents were seated at their desks when they weren't showing property. The large, blue-carpeted area was brightly lighted by overhead fluorescent fixtures. A door in the far wall led to a reception area with genuine Chippendale chairs and a

Sheraton pie crust table. Tasteful oil reproductions were mounted on the cream-colored walls. The reception room was lighted softly with glass-shaded lamps and a Tiffany ceiling fixture. Adjoining that expensively decorated room was a conference room similarly furnished in an eclectic mixture of modern reproductions and valuable antiques.

In the more Spartan sales floor area, half a dozen of the steel wood-tone desks were occupied this afternoon. A few of Myra's people glanced up and nodded respectfully to her as she strode past. At the end cubicle she stopped and addressed the woman seated inside studying listings on a computer screen. Darlene, whose duty it was to keep the Myra Raven Group Web site up to date. More and more listings were attracting buyers over the Internet.

"Is the new Central Park South listing on-site yet?" she asked Darlene.

The neatly dressed elderly woman at the computer waved her into the cubicle. "I was just polishing it, editing the virtual tour."

Myra stepped a few feet into the cubicle and watched as Darlene worked the mouse, and a video camera swept through the spacious luxury apartment. "Did we get the summer park view, as I asked?" Myra knew how desirable a park view was in the concrete world of Manhattan, which was why her office and her own apartment had one.

"Did we ever!" Darlene said. "I patched it in from a property we listed last July." She maneuvered the mouse so a view out the apartment's wide living room window filled the screen; then she zoomed in on what appeared to be a lush rectangle of green below.

"Marvelous!" Myra said.

Harold, one of her best salespeople, was behind her off

to the side. "Myra, can I talk to you about the McCallister closing?"

Myra nodded and left Darlene to her task.

Eleanor, last month's sales champion, was approaching Myra, head down, steps choppy, jaw set and determined. Myra knew what she wanted. She could read her people's minds. "I'll get with you on the closing after I talk to Eleanor about one of her listings," Myra said to Harold.

As Harold backed away a few steps, Myra said to a young woman passing by, "Amy, get me the file on 458K West Fifty-seventh."

"Myra," the intrepid Eleanor was saying, "I have some serious issues on that West Fifty-seventh property."

"Amy's getting the file," Myra said. To Harold: "I'm sorry, Harold, but I know what Eleanor wants and it'll only take a minute. When you see her leave my office, come on in and we'll get together on your closing."

"Fine, Myra."

Myra strode to her office, aware of Eleanor hurrying to keep pace behind her. She felt grand. The Myra Raven Group was humming.

She'd forgotten all about Web Thomas.

An hour later, still at her desk, she picked up the phone and made sure she had an outside line before pecking out the number of Prestige Available Escort.

"I need a male escort for this evening, dinner and drinks afterward," she said to the woman who answered the phone.

"Yes, ma'am. Have you used our service—"

"I'm in your computer," Myra said, telling the woman her PIN. "And see if Billy Watkins is available."

* * *

Rica figured the hell with it. She'd been sitting behind the steering wheel of a parked unmarked across the street from Helen Sampson's West Side apartment for the last two hours. There was no need to start the car's engine; she'd had it idling so the heater could be on. Which made the windows fog up. Which made it harder to see if the lights stayed on in Helen Sampson's apartment windows, or if Helen herself left the building. At least the rain had stopped before changing to sleet or snow. Rica was hungry, thirsty, and had to go to the bathroom.

Screw this!

She put the car in drive and pulled out of her parking slot, ignoring the blast of a horn behind her. A taxi pulled up next to her at the next stoplight and out of the corner of her vision she saw the driver working his gums and giving her hell for pulling out in front of him. She guessed he had a right, but she thought, *keep it up, asshole, and I'll put the cherry light on the roof and give you a bad time.*

This whole waste of yet another evening, she thought, was because O'Reilly was an idiot. Helen Sampson was as innocent as O'Reilly himself of Hugh Danner's murder. The woman was grief-stricken and despondent. You could feel it when you were close to her, hear it in her voice, see it in her facial expressions and body language when she didn't know she was being observed. O'Reilly seemed not to mind diverting people on the off chance that Helen Sampson might provide some kind of lead, meet with a known arsonist or something, or maybe start a fire when she didn't think anyone was looking. Department politics! That was the one thing about the NYPD that had surprised Rica when she finally figured out how things worked. Too much was done for purely political reasons. Made Rica want to puke. Say what you want about Stack; he was a hardhead and would never make captain, but it was because he was honest and he respected the Job. Everyone knew and said freely that he was one hell of a cop.

Rica and Stack and some uniforms from the Two-oh had been keeping a loose tail on Helen Sampson, which meant she wasn't being watched every minute, but was being observed intermittently in the hope she'd bust some kind of move that would mean something. Rica had tailed her most of the evening, watched her leave her bookshop, ride a bus, get some takeout at a deli, buy some magazines—some kind of fashion shit—then go home to her apartment and not come out. It was damn near bedtime now, at least for Rica. She was going home.

The cab driver blasted his horn at her so she'd look over at him, then made a violent twisting motion in the air with his middle finger. The guy wouldn't let it alone, so it was gonna be his problem.

When the light went green and traffic pulled away, Rica let the taxi zoom out ahead of her. Then she got on its rear bumper, rolled down the window, and placed the flasher on the unmarked's roof. She motioned with her left hand for the cabbie to pull to the curb.

She was going to ask him about that business with the finger.

Rica had given the cabbie a rough time, playing the game he'd started, liking the surprise on his face when he'd found out she was a cop. The fear when she threatened to have the bastard's job. The whole thing should have been a pleasure, a relief. So why was she crying here in her bed?

Her former husband, Rudy. The smart-ass cabbie. Stack. . . . *Men!*

She knew why she was crying. It was because Stack still loved his wife Laura. That was how it went: cops' wives got fed up with the life first and walked out. The cops, the wives, blamed the Job, and usually they were right. Eventually, both parties learned there was no going back.

The *eventually* was the problem.

There were more tears, over an hour's worth, before she fell asleep.

The next morning was cold but bright, with air so brittle it seemed if you sneezed you might shatter it. Rica and Stack drove the unmarked to the deli where Helen Sampson had bought last night's takeout. Before driving on to park outside Helen's apartment, Stack got them each a coffee and a danish and carried them out to the car.

Rica watched how his breath fogged and trailed behind him as he stepped down off the curb to cross the street, a big man ambling along with the gait he probably used years ago on his beat, wearing a long, dark coat of indeterminate color that, like the walk, might date back to those days. It was a simple, square-shouldered coat. Not what you'd call a topcoat, or a romantic trench coat with a belt and all those pockets. A sensible warm overcoat, was Stack's winter garment of choice. No zip-out lining for this boy. Old-fashioned kind of coat. Old-fashioned Stack. Fixed object in a shifting world.

When they pried the plastic lids off the cups, the steam made the unmarked's windows fog up, just as they had last night. Cozy, Rica thought. Nice and private. Stack peeled back a little plastic triangle from his cup's lid, then replaced the lid to keep the steam down so he could see better what was going on outside. Rica left the lid off her cup.

Stack, behind the steering wheel this morning, made no move to start the car.

"All Helen Sampson does is work, eat, and sleep," he said.

"She doesn't eat much," Rica said. "That's because she's grieving and has no appetite."

Stack grunted his agreement and sipped coffee through the little triangular hole in the plastic lid. He thought maybe it was time to tell O'Reilly that Helen Sampson checked out okay. That they were probably wasting time and effort that could be spent on other crimes instead of the Danner murder. Stack had a gut feeling this was one of those times in a case where the best thing to do was sit back and wait and see what—if anything—developed.

"We just gonna sit here?" Rica asked beside him. Something in her tone suggested she thought it wouldn't be a bad idea. She seemed to have edged closer to Stack on the car's bench seat. *If she weren't so pushy . . .*

"There wouldn't be any point in that," Stack said tersely. Throw some cold water on her. Them.

She said, "The city's got more than its share of unsolved homicides. Maybe it's time to think this might be another one." She knew he wouldn't consider her a quitter. Nobody ever accused her of that. It was just that they were going in circles on this Danner thing. "My gut tells me we should move on," she added.

He lowered his coffee cup from his lips and glanced over at her, obviously a bit surprised and pleased.

"Are our guts in sync?" she asked.

"In sync," he said, starting the car with his free hand.

"Let's cut Helen Sampson loose and concentrate our efforts somewhere else while we wait for any new developments."

"O'Reilly might not like it," Rica said.

Stack put the car in drive and accelerated away from the curb, sloshing a little coffee from the triangle in his cup lid so it ran down his thumb. "Screw O'Reilly."

"In sync," Rica said.

TWELVE

Dr. Lucette remembered now.

At least some of it.

He'd thought Sharon was back from downstairs, from her pedicure at Shear Ecstasy. But when he'd turned to look up at the figure standing near his chair, it wasn't Sharon. He wasn't sure who . . .

He winced as he recalled the object descending toward him, a club or sap of some sort. The flash of light and pain behind his right ear, then a dark downward spiral.

Above him a bright object sent out waves of glitter, making his eyes, his entire head ache. He tried to call out, to ask what was going on, but he couldn't speak. Something covered his mouth so tightly that he couldn't so much as part his lips. He could only moan. When he tried to raise a hand to rip away whatever was keeping him from speaking, he found that he couldn't move his arm. Nor his other arm or either leg. He strained every muscle against whatever was binding him. So immobile was he that he might as well have been sealed in amber.

He heard a strangled whimper. His own.

For God's sake, don't lose it! You've been in tougher spots. In Vietnam. Not so long ago. Take inventory. Figure this thing out!

He was lying on his back and must have been bound tightly for some time. His arms, folded beneath him, were numb from lack of circulation, his legs firmly pressed together at ankle and knee. The brilliant object above him—steadier and with less glitter now—was the kitchen light fixture. So whoever had struck him and knocked him unconscious in the living room had dragged him in here and tied him up.

But why?

A sole or heel made a scuffing sound, ever so softly, on the tile floor. Someone moving beyond the top of his head, beyond his vision. He tried with little success to turn his head, rolling his eyes, as he attempted to see whoever was there. But he couldn't. They remained just outside his field of vision. And now there was a strong smell, familiar, almost like gasoline.

Gasoline!

The doctor screamed against the tape over his mouth and his entire body vibrated so that his heels hammered on the tiles. Cool liquid splashed on the floor near him, then on his shoulders and chest. Into his eyes so that they stung. An instant before he had to clench his eyes tightly shut, he saw a wavering dark form looming above him, holding an object, a container. More of the cool liquid splashed on his stomach, his pelvic area, his thighs, and down his legs. He felt the coolness in his crotch, then beneath his buttocks. For God's sake! . . .

He smelled smoke!

Smelled fire!

At first the sensation in his legs and sweeping up his body was incredibly cold. He was reminded of the time years ago when as a child he'd fallen through the ice in the shallow lake behind the house. His mother—

Then came the heat. *The pain!* Even through his panic he knew enough to hold his breath as long as he could. Minutes! Hours! *Sharon!*

The air trapped in his lungs rushed from him in a hopeless sob.

He sucked in the pain! It entered him like a demon. The world was pain that would never end! He was choking! Either the floor was moving violently beneath him or he was writhing on it.

My God! Sharon! Help me! Mother!

Then he was floating through the pain. Into darkness as something in his chest exploded over and over again. He wondered if it would ever stop exploding.

Into darkness . . .

Dr. Lucette hadn't been a heavy man, but once the fat in his thighs caught, he burned well. As in more than a few prewar New York buildings, the apartment wasn't supplied with a universal sprinkler system, and he continued to burn. He wouldn't need any further attention.

"I'm really sorry about this," Sharon Lucette told Bonnie, her pedicurist, down in Shear Ecstasy off the lobby, "but cherry red looks more like vampire red to me. It's my fault. I thought I wanted it but when I looked at it, *Yech!* Don't hate me, okay?"

"It doesn't matter," Bonnie said. She wouldn't even think of hating anyone who tipped as well as Sharon. "It was only one foot and it's no trouble to paint over it." She adroitly dipped her small pointed brush into the new shade of enamel.

"Apple red," Sharon said, smiling down at her left big toe. "Much, much better!"

On the fortieth floor, the flames greedily consuming Dr. Lucette's foot sent out an exploring tendril, found the rubber kick plate beneath the sink cabinet, then snaked up a dish towel draped over a steel ring inside a wooden door. A few minutes later a slender tongue of flame emerged from the top of the cabinet door and cautiously tasted the glue where counter met cabinet, found it to its liking, and followed the bead of adhesive beneath the countertop to the corner, flicked out, and sampled the wallpaper seam where the paper had separated and protruded because of long exposure to dishwasher heat. It traveled up the thin edge of wallpaper . . . found the roll of paper towels and devoured it.

Found the drapes.

THIRTEEN

The dark form that was settled in the shadows beneath the trees in Central Park had a clear view of the fifty-first-floor apartment window in the Pierpont Building. Made visible from the park by the contours of the New York skyline, the window was four blocks away, but brought much closer by powerful binoculars. Flimsy blinds or curtains appeared to be closed, and there was no lamp glowing on the other side of the high window, so patience was required.

It was good that there was a breeze coursing through the park, even if it was a cold one. The stench of the dead doctor still clung to clothes and to porous flesh itself. The breeze would carry the odor of death throughout the city. People would breathe it in and not know, or choose to know—

Ah! The figure beneath the shadows sat straighter, peering intently through the binoculars.

There was a light now in Myra Raven's apartment window.

In a moment a shadow passed across the curtains; then only light remained. Hers was the only window glowing near that corner of the building.

The figure in the park lowered the binoculars, then jotted something down with a pen on a folded sheet of white paper.

Even without the binoculars, the window was now easily visible from the park. Against the black wall of the building it was like a fiery star burning against a night sky.

Or like a blazing eye high above the city, gazing back at the watcher.

"You Stack?" The tall guy in the FDNY uniform looked at Stack with a mixture of awe and curiosity, as if he'd recognized a movie star on the street but couldn't be sure.

Stack said he was Stack.

"Lieutenant Ernest Fagin, FDNY Arson." Fagin stuck out his hand.

"This is my partner, Sergeant Lopez," Stack said, causing Fagin to look at Rica for the first time. He shook her hand and smiled at her, trying to make up for bad manners. Give him that. He was young and gangly and looked like Abe Lincoln might have as a teenager without the beard.

They were standing in the middle of Dr. Ronald Lucette's living room on the fortieth floor of the Bennick Tower. The place was a blackened, waterlogged mess except for near the door where the flames hadn't reached. The stench of burned carpet, wood, upholstery, and flesh was acrid and overpowering.

"Was the fire confined to this apartment?" Stack asked.

"This apartment and part of the adjacent one on the other side of the east wall," Fagin said. "This could have been one hell of a fire. Traffic wasn't bad for a change, and we got to it in a hurry."

"I thought you guys didn't have the equipment to fight fires this high," Rica said.

"We don't have enough to do it from the outside. That's why response time's so important. We get to a high-rise early enough to use the elevator or stairs, and we blitz it and get it under control. We don't manage that, we can still sometimes outsmart the fire and contain the damage."

"Outsmart the fire?"

"Yeah, we hook up to a standpipe. Should be one on each landing, along with a coiled two-and-a-half-inch-diameter hose, sometimes in a cabinet. Then we pay out the hose and at least manage to contain the fire. But it's a battle of wits, because there's only so much pressure that way, so much water, and sometimes the standpipe systems fail. A bad fire, we sometimes direct streams of water from nearby windows of other buildings, using their standpipe systems. But if the flames get a chance to take hold and find plenty of fuel, they block fire exits and short out electrical lines so elevators are inoperable. Then the fire has us pretty much at its mercy."

It interested Rica that this guy talked about fire as if it had a mind, and an evil one at that. She had heard only that pyromaniacs talked that way.

"There's only one victim?" Stack asked.

Fagin nodded. "A Dr. Ronald Lucette. Lived here with his wife, Sharon. She was down off the lobby getting her feet worked on or something."

Stack looked at him. "Her feet? There a doctor's office down there?"

"Naw, a beauty salon. You know, getting her nails painted, her toes depilatoried, maybe. Hell, I don't know."

"A pedicure," Rica explained to the two of them. "Some women, they got the time and money, they get their feet looking good, calluses filed away, nails enameled by a pro, that kinda thing."

Both men stared at her. "You ever had one?" Stack asked. "No."

"The doctor is in," Fagin said, "if you want to go see him."

Rica was starting to like Fagin.

He led the way into the kitchen. Almost everything there was soot-darkened or charred, and there was about an inch of black water on the floor. Some techs were still there, wearing rubber boots and exchanging notes. The ME was packing up to leave. Dr. Ronald Lucette, who Stack knew had been the recent center of attention, was a blackened mess on the floor. He was lying on his right side with his knees drawn up, his arms behind him, reminding Stack of those photographs of the remains of long-ago volcano victims in Pompeii. His grotesque, darkened head was thrown back, mouth gaping, as if he still might be able to draw some cool fresh air and reverse the process that had left him in such a state.

"The fire started right where he is," Fagin told Stack and Rica. "Some sort of liquid accelerant was poured over and around him when he was on the floor tied up with something. Looks like cloth rather than rope or tape, but I couldn't tell you what kind. As you can see, it was a nasty, greedy fire. These prewar buildings are what everyone wants to live in, but some of them, with their solid walls and floors, aren't set up to support universal sprinkler systems."

"Was there a smoke alarm in here?" Rica asked.

Fagin looked at her, then motioned over his right shoulder with his thumb. The smoke alarm was above the kitchen door, its round plastic lid dangling to reveal that the batteries had been removed.

"If you find the batteries, let us know," Stack said. "There might be prints on them." But he knew there was about as much chance of finding fingerprints on the batteries as there had been of finding prints on the umbrella left at the scene of Hugh Danner's murder by burning.

"We already found the batteries," one of the techs called over. "No prints of any kind."

"The killer wear gloves?" Rica asked.

"That or the batteries were wiped," the tech said. "We dusted what we could of the rest of the apartment. We'll have to wait and see what we get other than the occupants' prints."

Stack looked at Fagin. "What about the wife with the neat feet?"

"She's in the apartment next door. She just sits and stares."

"I wouldn't want to see what she sees," Stack said.

He moved closer to the body and studied it from different angles.

Rica was peering over his shoulder. "Looks like the victim might have been bound with black cloth," she said, "but it's hard to know for sure, with everything in the place blackened."

"The lab might be able to tell you the original color," Fagin said. "Some dyes leave distinctive residues."

Stack straightened up.

The ME had moved closer, a middle-aged woman with ragged blond hair and a lot of loose flesh around her neck. A victim of gravity. Stack didn't think he'd seen her before.

"I can give you a preliminary autopsy report," she said. "Death by burning; soot in his mouth and, I'd be willing to bet, in his lungs. Which means the poor bastard was alive when he was set on fire."

"Like the last one," Rica said.

The ME nodded. "That's what I hear."

"If somebody makes a habit of this," Fagin said, "one of these days we won't be able to get to a high-rise fire and contain it, and that's everybody's worst nightmare."

"If it isn't the worst," Rica said, "it's in the running. What are the odds of one of these buildings catching fire high up and collapsing like the World Trade Center towers?"

"Pretty slim," Fagin said. "The WTC towers were struck by planes; then the fire was from thousands of gallons of jet fuel. And jet fuel burns at temperatures you wouldn't believe, and for a long time. Nothing like that here. A high-rise fire like this, we generally use a defend-in-place strategy, usually don't evacuate the whole building, just those people we think might be in some danger." He got a look on his face Rica had seen before on New York firefighters, and on some cops. "Not like the World Trade Center at all," he said in a different, softer voice.

Stack pulled a folded handkerchief from his pocket and wiped perspiration from his face. He wasn't feeling so good, wondering if he and Rica and the building itself would ever smell like anything other than charred matter. He stuffed the handkerchief back in his pants pocket.

"Thanks for your input," he said to everyone in the room. Then to Rica: "Let's go next door and chat with the new widow."

"Cheerful goddamn job," one of the techs said, as Stack and Rica were leaving.

In the hall they passed the paramedics on their way to remove the body. Two hefty guys chomping gum and discussing the merits of different Italian restaurants, their emotions and discipline to duty on two different tracks.

Doing their job with linguini on their minds; and when the body bag zipper rasped closed, their job was well on its way to being over for the evening. Stack and Rica, on the other hand, were knocking on an apartment door so they could talk to a woman married to ashes. One body with so many different meanings. Death sure was selective in its impact.

An expensively groomed woman in her fifties, whose only flaw was that she appeared to have been crying, opened the door. After Stack and Rica identified themselves, she led them to another woman slumped in a corner of a cream-colored brocade sofa that looked as if it cost more than a car.

Sharon Lucette was a tiny, attractive blonde in her forties. Her blue blouse was stained with tears. Her dark slacks were rolled up at the ankles and there were wads of cotton stuck between her bare toes, the nails of which were a brilliant crimson that Rica would describe as blood-red. She had been wearing sandals, but they were upside down on the carpet. Next to them were two red-stained cotton wads. When the neighbor who'd ushered in Stack and Rica introduced them to Sharon as police detectives, Sharon wailed.

"It's all right, Mrs. Lucette," Stack said soothingly. "We won't bedevil you at a time like this. Believe me, we know it isn't easy." He moved closer and touched her quaking shoulder. "It's one hell of a world sometimes, the things it can throw at you when you least expect it. An old cop knows that if he knows nothing else."

When the grief-tortured woman stopped sobbing and looked up at Stack, Rica saw that half her hairdo was perfectly sculpted, and the other half was wildly mussed and flattened to her head where she must have had her face buried sideways in a throw pillow. Her smeared mascara made her look like a stricken raccoon.

She seemed to draw strength from Stack. She sniffed and swiped at her nose with the back of her bare wrist. "I can talk. I'll try . . . I want that bitch arrested and punished!"

Stack and Rica exchanged glances. "You have some idea who did this to your husband?" Rica asked.

"I have exactly an idea," Sharon Lucette said. "Her name is Lillian Tuchman. She was suing Ron and his partners because of her navel."

Rica touched the point of her pencil to her tongue and began writing in her notepad.

Stack sat down next to Sharon on the sofa and patted her ever so softly on the back, a father calming a desperate child. "Her navel, is it, dear?" he asked gently.

"Yes. She claimed it wasn't where it should be."

"Ah," Stack said.

Sharon Lucette began to talk and couldn't stop talking. Stack spoke to her encouragingly now and then, guiding her in her grief and obviously feeling genuinely sorry for the distraught woman. These were the only sounds in the hushed apartment: Sharon's disbelief and pain set to words; Stack's solicitous, soothing voice; and the sharp point of Rica's pencil scratching paper.

Rica tried to write as fast as Sharon talked, making sure she wasn't missing anything pertinent, noticing that the smell from next door had permeated this apartment, too.

Probably it had permeated Sharon Lucette's mind and would never leave her, awake or asleep.

Rica wished Stack would talk to her sometime the way he was talking to Sharon Lucette.

FOURTEEN

Dinner was at Four Seasons, and on Myra. Billy Watkins accepted her generosity with solicitous charm. He was thirty-one, blond, looked like a college quarterback, and was getting tired of his job, though he liked Myra all right. She was one of the service's richest and least-demanding clients, and as far as he knew he was the only escort she ever requested. And though she was a bit old, she wasn't all that unattractive. Her body was still young enough.

Billy knew Myra liked him, too, but that she didn't love him. He'd learned a great deal about women, and this one was tough and vulnerable at the same time, and wary of love. They understood each other without having expressed it in words—neither of them would ever really love again. It made Myra sad. It made Billy strong.

In her soft bed in her expensively furnished apartment, she was as usual almost insatiable. She'd started out on top, as she often did, then let him turn her onto her back and thrust deeper and harder. She would beg him to be rough with her, biting his bare chest and shoulder hard in an effort to urge him on. Her nails would dig into his back, and her heels would batter his thighs and buttocks. Myra could be hard work, but Billy didn't mind. He'd dealt with more desperate and physical clients. Like the woman on East

Fifty-fourth who would only fuck in the tile shower with the water almost hot enough to boil lobsters. Or the one—

"Ah, Christ, Billy! . . ."

Beneath him, Myra had climaxed again. He'd spent himself almost completely the first time, an hour ago, and hadn't completely recovered enough to give her his best. But it had been good enough, which pleased Billy, though not as much as it had pleased Myra.

Raising his weight so it was supported on his knees and extended arms, he withdrew from her, careful not to hurt her as he rolled off her and onto his back. He lay there catching his breath. The ceiling fan above the bed was turning, the light fixture attached to it set on low. He bet the fixture, with its opaque delicate pink shade, cost a fortune.

It didn't surprise him to hear Myra begin to cry. Sobbing softly, she came to him and he put his arm around her and held her close. Her bare body was cool against his, though they were both perspiring.

She was the only woman he'd ever known who cried almost every time after sex, as if the act brought forth memories or a reality too painful to confront. Someday maybe he'd ask her what it was all about, what it all meant.

Her sobs were contained and quiet, as if she was ashamed of them. Billy knew they would build to a soft crescendo, then trail off, and she would mutter things he couldn't understand before she embraced her dreams and her breathing evened out. The same pattern, every time. People were captives of their pasts. He began stroking her damp hair and forehead softly, assuring her over and over that everything would be all right, that whatever they'd held at bay with their frantic coupling wasn't worth their fear. They both knew he didn't mean it, but they both wanted so much to believe.

Half an hour later, when Myra was asleep and snoring softly, he gently extricated himself from her and pulled the sheet up over her bare body so she wouldn't catch a chill from the fan's faint breeze. Then he worked his way over to the edge of the mattress and sat up, his toes digging into the plush carpet. From the street below, the sound of a car repeatedly blasting its horn was muffled and barely audible. This was one of Manhattan's more desirable prewar highrises, and the quietest apartment Billy had ever been in.

Almost silently, nude, he padded barefoot into the white-and-lavender-tile bathroom that was nearly as large as his bedroom. He stood before the commode and rolled and peeled a condom off himself, dropping it into the toilet's blue-tinted water. Then he relieved himself, watching the color of the water change to something ugly. *Like my life.*

He turned away as he flushed the toilet. It made a sound little louder than a whisper.

Maybe it was telling him in a hushed tone that life could change, *would* change, if you made it.

Myra had drunk quite a lot of wine at dinner, so she was sleeping soundly. Billy enjoyed these times after sex with her. It was almost as if they were a genuine devoted or resigned couple and he lived here and owned everything around him. As he had last time he'd been here, he decided that before showering he'd walk around and take inventory of his possessions—what might *be* his possessions, if he possessed Myra. He could pretend, couldn't he? That was all life was, anyway, pretend. Anyone in his business would tell you.

He noticed Myra had rolled onto her right side, wrapping herself in the white sheet, and was still sleeping deeply as he left the bedroom.

The apartment's living room was vast, carpeted in pale rose with a cream-colored soft leather sofa and matching chairs. There were steel or chromium-framed, modern oil paintings on the walls. Billy neither understood nor liked art that didn't look like identifiable objects. These things were all splotches of color and irregular shapes. One of them was simply three different-sized dots on a solid gray background. There was one painting that wasn't so bad, though. It looked like a nude woman seen from a lot of angles at once. He bet all the paintings were expensive, but if he owned them, he'd sell them, have them auctioned off at Sotheby's or someplace. The furniture was obviously quality stuff, though some of it was old. Why the hell, if Myra could afford that massive glass and gold coffee table that looked like the continent of Australia, would she own something like that rickety wooden chair with the curlicued wood back? Well, if this were his place he'd keep the table and ditch the chair. The big whitewashed-looking cabinet that held the TV and stereo, he'd keep that. Maybe get it refinished, though.

He walked over and glanced into the kitchen. Lots of white wood cabinets, big sink with a gray marble countertop, steel refrigerator and stove that looked like they came out of some restaurant. Well, piss on the kitchen. Who needed it? He and Myra would eat out every meal.

It wouldn't be so bad actually being married to old Myra. Billy might even have angled for it if she weren't so damned smart. Only when she was asleep, like now, did he hold any real advantage over her. Women were wily and indirect and usually doing more than one thing and thinking more than one thing at a time. And if it came right down to it, they wouldn't play fair. They were more difficult to read and deal with than men, who were usually pretty much transparent and direct, more honest. Still, Billy liked women even though they could be tricky. Especially Myra could be tricky. Not for the first time, Billy cautioned himself to be careful.

He took another turn around the living room, then the second bedroom, running his fingertips lightly over objects that could be or should be his own if only life were more fair. The third bedroom, Myra's home office, he didn't go into. Didn't even try the knob. He knew the door would be locked.

Billy glanced at the polished mahogany clock with its gold dial on the mantel. It was way past midnight.

He padded back into the bathroom and showered, then rubbed himself dry with a soft towel that was warm from being draped over a heated brass rack. His hair was short and dried quickly. He combed it, shot it with Myra's hair spray, then used Myra's roll-on deodorant.

Back in the dim bedroom, he found his clothes and put them on. It wasn't the best thing for his health, to go outside in the cold right after a warm shower, but it was an occupational hazard this time of year, and Billy had built up immunities. Besides, his thick Armani coat, out of style this season but still warm, was hanging in the closet in Myra's foyer.

After fastening his blazer button, he went to the bed and leaned over Myra. He kissed her on the forehead, once, twice, to be sure she was somewhat awake.

"Good night, Myra. You were wonderful, as always."

She managed a smile, then turned her face back to the pillow, muffling her words. "Nigh' . . . Billy."

He felt lonely, almost as if he were leaving his own

home and wife, as he walked from the bedroom and the sleeping woman behind him. In the entry hall he shrugged into his coat and turned up its black leather collar.

Glancing at his reflection in the gold-framed mirror, he smiled handsomely, blatantly admiring his boyish blond looks, telling himself the world wasn't always shitty. This had been a good night but he didn't yet know *how* good.

Myra paid the service direct or had used a charge card, but he knew there would be an envelope for him on the marble-topped credenza.

Next to the door.

FIFTEEN

On the forty-seventh floor of the Whitlock Building on West Fiftieth, six-year-old Eden Wilson rolled over in her sleep and moaned. She didn't quite wake up, and if she had, she wouldn't have known what awakened her. Something was penetrating even her deep sleep, making her uneasy. Something was different.

Her mother and father, Roy and Edith Wilson, slept soundly in the next room, unaware of any changes in their co-op apartment. They didn't realize their unit shared an air-conditioning duct with the adjacent apartment. The two halves of the vent were separated only by a thin vertical section of sheet metal, and between the units the heated metal had popped its tapping screws and pulled away from the sides of the duct. That allowed smoke from the apartment next door to find its way into the Wilson unit.

Then flame.

Only a tiny flame at first. Almost like a hesitant scout exploring in advance of a larger and more dangerous force.

That flickering red force soon arrived and traveled along a wallpaper border that had a bunny-and-flower pattern. As the flames worked their way around a smoke alarm whose batteries had run down, pieces of the wallpaper border curled and dropped burning onto the synthetic fiber carpet.

Eden sighed and rolled over in her sleep as a cinder glowed brighter among carpet fibers and began spreading its pulsating redness in a rapidly enlarging circle.

The glowing circle became flames at its circumference, and the flames grew. They grew tall enough to reach the kicked-off bedsheet draped to a few inches above the floor. The taste of material emboldened the fire and it spread along the stitched seam edging. The growing ring of flames on the carpet had reached the closed hollow-core wood door, thin particleboard sheets braced inside only with cardboard tubing. Flames devoured the adhesive along the edges of the door and began working on the particle wood and the enameled door frame.

At the foot of Eden's bed, the flames worked higher toward the box springs and mattress. They found a blond doll balanced on the corner of the mattress and enveloped it. The doll melted, contorting as if in play death, and dropped onto the floor.

Eden awoke and sat bolt upright in bed, gazing around her in wonder. Then she drew up her legs, clutching her knees, and began to scream.

In the next room her mother and father were choking, lost in a suffocating pall of black smoke, trying to crawl in the direction of the door, unable to find even each other.

Rica awoke with the phone chirping in her ear. As she fought her way up out of sleep and reached for the receiver, she noticed the clock's red LCD display: 3:21 P.M.

Too early, she thought. Way too early. And too cold. The

radiators weren't clanking and wheezing, or doing much heating. She'd have a talk with the super again, tomorrow. Misery, she thought, licking her lips and propping herself up on one elbow. Misery. The caller better have a good reason to rouse her.

She thumbed the phone's illuminated *on* button and pressed plastic to ear. Mumbled something even she didn't understand.

"Rica?"

It was Stack. "Yeah. Me. Here. Half awake."

"Make it the rest of the way," Stack said. "We got another co-op fire, on East Fiftieth near Second Avenue. Forty-seventh floor."

Awake now. "Jesus! The FDNY equipment can't reach that high."

"I'll be by to pick you up outside your building."

"Give me fifteen minutes," Rica said.

"Make it ten. I'm on a cell phone and on the way."

"Great," Rica said. "I'll have time to put on shoes."

He was there in nine minutes. And she was waiting, Stack noticed with satisfaction, as he steered toward the curb. He worked the button that unlocked the doors and she slid into the seat beside him, huffing and shivering from the cold. She said nothing, staring straight ahead as she buckled her seat belt. She might be angry, or simply distracted, or not all the way awake. He had no way of knowing and decided not to push to find out.

Stack stomped the accelerator, pulling the car back out onto cold and vaporous streets that by Manhattan standards were almost deserted. He'd encountered no more than twenty or thirty vehicles, mostly cabs, all the way to Rica's apartment. The city that never slept was catnapping. Stack didn't use the cherry light or siren, but he took the corner fast, breaking through a mist of steam rising ghost-like from a subway grate.

"How'd you get the call?" Rica asked.

"Fagin, the FDNY guy."

Rica remembered Fagin, young Abe Lincoln at the Dr. Lucette fire in the Bennick Tower. "He say anything about it?"

"Said it's been burning quite a while, but he didn't tell me what the exact situation was. We didn't talk all that long. He was busy."

"I'll bet."

A cab came out of nowhere, skidding to a stop just inches from slamming into the unmarked. A horn's angry blast followed them.

"Prick was going too fast," Rica said.

Stack smiled. He got out the cherry light, rolled down his window, and placed the light on the car roof. Then he kicked in the siren and cranked the window back up. Good Stack. Law and order personified.

"That cooled it off in here," Rica said, tightening the scarf around her throat as if cold air were still blasting in. She wished she'd brushed her teeth. She felt as if she had a mouthful of moss and must have had breath like diesel exhaust.

Stack sped through the next intersection, letting the siren yodel that they were coming, they were going. He glanced over at Rica, who was wrestling something from one of the big pockets in her bulky coat.

He was surprised when she drew out a steel Thermos bottle.

Carefully, while he was on a straightaway, she unscrewed the black plastic cap and poured steaming coffee into it.

"We'll have to use the same cup," she said. "Intimate." She handed the cap to him to sip from first.

Stack took a long pull, burning his tongue and not caring, then lowered the cup and smiled. "Thanks, Rica! That brought me all the way to life."

"I'd make somebody a good wife," she said.

"Somebody."

He handed the plastic cup back to her, then tapped the brakes and turned the corner onto Second Avenue. Far down the street they could see a reddish glow in the night sky, as if a smaller sun were paying a nighttime visit.

"My God!" Rica said.

"Better drink your coffee now," Stack told her, stomping the accelerator pedal so she was pressed back against the seat.

They flashed ID and walked among the haphazardly parked fire equipment and ambulances, careful to stay out of the way. An aerial ladder reached ineffectively up the side of the building, and a firefighter clung to it and held a hose, playing a stream of water almost straight up toward half a dozen fiery windows. Other streams of water, from street level, were trained on the floors beneath the fierce red glow that was at times trying to escape through heat-shattered glass. Stack guessed the idea was to try to keep the fire from working its way downward. At this point, not much could be done about upward. Several patrol cars were parked among the FDNY vehicles, and there were uniforms holding back a crowd that was probably mostly made up of tenants who'd fled the building. Stack motioned for Rica, and they walked over to where a uniform was standing near the front of one of the cars.

Stack and Rica identified themselves. At the mention of Stack's name, the uniformed sergeant, whose name was Mosher, straightened his posture noticeably. He was a graying, portly man in his fifties, and he focused entirely on Stack as he gave an account of his recent actions and what he knew.

"My partner Vinny and I got the call about forty-five minutes ago. We got here, we could already hear the fire department sirens. Right away we learned from tenants in the lobby that the fire was on the forty-seventh floor. The elevators were working hard, carrying tenants down. Couple of other uniforms from the One-seven arrived, then the FDNY in force. After the elevators were made off-limits so nobody'd get trapped in them, we helped tenants use the fire stairs in back to leave the building; then we got into crowd control."

"You One-seven?" Stack asked.

"From the One-nine, but we were close, so we got here in a hurry when we heard the call."

Stack knew that many of the police personnel on the scene were from surrounding precincts. This fire was already a major disaster and might get worse in a hurry.

He gazed up where Sergeant Mosher had been looking. The building had a fancy stone facade that rose about five stories, then became drab brick. There were people in some of the upper-story windows, above the level of the fire.

"Not everybody got out," Mosher said unnecessarily. "Some can't leave because of the flames or smoke. A few refuse to leave, if you can believe it."

"I can," Stack said.

Rica, stamping her feet and blowing foggy breath, prodded Stack in the ribs. "Fagin."

Stack thanked the sergeant, then turned to see the tall, angular Ernest Fagin making his way toward him, sidestepping equipment and dancing over thick networks of fire hose as if he'd run this obstacle course a hundred times before. Maybe he had. He was wearing boots and a long gray slicker with two broad yellow horizontal stripes but his head was bare. He said hello to Stack and nodded to Rica.

"You two get filled in?" he asked, shooting a glance at Sergeant Mosher.

"Not all the way," Stack said.

"The fire's still confined to the northwest corner of the building, but there's no way we can get water or foam that high from street level."

"What about the people trapped up there?"

"We can't get an accurate count of how many there are. We've got a team working its way up the fire stairs, seeing if they can clear them and get everyone down safely, then move equipment up to the floor the fire's on."

"Standpipe hose?" Stack asked, remembering an earlier conversation with Fagin.

"We tried," Fagin said. "The standpipe valve's not working, but we think we can get it fixed."

"Is there a chance?" Rica asked. "I mean, before a lot of people die?"

"Not much of one," Fagin told her honestly, pulling a

long face as he spoke. Rica thought she saw tears glistening in his eyes, though it might have been the acrid dark haze irritating them. "Do you think this is the work of your guy?" he said.

Rica shrugged. "No way to know yet." She glanced up at the fiery show above. "If ever."

"We can find out," Fagin told her grimly. "We can put it back together enough that we can know."

A large man wearing a FDNY captain's emblem on his fire helmet appeared and waved Fagin over. With a backward glance, Fagin left Stack and Rica.

There was an increased flurry of activity, and several firefighters moved toward the side of the building.

"I feel useless," Rica said.

"The best thing we can do," Stack said, "is stay out of the way."

An engine roared, and a loud air horn blasted as FDNY equipment began repositioning itself. Something was sure as hell going on.

Fagin jogged around a parked ambulance and came halfway to where Stack and Rica stood. He was wearing a fire helmet now. He grinned and pointed skyward, then made an upward walking motion with his forefinger and middle finger.

"They must have cleared the fire stairs," Stack said, watching Fagin wave to them, then hurry back out of sight so he could get to work.

Standing across the street in the cold, Stack and Rica waited.

Within fifteen minutes more tenants began streaming from the Whitlock's entrance. Most of them looked okay, though some were dazed and staggering. A few were on stretchers or being helped by fellow tenants or paramedics. Stack figured they must have been coming down the fire stairs while the FDNY was lugging equipment up. Which meant there was probably no guarantee the stairwell would remain clear enough of smoke or flames for passage. It wasn't the first time Stack was glad he'd chosen the police and not the fire department as a career.

A familiar thrashing noise broke into his thoughts and grew louder, and he looked up to see two helicopters suspended above the building. He'd seen a movie once about a fire in a high-rise building, where the people trapped in the upper floors and on the roof were raised by rope or cable to hovering helicopters to escape the flames. It didn't seem a practical idea even in the movie. He wondered if it was going to be tried here.

But the helicopters remained pretty much in place for a while, then tilted to the west and disappeared.

Almost an hour had passed when Fagin crossed the street to where Stack and Rica stood. His face was soot-blackened except for around his mouth and eyes, and he looked exhausted.

"We're okay," he said. "We got the beast under control. I think you two better come up with me, if you don't mind climbing forty-seven flights of stairs."

Stack and Rica stared at him.

He grinned in blackface. "Only kidding. We got the elevators working."

As they walked with Fagin across the street to the Whitlock, the figure that had observed Myra Raven from Central Park now observed Stack and Rica.

The media had made no secret about who was in charge of investigating the co-op burning deaths. Detectives Benjamin Stack and Rica Lopez. It had been easy enough to find out a great deal about them.

And tonight, to get a look at them in person.

SIXTEEN

Stack fell back into bed at seven A.M. and slept until the alarm woke him at nine. He didn't mind waking up. He'd been dreaming about flames and black smoke and faces pressed against high windows. It was a relief to realize he was home in his apartment, breathing cool, smoke-free air.

But last night had been no dream. In the corner unit of the Whitlock Building, where the fire apparently originated, a burned body had been found in what had been the kitchen. Another body was discovered in the adjacent apartment, and a woman and a child were hospitalized with third degree bums.

At this point, that was really all that was known. Fagin from Arson and the ME were sorting things out, and Stack would get the information today.

Stack had an hour before he was supposed to swing by and pick up Rica. He showered and dressed quickly, so he'd have time to stop at the deli two blocks down and have some breakfast. Before leaving, he glanced at the Uncontested Divorce Summons with Notice UD-1 form on his desk. His attorney, Gideon Fine, had instructed him to fill it out as best he could, then send it to him so it could be completed and filed with the state. Stack and Laura's divorce was moving smoothly enough through the system.

Neither party was having second thoughts, and no blood would be shed over who got the TV or blender. So far there was no animosity; it was a matter of two people finally admitting the tension had at last eroded what they once shared. Laura was always reasonable, and Stack figured they'd remain friends after parting. He told himself he felt good about that. You took away what you could.

No time to worry over the divorce form now. He wrapped his plaid muffler round his neck, slipped into his coat, and left the apartment.

In the hall, he noticed that the coat still smelled strongly from the fire. He decided to walk to the deli for breakfast, then back, rather than give up his parking space. That way the cold air could maybe cleanse his clothes of their acrid burnt scent.

He stopped in at a shop next door to the deli to pick up a newspaper, and noticed the *Post* headline: TORCHER SETS ANOTHER HIGH-RISE INFERNO.

Great, Stack thought, reading the paragraph below. The media already knew more than he did, or they were assuming, and they'd settled on a name for the killer: "the Torcher." The *Times* mentioned the fire on the front page, but beneath the fold, and they didn't speculate on how it had started. Stack reached over the *Times* and picked up a *Post.* He was curious about how the paper would treat the Torcher murders, what the angle was, what information might have been developed after he'd left the scene. Smiling slightly, he realized he was already thinking of the killer as the Torcher; probably the nickname would catch on.

He managed to find a small booth by the window and settled in with the toasted corn muffin, orange juice, and coffee he'd bought at the counter.

After arranging the food before him, he gulped down the cold juice, then spread out the paper and read while he munched the corn muffin and sipped coffee.

The sobriquet "Torcher" was used throughout the story; better get used to it, all right. The reporter listed two casualties, a James Healy, in whose apartment the fire had started, and Roy Wilson, who'd died of smoke inhalation in the adjacent apartment. His wife, Edith, had managed to rescue their six-year-old daughter, Eden, but both had been badly burned. Cause of the fire had not yet been determined. FDNY response time was fast, but the call hadn't come in soon enough. It was only after a heroic struggle up the fire stairs in the rear of the building that tenants on the upper floors could be rescued. Several tenants had suffered from smoke inhalation, and one man had suffered a minor heart attack, but there were no other serious injuries or fatalities from the fire. There was a photo of firefighters leading frightened and stunned tenants from the Whitlock Building's canopied exit. Stack thought a woman in the background might be Rica.

Rica.

He looked at his watch and ate and read faster.

The rest of the piece was mostly speculation about the dangers of fires in high-rise apartment buildings, how those on the upper floors were in grave danger. Readers were assured that stores in and around Manhattan were stocking up on smoke alarms and fire extinguishers. Sound advice, Stack thought.

When he was finished with his corn muffin and paper, he stood up, put his coat back on, and took a final sip of coffee.

Before leaving, he folded the section of paper containing the photo of the woman who might be Rica and tucked it under his arm.

In a diner not far from where Stack had stopped for breakfast, someone else was sitting over coffee and a newspaper. Both the *Post* and *Times* lay on the table, but it was the *Post* that was being read, evoking a reaction.

Torcher, was it? Well, that was all right; let them wonder. How could they know they were dealing not so much with a torcher as a watcher? Watching, waiting, weighing, whetting, that was the essence and the planning of it. The fire was the culmination, the flames the destiny and destruction. But it had to be watched all the way through, until ash was becoming ash. So the Torcher watched.

Not much was all right about the rest of what was in the news account. Certainly not the man in the next apartment, the child and her mother in the burn unit at Roosevelt Hospital.

Learning about them had been stunning, like an actual punch in the stomach.

That wasn't supposed to happen! The building wasn't all that old; it should have had a sprinkler system. And the people next door—didn't they have sense enough to install smoke detectors? Especially in the kid's room.

It was brutal. It was almost disabling.

It was also fate. It *had* to be fate.

And there was another fate. A mission. Surely fate had arranged for the mission. This wasn't going to stop the Torcher. It couldn't. Collateral damage; that was what the military called it. Entry into hell was already built into the deal. Deaths that were accidental wouldn't change the larger picture, could hardly be held against anyone. Accidents. They were accidents.

The Torcher had only one purpose now. A single focus. There would be grief. Perhaps crushing grief. But nothing worse than that already borne. There was always more than enough grief to go around in this world.

That was the truth of it.

It changed nothing.

That was the horror of it.

SEVENTEEN

"That's not me," Rica said, when Stack showed her the Whitlock Building fire photo in the morning *Post*. "That woman's twenty pounds heavier than I am."

"Maybe it's the coat," Stack suggested, as they drove along Broadway.

It was the same coat Rica was wearing this morning. Her hand slipped beneath its lapel, toward the underarm holster concealed by her blue blazer.

Stack was quiet the rest of the drive to the Eight-oh.

In the squad room they went over what new information had come in about the Whitlock fire. An accelerant had been used to start the blaze, which had originated where the body was found in the Healy co-op. The ME's preliminary report said the victim had been alive when the fire started. The bound and blackened corpse was presumed to be that of the apartment's owner-occupant, James Healy, but they were awaiting dental identification to confirm.

"It's our firebug's work," Rica said, seated next to Stack at his desk.

"'fraid so."

The desk phone rang and Stack snatched it up and identified himself. It was Sergeant Redd out at the booking desk. He told Stack that Commander O'Reilly left instructions for Stack and Rica to come immediately to his office when they got in.

"He's in a bad mood," Redd added, "even for him."

Stack had to smile. There were few other cops in the precinct house whom Redd would have so confided in. He thanked the grizzled desk sergeant and hung up. "Commander O'Reilly politely requests a confab," he said to Rica.

"Gee, maybe he heard there was a fire."

"Put away the mock innocence," Stack told her, standing up behind his desk. "It won't play well with O'Reilly."

"He'll probably assume I'm serious."

"That's what I mean."

After Stack knocked perfunctorily and they entered O'Reilly's office, O'Reilly said nothing as he continued concentrating on what he was writing before him on his desk, making them wait.

"Sorry," he said without sincerity, after about half a minute. He replaced the gold-tipped cap on a fancy green pen, then sat back hard in his padded desk chair as if he'd suddenly become limp. "From what I hear about the Whitlock Building fire last night, it seems we got the latest in a series."

"It looks that way," Stack said.

"That's the way the *Post* sees it," O'Reilly said.

Rica shrugged. "The *Post*—"

Stack felt like grabbing her by the neck.

"Has lots more readers than you got fingers and toes," O'Reilly finished for her.

"Among them the mayor and police commissioner," Stack added in a neutral voice, trying to defuse the situation before the glare O'Reilly was aiming at Rica caused her to ignite.

"Pre-fuckin'-cisely," O'Reilly said, at last looking away from Rica, who seemed unaware that she'd angered him.

"If the arsonist is our man," Stack said, "there's something different about this fire. He didn't kill only his intended victim. That might mean something, if it was deliberate or an act of callous disregard."

O'Reilly stared at him the way strangers regard other strangers across the aisle on the subway.

"Between the two, I'd bet on callous disregard," Stack continued. "Most likely it was a simple accident that there was collateral damage. The fire got out of hand."

"I don't know," O'Reilly said. "This firebug isn't exactly a humanitarian. You and I have both seen plenty of sickos that'd go out of their way to kill anyone if only it were legal. The kinda people that still torture and kill bugs for sport."

Still? Stack wondered if O'Reilly had ever killed insects for pleasure, and at what age he might have grown out of the sport.

"What about terrorism?" O'Reilly asked.

Stack had thought about it. "I rule it out. Our firebug goes for a particular victim, when he might try to burn down the entire building. There's nothing strongly political about the victims. Also, no terrorist organization has claimed credit for the fires."

"That's how I see it," O'Reilly said. "But we keep our minds open."

"Always."

"Since we have a serial killer here," Rica said, "there

might be that part of the equation that makes him want to be caught. He might be the type who'd be bothered by his conscience. So far he's only picked on adults. But this time a little girl was badly burned. Maybe he has a daughter about the same age."

"I wouldn't be too optimistic about any guilty conscience figuring into this," O'Reilly said. "And I never completely bought into that catch-me-before-I-kill-again psychology crap. I think these scumbags just get more and more compulsive and out of control, and finally it makes them careless and they screw up and get caught."

Stack thought O'Reilly might be right. Sociopaths were usually more driven than they were complicated. Of course, there were always exceptions. They were the hardest of all to track and bring down.

"Soon as the ID's confirmed," he said, "we'll find out what we can about the dead man, Healy. Meantime we can talk to some of the neighbors, see if they saw or heard anything suspicious."

"I've already got officers canvassing the building," O'Reilly said. "You'll start getting the results fed to you this afternoon. There's another angle here I want you to pursue." He slid a sheet of paper across the desk toward Stack. "This is a list of known arsonists living in the New York City area. I'll borrow a couple of suits to help you, and I want everyone on that list talked to and evaluated to see if they might fit these murders."

"Makes sense," Stack said, before Rica could chime in. He picked up the list and looked at it. Sixteen names. It would take a while to find them all—the ones who could be found. But O'Reilly was right; it was a job that needed doing.

* * *

After leaving O'Reilly's office, Stack and Rica linked up with Eight-oh plainclothes detectives Nancy Weaver and Jake Jones. Weaver was an attractive woman about forty, wearing a drab gray skirt and blazer that would never be allowed in Rica's closet. She'd come out of Vice and looked like a cop except for a devilish glint in her eye. Jones was a sloppy, grossly overweight guy with about as many years to retirement as he had hairs on his head—three. Rumor had it there was something between the two, but Stack didn't believe it. Still, there was that glint in Weaver's eye.

Stack and Rica took the first eight names on the list and gave the others to Weaver and Jones. Acting individually or as a team, they would check out the names and locate the former arsonists, using whichever method they thought best for each name on the list.

The first thing they did was run the names through local data banks and VICAP to see what they were dealing with.

It didn't take long to learn they were dealing with just about everything. Some of these guys had simply burned down their own homes or businesses for insurance fraud, and others had been setting serious and sometimes fatal fires for decades. Some seemed to be in it for profit, and others for the high that only pyromaniacs, and sometimes arson inspectors, really understood. Stack didn't think any of them would be surprised that the police wanted to talk with them about the recent rash of fatal apartment fires.

It was ten-thirty before they had all the information they needed to set out on the street part of their task. They went over the names again with Weaver and Jones, and this time split them up according to geography so a minimum amount of time would be spent driving around the city.

Weaver and Jones had just left, and Stack and Rica were about to leave the precinct house when Sergeant Redd brought them more information on the Whitlock Building fire.

Sitting back down at Stack's desk, the two detectives went over these fresh developments before adding them to the murder file.

James Healy was James Healy, all right. His dentist had made the positive identification, though some of the base metal in Healy's fillings had melted from the heat of the fire and made the job more difficult. But according to the dentist and the ME, there was no mistaking the exterior stratification of the upper right bicuspid. Uh-huh. Healy was—had been—single, forty-six years old, and a buyer for a chain of shoe stores.

"Ever hear of Soles on Nice?" Stack asked.

Rica nodded. "They've got stores here and there around town. Women's shoes, medium-priced. I never shop there. The stuff they carry's more for teenagers. You know, plat-form pumps, see-through sandals, crossover jumpers."

Stack nodded his head and grunted. He had no idea what the hell she was talking about. He read further. Im-mediate neighbors said Healy was quiet and polite and spent a lot of time on the road for his company.

There were two more items of interest: the accelerant used to start and feed the fire tested out the same as in the earlier murders; and Healy had been bound with strips of cloth before being set on fire.

When this thing with the known arsonists—which prob-ably would lead nowhere—was finished, Stack would make it a point to meet with the detectives questioning Healy's neighbors and coworkers in depth. This case was growing and becoming more important, and he didn't want it to slip out of his hands completely and into O'Reilly's.

He looked up, surprised by his thoughts. Was he becoming proprietary and ambitious?

Maybe. Laura was gone and their marriage would soon be officially ended. All that was left for him was the Job. He'd always taken it seriously. Was there a danger he might take it too seriously? He'd seen other longtime cops do that. No wife or other family that really mattered; no friends other than cops; no life other than the uniform or the badge. It could lead to eating the gun.

Rica studied him, the expression on his face. What the hell was he thinking?

"Some oral sex for your thoughts?"

He stared at her. "Damn it, Rica, stop that kinda talk!" He glanced around, worried. No one else seemed to have heard.

"Okay," Rica said. "I was only trying to jolt you out of your dark mood. Kind of like shock therapy. Did it work?"

"I feel great now," Stack growled at her. He stood up and grabbed his sport coat from where it was draped over a nearby chair. "Let's go talk to some firebugs."

He strode toward the door, not waiting for her. She hurried to keep up, noticing that asshole Mathers smiling at her and doing something to the inside of his cheek with his tongue.

Maybe I did go too far, Rica thought. Briefly.

The first three names on Stack's and Rica's share of the list didn't pan out. All three firebugs had alibis. The third said he was home alone sleeping in his house trailer in New Jersey. A neighbor two trailers down said the suspect had been with him and several other trailer park dwellers the night of the Whitlock Building fire, drinking beer and scarfing down hamburgers and hot dogs. Having a barbecue. The guy had been taunting them, Stack figured. Firebugs liked to do that sometimes, play with fire in more ways than one.

Before leaving the trailer park, Stack pulled the unmarked onto a gravel driveway that led only to a grassless rectangle where a trailer had been.

"This is another one of O'Reilly's wheel-spinning assignments," Rica said. "He oughta have uniforms doing this kind of work. We should be talking with Healy's neighbors, his employer. Instead we're exchanging chitchat with characters who get all sexually satisfied whenever somebody strikes a match."

"We got nothing here," Rica continued. "A waste. A lighter that every time isn't going to work."

"You're essentially right," Stack said. He got the list out and unfolded it, studying it. "The rest of our addresses are in Manhattan. Why don't we split up to save time? I'll drive to the first one and leave you while you do the interview." He placed his finger on another address. "This one's only ten blocks away from where you'll be. I'll go there and do that one, then drive back to the first address and pick you up. We can double up on these and get them out of the way so we can get down to more serious business that's more likely to bring results."

"Suits me fine," Rica said, as Stack put the unmarked in gear. Gravel pinged off the insides of the fenders as he reversed the car, then drove back out onto the street.

"Stack, you ever think about Laura?"

"Sure. We were married eighteen years. I'm divorcing the woman."

"I mean think of her in that way . . . the way you used to before you were married."

He glanced over at her. "You trying to get me to open up and reveal my inner soul? You think I'll feel better if I talk things out. Right?"

"Naw, that's psychobabble rot. I'm gonna tell you something I never told anybody else, trust you with it. A few years back I got to thinking about my divorce even though it'd been years before, then some other shit in my life, what mighta been if I hadn't done this, had done that. I was bothered by my thoughts. I mean, really bothered. I didn't wanna go to the department shrink, have it on my record, so I went to a private psychotherapist who put me in a cognitive therapy group."

Stack was surprised. This was a new side to her. "It help?"

"Some. The others in the group had thoughts like mine, lots of them suicidal. Then the World Trade Center towers went down, and when the group met later that week everybody was talking about how scared they were about being killed by terrorists. I said, 'Wait a minute. We got nothing to worry about. We're suicidal!' I mean, the week before, all our discussion had been about how to conquer our suicidal impulses, our wanting to be dead, and then there we all were, worrying about getting killed. You see what I mean?"

"I don't know."

"I couldn't buy into it. The whole experience gave me perspective. Suddenly. Like *that*. It *did* help. You choose some group or some person to talk to, and you never know what's going to happen, how the breakthrough will come. So why don't you talk to me, Stack?"

He gripped the steering wheel, staring straight ahead. "I loved Laura when we got married. Then I began to ignore her because of the Job. She resented it, the uncertainty about whether we'd grow old together, my attention to my work more than to her, all the time I spent away. We grew apart. She no longer wanted to be a cop's wife. I don't blame her. That's it."

Rica turned her head and stared at him. "Well, I'm glad that came flooding out. That's really *it?*"

"Pretty much so."

"All your fault, huh?"

"Yes." He took the car around a corner faster than he'd intended. A pencil on the dash rolled onto the floor. "You still in that therapy group, Rica?"

"No. I don't need them anymore. I don't need anybody because I got me."

Stack realized he was smiling. "Rica?"

"What?"

"Never mind."

Damned if he didn't feel better after talking to her. Maybe it helped, spilling your guts like that.

When they reached the first Manhattan address, Stack braked the unmarked and parked at the curb near a mailbox with white and yellow graffiti spray-painted all over it. Rica looked out the car window at a ratty-looking walk-up apartment building.

"If our guy lives here," she said, "he's not a very successful firebug."

"Maybe he's only visiting," Stack said. "No telling where O'Reilly got these addresses. His contacts tend not to like him, so sometimes they feed him wrong information."

Rica reached for the door handle. "Like you said, let's split up and get this business out of the way."

"There's a diner down at the corner," Stack said, when she was getting out of the car. "If you finish before I do, go there and I'll meet you."

Rica nodded, turned, and walked toward the old brick building. She heard Stack drive away behind her. That was okay; she didn't feel alone or in any danger out of the ordinary. Maybe this firebug, Larry Chips, wouldn't even be home.

Nobody had to buzz her into this dump. The vestibule smelled like tragedy and stale vomit. There was no name in the slot for the apartment number on O'Reilly's list. She pressed the intercom button but without much hope. The button barely moved under ancient layers of paint.

Naturally the apartment, 5D, was on the top floor. The penthouse, Rica thought, as she sighed and began climbing creaking wooden stairs.

Her breathing was a little ragged by the time she reached 5D and knocked on the door. A faint female voice sounded from inside the apartment; then there was silence. Rica knocked again. "Larry Chips? Police. Open up so we can talk." She moved to the side, not liking it that whoever was in there hadn't come right to the door.

Finally the door opened and a skinny African-American man in his thirties peered out at Rica. The unmistakable scent of marijuana smoke wafted from the place. Rica decided to let that one go; she wasn't here for a drug bust.

She flashed her shield. "I'm looking for Larry Chips." She knew Chips was white.

"Not here," the black man said. He had huge almond eyes that wanted to focus anywhere but on her.

"Does he live here?" A toilet flushed inside the apartment. The stash going into the New York sewer system?

"Naw. He been stayin' here, is all."

"So, is he here now? I only wanna talk to him."

"He ain't been here for a long while."

"You expect him back soon?"

"I mean, been three, four days since he been here." The dark eyes slid to the side, couldn't help it. "He got himself parkin' tickets or somethin'?"

"Something," Rica said. This guy was playing for time. Maybe Chips was on his way down the outside iron fire escape even as they chatted. "I'm coming in," Rica said in a neutral tone, and moved forward.

The man backed away from her as she opened the door all the way. He was even skinnier than he'd looked from the hall, wearing ragged, faded jeans too short for his bony legs, a torn gray T-shirt, and jogging shoes without socks. Rica got a glance at trash all over the place, very little furniture, a diminutive black girl in a dark jacket standing motionless near a wooden chair.

Jacket. Jogging shoes without socks.

Rica caught movement outside the dirty window, saw a hand disappear from gripping the iron rail of the fire escape, just as the man in the jogging shoes bumped into her, shoving her hard on his way out the door. The girl broke and ran at the same time.

Rica ignored them, regained her balance, and rushed to the window. What the hell was Chips doing, if the runner was Chips? Possibly all this was about was the drug thing. But the toilet had flushed, and there'd been time to flush it again if necessary.

Rica reached the closed window and wrestled it open, wincing at the blast of cold outside air. She was about to throw a leg over the sill when the glass pane shattered and she instinctively fell back.

Lying on the floor, she shook her head and stared up at the bullet hole in the glass.

He's shooting at me! What the hell did I stir up here?

Rica scrambled to her feet, pulled her two-way out of its belt holster, and held down the transmit button. "Officer in need of assistance. Need some backup here!" She barked the address, along with brief information as to the suspect's position.

Then she carefully edged back to the window, wishing her heart would slow down. It was making her entire body tremble. Gun drawn, she craned her neck until she could peer down the fire escape.

About two floors down, a blond man, wearing one of those distressed brown leather bomber jackets, paused and gazed wistfully back up at her. *He really doesn't want any of this to be happening.* He held tight to the fire escape ladder with his left hand as his right came up fast from his side. As Rica drew back inside, a bullet pinged off the maze of iron outside the window, raising a cloud of rust.

Rica held her breath and poked her head and gun hand back out the window, ready to return fire though she figured the sprinter would be on the move again.

She was right. The man was leaping from the first-floor balcony, not bothering with the gravity ladder.

He was running when he hit the pavement, almost fell but maintained his balance, arms flailing, then kept going.

Rica was aware of people in the alley below, a couple of what looked like teenagers cutting through, a wino searching through a trash container. The teenagers had broken into a run at the last shot. The wino was frozen. Rica couldn't shoot down there and send a 9mm round ricocheting all over the place looking for a home.

The suspect could move. He must have broken an unofficial record as he sprinted to the mouth of the alley and disappeared around the corner.

At the opposite end of the alley a police car pulled up. Two uniforms piled out. One of them tackled the front teenager. The other gave chase as the second boy banged into a trash can but made it around the corner before he could be grabbed.

"The other way!" Rica shouted, pointing in the direction the blond man had run. "The other goddamn way!"

The cop who'd tackled the teenager had him on the ground and was finishing cuffing him. He looked up at her and held his hand cupped to his ear to indicate he hadn't understood.

"Fuck it!" Rica spat in disgust, knowing that the blond sprinter—Chips?—had made his escape. She ducked back inside, careful not to cut herself on any broken glass lying around.

Glad to be in out of the cold, she looked carefully at the apartment for the first time. Not just messy, a horror. There was no furniture other than a soiled mattress and the wooden chair. Rags were piled in a corner. There were burn spots on the old hardwood floor where fires had been built, probably on what looked like a blackened cookie sheet near the mattress. Rica was sure nobody lived here, only camped out.

Still with her 9mm in hand, she carefully checked out the tiny L kitchen that was barren of appliances, then the bathroom.

She was alone, as she'd thought. The skinny guy and his girl companion had probably taken the stairs and reached ground level before Chips. Or maybe had a way off the roof.

She raised the toilet seat lid and backed away, making a face as the stench and revulsion hit her. This wasn't the toilet she'd heard flushing. Must have been from the floor above. The water service was off here, though that hadn't slowed down anyone wanting to use the facilities. On the cracked tile floor was a bent, flame-blackened teaspoon, a small length of rubber tubing. More than weed was on the menu here. Maybe the man and the woman who'd fled had good reason to run.

And had probably taken the reason with them.

Rica heard voices, a lot of clomping around in the hall.

She walked back into the destroyed living room. "It's okay. In here."

She holstered her gun and stood watching as three blue uniforms stormed in.

"We didn't get him," one of them said, a big guy with a bull neck and a white mustache. "We got two teenyboppers down in the alley. Black males, claim they know zilch."

"Witnesses," Rica said. "Treat them like witnesses or Al Sharpton'll get you."

Two of the uniforms left. White Mustache stayed with Rica. He wrinkled his nose. "Smells like shit and weed in here."

"That's exactly what we've got," Rica said.

EIGHTEEN

"What's with this Larry Chips?" O'Reilly asked the next morning in his office. He was standing behind his desk, apparently too irate to sit. Stack and Rica sat in the matching chairs facing his desk. "Why'd the guy do a rabbit when you knocked on his door?"

"We can't know for sure why anyone in the apartment ran," Stack said. "The place was supposed to be unoccupied; it had been vacant for more than a month. The owner's an absentee landlord who lives in White Plains, and he said he has no idea who was in there when Rica knocked. Had to be squatters."

O'Reilly crossed his arms and stared at Rica. "Any ideas why these squatters all took off like they were scalded?"

"Drugs would be my guess," she said.

"There was no sign of anything in the place other than a trace of weed. Not enough to justify fleeing from a cop with a gun."

"Could be they took most of their stash with them," Stack said. "Coulda been anything."

"Maybe," O'Reilly said, "but I gotta tell you the apartment isn't the kind of place where you usually find major league drug dealers hanging out. More like a dive for transients." He was still looking at Rica.

"That's the way I see it," Rica said, not so much mind-ing agreeing. When somebody was right they were right. And she thought maybe *she* was right in how she figured this. "Chips was the first one out of there, and we all know why he might have been eager to leave. It's possible he bolted and started a panic. That kind of thing can be con-tagious. The other two caught the mood and fled. Everyone there wasn't necessarily running for the same reason."

"You think Chips is our firebug?"

"It's possible. It'd explain why he'd risk a bullet to get away."

"If he had a stash of coke on him, that'd explain it, too," O'Reilly said.

"He only has a drug record for minor possession," Stack said. "Two arrests, one conviction for marijuana posses-sion. His drug of choice is fire."

"So you're with Rica on this? You think Larry Chips is the Torcher?"

"Neither of us thinks it for sure," Stack said, with a glance at Rica. "We both see him as our strongest suspect. He's a known arsonist, ran when Rica knocked on a door, took a shot at a cop rather than stop." He shrugged. "He looks good for it."

"Not to me," O'Reilly said. "Chips is a firebug, all right, but one that's turned it into a business. You look at his record and it's all setting fires for purposes of insur-ance fraud, work for hire, that kinda thing. A sickness but also a business."

"People change," Rica said.

"Not firebugs. It's like a sexual thing to them, fire."

Rica thought O'Reilly seemed to know a lot about it.

She thought she'd prod a bit. "What do you mean, sir, a sexual thing?"

O'Reilly looked uncomfortable. He cleared his throat and turned it into a cough. "You know, they relate fire to sex in some way. Pyromaniacs have been known to have orgasms at major fires."

"You're kidding me!" Rica said.

O'Reilly gave her a look as if he might be wondering if *she* was kidding *him*. About time, Stack thought.

Rica crossed her legs so some thigh showed, then sat slightly forward so her breasts were prominent. "Come to think of it, lots of words related to fire are used in sexual talk. "Hot stuff.' 'Hot mamma.' 'My old flame.' 'She's *hot!*'"

O'Reilly coughed again and tried not to look at Rica's legs.

"It would get the higher-ups off your back if we named a suspect," Stack said to him, trying to shut Rica up. "And right now we don't have anyone more likely than Larry Chips."

"And I'd look like an ass if the Torcher turned out to be someone else."

That explained it, Stack thought. O'Reilly was as usual interested mostly in self-preservation and advancement. Larry Chips didn't fit airtight as a suspect, and the Torcher murders had developed into a high-profile case where a wrong guess could haunt an ambitious cop.

"I'll leave the guesswork to you two," O'Reilly said, finally sitting down in his desk chair. "As of right now, Larry Chips isn't even a suspect. But I've got a query in to the LAPD about him. Los Angeles is where he lived most of his life and set most of his fires. We oughta at least find out how long he might have been in New York. What else he might have been up to the past year or so. What I gather so far is that this guy's a punk with a quirk. Too soft to be a killer."

"I don't want to get off him too soon," Stack said. "I still think he might be our firebug. And if he isn't, I'd like to hear it from him."

"And I think we oughta look under other rocks," O'Reilly said. "Especially now, with the kid's death putting more heat on us. Let's get the full lab and ME reports, the story on Larry Chips from the LAPD. My guess is he's only a diversion. Making him the focal point of the investigation won't be productive at all."

"What do you mean, 'the kid's death'?" Rica asked.

"You haven't heard? The six-year-old Wilson girl, Eden, died from her burn wounds late last night."

Rica felt herself tighten up inside. Six years old . . . "The bastard has to feel bad about that. Feel guilty."

"Why?" O'Reilly asked. "Because you would?"

"Because anyone human would."

"Not a sociopath firebug."

"So who or what should be the focal point?" Stack asked.

O'Reilly looked at him as if the question were absurd. "Why, the victims. What I want you and Rica to do is stay on the victims, talk to people who knew them, worked with them, hated or loved them. Find some common thread among the victims. You think this Torcher freak just chooses victims at random?"

"It happens," Rica said. "Maybe especially with the sociopath firebug you just described."

O'Reilly gave a hoarse laugh. "Tell her, Stack. Give her a refresher course."

Stack didn't like it, but he told her. "It doesn't happen very often. Usually a serial killer has a compulsion that causes him to gravitate toward certain types of victims. Trouble is, what marks them as types in the killer's mind isn't necessarily obvious to anyone else. If we're looking for a serial killer whose motive's something other than compulsion, there still figures to be a common denominator among the victims. If nothing else, they probably knew their killer before he committed the crime."

"There's another possibility," O'Reilly said, "if slim. So far this firebug has set his victims ablaze in apartments."

"Maybe there's something in common about the apartments!" Rica said.

O'Reilly smiled at her. "Sometimes, Stack, your protégé shows promise."

"In flashes," Stack said. He doubted that some kind of similarity in apartments was setting off the Torcher. "What do you think might be the killer's problem, he hates Berber carpet?"

"Don't wise off with me," O'Reilly said. "See if you can use all that cleverness to outsmart this killer. In other words, do your job."

Stack would. They were searching for the killer of a child now. If the high-rise fires continued, it was inevitable that there would be more innocent victims, including chidden.

O'Reilly pulled a file folder over to him and began reading its contents with an expression of mock concentration. Stack had been sufficiently reprimanded and dismissed. He went to the office door and held it open for Rica, then turned back to O'Reilly. "How's Vandervoort doing?"

"It doesn't look good for him," O'Reilly said, ignoring the implied disdain in Stack's question and studiously not looking up. "I'm told he's going to start chemotherapy next week, maybe radiation to go along with it."

Doesn't look good, all right, Stack thought.

Out in the hall, Rica said nothing as she hurried to keep up with Stack. She knew he was fuming, and she didn't want to heighten his anger and embarrassment.

As soon as they entered the squad room, Sergeant Redd approached them.

"Your wife wants you to call her," he said to Stack. "She says it's important."

Stack thanked Redd and veered toward his desk and a phone. Rica kept right on walking toward the coffee machine, not wilting under the force of all the eyeballs aimed at her.

At his desk, Stack punched out the number of the publishing house where Laura had gotten a job as some kind of assistant. After asking for her and holding for a while he listened to an orchestral arrangement of Eric Clapton's "Bad Love" before Laura's voice came over the phone.

"Hello, Ben. Thanks for calling." It was a shock to hear himself referred to by his given name, and he realized Laura had been just about the only person in his life who used it.

Stack felt awkward, almost as if he were talking to a stranger. Time apart had added to the void between them. "How's the job?" he asked.

"Fine. I like it here and they seem to like me. They're going to make me a copy editor."

He remembered she had edited medical textbooks somewhere before they'd met.

"I need a favor, Ben. I bought a co-op and I need some help."

Was she going to ask him for a loan? He was in no position. "Help? Sure, if I can, Laura." He was trying to digest the fact that she was already moving out of the tiny apartment she'd rented by the month and had bought a place. Moving up in the world. Moving fast.

"I don't want to borrow money or anything like that," she said. "I need a reference, is all."

"For the loan?"

"No, for the co-op board. They go through the formality of approving prospective owners, and I don't want to blow this deal by being turned down. I can afford this place, but I need for them to know that. To know me, and how I'll work a second job, if it comes to that."

"I'll be glad to write them a letter."

"That's great, Ben. A character reference, is all. Don't overdo it. You know, I'm not asking you to lie for me, or even to exaggerate."

"You have character," Stack said, "and I take your word you can afford what you're buying. Don't worry, I'll make you a cross between Mother Teresa and Ivana Trump."

She laughed. The conversation had loosened up. Maybe they could actually be good friends after the divorce was final. "Thanks so much, Ben. I really do appreciate it."

She gave him an address on East Fifty-third near First Avenue. He knew the neighborhood. It wasn't bad, near the UN Building.

As he was hanging up the phone, Rica approached the desk. She was carrying two cups of coffee. She set one down on the desk, then took a nearby chair.

"She wants a reference letter," Stack said, knowing Rica would ask. "She's buying a co-op."

Rica sipped her coffee, thinking about that. "Have you stopped to consider?" she asked.

Stack tested his coffee with a tentative forefinger and found it too hot to drink. "Consider what?"

"That you're being asked to write a glowing letter of recommendation for someone you're divorcing and might do battle with in court."

"Not so long ago you were trying to get me to reveal any leftover tender thoughts about her."

"I was *not*. I wanted you to admit to yourself how you felt so you could let her go."

"You mean get in touch with my feelings so I can get on with my life?"

"And feel good about your new empowered self. Don't patronize me, Stack. It's too soon after your lecture on serial killers. I just want to see you straighten out your emotions so you don't get roughed up too much in divorce court combat."

"It isn't like that," Stack said.

"Like what?"

"Combat."

"It might become so," Rica said. "Please listen to me and don't sign or even write anything without your lawyer's approval."

"You really think that's necessary?"

"I think it's why you have a lawyer."

Rica stood up with her coffee and stalked away, giving him privacy. Stack sat and watched her. Women were so damned practical. And insightful.

That one, anyway.

He dragged the phone over to him and called Gideon Fine.

* * *

The incinerator. They all had to go to the incinerator.

The Torcher stood staring at the stack of New York newspapers whose headlines screamed and captions ranted about recent deadly fires. Someone mad, the writers speculated. Someone insane must be responsible.

The Torcher laughed. Was it possible to be insane and responsible simultaneously? Maybe the newspapers deserved a letter asking that very question.

No, there was no reason to write letters, to ask or explain. The flames would explain eventually, would purify and explain and end. After the fire came the long night of the soul.

The incinerator waited for the newspapers. To keep them because of vanity would be running a risk. To keep them would be inviting suspicion, if anyone happened by some remote chance to see them. So they had to be destroyed, with all their accounts and speculation and terror between the lines. Flame to fame to flame.

The Torcher picked up the stack of papers and curled it so it fit into a grocery sack. A neat bundle now, ready for its plunge through darkness to the building's bowels and the waiting flames.

Like a chute to hell.

NINETEEN

Stack and Rica spent the next several days trying to link the victims together. But for all their work they came up zero. The Torcher's victims seemed to have virtually nothing in common other than that they all lived in apartments. They were respectively a tax attorney; a plastic surgeon; and the latest, James Healy, who'd made money buying and selling taxi medallions—a lucrative and distinctly New York business. For the last few years Healy had fancied himself a day trader and bought and sold stocks at his home computer. Roy Wilson, who died in the apartment adjacent to Healy's, didn't count. His death had been accidental, as had the death of his daughter, Eden.

The deliberately killed victims were male, reasonably well-off financially (which they would be in order to live where they had), but beyond that were downright dissimilar. As far as Stack and Rica could determine, the victims' paths had never crossed. Two were single, one was married. All had stock or bond portfolios, but who didn't these days if they had a few extra dollars to rub together? Photographs of the three victims before death were no help. The three men looked nothing alike. It would be a real stretch of the imagination to think anyone could see them as the same type.

That there was no forced entry didn't necessarily mean killer and victim were acquainted. Maybe only that the victim had answered a knock on the door.

Stack knew what the next step had to be, and O'Reilly instructed them to do just that: get off the victims, for a while at least, and look for some commonality in where they'd lived and died. The physical properties. If those apartments had something in common, that something could be the catalyst that led to murder. Obviously the killer had to be someone who'd been in all three. That narrowed the list of possible suspects considerably among the millions of people who lived in or were a short train or plane ride from New York City.

Stack and Rica had come in early this morning and sat for hours studying crime scene photos of the burned apartments where Torcher victims had died. It had taken Rica about fifteen minutes to realize they were wasting their time.

"All we're looking at is charred wood and drywall and ashes," she said, leaning back in her chair and stretching. She threw her shoulders back, putting on a breast show, but Stack ignored it.

He agreed with her but kept shuffling through the photos in each murder file. "What we need are shots of the apartments before they were burned."

"Just the kitchens," Rica said, "where the bodies were found."

"Not necessarily. If the apartments rather than the victims had something in common that might have set off our firebug, it might show in photos of the other rooms."

"Or the other rooms themselves." Instantly Rica wished she could reach out and grab her words before they reached Stack. She knew he wouldn't let them pass.

Methodical, relentless Stack. She thought she'd say it before he did: "I suppose that's our next move, visiting each of the apartments."

"Nope, we're going to the funeral," he said. "Eden Wilson's going to be buried this morning."

Rica should have remembered. They would go to the funeral and watch for anyone in any way suspicious. It wasn't unknown for killers to give in to a compulsion to attend their victim's funeral, and their firebug was driven by compulsion. And maybe this time, guilt. At least they could hope.

"Then," Stack said, "we visit each of the apartments."

The man could be frustrating, but he made her glad she wasn't a criminal.

Eden's funeral took place after a service in a small mortuary in Brooklyn. Her mother, who'd buried her husband and Eden's father only days ago, looked numbed from grief and medication. The girl's grandparents looked old, much older probably than they had last week.

After the service, Stack and Rica drove the unmarked in the funeral procession to a cemetery situated on a slight hill and crowded with headstones and religious statuary. It was near a busy highway and would seldom be silent. No place for a child to be laid to permanent rest.

Hunched against the late-morning cold, Rica read the engraving on Eden's headstone: *In the violent world around us, in God she is secure.*

Rica sure hoped so.

Standing near a concrete Christ with outstretched arms, she tuned out the graveside service and let her gaze slide over the group of mourners. They all appeared profoundly grief-stricken, many of them crying. The death of a child . . .

Rica and Stack had studied the mourners earlier in the mortuary, if or how they approached the closed casket with the girl's photograph resting on it, how they interacted with each other. Everyone there seemed to be known to at least one other person. No one behaved in any way unusual under the grim circumstances.

Rica was sure that attending the memorial service and funeral had yielded her and Stack nothing. It had to be attended, though, and by the chief investigators themselves rather than the NYPD representatives who'd covered the other, adult victims' funerals, whose reports Stack and Rica had read, dismissed, and filed away as useless. It was all a sad part of routine police work, of the deceased's devolution from person to a set of facts and statistics.

The funeral ended the way they all do, with a tentative, heartbroken sense of loss and sad new beginning. Eden Wilson was completely gone now, and her brief existence had been summed up. All that was left was memory losing its battle against time.

Gray clouds had become darker and caused the shadows of the tombstones to disappear. The wind was colder and carried light rain like specks of ice that seemed to burrow into exposed skin like acid.

Rica was never more glad to leave a place.

The next evening, Stack and Rica sat wearily on a gray sofa in the lobby of the Whitlock Building. Other than a section of carpet that had been removed and awaited replacement, dark scrapes on one of the walls, and scuff marks on the marble floor, there was little indication that a major fire had occurred here. Life did go on.

They were both bone tired. They'd visited the apartments in the order in which they'd burned, carefully examining and then photographing each. They saw nothing linking them together. They'd concluded that Danner had owned no valuable art; Dr. Lucette had possessed only moderately expensive and rather tasteful erotic art; Healy's taste in art ran to dogs playing poker. None of any sort of art seemed to be missing. Art theft seemed not to be a motive. Nor for that matter theft of any kind. Plenty of jewelry and cash had been left behind in each apartment.

All indications were that major amounts of money hadn't been kept in the apartments. Only the twenty thousand dollars in Danner's bedroom safe had been a considerable enough sum to suggest motive. And of course the money hadn't been removed from the safe.

"White," Stack said in a tired voice.

Rica looked over at him. "What?"

"All three apartments were painted one shade or another of white."

"Almost every apartment in New York is white," Rica said. "It makes them look larger."

Stack realized his own apartment was white.

"It's like some kind of game with him!" Rica said in frustration. "Only he can see and we have to play in the dark!"

"It's a game with all of them, but a damned serious game."

Stack's cell phone chirped. He glanced at Rica as he pulled it from an inside suit coat pocket, pressed it to his ear, and said simply, "Stack."

Rica sat staring at the scrapes on the wall and listening to his end of the conversation:

"Yeah, I'm sorry . . . It isn't me saying no, it's my lawyer . . . For God's sake, we both have lawyers, so it makes sense that we oughta listen to what they say, take their advice . . . Yeah . . . yeah . . . yeah . . ."

One of The Beatles, Rica thought.

"Yeah . . ."

Nope. Too many "yeahs."

"Yeah, that makes sense . . . I don't mind, Laura, but I've gotta let Gideon Fine know. That's right, because he is. Yeah . . . yeah . . . yeah. No, it sounds reasonable, and I can't think why I shouldn't, but then I'm a cop, not an attorney . . . yeah . . . yeah . . . yeah."

Stack hung up. "Laura," he said.

"Yeah."

"She's ticked off because my lawyer told me not to write that letter of recommendation for her. He said it was unwise to put sterling praise in writing about someone I might yet be engaged with in litigation."

"She must see the sense in that."

Stack made a face. "Hell, I don't know. Why does a divorce between two people who aren't contesting it have to be such a walk on eggs?"

"I couldn't tell you," Rica said, "but it is. And eggs break real easy."

"Since my lawyer told me not to put anything in writing," Stack said, "Laura wants me to drop by and talk to this co-op board in person."

"You mean, like, testify before them?"

"No, no, they're not a panel of judges or a grand jury. It'll be more of a conversation, is all."

"See what your lawyer says about that," Rica suggested.

"Oh, I will. I never liked it when lawyers played cops; I'm not gonna try playing lawyer."

"I know you can be persuasive, Stack. You're a nice guy and want to help Laura. But don't try to talk your lawyer into giving you the okay."

"I won't."

But she knew he would.

They sat silently and watched an elderly woman walking a small, sweatered dog that looked like a schnauzer but probably wasn't enter the lobby. She nodded, smiling at them, as she crossed to the elevator. Rica thought she remembered the woman from the night of the fire but couldn't be sure. She *was* pretty sure about the dog, though, that had been weaving around legs in the crowd of tenants watching their building burn.

What kind of cop am I, that I can remember a dog but not a person? Height about sixteen inches, eyes brown, hair gray and brindle, clothing red sweater with leg holes.

The dog glanced back at her as if it knew her thoughts.

"So we come up empty again," Rica said, when the elevator door had glided shut behind the woman and her canine. "Not surprising, since we have no idea what we're looking for."

"I know what to look for," Stack said. "Larry Chips."

"Gut feeling?" Rica asked.

Stack took a while before answering. "I'm going with my head this time. Chips is the best we've got." He met her eyes with his steady gray appraisal. "How do you feel about it?"

"You ever get in your car and have the feeling you're going to have an accident, but you ignore it and go ahead and drive off anyway? Then it turns out you were right to ignore the feeling and you didn't have an accident?"

He kept studying her. "Yeah."

"Well, that's how I feel about Larry Chips."

TWENTY

Etta Daggett said, "Let's do it."

She was Leland Brand's unofficial campaign manager. Not that Brand had declared himself a candidate for the next New York City mayoral election. The next such election was years away, and he was still, after all, an aide to the present mayor. But the present mayor had announced that for personal and business reasons he wasn't running for another term. The Office of Public Safety, the Division of Safety and Health, and several other city departments were about to be combined into one new office, the Department of Public Well-being. To be appointed commissioner of that office was an obvious stepping-stone to the mayoral candidacy, if the new commissioner played the game cleverly enough. That was where Etta Daggett came in.

On hearing of the proposed departmental realignment, the first thing Brand had done was quietly hire Etta Daggett. She'd handled several present elected officials and had a reputation as a mudslinger and a ball-kicking political infighter. Brand didn't have much stomach for that kind of thing, but one did what one must.

"What's the mayor say?" he asked. He was almost Etta's physical opposite, short while she was tall, military erect while she was stooped, blond while she was dark, alert and handsome while she was deceptively drowsy looking and sporting a mustache of fine dark fuzz she defiantly preferred to depilatories. Brand wore tailored pinstriped suits, white shirts, and drab ties without pattern. His hair was cut short and expensively coiffed, his collars made rigid with plastic stays, his pants pressed as if the creases were sewn in, his colors coordinated as if by computer. Next to him, Etta appeared to have dressed in the dark.

"The mayor is leaning toward appointing you commissioner of the Department of Public Well-being," she told Brand. "That means you can stake out your claim for the foreseeable future. Ask the right questions and provide the right answers. High-rise apartment fires are a major threat to a city built mostly in the air. Why wasn't New York ready for this threat?"

Brand raised a golden eyebrow. "The mayor will go along with that approach?"

"Sure. Because there's something to it. The technology isn't there to fight fires hundreds of feet in the air. Not on a city budget, anyway."

"I read about some special helicopters equipped with fire retardant sprayers—"

"So don't tell anybody," Etta said. "Most of that shit doesn't work anyway. It's usually some guy who invented something in his garage and wants to take advantage of a bad situation. You're above that. What can we do *now?* That's your approach. You make a success of this commissioner's job, then use that success for all the media time you can get, especially in periods of crises."

"You really don't think it's a little early to be moving on the next mayoral election?"

It's a little late to be changing your mind about it. Or your guts. "Not the way politics are, what they've become. You've got no choice but to spend a long time laying the groundwork for a successful campaign. The voters can spend the next several years getting used to depending on you for their safety, their lives, because you know what to do. And then you promise that if elected, you'll damn well do it."

"If I may play devil's advocate," Brand said, "do what?"

"You mean as mayor?"

"No, too soon for that. As commissioner."

"Call a fucking meeting with experts! How are you supposed to know off the bat what's needed here? Fighting fires isn't your field. You don't want to go off half-cocked and shoot your dick off. Find out what the experts say about this situation before you act and maybe do more harm than good."

"The mayor was talking about appointing a committee as well as combining departments."

"Doesn't mean squat. There are already so many committees a committee is needed to figure out how to tell one from the other."

"Still, committees work even if they don't work. They give the impression something's being done."

"The plan is," Etta forged ahead patiently, "the mayor will pretend you're ahead of the curve on this issue and agree with you once you've established your position as the new commissioner. That way the public remembers and gives you credit in the voting booth. You'll still be the Department of Public Well-being commissioner. If things are going crappy, we convince them they can't switch horses now. Too dangerous. If things are going smoothly, you're the reason. Win, win."

"You really think voters are still that gullible?"

"They're dumber than they ever were, especially if they think they're sophisticates."

Etta slouched over to a credenza near the window and poured herself a bourbon straight up, then sampled it. She had no idea what kind it was, since it was in a crystal decanter, but it was smooth.

When she turned, taking a second sip, she saw that Brand was standing there looking mildly confused.

"I'm hired only to advise," Etta said. "It's ultimately your call, Leland. But if the mayor appoints you the new commissioner and his obvious heir apparent—and he will—I do advise you to make this high-rise fire thing your issue. It's a sure winner. This Torcher creep will start a few more fires, cause some more Sturm und Drang while you go up in the polls as his adversary. Then he'll get caught like they all do, and you can claim some of the credit for that, too."

"And if he isn't caught right away? If he keeps setting fires and real panic sets in and more people die?"

Etta smiled. "Then it's *I told you so* time. You were the one who jumped on this problem early and demanded something be done. If only people had listened! There's always a silver lining, or one you can paint that color."

Brand shook his head. "Pathetic, but probably sound reasoning."

"I've gotta talk freely, Leland, in order that we can work together. You came up through the ranks in New York politics, so you're no cherry. But in the past few years, while you've been doing a damned good job *in* City Hall, the game of getting *to* City Hall or anywhere else has gotten rougher. If somebody doesn't have the stomach for today's politics, or tomorrow's, he better grow one."

Brand walked over to the window and looked out at Lower Manhattan, at the bundled pedestrians and clogged traffic, at the city he really did love. He'd never had any illusions about political life; if he hadn't known how the game was played, he wouldn't be an aide to one of the most successful mayors in New York's history. And he knew Etta was right about how much lower the gutter had slipped in recent years. "What if my opponent, whoever he or she turns out to be, takes the line that I shamelessly worked a human tragedy to my advantage? That my ambition exceeds my morality?"

"You remind your opponent—and the voters—that you goddamn *did* something about the situation. Or at least you tried. Which, if you stop to think about it, will be true." She noticed he was nodding slightly in agreement, maybe not even aware of the abbreviated little bobbing movements. "You start talking it up now and the mayor won't have any choice but to appoint you. And the cops'll feel the pressure—I'll help see to that. Then whoever's going around burning people in their apartments will feel the pressure, too. And the thing is, you might really be contributing to ending the city's latest nightmare."

Brand grinned at her with something like admiration. "You're definitely persuasive, Etta."

She smiled. "No, Leland, *you're* persuasive!"

"And persuaded," he said, and walked over and poured a bourbon of his own.

"There's gotta be *something* linking these victims to each other besides their killer," O'Reilly was saying. He plopped back down in his desk chair and stared at Stack and Rica, seated across the desk from him. It took a while for his chair cushion to stop hissing. "There must be something you two are overlooking."

Stack said, "Maybe that something is Larry Chips."

O'Reilly flushed with anger. "Him again? I told you, he's a small-timer and a fuckup. Strikes the match in fire insurance scams because he doesn't want to or can't turn an honest dollar."

"Then why'd he bolt on Rica?"

"Who knows for sure? Maybe he was planning on burning down the building and thought we somehow found out about it. A guy like that rabbits out of a drug-dive apartment and you got him built up like Oswald. Chips probably had a dozen reasons to run when he saw a cop."

"Name Chips as our suspect," Stack said, "and we relieve some public angst. There'll be a lot of media play, and maybe somebody'll actually spot him somewhere."

O'Reilly shook his head violently. "This is the NYPD, not *America's Most Wanted.* Chips is a nonissue."

Rica said, "Maybe so, but it still might help to get his name in the papers and on TV as a prime suspect. Getting a suspect's photograph plastered all over television has brought results in the past. If Chips isn't our firebug, it still might shake some information loose out there. He split from that apartment and risked killing a cop or getting shot himself for *some* reason."

O'Reilly sighed and leaned back in his chair, studying Rica. Stack thought of a naturalist observing some kind of animal life that didn't care one way or the other if he existed, but was nonetheless keeping an eye on him. O'Reilly said, "Has it occurred to you, Rica, that a wacko like Chips is very often not thinking clearly?"

"Sure. There are times even I don't think clearly."

O'Reilly continued with his analytical gaze, maybe now trying to decide if she was messing with him. She met his stare with admirable neutrality. Stack would have said something to break the tension, only he was becoming amused.

Rica's equanimity seemed finally to bother O'Reilly and he shifted his weight forward so the chair tilted with him. He propped his elbows on the desk and assumed a pose of concern, letting his gaze roam now between Rica and Stack. "What you gotta ask yourself, you two, is do you really think Larry Chips is good for these barbecues, or is it that you've run through every other possibility you can think of and he's all that's left?"

"If you're looking for an honest answer," Rica said, "it's a combination of both. And it's not as if we'd be badgering a law-abiding citizen—this guy took a shot at me, remember?"

Stack wished he could reach over and prod her in the ribs, make her go a little more cautiously here. Who could tell when O'Reilly might look for a scapegoat so he could set right Vandervoort's poor administrative procedures?

There was a knock on the door, and a clerk Stack hadn't seen before walked in and handed O'Reilly a folded sheet of fax paper. She was young, cute, and had an almost impossibly turned up nose. No words were exchanged as she made her way back out of the office without looking at either Stack or Rica, while O'Reilly read whatever was on the paper.

"Here's why Larry Chips took a shot at you and ran," he said, dropping the paper on the desk. "LAPD says there's an active warrant on him for a homicide out in LA. He shot and killed a man at a fire he set. Outdoor security camera caught him running from the scene." He stood up behind the desk so he could look down at Stack and Rica, who remained seated. "So, let's view Chips as a shooter, not a burner of people."

"What kind of fire did Chips set out in LA?" Stack asked.

"Not an apartment fire like the ones you're investigating. He torched a house. The victim rented it from whoever owned the building and probably hired Chips. The tenant's burned corpse had four slugs in it. Any of our apartment fire victims have slugs in them?"

Stack admitted that none had. Rica said nothing.

"Okay," O'Reilly said.

You think so, asshole? Rica thought.

Stack stood up, so she figured she'd better also.

She wasn't surprised when O'Reilly came up with something else to ask when they were almost out the door. The Columbo syndrome.

"You two looked into the sex lives of whoever was romantically involved with or married to these victims? You know, kinky stuff, that kinda thing?"

"Kinky stuff?" Rica asked.

"Not yet," Stack said.

"That one boggles the mind," Rica said, "considering half these people's sex lives have gone up in smoke."

"Or a third," O'Reilly said meaningfully.

Rica was formulating a reply when she felt Stack actually push her out the door.

In the squad room they saw the new young clerk busy at an open file drawer. Stack and Rica walked over to her.

Stack introduced himself and Rica to the young woman,

called her *dear,* melted her heart with his smile. Made Rica sick, but the girl didn't seem to see through him.

"Did the commander ask you to bring that form into his office as soon as it came in?" Stack asked.

"No," said the clerk. "It came in by fax over two hours ago. He told me to wait twenty minutes after you entered his office, then bring the information in to him."

"Thank you, dear," Stack said.

As he and Rica strode from the building, Rica could hear him breathing hard with his anger.

She thought she might even be able to feel heat emanating from him.

TWENTY-ONE

Stack knew Gideon Fine didn't like it, but what else was there to do? Stack and Laura were trying to end their marriage with as little stress as possible and without lasting animosity, but the system kept getting in the way. Caution became distrust became betrayal.

And why in God's name *shouldn't* he simply stand in front of a co-op board and tell them the truth about Laura? She would be financially okay and could afford the co-op; she had no felony convictions or destructive addictions and had never been evicted for whatever reason from anywhere.

"Well and good," Fine had said, "but as your attorney I have to inform you that you can't get in trouble if you don't say anything one way or the other about Laura. If you go on the record—any record—what you say might be taken out of context, misrepresented, misinterpreted, and be used to do you harm."

But Stack would have none of these intricacies and intrigues. With the people you loved, used to love, and trusted, you hung the truth out on the line. There was too much damned subterfuge in the world, and nobody knew it better than an old cop.

He stood on the cold street corner and through the fog of his breath studied the building and block where his former wife was going to live, feeling proprietary, feeling protective, feeling like a husband. The co-op Laura was trying to buy was in a prewar brick building in the lower Fifties near First Avenue. It was a fair neighborhood almost on the edge of upscale. A safe enough neighborhood, Stack decided. He withdrew his hands from his coat pockets and crossed the street.

The Norwood, as the building was called, didn't have a doorman, and the outer lobby was veined gray marble that could use polishing and mirrors that could use resilvering. There was a cluster of new-looking but mismatched upholstered chairs around a table with a fanned arrangement of outdated magazines on it next to a lamp. Several of the magazines were Spanish issues, one French.

Stack pressed an intercom button, identified himself, and was buzzed into the main building. He rode an elevator to the second floor and went to a door marked 2B, where he'd been told the Norwood co-op board was meeting.

A short, balding man in a white shirt with his tie loosened opened the door before Stack had a chance to knock, then smiled and invited him in. Shaking hands with Stack, he said his name was Hank Upman and that he was president of the board.

Stack found himself in a vacant unit without furnishings except for a long folding table with a white cloth over it, two new-looking mismatched chairs that expanded the decorating motif of the lobby, and a row of wooden folding chairs behind the table. On the folding chairs sat six board members—three men and three women. The chair in the center was empty, obviously Upman's. It was cool in what was apparently the unit's living room, and smelled faintly of cleaning fluid or insecticide. Stack unbuttoned his coat but left it on.

Quickly Upman introduced the rest of the board members in a flurry of names, only a few of which Stack could remember, then told Stack he knew his time was valuable and thanks for coming and would he please sit in one of the upholstered chairs facing the table. And would Stack like a cup of coffee? Stack said no, and Upman walked around the long table and sat down in his chair. He was a jittery kind of guy but it seemed not so much inner-driven as for show, as if he might be trying to convince himself and anyone watching that he was busy and important. Inside, he might be perfectly composed. His intense dark eyes were steady, and his broad features were calm, even as his body motion was a series of shifts and twitches and his hands were never still.

"We've talked briefly to your former wife, Mr. Stack, and—"

"Present wife," Stack corrected. "The divorce isn't yet final. And it's Detective Stack."

"Yes, sure." Upman began picking at the flesh of one hand with nervous fingers of the other. "What we'd like from you is a character reference. Since you, uh, expressed hesitancy about writing a letter of reference, I . . . we all want to assure you that what you tell us won't go beyond these walls."

"It wouldn't matter if it did," Stack said. "There's nothing secret or sinister about Laura. She's simply a cop's wife who's finally had too much of irregular hours, regular worry, and a husband married to his work."

"You make it sound as if the divorce is all your fault," a middle-aged woman at the end of the table said. She wore violet-framed glasses with a woven cord dangling from their sidebars and draped behind her neck. Stack thought her last name was Hart but decided not to risk it.

"It is," he said simply, almost hearing Gideon Fine groan. *Better get control of that, quit shooting off your mouth. The truth can kill you in court.* "What I mean is, there's no dislike or trouble between us. It's just that our marriage is over. I'm confident that if I tell you about Laura you'll be more than glad to accept her as a resident here. There's simply no reason not to."

"That's very reassuring," Upman said, not sounding at all reassured.

"It's refreshing to hear a husband who's being divorced talk that way," said the woman whose name might be Hart.

"What about unusual friends?" A slender blond man, quite old and seated on the other side of Upman, had spoken. He had a downturned mouth and dewlaps blemished with liver spots.

"Unusual how?' Stack asked.

The man shrugged. "Habits, associations, creeds—"

"Not creeds," Upman cut in. "Affiliations, more like."

Colors, more like, Stack thought, noticing that everyone on the board was white. "If I'm not mistaken, she's in a garden club. She likes to grow geraniums."

The board stared at him as if he'd gone insane.

"There are strict rules about plants and containers on the balconies," a dark-haired man wearing a gray knit sweater said. Warren, Stack was pretty sure was his first name.

"I'm sure Laura will conform to the rules. She'll probably even resign from the garden club if you ask."

"Hardly necessary," snapped a tall woman seated on Upman's right. She was tuned in and knew sarcasm when she heard it. She was wearing a brilliant silk scarf wrapped around her head and had on the largest gold hoop earrings Stack had ever seen. "Does your wife subscribe to the *Times* or the *Post?*"

"We always got the *Times* delivered," Stack said, "but we used to read both."

"The *New Yorker?*"

"Pardon?"

"Does she read the *New Yorker?*"

"No."

"Would she understand the cartoons?"

"Very well, I'd imagine."

"These kinds of questions might seem strange to you, Detective Stack," Upman said, "but their purpose is for us to get a feel for what kind of person your wife really is. I'm sure you ask the same kinds of questions in your interrogations."

"No," Stack said. He had never inquired if a suspect understood *New Yorker* cartoons. But maybe it wasn't a bad idea.

"There are various reasons for divorce," Warren said. "What can you tell us about your wife's lifestyle?"

Stack wasn't sure quite how to answer. "She's quiet," he said. "Doesn't keep late hours or play the stereo at top volume."

Warren sat back and seemed to be carefully composing his next question. "I mean, what are the chances of her ever remarrying another man?"

"Or going out with . . . dating another man?" asked the old blond guy who'd inquired about unusual friends. Something about the emphasis on *man.*

"I'm not sure how to answer that one," Stack said.

"You can answer generally," Warren said. "That's all we ask of you."

It took Stack a moment; then he was astounded. "Are you asking me if she's a lesbian?"

No one on the board looked surprised by his response.

"That wasn't the question," Upman put in quickly. Stack understood why he was board president. It took somebody with sense to steer these people away from trouble.

He stared hard at Warren. *"Was* that your question?"

"Of course not," Warren said.

"Laura isn't leaving me for another man or woman," Stack said. "Since you haven't asked."

"And we haven't," Upman reaffirmed. Gideon Fine would approve of Upman.

The woman with the violet glasses smiled. "Outstanding debts?" she asked, switching onto a safer track.

For the next twenty minutes Stack fielded more conventional questions, but still some of them probed where the board had no business going. Some of the questions, Stack simply refused to answer. None of the board members objected to his refusal, or pressed him, but Stack had the feeling that if he were someone else, someone not NYPD and without a decidedly menacing aura about him, they would have been more demanding and threatening.

At the end of the interrogation—and that was what it had become—he wasn't sure if he'd helped or hurt Laura's chances of being approved by the board.

The board members all smiled amiably and thanked him profusely for his time, and Upman politely ushered him out. As he was leaving, Stack heard them discussing whether they should adjourn.

Probably, Stack thought, so they could talk off the record.

As he pushed the street door open and emerged into crisp cold air, he couldn't help thinking it might have been a mistake to come here. Rica had been right again.

It seemed to be happening more and more often.

Or maybe he was listening to her more often.

TWENTY-TWO

May 2000

"There is one problem," Myra told Ed and Amy Marks, "but then there's always at least one."

They were in Five-'n'-Dine, an inadequately air-conditioned diner around the corner from the co-op the Markses were buying. It was a sunny and glorious day on the other side of the window next to their booth. Inside the diner, the scent of frying onions seemed incongruous with the outside view of sun-brightened traffic and the potted decorative trees lining the other side of the street.

Ed Marks stared at Myra in a way that suggested he wasn't surprised by this turn of fate; he was a man who seldom believed his luck would hold. Amy stopped sucking the straw in her strawberry milkshake. Her cheeks that had been hollowed to fashion-model gauntness by vacuum force suddenly regained their youthful plumpness.

"Problem?" she asked, as if it were a new word to her.

"Nothing so out of the ordinary," Myra said, smiling reassuringly. "It seems we need an additional sum to secure board approval for your residency."

Amy fingered the straw, kinking it. "You mean some sort of tax or residence fee?"

"Residence fee would be accurate," Myra said. "This isn't at all unusual in New York real estate transactions, where space is at an absolute premium. Wheels within wheels, you might say."

She could see what Ed Marks would say, only he didn't: *Payoff.* He wasn't as naive as he seemed. He was, after all, a cop, even if still a probationary patrolman. Maybe he'd broach the subject later to his naive but spirited young wife, then clue her in on how the world worked.

"How much?" was what he actually said. To the chase, like a good cop.

"Twenty thousand dollars, but I don't want the amount to frighten you away."

"Twenty thousand dollars? Why shouldn't it scare the hell out of us?"

Myra smiled, patient with the boy. "Because I've arranged for long-term financing of the fee so your total payment will only slightly increase. You might even view this as insurance. In fact it will be a separate monthly payment. And don't worry even a little about the loan. I've arranged financing—I do it all the time for my clients."

"And you say this is the usual thing?" Amy asked.

"Unfortunately, yes."

Ed Marks sighed. "Do we have a choice?"

"The deal's not so locked in that you can't back out," Myra said.

"Ed—"

Marks raised a hand for his wife to be silent. "That's not what I meant. What kind of payment are we talking about?"

"Separately made, but of course figured in as part of the mortgage payment . . . Let's see. . . ." Myra got an amortization schedule from her purse, calculated, and wrote a figure on a paper napkin for the Markses to look at. "With your mortgage installments," she said, "principal, interest, and taxes, total monthly payments will be . . ." She scribbled another figure, then looked across the table at the Markses with a serious expression. "Can you swing that payment?"

"At the outside," Ed Marks said.

Myra nodded, smiling. "As your equity builds, you'll see you've made the right decision."

"I hope so," Ed Marks said, and bit into his grilled Reuben.

"I know so," Amy told him, and went back to her milkshake.

TWENTY-THREE

February 2002

Death itself wasn't the object, the Torcher thought. Fire and change and balance and justice, those were the objects of the purity of flame. The man and his child weren't supposed to die. The Torcher felt sympathy for the woman who was left; how deep must be her loss. But in a way, it was fate. Loss was always fate. Once alive the flames gained a strength and will of their own. It was terrible what happened at the Whitlock Building fire. A loss that carried the living not to hell but to a cold darkness forever. And the dead? Who could know but the dead? That was the terror.

Where was the blame? Well, look to the reasons. The roots of the fire were firmly and deeply planted; the old building was a firetrap; the fire department's equipment was inadequate for high-rise fires; no one had warned the public that after approximately ten floors high, those trapped above by high-rise fires could make cell phone calls or come to their windows and make their frantic, poignant gestures of helplessness and hope, or drop objects and notes to loved ones, missives of desperation. But the fire once vital and large enough not to be overcome would inevitably ascend to them, and their choice would be to burn or leap to their deaths.

Two simple choices. Death. Or a different death. Reasons? Explanations? The fire simply had its way. It always had. It always would. Nothing in human history had worked more, and more profound, changes. Nothing was more elemental and powerful, in a struck paper match or a nuclear explosion. Fire had a way and a will.

Unintended death was tragic, especially the deaths of the innocent. The horror of it was enough to make a strong man sob.

But guilt?

No. There were, as the psychobabblers were prone to say, larger issues in play here.

Put simply, the fire had had its way.

It would again. Soon.

Right now, tears were unstoppable. Tears that stung the eyes but changed nothing. Look at everything else that had happened despite tears.

"Look at this crap," Rica said, tossing the folded newspaper to Stack. She was perched on the corner of Stack's desk, the way she'd seen Marlene Deitrich perch on a barrel in that old move, *The Blue Angel.* Toned down some, but not much. Rica knew men were the same suckers as their grandfathers.

Stack had already read the *Times* over breakfast. Leland Brand was making an issue of high-rise fires in his transparent effort to curry favor with the mayor and the public. Stack had come to understand such matters. Rumor had it that Brand might be appointed commissioner of the new and powerful Department of Public Well-being that was shaping up. Eventually Brand would run for mayor. Brand could use an issue, and Stack knew the mayor had given him this one to play with. The question was, why? Did the mayor see it as a win-win situation that would make his choice of Brand for commissioner look all the wiser? Or did the mayor see it as rope with which Brand might hang himself? A test, of sorts.

Brand had set up an interview with a reporter who acted more like a publicity flak than a journalist. The questions might have been written by Brand as launching pads for his own queries that were designed to make sure the public knew yet another crisis was afoot, as well as who was taking it upon himself to rid the city of it. Was the FDNY prepared to fight fires near the peaks of buildings that rose like angular mountains? (Stack was sure Brand hadn't written that one.) Were they adequately familiar with their newer equipment? How high would their ladders reach? Did most New York skyscrapers have evacuation plans in case of fire? How *did* people escape from a burning building if they were on a high floor? What was the survival rate? Was the FDNY properly trained? The public had a right to know this sort of information. It was the public whose lives were at stake.

"He could have gotten his answers if he'd asked a firefighter," Stack said, tossing the paper aside.

"He wants to start a healthy public dialogue," Rica said.

"He wants to be appointed Public Well-being commissioner, then run for mayor."

"You figure? The election's years away."

"He's the kind of pol who'd start early."

"The two things aren't mutually exclusive," Rica said, "political ambition and a desire to serve the public."

"Uh-huh. Do you like *New Yorker* cartoons?"

Rica smiled. Sometimes a cop and a cop's partner could understand each other almost too well.

Across town, Larry Chips thought he could go for the busty blonde sitting alone at a table in Eb's Irish Lounge. The lounge was Chips's idea of a bar. Of a dive, actually. It was narrow and dim and still smelled of last night's stale beer. A dank cave of a place, at this hour. Which is why he was drinking here when it wasn't even noon. Even cops didn't like going into a place like Eb's at this time of day. It was so unlike the sunshine outside.

Except for the blonde. She could be a bit of sun and warmth, Chips thought. It had been a long time since his last woman, and in truth he hadn't much felt the urge lately, what with all the stress in his life. But this bitch, he figured, might be a great stress reliever. It was very possible she was a hooker, he thought, the way she was sitting there drinking margaritas in a place like this at this hour of the morning. Little Miss Nonchalant, with a tight skirt and a blouse like white paint, legs crossed, showing good ankles made better by four-inch heels. Well, he didn't care if she was peddling ass. He wouldn't have to pay. He could talk his way into it.

She looked in his direction through the dimness and he smiled at her. She looked away. Looked back. Might have smiled.

Might was enough. Chips swiveled around off his bar stool and carried his Wild Turkey on the rocks over to the blonde's table. Smiling big, he sat down without asking, "Pardon me if I'm pushing it," he said, "but did I notice you notice me?"

"Not noticeably."

"But some?" Wider smile.

A smile back. "Okay, some."

"I'm Larry."

"Mirabella."

Sure you are, Chips thought, gently shaking her extended hand. The back of her hand looked older than her face, maybe mid-forties. And her wrists were thin. She was, in fact, kind of gaunt except for the great rack of tits. Maybe she was some sort of addict. Maybe the tits weren't real. Chips didn't much care what was real or not, or if Mirabella was a real name and not just some magazine, if he had the name right. Something like that, anyway. The bitch was real enough, what he was interested in, here in Eb's Irish Lounge.

"You Irish?" he asked, getting her talking, chatting her up so he didn't have to come right out and ask if she was working.

"I used to be," she said. She had a nice voice, kind of throaty.

"How could you used to be?"

"I was married to a guy named Rourke."

He gave her a grin, as if to say it was okay with him if she wanted that to mean she used to be Irish. Maybe she needed to used to be Irish.

Chips saw that her glass was low and signaled the bartender for fresh ones.

"It didn't work out very well," she said.

"That's a real shame. He beat up on you?" Showing he was a concerned and sensitive guy. New Age type that might do the dishes and keep a florist in business.

"Why would you ask that? Are you stereotyping the Irish?"

Whoops! Too far. "No, no, Mirabella, I didn't mean it that way."

"I didn't know if the son of a bitch was really named Rourke or was Irish, but he said he was and we used to come in here and he'd drink rye whiskey. And he didn't beat me. I wish he would have. He didn't care enough. He beat up on somebody else."

I think we're gonna get along swell. "You've gotta excuse my manner, me blurting out something now and then. I spent too much time in the bush."

She looked inquisitive, which kind of wrinkled her nose in a way that was cute. "Bush?"

Yours later, sweet. "I been working up in Alaska, on the pipeline." *What I want to do is lay some pipe in you.*

Mirabella grinned. "I thought they finished building that pipeline twenty years ago."

"Everyone thinks that. Me and the rest of the guys that work on it don't set them straight. The pay's still damned good, if you don't mind living out in the bush for months at a time."

"You mean the tundra?"

"Huh?"

"Never mind. I think you're full of shit, Larry."

"You mind?"

"Not much." She accepted her fresh drink from the old guy who'd walked out from behind the bar to bring the order to the table. Chips made a mental note to leave a tip, but not too large a one. He didn't want to be remembered later.

"To us," Chips said, raising his glass of Wild Turkey.

"Why not?" She toasted with him and took a long pull of her Margarita, then made a deal out of licking salt from the glass rim.

"You could be arrested for illegal use of the tongue," he said, grinning.

"It wouldn't be the first time."

"Mirabella, don't take this wrong but you're not in here . . . uh, you know? . . ."

She smiled and shook her head. "I'm not a working girl. Not anymore. Not Irish, not a working girl."

A lush? Chips wondered. "You got a deep, dark secret?" he asked, leaning over the table to look deep into her eyes, keeping his voice and expression somber. He'd pulled this one before. It was surprising, some of the things they'd admit if they were a little drunk and you asked them right out. If they really thought you were curious about them and their fucked-up lives.

It worked with this one. She was smiling but her eyes were dead serious as she leaned toward him so their faces were only inches apart. He could smell her perfume, smell the booze on her breath. "I've got a feeling you're gonna be my deep, dark secret," she said in that husky voice, as if she needed a throat lozenge. As if she needed something and everything.

Surprising, but not surprising. Chips rolled with it. He gave her a light kiss on the lips. Waited. She sat back, but she was breathing hard, the major bazooms rising and falling beneath the thin material of her blouse. Nipples visible now, hard, definitely hard. Chips knew he'd started the fire.

They left together even before they finished their drinks.

The Torcher looked around Bruni L'Farceur's apartment, at the designer furniture and the artwork on the white walls.

L'Farceur was a rich and successful woman who owned a gallery in the Village where some of the city's—the country's—most talented and accomplished artists displayed their work. It was only coincidental that most of the art in the apartment would be spared destruction, unlike its owner.

How quiet it was here, high above the city and its noise and confusion and problems. Problems for some, thought the Torcher, gazing around at the sleek modern furniture, the sea of plush white carpet. The paleness and sparseness of the apartment set off the colors of the furnishings and artwork, yet nothing seemed to clash or be incongruous except intentionally, a clever and daring decorator's trick. The Torcher wondered what it would be like to live here. Or to die here?

Like dying anywhere else, once the fire becomes the everything. Once the agony becomes the end and the beginning. A place like this, any place, it makes no difference to the fire.

The kitchen was what most interested the Torcher, and it was pretty much as expected: expensive. Lots of copper and light marble and pale stained paneling. Two of everything—dishwashers, refrigerators, freezers, wine cases, sinks, stoves, and ovens, even twin elaborate, copper-trimmed blenders on the wide countertops.

L'Farceur would be the richest one yet, so maybe the most deserving.

The Torcher had experienced a learning curve as well as a guilt curve. The ceramic tile floor wouldn't burn, of course. The copper and marble were also safe. Curtains had to be dealt with, perhaps soaked and placed in the sink. That was no problem, since it had four separate basins. The main thing here was, this was a newer building—constructed in the eighties, so it was classified as "fire-resistive." That meant the floors and ceilings were fire-retardant material, so that each floor was sealed off from the ones above and below. Almost like a ship with waterproof compartments. Air-conditioning and heating ducts and vents were also equipped with mechanisms that sealed them in case of fire. Most important, the thick and solid walls of older buildings that made installing sprinkler systems a problem weren't part of this construction. The building was equipped with a sprinkler system of a brand and type familiar to the Torcher. The learning curve. Outside the kitchen, the fire would have to travel along a tiled hall to reach carpeting, and there was a sprinkler head set in the hall ceiling. Excellent compartmentalization.

All of this was important to the Torcher, since FDNY aerial ladders would reach only approximately ten stories. Bruni L'Farceur's apartment was on the fifty-second floor.

It was Ernest Fagin who called the meeting with Stack and Rica. The three of them sat in a booth of a diner on Amsterdam on the Upper West Side. Stack and Rica were having only coffee, Fagin a cup of hot tea and an aromatic warm cinnamon bun that was mostly frosting.

"After reading the *Times* piece where Leland Brand tries to make it seem like there's a crisis in the FDNY, I thought I oughta talk to you two," Fagin said. He took a generous bite of cinnamon bun and chewed. Rica hated him for his gawky, skinny build and his big appetite.

"Is there some kind of crisis?" she asked. "High-rise fires are nothing new in this city."

Fagin stirred sugar into his tea and sipped. "You might say we've been lucky so far. But crisis? . . . I don't know. You'd have to be the judge. What we can do in a high-rise fire has always been more limited than most people thought."

"What exactly is your definition of a high-rise fire?" Stack asked.

"One that's on a floor higher than your tallest ladder."

"What floor is that?"

"Well, our aerial ladders will reach seventy-five feet, sometimes ninety. The rear-mounts up to a hundred feet."

"Ten stories," Rica said.

"About that. If a fire is on, say, the twentieth floor, it's like I told you: firefighters use the elevators, if they're operable, to move equipment to the upper floors and the fire. Sometimes the elevators don't work or are too dangerous; then we got real trouble. We lug the equipment up the fire stairs and hook a hose into a standpipe valve on the landing below the fire. Then we pay the hose up the stairwell so someone can direct the stream of water toward the fire from that landing."

"Sounds reasonably effective," Stack said.

Fagin smiled. "Really? Well, it can be if the fire's not too large. And the stairwells aren't full of smoke. And the standpipe valves work as they should. And if nothing interrupts the water pressure."

"Does the FDNY know what floor the fire is on when the alarm or call comes in?" Rica asked.

"Usually. It's vital information in New York. We know what address and floor we're going to, and we can know what kind of equipment we'll need. Ladder trucks, pumpers, what kind of attack we're going to be involved in."

Rica blew on her coffee to cool it. "You make it sound like a war."

"It is," Fagin said. "We get there in force as fast as we

can. The truth is, in your average high-rise office building, with a twenty- or thirty-thousand-square-foot floor area per story, we sometimes can't extinguish a fire with one or two hose streams from standpipe valves. A fire hose with a two-and-a-half-inch nozzle produces three hundred gallons per minute. Sounds like a lot, but it puts out a fire on only about ten percent of the floor space fire we're talking about. What we're really trying to do is contain the fire to that one floor until everything burnable is consumed."

"Then it goes out by itself?" Rica asked.

Fagin sipped some more tea. "Just like the half-smoked cigarette you flip away. No fuel, no fire."

"What if you're an occupant on that floor and the flames are between you and the fire stairs?" Stack asked.

Fagin shook his head. "That's why I wanted to talk to you two, let you know what might happen here, how really serious the situation could get."

"Then Brand is right," Rica said.

"He doesn't know jack shit what he's talking about," Fagin told her, "but he's got the essential problem nailed. If our blitz tactic doesn't contain the fire, we need about three times as many firefighters and lots more equipment. It goes from a battle to a war. Besides directing water streams through broken windows from adjacent buildings, we try other things, slinging lines, setting up nets for jumpers, using high-powered fans. But the truth is, not much in the way of exterior attacks works well in a high-rise fire. It's interior work, grunt work in flames and smoke and superheated air full of toxic fumes."

"You make me glad I'm not a firefighter," Rica said.

"We earn our pay," Fagin said, not smiling.

"Haven't we seen enough to realize that," Stack told him. It wasn't a question.

"Learning about a high-rise fire as soon as possible is everything, since we have to get so much equipment there, then transport it up as many stories as it takes. If the fire's taken hold and extinguishing it is out of the question, we can only begin our defense and containment. If we fail, and the flames and smoke move to the floors above or below . . . well, it can be one hell of a horror."

"You wanted to warn us how much of a horror," Stack reminded him. "And you wanted us to know how many people might die."

"Horror's relative, I guess. And as to casualties, I'm afraid you can just about choose your number."

"High-rise hell," Rica said.

"The FDNY is going to have to defend itself against Brand's attacks," Fagin said. "And so are you two. I thought it best you had some idea what you're talking about." He glanced at his watch, then snatched up the check that had been left on the table. "I've gotta get going. This is on me. I'll get it on the way out."

Stack and Rica thanked him, then sat and finished their coffees while Rica picked on the half of cinnamon roll Fagin had left.

"He paints a grim picture," Rica said, after they'd both been silent for a while as they digested what Fagin had told them.

"Grim seems to be all we get in this investigation," Stack said, "other than confusion. Maybe because we started out looking for a serial killer, and now we seem to be looking for an arsonist."

"And the difference?"

"Motivation. Is our firebug more of a murderer than a pyromaniac, like any other psychosexual serial killer? Or is it vice versa?"

"Sex and fire have always gone together," Rica said. "Haven't you ever shared a candlelight dinner?"

Stack ignored the question.

"I don't know if I can buy into the quirky sexual motivation," Rica said, "with all the victims being men. And as far as we know, heterosexual men."

"Could be their sexual orientation makes no difference to the killer. After all, we're dealing with somebody abnormal here from the get-go. Who knows how he thinks above or below the belt? Maybe it's the sexual kick, the power trip, our firebug is after, not the fire itself. In other words, he isn't a firebug any more than someone who shoots people is necessarily a gun nut."

"It might be a distinction without a difference."

"We'd be looking for a different kind of killer," Stack said. He drained his coffee mug, then glanced into it and made a face as if he'd ingested poison.

"Another possibility," Rica said, "is that our killer is liking fire more as he goes along, is becoming more and more of a pyromaniac."

"A work in progress. Yeah, it could be that way: Problem is, there's only one way to find out for sure, and that's ask him."

"I forgot to ask you," Rica said. "How was the interview session with the co-op board? The one your wife talked you into but you shouldn't have listened?"

Stack placed his empty mug on the table too hard. "Like a fire in a high-rise."

TWENTY-FOUR

Bruni L' Farceur pointed and said, "Put that there."

The mover from Fragile and Agile obeyed. He was over six feet tall and an easy two hundred pounds, and the delicate scrap-iron sculpture, heavily framed in two-by-fours, seemed almost weightless in his grasp. Bruni found herself wondering what he'd be like in bed.

The mover, with the name *Biff* embroidered over the pocket of his white coveralls, left to go back down to the truck. His partner, a chubby little man whose coveralls proclaimed him to be *Lou,* entered with a long wooden case that was strapped to a hand truck. Bruni, dressed for the occasion in designer jeans, leopard (synthetic)-topped boots, and an oversize black sweatshirt, told Lou where to go with the case, which she knew contained a variety of steel rods that the artist would later assemble into a work titled *Tall in the Saddle,* a representation of the white man's maltreatment of nineteenth-century Native Americans.

Behind Bruni, at the other end of the loft space on Mc-Dougal in the Village, painters were still working to color everything but the floor white. Every beam and support pole and conduit and plumbing pipe and heating duct and corner brace and window frame and steam pipe—pure white. *Blanco.*

This place would be perfect for her America in Motion exhibit. Her gallery uptown wouldn't have worked. Not only was it too small and the ceiling too low for massive mobiles, but the building itself, the neighborhood, wasn't right for the sculpture exhibit of pieces that sometimes ran hundreds of pounds and depicted inconvenient truths. Just when Bruni and her partner in the gallery, Mil, were out of ideas and in an absolute blue panic, a customer had suggested staging the exhibit somewhere else, some vast and suitable place. Perhaps they should contact a real estate agency. "Illumination!" Bruni had cried, and dashed for the phone.

The real estate agency happened to have just the thing, an unfinished loft space whose owner was being assigned an important executive position in Switzerland. He'd been about to decorate the loft, but he'd be glad to have it rented for a short while, and any cosmetic changes would be all right with him. He might even be able to incorporate them into his decor whenever he returned to the states.

Movement caught Bruni's eye, and she expected to see Biff returning with another load from down in the street. Instead it was the real estate woman, Myra Raven. Big in the biz, Mil had said of her. After meeting her, Bruni and Mil began referring to her as Raven the maven. Not to her face, of course. There was something about Myra Raven that suggested she was not to be treated in any way risky. Annie Liebowitz should photograph this woman. It was hard to look at her without the word *bitch* leaping to mind.

"Myra, you peach!" Bruni cried, and tottered to her in the high-heeled boots. The two women air-kissed. "Everything is going marvelously," Bruni said. "This place you found for us will be perfect!"

Myra, dressed Upper East Side in every way except there was no Yorkie under her arm, looked around and said, "I came by to tell you the owner will agree to a third month on the rental agreement, at your option."

Bruni threw up her arms as if in tribute to a superior being. "You are truly a negotiator in the Trump mold, Myra! Now if the exhibit is the spiraling success I think it will be, we can extend it an extra month. You, of course, have a free pass for every night if you want. And do bring a friend! Some of the pieces are titillating to die for."

"Maybe I will," Myra said. "Maybe I'll buy something."

No kitsch for sale here, sweetie. "Don't feel at all obligated, Myra. My God, you've done enough already!" Bruni laughed and winked. "Of course, that wouldn't prevent you from getting a special, special price."

"Where do you want this box?" asked a husky male voice. Biff had returned from the van with another crated sculpture section of a piece Bruni knew would, when assembled, represent the Brooklyn Bridge with teepees for stanchions and strung ceremonial beads for support cables.

"Over there by that large arrow," Bruni told him, and pointed.

Both women watched as Biff muscled the heavy case of steel parts to where Bruni had instructed.

"Isn't he absolutely Romanesque!" Bruni said.

Biff had heard, and turned briefly to glance curiously at her before returning to work.

"I wouldn't be opposed to Greek," Myra said.

Bruni loved it.

* * *

Stack had just won a coin flip and sent Rica for coffee when his desk phone rang. When he picked up, Sergeant Redd told him his wife was on the line.

Stack pressed the glowing button on his phone. "Laura?"

"I called to thank you," she said.

At first he wasn't sure what she meant. Then he understood. "You got approval for the co-op?"

"Yes! Your appearance before the board made the difference."

"I didn't think I impressed them all that much."

"They thought you were arrogant and sarcastic and uncooperative, which assured them that you were at fault in our divorce. They all told me they felt much reassured after meeting you."

That rankled Stack. *They* called *me* arrogant?"

"They're pompous asses," Laura said, "but I needed their approval. And I was serious about thanking you. If you hadn't taken the time and trouble to show up and let them grill you, I might have been rejected. It couldn't have been fun for you."

"They could give the police lessons in interrogation," Stack said. "You're not moving in with nice people, Laura."

"They don't actually represent everyone in the building. The ones who want the power take over those boards quite often, and discourage prospective board members who want to serve in a reasonable way. You wouldn't believe some of the interviews I've had the past few weeks. It's humiliating, dealing with those people, and I didn't seem to be getting anywhere—a divorcing woman, new at a job. I really wanted this apartment, which is why I asked for your help with the co-op board. I figured the least you might do is scare them."

"I hope I scared the holy shit out of them," Stack said.

"You scared them enough," Laura said, "Thanks, Stack."
Not *Ben* anymore. "If you need some more help . . ."

"Your lawyer couldn't have approved of your helping me this time. I'll make sure what you did doesn't come back to haunt you in court. We don't have to do everything our attorneys say, Stack. We can be friends when this is over."

Stack wished she were right, but he wasn't so sure. Wasn't so sure he didn't want them to be more than friends. "I better not tell my lawyer you said that."

She laughed, and thanked him again before hanging up.

He sat there and felt a certain satisfaction after the call. People didn't have to buckle under the weight of the system, to be reduced to pawns by a litigious society.

Rica was back. She placed a foam cup of steaming coffee on Stack's desk, then sat on the corner of the desk herself. Another offering. "You're smiling."

"Sitting here thinking how unnecessary half the attorneys in the world would be if we quit taking their advice."

"Your wife called."

"To thank me. She got the apartment. She said it was because of my appearance before the co-op board." He dipped his fingertip in his coffee to test how hot it was. *Yeeowch!* "You wouldn't believe those people."

"Question might be," Rica said, "would a divorce court judge believe them?"

Larry Chips drove Mirabella's five-year-old Neon along Deering Street in a suburb outside Newark. He made a left, then another into the lot of a strip shopping mall, drove past the row of small shops and the Big-K that anchored them, and pulled up to one of the self-serve gas pumps in the station at the corner. The pay-at-the-pump kind. He liked those, nobody remembered you there even if they happened to glance at you. Using Mirabella's Visa card, he waited for authorization, then pressed the 92-octane button on the pump. He braced the nozzle so it wouldn't fall from the fill pipe, and while the tank was filling he walked back to the trunk and got out a battered red spare gas can. When the Neon's tank was full, he withdrew the nozzle and filled the red can, then returned it to the trunk.

He made one more stop, at the supermarket at the other end of the shopping strip, and bought ten half-gallon glass bottles of orange juice. The checkout clerk asked him if he had a vitamin C deficiency, and Chips laughed convincingly as if he thought the dork was funny and said no, his vision was fine, thanks. Give him one back, and plastic rather than paper, please.

Back on Deering Street, he drove to Mirabella's house and made a right turn into the driveway.

The driveway was long and needed paving or some more gravel dumped and spread around on it, and was crowded by fir trees and overgrown juniper bushes. That was fine with Chips. It made for more privacy. People were less likely to use a driveway like that to turn around in, especially since they couldn't quite make out what was behind the foliage at the far end.

He'd dropped Mirabella off for work in the city a few hours ago, at a place called Claybar's where she waited tables and sometimes danced, so he had privacy now.

The modest clapboard house, in the bedroom of which he and Mirabella had made desperate and lonely love the last two nights, sat next to an even more run-down garage. The house merely needed paint. The garage needed siding replaced, and the roof sagged in the middle. Chips couldn't walk into the thing without thinking it was about to collapse around him.

He left the Neon parked outside and struggled to open one of the garage's heavy plank doors. The door resisted all the way, scraping on the loose gravel. One of Chips's feet slid out from under him and he almost fell, cursing and banging an elbow on the balky door.

Chips stood for a moment rubbing his elbow and peering into the garage. Once his eyes adjusted, it wasn't so dim in there. Enough illumination streamed through the spaces where the siding was missing that there was no need to turn on a light.

He got the red gas can from the Neon's trunk and carried it inside, listening to and feeling the liquid slosh around in it with each step. He set the can on an ancient wooden workbench that sat against the garage's east wall. Then he went back to the car, got the plastic grocery bags containing the orange juice he'd bought, and carried them inside the house.

Carefully removing the bottles from the bags one by one, he poured the contents of each down the drain in the sink. He washed the empty glass containers, put them back in the plastic bags, and carried them out to the garage. It didn't matter that he'd bought orange juice or any other kind of liquid, just so the containers were glass. Gasoline, all petroleum products, had a way of eating through waxed cardboard or plastic containers.

In the garage, he used a funnel he'd noticed on a shelf to transfer the gas in the red can to the empty orange juice bottles, carefully capping each bottle when he was finished. When the can was empty, he went out and used a short section of garden hose to siphon more gas from the Neon, then repeated the process. He smiled, satisfied. Now the liquid was in smaller, more manageable containers.

Chips hid the bottles in a box of old rags beneath the workbench, then replaced the gas can in the Neon's trunk—with the airless spare tire, the way Mirabella was used to traveling—so she wouldn't suspect anything had occurred. He pulled the Neon into the garage and wrestled the wooden doors shut.

In the house, he washed his hands thoroughly so there was no lingering scent of gasoline. Then he went to the refrigerator and got out a can of Budweiser that he opened and carried into the living room. He settled down on the sprung sofa before the TV, used the remote to get a classic replay of an old Cards and Detroit World Series game on ESPN, and propped his feet up on an overstuffed hassock.

The beer was plenty cold, he was comfortable, and Bob Gibson was pitching. They didn't make hard-nosed pitchers like Gibson anymore, which was why so many of these wuss batters could lean out over the plate without getting knocked on their ass by a fastball.

After the game and a few more beers, Chips would take a nap, then drive into the city to pick up Mirabella at Claybar's, maybe have a few more beers, then come back here to restart the sex machine.

Life was tolerable sometimes, Chips thought. Sometimes it was almost fair.

TWENTY-FIVE

Otto Kreiger was executive vice president of the Belmire Tower co-op board. He ran the meetings with precision, fairness, and promptness. He told that to everyone who would listen. A tall man of great girth, he kept his balding head completely shaved and had grown a neatly trimmed and fierce goatee so he resembled an aging professional wrestler. Only his tiny wire-framed spectacles suggested a mean intelligence buried in all that aggressive bulk.

"This William Matoon," Molly French of 32B said from halfway down the polished mahogany conference table Kreiger had purchased with board money, "I certainly can't recommend him as a tenant."

Several other board members began agreeing with French.

Kreiger pounded on the table with the *Robert's Rules of Order* he used as a gavel, then stood up. The other board members were silent.

"He has a police record!" Lewis Adams of 4C blurted out. He particularly disliked Kreiger and couldn't wait for his two year term on the board to expire. He, Adams, would walk away, for he knew when Kreiger's term expired on the same date, Kreiger would run again for board president and would find whatever way necessary to win.

Adams was intimidated by Kreiger and loathed him as well, and had had enough of the man, who reminded him very much of an overgrown boy who'd bullied him unmercifully forty years ago in prep school.

Kreiger glared at him until a few seconds of silence had passed, then spoke:

"Mr. Matoon has some things on the plus side of the ledger. He placed fifty percent down on his unit, so he can well afford to live here. He is single and without pets or loud hobbies or egregious habits. That is to say, he doesn't record live drum music in his home or collect police sirens. And he owns his own investment firm."

"That sounds good," Adams said, "but what do we know about his investment firm other than the books he showed us that were probably cooked by his own accountant?"

"We know it earns him enough to live in the Belmire," Kreiger pointed out. "In fact, Lewis, his annual income far exceeds yours."

"Or he has a dishonest accountant," Adams persisted.

"I should remind you, Lewis, that minutes are being taken here, and you might be putting the board in legal jeopardy with careless and groundless accusations concerning matters about which you and the rest of us can know nothing."

"What we don't know is irrelevant," Molly French said calmly, "compared to what we do know—that Mr. Matoon has a police record."

"Embezzlement, fifteen years ago. Mr. Matoon served his time and has apparently been a solid citizen since. Be charitable, Molly. This is the land of the second chance."

"I was thinking of the child molestation charges."

"Charges only," Kreiger said. "Mr. Matoon was found innocent both times. This is also the land of the litigious. Children tell tales, and suspicious parents sue." He shrugged his massive shoulders. "Haven't we all made mistakes?"

"Like child molestation? No, we haven't."

"There you go acting the jury again, even though Mr. Matoon never went to court on those false charges. I was referring to the embezzlement charge."

"He went to court on that one and lost," Adams pointed out.

"I'd like to get through this matter," Kreiger said, "so we can get on to other business." He stared at Mr. Henries from 27C, who had been made aware that if William Matoon was approved as a resident, the money for more exercise equipment would be forthcoming from the general fund. Henries looked away. Mrs. Vendable of 43B didn't look away; she was staring directly at Kreiger, reminding him he'd promised to see that the noise abatement rule would be followed so the lunatic in the unit next to hers would stop playing his stereo at top volume late into the night. That would be, to her way of thinking, her back being scratched in return. As with Mr. Henries, the tacit arrangement had been struck.

Kreiger forged on confidently. He wasn't going to change French's or Adams's mind anyway. "I think we need to remember," he said, "that we're all human and make mistakes. Mr. Matoon has a spotless record going back years, and is now a respected businessman in the investment community. Are we so haughty that we can't find it in ourselves to overlook past sins even as we'd like our own to be overlooked?"

"I never molested a kid," Adams said.

"But you *are* out of order." Kreiger glared at him for a

good five seconds, then continued: "I don't know about the rest of you, but I don't glom onto a few unsavory ancient episodes and use them to bury someone who's trying to lead an exemplary life now. And here's something else to consider. Mr. Matoon is more than qualified for residency here in every way other than his youthful scrapes with the law. And as I said, ours is a litigious society. We might well be liable if we turn him away as a neighbor."

"There are laws protecting co-op boards and you know it," Molly French said.

Kreiger looked at her with an expression of strained tolerance. "If we had the time, I could wear you down citing examples when the fine points of the law were no excuse when it came to a jury or a lenient judge. I wouldn't look to the law to protect us in what many would see as a heartless and unnecessary shunning of a fellow citizen. And politically we are in the midst of what some commentators call class warfare. Snobbery, real or imagined, is paying a heavy price these days in court, whether or not the law is on its side."

"Jury nullification," chimed in Mrs. Vendable.

"I move that we vote on the matter," said Mr. Henries.

Kreiger and Mrs. Vendable seconded the motion together.

William Matoon was approved for Belmire Tower residency by one vote.

Expenditures for the exercise equipment were less of a problem. Stronger enforcement of the noise abatement rule was unanimous.

After the meeting, Otto Kreiger went up to his fifty-seventh-floor unit and had a glass of a chocolate high-protein drink while he sat at the dining room table leafing through a catalogue of exercise equipment. He was aware he'd been gradually breaking down the motorized treadmills with his bulk, and one or both machines would have to be replaced soon regardless of how the board had voted.

Kreiger flipped pages to the back of the catalog, where the heavy-duty equipment was listed. If the board objected to paying more for industrial-strength treadmills, he would be generous and pay part of the difference from his own pocket. An act of generosity he could remind everyone of later.

Bruni L'Farceur rode the elevator to her fifty-seventh-floor co-op in the Flanders Building on the Upper East Side. As she walked along the plushly carpeted hall to her apartment door, she reflected with a sense of satisfaction that art was one hell of a business.

What it took was an acceptance of the fact that art patrons wanted to be, yearned to be, convinced of a new artist's talent and sales potential. Once someone like Bruni found the proper proportions of metaphysics, commerce, and bullshit, the rest naturally followed. The rest being a luxury condo on the East Side, a juicy stock and bond portfolio, and *real* art to hang on her own walls. *Objets d'art,* sexual playmates, tangible currency, cars or boats, rare this or rare that owned by no one else, stuff, things. That was quite simply what it was all about, and the sooner learned the better.

She keyed her apartment door and went inside, feeling as she always did when returning home that hush of isolation and altitude, of distance from the daily fray. Here, among what she most valued, she renewed herself.

After hanging her coat in the entry hall closet, she removed her boots so she wouldn't track anything on the carpet, then padded in nylon-clad feet toward her bedroom.

On the way there, she stopped. Something wasn't quite right. She stared at her prized Pollock mounted on the wall, lost for a second in its colorful multilayered complexity. Bruni wasn't at all frightened, not here, but still . . . She glanced around. Everything seemed to be in order, from her Rodin reproductions to her genuine Seurat.

No, wait . . .

The entry to the kitchen. There seemed an inordinate amount of light streaming from the doorway, as if the kitchen were illuminated with Kleig lights, like the time *New York Style* had taped a TV spot here.

Curious, she padded toward the kitchen and stood in the doorway.

It was immediately apparent what had happened. The taupe sheer curtains that softened the light were gone from the window. Fallen, perhaps.

Bruni stepped all the way into the kitchen and was surprised to see something—the curtains!—wadded and soaking in all four of her sinks. As if they were being washed. They must have fallen straight down.

This is absolutely absurd! But won't the explanation make a great story? Mil will be first to hear, then others before Mil has a chance to repeat.

Must get them out of the water, though . . .

What on earth? An umbrella, leaning there against the cooking island. Now who—

Bruni never finished her thought. She neither saw nor heard the descent of the brass reproduction of Rodin's *The Kiss* as it arced through the air and struck her behind the right ear.

* * *

Bruni smelled something. Was there a car about? Where on earth was she? Why couldn't she move? She must call Mil. Yes, Mil. She must wake up from this dream and walk in the real world.

Then she saw the dark figure looming above her, heard the rasp, and saw the spark.

Realization became fire became pain that was so excruciating it was art. For a brief moment it was art!

TWENTY-SIX

Billy Watkins, sweating as if he'd just staggered out of a sauna, lay in Myra Raven's bed beside Myra. Like Billy, she was still breathing hard. The covers were thrown back, the ceiling fan was on, and both of them were nude before God and glistening wet from their efforts to get into hell.

She stirred beside him, sighed, and reached over to gently touch his forearm that lay near her hip.

"You were something, Myra," he said, his mind doing slows turns like the fan blades above.

"Aren't I usually, Billy?"

He grinned, looking over and making sure she saw him. "Not usually—always! But this time you were so . . . I guess you'd say *needy*."

"Insatiable, you mean?"

"Yeah. Like you wanted something nobody could give you."

"Not even you, Billy?" Teasing him now, but in a sad kind of way. That's what she was tonight, sad.

"I don't know. You tell me."

"You helped immensely. You always do."

"You're a puzzle, Myra."

"Women always are, Billy. You of all people should know."

"I do, Myra. But I don't think of you as I do the others. You know you're special to me." That ceiling fan, white with the gold trim and the gold-scalloped blades, he wondered what it cost.

"You getting cold?" Myra asked.

"Not hardly, so soon after you. But you have goose bumps." He sat up effortlessly, the muscles of his flat stomach tensing, and reached down and covered her with the silk sheet.

"I needed comfort tonight, Billy. You gave it to me."

"That's why I'm here, Myra, what I want to do."

"You treat me so nice, Billy." Her voice was still husky from recent sex, her words still slightly slurred from the scotch-on-the-rocks she'd downed one right after the other before they came into the bedroom. Billy didn't agree with her about how puzzling women were; he knew women. This was one with a sorrow she couldn't drown. That was obvious and simple enough, even if the sorrow wasn't.

"I like treating you nice," Billy told her. "You bring that out in men."

"Not all men. Not most men."

"This man." He tucked the top edge of the sheet beneath her chin. "You okay now?"

"Okay as can be."

He lay on his back silently beside her, watching the rotating fan blades. Getting a little bit cool himself from the breeze, but it felt good. He knew that later they would probably take a warm shower together. She might want to go again. Billy thought that would be fine; he had it in him and he had no place better to be. Anyway, it was his fucking job. It was his job, fucking.

Beside him, Myra began snoring lightly. After about five

minutes of listening to her, he slowly swiveled on his hip, sat up, and stood gradually so as not to disturb her. He curled his bare toes into the deep pile of the expensive carpet. He loved doing that when he was in her apartment. He felt good, almost rested now, but he had to take a piss. Walking softly, he made his way out to the hall and the main bathroom. He figured if he used the bath off the bedroom, he might wake Myra. He didn't want to do that just yet.

Once inside the bathroom, he stood as he often did and took in the luxury he so longed for and that was so beyond him right now. But someday he'd have a bathroom like this, all the marble, the walk-in shower almost the size of his bedroom, the long vanity with its gold-framed mirrors. There was a phone by the commode, and another by the sunken bathtub with its Jacuzzi setup. It was a large Jacuzzi. He recalled making love to Myra in it the second time he was with her.

That had been a few years ago. Aware that time was undermining him, Billy studied his blond handsomeness in the mirror. He could still pass for a California surfer who'd somehow wandered to Manhattan and just gotten off the bus at Port Authority, but not on close examination. The artificially tanned flesh was beginning to crinkle at the corners of his eyes, and he knew that beneath his tousled blond curls, his hairline was receding. A man couldn't do this kind of work forever. He had to grab his opportunities when they were within reach.

He stood at the commode with his fists on his hips and relieved himself, then pressed a gold button on the toilet tank. As always, he was impressed. You could hardly hear the damn thing flush.

At the washbasin, when he was running water on his

hands, he noticed among the scented soap dishes, candles, and woven basket of guest towels, a flat silver cigarette lighter. After drying his hands on one of the towels, he picked up the lighter and flipped open its lid. Billy knew quality when he saw it, and this was it. Silver plated over brass, probably, heavy for its size, and with an inlaid design on the lid that looked like real gold. There was no personal engraving on the lighter, which meant it couldn't be easily traced. Myra didn't smoke, so what was it doing in her bathroom? Maybe to light the scented candles, for later.

He was standing there considering stealing the lighter when Myra's voice, coming from directly behind him, startled him.

"Billy?"

He jumped and almost dropped the lighter into the marble basin, catching it just in time with his left hand. "Jesus, Myra!"

She smiled. "Didn't mean to scare you. Thought it might be shower time." Reaching for a washcloth, she seemed to notice for the first time the lighter in his hand, and raised her eyes to match his gaze. He hoped he didn't look guilty because of what he'd been thinking. He wasn't actually going to steal the lighter, anyway.

"I thought I might light some of these candles for us," he said, congratulating himself for thinking fast.

"That's why the lighter was in here," Myra said. "I was going to light them."

"I figured. I knew you didn't smoke." He held the lighter up near the fixture over the mirror. "Nice lighter. You don't see many like this anymore. Mostly throwaway plastic Bics, that kinda thing."

"Going the way of fountain pens," she said. "It used to belong to my husband."

"Husband? Myra, you're not—"

"A long time ago, Billy. He's been gone for years and years. Would it bother you if I were still married?"

Hit her with the boyish grin. Still boyish enough. "Truth?"

"Certainly."

"It wouldn't make a bit of difference. Not where you're concerned."

She studied him for a while, then smiled, came to him, and kissed him gently on the cheek.

"I'll start the shower," she told him. "You light the candles."

"Great idea."

He watched her reflection in the mirror, a bony, graceful woman, like one of those whippet dogs, as she walked into the tile shower and turned on warm needles of water. Then he moved some candles out from near the soap dishes and guest towels and flipped open the lid of the silver lighter.

It worked the first time.

Stack and Rica stood with Ernest Fagin inside the door of Bruni L'Farceur's apartment. The smell of charred wood and roasted flesh was in the air, eerily incongruous with the eggshell-white walls and their symmetrical display of artwork, the statuary and museumlike quality of the rest of the co-op.

"Looks like an extension of MOMA," Rica said.

Fagin nodded. He looked exhausted and a lock of straight dark hair dangled over his left eye. "I'm told a lot of this stuff is original, and even the copies are worth a mint. The only damage is in the kitchen. Wanna peek?"

Stack and Rica glanced at each other. Neither really wanted a peek. This case was wearing them down in body and mind. There was a saturation point for all the char and gore here, a time when the nerves recoiled, for everyone but the killer.

Without answering, they followed Fagin into the kitchen. Everything here was different from the rest of the apartment. The walls and ceiling were charred and water stained, the stench was overwhelming, and in the center of the ceramic tile floor, resting in about an inch of water, was the blackened corpse of a woman assumed to be Bruni L'Farceur. She glistened darkly, raw as a peeled grape, still moist from the sprinkler system. What was left of her jaw was agape, one cheek completely burned away to reveal blackened molars in a horrible grin. She was arched backward, though she didn't appear to have been hog-tied. Her arms were folded and bound together behind her with what looked like the remnants of strips of cloth. It was also obvious that her legs had been tightly bound together.

"Like the others," Stack said.

Rica moved a hesitant step closer to the corpse. "No gag this time."

"There was one," Fagin said. "Duct tape would be my guess. I removed what was left of it to feel inside her mouth. What was left of it. There was soot on the roof of her mouth. She was alive for a while after she was set on fire, breathing in the smoke of her own body burning."

"Dear God," Stack said.

Fagin shook his head sadly. "Sometimes I wonder."

Rica nudged Stack and pointed. He looked and saw a black umbrella half folded in a corner.

"Our firebug," Stack said. "No doubt about it." He stepped toward the multiple sink basins and saw masses of something floating in them. "What's this?"

"The curtains. Looks like they were taken down ahead of time so the fire wouldn't spread after the Torcher left. Damage control."

"You're saying the killer wanted to contain the fire?"

"Uh-huh. That's sure what it looks like. A guilty conscience after the Wickham Building fire?"

"Serial killers aren't bothered by that," Stack said.

"Maybe all the publicity warning about high-rise fires, all of Leland Brand's ranting, has actually done some good," Fagin suggested.

"A professional profiler would laugh if you told him that," Rica said.

"There's something else you oughta know about this one. It was reported soon after it started. An anonymous phone call. The voice was disguised. I heard the recording. Sounded like some guy with a mouthful of marbles talking in an echo chamber."

"Then there's no getting around it," Stack said. "Whether because of guilt or some other reason, the Torcher didn't want this fire to spread. Selectivity is being practiced here. The victim was to be the only one killed, which means murder and not the fire itself was the object."

"I don't buy that last part completely," Fagin said. "I know the work of a firebug when I see it. It's hard to explain, but it's like something sexual, or somebody practicing a religion. Fire does that to some people. The idea might have been to kill only Bruni L'Farceur, but if the fire isn't part of the compulsion, why doesn't the killer just use a gun or knife?"

"I'm not saying the Torcher isn't a pyromaniac," Stack said. "I'm talking about motive. There's some kind of profound and particular link between victim and killer. It's that way in the killer's mind, anyway. Or maybe it's some kind of devious insurance scam, though we see no sign of it. Not yet, anyway." Larry Chips's game, Stack thought.

"It could be we're seeing simple compassion here," Fagin suggested. "I mean, for the other occupants, considering what happened last time when the flames took control."

"Maybe," Stack said. "But that would be unique in this kind of case. We're almost always dealing with a sociopath unburdened by empathy and remorse."

"There can always be an exception," Fagin said.

"If serial killers ever do feel compassion, it's only after the crime's been committed, so it doesn't stand in the way of their compulsion, their mission."

"But we do agree there was an effort here to confine the fire to the kitchen."

Both men looked at Rica, as if at the same time they'd just remembered she was there. "So what do you think?" Fagin asked.

Rica turned her head and spat off to the side, into a Kleenex she'd found folded in her pocket. It wouldn't do to have her DNA floating around the place. She felt like spitting again but resisted the temptation. The sweet, burned stench was horrible and created a terrible taste along the edges of her tongue.

"Maybe the bastard's an art lover," she said.

*   *   *

The Torcher enjoyed in particular the restaurant on Second Avenue because the bar featured a fireplace. It was the large stone kind, and real wood was burned so that it crackled and sometimes made sparks fly to be drawn up the flu and into the cold night.

It intrigued the Torcher how, when you stopped to think about it, fire was everything to everyone. Always had been. Always would be. Of course few people stopped to think about it, but while they went about their business, there was the fire down in the boiler rooms of their buildings. Upstairs in their homes, while they were comfortably watching television or reading a book, there was the fire down in their basement furnaces, pulsing and living at the burning hearts of their lives. When they left their beds and stepped outside in the morning, there in the east was the fire blazing on the horizon and turning the clouds blood-red. Everything to everyone.

One of the waiters approached the fireplace with iron tongs to cast more fuel to the flames. The Torcher always liked to watch this procedure. At times, when a fresh log was thrown on the fire, insects would feel the heat and emerge from the log's cracks and their hiding spaces beneath the rough bark, only to be consumed by the twisting, seeking flames.

There was no escaping the flames. Even when the great logs were burned down to a heap of glowing embers, the fire seemed only to be resting, waiting, catching its breath and testing the oxygen. It seemed to know living creatures. It seemed to know flesh and be drawn to it.

Sometimes the fire could be exquisite.

TWENTY-SEVEN

June 2000

Myra Raven sat across from Hugh Danner in the coffee shop located on the northeast corner of the Ardmont Arms. They were both having iced tea and pieces of each other. Myra was gripped by a barely controlled fury. Danner was just as acrimonious but even more contained, and parrying insults with what sounded like simple logic. He knew he wasn't fooling Myra with his slick sophistry, but what did it matter? He had the conniving bitch by the cunt hairs, and there was *nada* she could do about it.

She took a slow sip of tea, failing to prevent her hand from trembling. "We had an arrangement," she said.

He lifted his glass and sipped. Hands steady. *Notice, Myra?* "Arrangements change, Myra. Everything in life changes sooner or later. Besides, this is business. That's how you defined it, anyway, when you first approached me."

"You can bet our business is finished forever. That's something that sure as hell isn't going to change."

"Of course, I see your point. Now please try to see mine. The resident whose application I pushed through the board is, according to my sources, due to receive a very influential judicial appointment."

Myra glared across the table at him. She hated his smoothness, the pink glow of his skin after a close shave, the primitive jungle of black hairs on his bare forearms, the suave perfection of even his casual clothes, the court-room manner the bastard probably slept with and no longer even had to practice before a mirror. Whoever he really was—and she was finding out who—he was lost in-side the facade he'd built for himself. She understood that about him, probably better than anyone he'd ever met.

"And the judge will owe you a favor," she said bitterly.

"Oh, more than that. He'll owe me for not mentioning that he paid someone off to make sure he got the co-op his young wife insisted on having as a city pied-à-terre."

"And he'll know what a dishonorable asshole you are."

"Oh, sure. You might say the future judge and I are now partners in crime. It's a safe arrangement. It wouldn't be-hoove either of us to talk about our relationship. Just as it wouldn't behoove either of *us*."

"That's all it is with you, maneuvering to see who can get the other party down and stand with a sword to his heart."

"That's well put, Myra. But I prefer to think of it as col-laring and leashing the other party. Much more productive that way. And I'm the one holding the leash, because a judge will have much more to lose than I would. He'll get up and follow when I tug on the leash."

"You are truly contemptible."

"As you are, if whoever's passing judgment doesn't un-derstand how the world really works, the true business of the world. You do understand, Myra, which is why you're so disturbed by what's happened. I've bested you in a busi-ness deal, beat you at your own game."

"I don't live in the same scummy world of blackmail you do. Which is what you're planning on doing with that judge, blackmailing him."

"However you choose to define it, he'll feel secure as long as he cooperates. And he isn't completely without power. Remember, if I destroy him, he can at least hurt me. I wouldn't want that. And he won't hurt me, because I can destroy him. Just as you won't hurt me, or him, because it would destroy you. Your client, the young cop, how can he step up and complain that the bribe he offered wasn't productive? And how can you afford to see it made public that you grew your company into the most successful real estate agency in Manhattan by paying off influential co-op board members to ensure that your clients would be approved for residency to the exclusion of all other applicants? It's in everyone's best interest that none of us reveals any of this. We have a balance here, Myra. And in the end, we'll all see that it isn't disturbed."

More than Myra's hand was trembling now. She tried to keep it inside, this developing earthquake of emotion, but she could see that Danning knew she was seriously rattled, and *that* rattled her all the more. She leaned toward him over the table, clasping her hands in her lap. "Listen, you despicable, butt-sucking scum ball, you don't realize who you're playing games with here. I swear to you you'll be sorry if you don't return that boy's money."

Danner smiled. He really enjoyed this, she could tell. "I'm afraid you're going to have to return his money, Myra. Unless you want to use it to buy more cosmetic surgery. Should I tell you where it would do the most good.'"

She raised her right hand and closed it around her iced tea glass. He saw what she was thinking and merely waited for it to happen, for the cold tea and maybe the glass to follow, striking him in the face. Grounds for litigation, surely. More for him to hold over her head. More control.

But she merely sat there, staring at him.

A little more goading, perhaps. "Vulgarity doesn't become you, Myra. It doesn't fit with the kind of phony image you created years ago to hide behind. I've checked into your background, Myra Ravinski."

"My background has never been a secret."

"Not exactly a secret, but something you wouldn't want emphasized, especially in a highly public trial about real estate fraud. The point is, Myra Ravinski, I understand you and I understand how it is. Now you should understand. Get used to your collar, Myra, and it won't chafe so much. And don't be so sure that after you think things over, you and I won't be doing business as usual."

Something broke in her, but not in the way Danner had planned. Her hand relaxed on the glass and she raised it and took a sip of tea. No trembling this time. A stillness and a coolness grew in the core of her. There was ice at the pit of her being. If Danner had known about it, understood it, he would have been alarmed.

She sat back and sighed, regarding him without blinking. "I suppose the truth is you're right, it's only business."

"Exactly. So you might as well put it behind you."

"Yes, I intend to." She could see he sensed a balance had shifted. Men like Danner could always tell when that happened. She was surprised it had taken him a little longer than most to recognize it. He didn't like this, didn't understand the subtle change in her.

"It's what happens sometimes in business," he said softly but in a patronizing tone, trying to retain control.

"You got fucked, Myra, and there's nothing you can do about it."

She nodded and stood up, leaving the check for Danner to pay.

"That's how people get AIDS," she said, smiling as she walked toward the door.

Ed Marks became an honest cop on the day Myra told him he and Amy weren't going to get the co-op after all. She repaid their $20,000 loan from her own pocket, he knew. What bothered him was how Amy cried, and how he longed to go see whoever on the board had rejected them and use his nightstick to beat him to death.

But what bothered him most was that a slimeball he didn't even know had possession of the knowledge that Ed Marks, a cop and a cop's son, was dirty. This wasn't free meals at some hash house so he'd hang around and prevent trouble, or a merchant's key so he could get in out of the cold sometimes. This was the kind of thing—twenty thousand was big enough money—that would kill his career and make him want to kill himself. He knew what it felt like now, and how it would feel if he gave in to the temptations of the Job again. It was all out there on the street for the taking, something beyond a cop's salary, a cop's pension; all a cop had to do was nod or look the other way at the right time. Not Ed Marks. Not if this was the way it could feel afterward. Nothing like this would happen to him again—ever.

The Markses had to get out of their apartment within days. Myra Raven helped them to locate a fourth-floor walk-up to live in temporarily while they continued looking for something better and affordable. The place was decrepit, and Marks wished it had an elevator. It was a good thing Amy didn't have to go out much, a woman carrying twins taking four flights of stairs. It wasn't right. It wasn't fair.

Ed Marks found himself thinking more and more often that he'd like to find the bastard who put them in this position and do something about him.

Myra couldn't shake what had happened between her and Danner. It bothered her all the time she was trying to unwind the deal with the Marks family. She could still see the wife, Amy's, face, almost like her own younger face, register the despair when she realized the move wasn't going to happen. Not the move she wanted, anyway.

Instead she was going to a Lower East Side walk-up— only for a while, both Myra and Ed Marks promised. An indefinite while. So far Myra'd had no luck in locating another co-op or condo they could afford and that would suit them.

As the days passed, Myra became more bitter and moody, sometimes snapping at her people in the office. She was on edge, and she was drinking too much, having rediscovered martinis. She wouldn't have her personal life affecting her business persona. Myra simply would not allow that to happen.

She sat for hours at her desk, later and later into lonely evenings, sometimes simply staring at the paperwork before her, not really seeing it. Finally she made a phone call she'd never dreamed of making. Another mistake? Maybe, but she was willing to take the chance.

The next night, when she buzzed up her visitor from the

lobby and later opened her apartment door to his knock, she somehow knew that what she'd done was going to work out okay. The tousled blond hair, the twelve-year-old's kind of grin, the boyishness that somehow went with the lean handsomeness, all of it was strangely reassuring as she stood there staring at him and thinking, *Sonny, you are in the right business.*

"I'll go first," he finally said, widening the grin and extending his hand. "Hi, I'm Billy Watkins."

TWENTY-EIGHT

February 2002

Sometimes cracks were barely visible, and only in the right light.

Like the yellow lamplight from the other room, angling in through the half-opened door. What the cracks might mean, that was something else.

Mirabella lay beside Larry Chips and stared at the cracks in the bedroom ceiling of her house in New Jersey, trying to read some message in them, like with her horoscope. Chips had picked her up from work, where they'd had a few drinks before leaving; then they'd driven straight here with Chips behind the wheel. He'd told her to call him Chips, said everyone did, like it was some kind of gambler's nickname and glamorous. Mirabella hadn't seen Larry Chips as glamorous from the beginning, only a little better than average looking with a pathetic line of bullshit. He didn't even realize she was the one who'd picked him up.

Sex the first night had been great. And the second and third. Chips had moved out of his rat trap apartment he'd probably rented by the hour and into her house, promising to pay half the rent when he got some money. Mirabella knew better than to plan on how to spend her windfall.

As they'd settled into a routine, the sex became less passionate and inventive, and less frequent. Chips continued to talk a good game, but when it came time to do the deed, he often preferred to sleep off all the alcohol he'd consumed beforehand. She was sure he sometimes only pretended to fall asleep, rather than have sex with her.

She knew he still found her attractive. He wasn't simply using her so he could live in her house, eat her food, and use her car. Mirabella understood men. She had known enough of them to learn plenty. Chips was brighter than he seemed and was preoccupied with something. After only their first few nights together she realized he wasn't standard issue. He came across as a small-timer, and in many ways he was one. But she had a hunch that in some ways he wasn't small time at all. There were depths and dark sides to this one. She wondered if she really wanted to know what preoccupied him.

Of course, that he was different was what made her curious about him, and all the more attracted to him. She'd drawn so many losers that she thought this one, just because he was different, might be better. How could she not be intrigued? It was the usual beer and football male shit, like with all the others, and then suddenly his behavior would change and confuse her.

Like the night she couldn't find him and finally went out onto the porch, and there he was, sitting in the dark on the top step, lighting match after match from a book of paper matches from the Claybar. He was staring at each of them as if hypnotized until they almost burned his fingers, before flipping them out into the dark. They looked like miniature shooting stars arcing out toward the concrete walk leading to the driveway.

When she tried to talk to him, he seemed barely aware she was there. Preoccupation again, she thought. He'd mentioned without realizing it one time that he was from California, so maybe he needed his space. Mirabella didn't know how long he'd been sitting out there, but in the morning she found at least a hundred bent and burned matches lying there on the cracked walk like lifeless cremated worms.

That was her Chips, unpredictable. He sure made life interesting and sometimes a little scary, like unknown territory. That was what got her more involved with him than she'd first planned, and what kept her interested. Always something to make you wonder.

Tonight was another example. She got up after he was asleep and walked into the kitchen to get a drink of water, because there was no glass in the bathroom. And there was something orange-colored splashed around and dried on the bottom of the sink.

She touched it with her finger and tasted it. Orange juice. But she was sure there was none in the refrigerator.

She opened the refrigerator to make sure. No orange juice. So where did he get the juice and where was the rest of it? And why had he poured some of it in the sink, probably down the drain deliberately? What was going on here? Was this guy with the CIA or something, or maybe just a secret screwdriver drinker?

She drank her water, then turned the faucet back on and used the stream of water and her glass to wash the residue of orange juice down the drain. Then she went back to bed and decided not to ask Chips about the orange juice. This was partly because she was for some reason afraid to ask, and partly because she somehow knew she wasn't ready for the answer. She grinned into the darkness. *What the fuck was he doing with orange juice?*

It would be interesting to bide her time and find out. He was good at sex and games when he wanted to be, and he didn't put her down or beat her, and he had that unsolved puzzle quality about him. The only other man she'd known with that same kind of quiet, unreadable way about him had been a good guy and steady; then one night he'd snapped and beaten two men to death with a Derek Jeter model baseball bat.

She couldn't imagine Chips doing anything like that. There didn't seem to be any sort of violent undercurrent about him, as there'd been with the Derek Jeter fan.

She would ride with this guy for a while.

See where it went.

Orange juice.

O'Reilly had wanted to see Stack alone in his office.

So here Stack sat, staring at the backdrop of plaques and photos and commendations that were mostly Vandervoort's, and waiting for O'Reilly to finish writing whatever it was that was so important on his desk. The office was too warm. And it was dim because the heat caused the window to fog up, blocking the light. The air was still and smelled like O'Reilly's cologne or aftershave. Stack waited patiently for his boss to finish his busy act and get to what he wanted. Stack had work to do.

Finally O'Reilly capped his ridiculously expensive pen,

peeled off his reading glasses, and crossed his arms on the desk as he leaned forward to address Stack. "Sorry to keep you waiting."

"I thought maybe crime had taken a holiday."

"Wouldn't it be loverly?" O'Reilly said, ignoring the sarcasm. "I called you in here to talk about something personal."

The hair on the nape of Stack's neck stirred. He was in no mood for what he knew was coming. He waited for O'Reilly to say it.

"Rica."

"A top-notch homicide detective," Stack said, playing hard to get.

"How do you feel about her?" O'Reilly asked.

"I just said."

O'Reilly uncrossed his arms and leaned back in his chair. Now he rested both hands on the desk as if he were about to drum his fingers. Only he didn't. "C'mon, Stack, you know what I mean. But if you don't, I'll give you some clues. Everybody in Mobile Response and most of the precinct cops know what's going on, or think they do. Which is that you're playing the meat trombone with Rica."

"What the hell is that supposed to mean?" Stack trying to believe what he was hearing.

"Simple. That you're porking Rica."

Stack felt his face flush in the warm office. The idiot O'Reilly would take it for embarrassment, not knowing Stack was tempted to fly across the desk and grab him by the throat. He said simply, "They're wrong."

"Not that most of them wouldn't blame you."

"Blame or no blame," Stack said, "it's all the same to me."

O'Reilly flashed a nasty, knowing grin that made Stack even madder. "Aw, don't get coy with me. You're going through a divorce, spending all that time with Rica, who's so obviously wrapped up in you that she might spontaneously combust. You telling me you've never noticed?"

"No," Stack said, "I'm telling you we don't sleep together."

O'Reilly looked dumbfounded. "Why not? Oh, maybe the strain of your divorce and all."

"We don't sleep together because we're both professionals," Stack said. "We do the job instead of each other."

O'Reilly laughed. "Stack, have you ever *looked* at Rica? The woman is made for recreational sex."

"You called me in here to ask if I was fucking her," Stack said, not realizing he'd stood up and was glaring down at O'Reilly. "I've answered you."

"You've goddamn lied to me."

Stack took a step toward O'Reilly, who for the first time seemed to realize he was maybe going too far here. "You can see it any way you want," Stack said. "You asked your question. You got your answer. Anything else?"

"Yeah. I want you two to quit making it so obvious."

Stack leaned over with both fists on the desk. "It's only obvious to some fuckhead who thinks that way because he can't understand why we wouldn't be clawing at each other in the backseat of the unmarked. You know why he thinks that way? Because that's what he'd be doing."

"This fuckhead," O'Reilly said, dead-eyed and cool now. "He got a name?"

"You name him."

Stack started toward the door. It was one direction or the other now, and toward O'Reilly meant a breakdown of self-control; then there'd be an IA investigation, disciplinary action, and possibly the end of Stack's career. O'Reilly knew that and knew Stack knew it. He was deliberately baiting Stack now.

"Keep in mind," O'Reilly said, "I won't have two of my officers hammering each other while on duty. And I won't have this kind of talk about them, which both of us knows is true, continuing on my watch."

Stack turned around. "Or?" His voice was tight, and he saw O'Reilly blink, having second thoughts. Maybe professionalism and a regard for regulations wouldn't restrain Stack. Stack with the bad-ass reputation that O'Reilly *did* know was true because he'd seen the bodies.

"There's no *or* about it," O'Reilly said. He had his balls again and was staring hard at Stack.

Stack returned the stare for a while, then slowly turned his back on O'Reilly and went out the door. His throat was dry and his heart was banging away, but he had himself under control.

"If it ain't true," O'Reilly said behind him, "what you need's a shit-pot full of Viagra."

Stack made a mental note to send Vandervoort a *Get Well Soon* card.

Victoria Pike settled into a sagging, overstuffed chair and propped her aching feet up on a hassock. Her apartment had seemed a great idea when she'd bought it last summer, and now she was pretty much stuck with it. Her financial history was such that it would be all but impossible for her to obtain another mortgage loan, so even if this place was drafty in the winter and sometimes assaulted by what seemed like legions of cockroaches when the weather was warm, here she would stay for the foreseeable future.

She figured at least she wasn't flat broke. Her job at the restaurant was tolerable, and the way she'd found to receive an occasional windfall wasn't the worst thing she'd ever done. This wasn't prostitution, which in her college years she'd once considered. This wasn't some of the things she'd done for drugs.

She was a graying woman in her forties who looked like one in her fifties. Her figure was still reasonably trim but her eyes were defeated, her features drawn, and her complexion spotty. She'd never figured out what caused the damned brown spots here and there on her face and neck, like liver spots on the very old.

Some life had returned to her legs. She made herself climb up out of the chair, then trudged into the kitchen and removed a frozen chicken teriyaki dinner from the microwave. Carefully, so as not to burn her fingers, she peeled back the cellophane over the plastic tray and examined its contents. The dinner looked done, but when she prodded the chicken breast with her finger it was still cold in the middle. She slid the tray back in the microwave and set the timer for a minute and a half. She could have eaten cheaper at work, and the food was better, but by now she was tired of it.

Victoria hadn't always been a waitress in a restaurant that couldn't figure out what kind of food it served. Not too many years ago she'd been a stock analyst at Voss, Bauer and Murray, a large Wall Street brokerage firm.

That was before her looks had left her and she'd been a favorite guest on the financial channels, where she'd
confidently explained the machinations of the markets and
dispensed advice.

But she'd misread her computer model and made a call
for the market to rise, just before the tech stock bubble
burst. She'd stubbornly continued her buy recommendation for months, even as tech stocks plunged and dragged
virtually every kind of stock down with them. Finally Voss,
Bauer and Murray had bought out her contract, and she
was unemployed.

It wasn't her first mistake. Back in '97 she'd misinterpreted the market's direction and cost another brokerage
firm's clients millions. She'd been fired then, too, just like
after the tech stock massacre a few years ago.

The tech wreck caught her at a particularly bad time.
She'd just come off a horrible love affair that had turned
violent. Again. So many of the men she loved eventually
came to abuse her psychologically and physically. Did she
know that going in? Was there a pattern? Her analyst had
said yes to both questions. Before she could no longer afford to pay him. At which point he said nothing, refusing
even to speak with her on the phone.

Victoria had always been a drinker, but after her health
coverage lapsed and she could no longer afford analysis,
she developed a closer relationship with the bottle. Gin,
wine, beer . . . it made little difference to her. It was the
oblivion at the bottom of the bottle that attracted her. If she
hadn't been totally unemployable before on the Street, she
was now. Word of her drinking problem had circulated like
a major stock split rumor.

This time the rumor was true enough, Victoria had to admit.

With a great deal of willpower and an effort that left her limp and scared, she'd managed to give up alcohol. Only to discover cocaine.

Kicking hard drugs was the toughest thing she'd ever done. But she did it, and hadn't had a drink, a snort, or a smoke in over a year.

Now she worked hard hours in a job where hardly anyone knew about her past, about how far she'd fallen. After work she spent most of her time in her apartment, sleeping, watching TV, or in a melancholy stupor simply staring off into memory, sorting through the past and searching for something that attracted and frightened her.

At least at work she could lose herself in her labors. Actually forget for a while.

It wasn't much of a job, and it didn't pay well except on unusually heavy nights. But it was a living and it was a life.

Victoria earned enough to get by if she disciplined herself and watched her pennies. Besides those pennies, she again had at least some money that stuck. Money of her own.

Money.

It was something Victoria Pike understood better than most people.

Money was what made life smoother. It was what got your ticket punched for the next ride.

Meanwhile, Victoria stayed clean with the law and worked, saving money. When she had enough, she'd know what to do with it, how to parlay it into a fortune.

She would get her ticket punched again. She would take

the roller coaster ride again. And maybe this time get off at the top.

She knew it was probably only a dream, but it was one she desperately needed.

TWENTY-NINE

Otto Kreiger said good night to his wife, Gertrude, who left to attend the New York Macramé Museum board meeting, as she did the first Tuesday of every month. Every Wednesday it was Tai Chi classes, and every Friday it was Cooking with Claire. The last seemed a waste of time to Kreiger, because Gertrude was pretty much a stranger to their own kitchen. But maybe she took part in all these activities to get out of the apartment, maybe even to get away from him. Kreiger didn't much care. He enjoyed his time alone, without Gertrude's constant chatter and movement. Probably, he decided, she had all those planned activities and lessons simply because she couldn't be still.

And it wasn't as if Gertrude and Otto Kreiger couldn't afford them. Otto had made his pile, and now he was damn well going to enjoy life. There were plenty of ways for him to do that. Plenty of board memberships, golf games, poker nights. Winning, running things, coming out on top, that was what Otto Kreiger was all about. He knew it and made no apologies. Probably a woman like Gert, a beautiful redhead twenty years younger than Kreiger, stayed with him because he was a winner, had the spoils. Hell, she was part of the spoils and she knew it. Had to. She wasn't *that* dumb. That was life, and so be it. Let Gert sign up for and join anything she wanted. Far as Kreiger was concerned, she could join the goddamn navy, as long as she came back a few times a week and spread her legs.

Kreiger had just toweled off after taking a shower and wore only an oversize white terry cloth towel wrapped around his pink and ponderous body. He was going out in about an hour to play stud poker at his club, take some more money from those whining amateurs who supplied his pocket change. He'd wear his new gray sport coat with the leather elbow patches. His charcoal Armani pants with all the pleats. And gold cuff links, goddamnit! The ones with the diamonds set in them. Let the whiners know who might run them out of the game if the pot got worthwhile. Play with the big dog and you might get bit. Might get your damned throat ripped right out.

It was almost like a premonition. Kreiger could feel luck running through him like a dark, magnetic force in his blood. Something beyond mere brain knowledge. His night, his might, his right. He knew it deep in himself, the way birds know there's a south.

He decided to work on a drink while he dressed, set the mood for the evening. As he walked from the bathroom, his bare feet left damp footprints on the plush carpet for the first half dozen steps. The footprints faded as he trod to a credenza and poured two fingers of Absolut into an on-the-rocks glass, then headed for the kitchen to get some ice.

He remembered placing his bare left foot on the cool tile floor. That was when the kitchen ceiling swung down as if it were on hinges and slammed into the back of his head.

* * *

What the hell is this?

Otto Kreiger couldn't move, couldn't breathe, couldn't talk. His head ached and he was lying on his back on the kitchen floor. His arms were jammed behind him, causing his nude belly to bulge so he couldn't see his feet. He couldn't separate his legs, only bend them slightly.

Somebody had sapped him as he was entering the kitchen, he realized, then tied him up. And tight!

Kreiger tried again to move, but managed only to start a cramp in his side that he had to assuage by lying still and limp. Bastard who'd done this to him knew what he was doing. A pro. By now had probably robbed him fucking blind! A faint admiration for whoever had the balls to do this to him crept into Kreiger's mind, but that wouldn't stop Kreiger from killing this joker if he ever found out who he was. *Fuck with the bull, you get the horn.*

Jesus, he was cold! He hoped somebody would find him before Gert got home. Not only did he want to get warm, but he wanted to save himself the embarrassment of being found this way by his young wife. Also, he wanted to see what the bastard who'd hit him had stolen.

Then with a start it occurred to him that he might not have been unconscious all that long. Whoever had sapped him might still be in the apartment. He tried to move his head but couldn't. Rolled his eyes but could see only the ceiling and the top eighteen inches or so of the cabinets on the wall behind him. He lay still, listening.

Yes! He heard something, a slight noise above—behind him! Someone was here with him!

Not to help him! Not saying anything!

Courage ran from Kreiger and he fought to control himself, wondering if he was urinating. For a moment he thought he might have a heart attack. Then he concentrated on lying very still. That might be his best strategy, be motionless and so unnoticeable. No, that was crazy! But whoever was there might think he'd lost consciousness. Whoever had broken in might even forget about him as he went around collecting loot. No sane thief wanted a murder charge!

Then Kreiger realized he was colder than he should have been. It wasn't just that he was nude and lying on a tile floor. There was something . . . Yes, he was wet, and not from the shower. He'd dried off from that. He was lying in a puddle. Not a warm one like urine. His body heat had warmed it slightly, but not even to room temperature. It was cool like alcohol. Or—

Terror struck him like an ax and made his eyes bulge. His chest heaved, his heels hammered, and despite the headache he kept banging the back of his head against the floor. A voice said something he couldn't understand. It might have been his own. Very cold liquid—*Yes, my God, gasoline!*—splashed over the length of his body. Some of it got in his eyes, though he'd clenched them shut.

When he opened them he could barely see through the stinging blurriness that someone was standing near him, over him. He saw something dark mushroom above him, like an enormous bird spreading its wings, and it took him a few seconds to realize what it was. An umbrella!

Kreiger stiffened his body and began to scream. The sound came out of his taped mouth as only a moan, but it ranted like an air horn inside his head, tried to escape through his ears, his nose. Not enough noise to be heard by anyone out there, though, he knew. He *knew!*

The black umbrella was directly over him now. He tried

to fix his eyes on it and lose himself in its blackness, be safe and unseen there as in shadow. The scream echoing inside his skull continued. Even through the pain he continued to scream. The pain and the scream became one, and was the last thing he experienced. It carried him like a dark bird into death.

The Torcher backpedaled from the kitchen, then lowered the umbrella and tossed it half folded into a corner. As always there would be no fingerprints. Gloves would prevent them. Since it wasn't raining outside, the umbrella, taken from Kreiger's closet, might attract attention.

The flames along the tablecloth edge were still high, though the sprinkler system, compartmentalized and confined to the kitchen, where the fire was, continued to spray water. Kreiger lay blackened and glistening like a huge rotted whale on the floor. He was still burning slightly, sizzling, actually, where the water hit.

Look away! Time to leave, not too quickly.

The dry coat slid over wet clothing. The boots were wet but wouldn't be memorable; there was still plenty of snow and slush outside.

Everything was as planned. The alarm system wired to the sprinklers had been easily neutralized. But soon the smoke, which the showers of water helped to create, would escape the apartment and cause an alarm to sound, or the smoke would be smelled or noticed by someone in the building.

Already it was detectable out in the hall.

Not in the elevator.

There was no one even to notice the Torcher until the

lobby. Half a dozen people were there, laughing and leaving together. On their way to dinner and a Broadway show, maybe. Living life, having fun.

The Torcher joined them as they went out the glass doors into the maelstrom of the city, past the doorman who was looking the other direction anyway for a cab to hail for them. They would need two taxis, the Torcher thought. Busy doorman.

Away. Walk slowly.

The tone of the conversation and laughter, fading now, didn't change.

Into the dark. Alone.

As water pressure dropped, the sprinklers in the Kreiger kitchen sputtered, then were reduced to emitting only a drizzle. Pockets of fat, what Gert sometimes called Kreiger's love handles, were sizzling now like bacon. A spark jumped. Another. One landed on the bath towel lying on the floor near the inert Kreiger. Having been shielded by the umbrella, the thick terry cloth towel wasn't so damp that it couldn't hold the spark, nurture it to flame . . . slight at first, then larger.

The single flame was joined by others, and they writhed and danced along the unfurled towel to the cooking island whose counter had acted like a roof and kept the cabinetry below it dry. The laminated-wood cabinet doors began to smoke, then glowed and flamed. Behind the cabinet doors, the flames found cleaning fluid, rags, a box of folded plastic wastebasket liners.

It wasn't long before the cooking island blazed, superheating the gas in the stove's lines to the burners until fumes found an opening and became flame that wove and twisted its way to the ceiling.

The kitchen was sucking in air now from the rest of the rooms; the fire was in control and the fire had to breathe! It flattened itself and spread over the kitchen ceiling, blossoming out and down to attack more prey along the walls, the walls themselves. It was strong enough now to have a voice, a constant sibilant sigh that was becoming throatier and throatier. It would soon become a roar. The fire was strong enough now to leave the kitchen, to steal up on, then burst upon and devour whatever was in its path. It was feasting and craving and growing by the minute, by the second.

It would soon be powerful enough to explore, to go where it chose, to claim what it needed.

THIRTY

In the living room alcove office of his co-op on the fifty-eighth floor of the Belmire Tower, Alan Warner was hunched over his computer keyboard. The alcove could be transformed into an office simply by opening the antique Victorian hutch Warner had paid someone to fashion into a workstation that contained his computer, printer, and fax machine, with space for a file cabinet and a few reference books.

He was diligently working on chapter fifteen of his next book in his series of *Guntrader* western novels. Warner was prolific and had a strong story sense, and while he wasn't a household name, his westerns sold well and had countless times been adapted for TV and the movies, making him a wealthy man. But he had to work hard to meet deadlines, and sometimes he felt as if he were running—or typing—in place. It was his habit to catnap during the days and work evenings, which was why he was seated now hard at his task while his wife Niki had gone to bed early to read.

Warner, a middle-aged, stocky former Brooklynite who wore his dark hair long in back like his fictional western gunslingers, sat back from the computer and cursed. He was trapped in a box canyon. His main character, Max Dill, was under siege in a desolate ranch house surrounded by dozens of hired guns who'd been rustling horses and selling them to the U.S. Cavalry. Nobody other than the rustlers knew Max was there, and he was fast running out of ammunition.

How the hell am I going to get him out of this? Warner asked himself. He didn't want to have the cavalry ride in to the rescue; that didn't quite compute, since they were the ones buying the horses.

He sat back, waiting for an idea to hit him as they always did, and nodded off, maybe for only a few seconds.

He came awake smelling something burning, and thought at first the rustlers had set fire to the ranch house in an effort to flush out Max Dill.

Then he realized he was staring at his computer monitor and had dozed off. But he hadn't slept very long, because there were no wild mustangs galloping across the monitor; the screen saver hadn't come on. So he'd been dreaming.

Wait a minute. He could still smell something burning. From the apartment below, he'd bet. Gertrude Kreiger attempting to cook again. Warner had an eye for female beauty and appreciated Gert Kreiger, but cooking wasn't part of the repertoire he imagined her to possess. Cooking ability wasn't something a woman like her needed, especially married to that rich sidewinder husband of hers, Otto. Warner's dislike for Otto Kreiger fell short of hate because of the time he'd found a statement from Otto's brokerage firm stuck to the inside of the incinerator shaft. Obviously it had escaped from Otto's trash during its plunge to the basement and fiery destruction. It listed all of Otto's stocks. Warner had taken the statement to his apartment, researched some of the stocks, and bought them. He'd more than doubled his money in three months, then sold the stocks and bought a two-year-old Mercedes 500SL. Thanks, Otto.

"What's going on?" Niki asked behind him.

Warner turned to see his attractive blond wife—attractive enough, he thought, to maybe someday play the rancher's daughter in a Max Dill movie—standing outside the open bedroom door. Sexy, he thought. Maybe the cavalry would work after all and he could finish this chapter, then . . .

"Alan?"

"Oh! Wrong? I dunno. Gertrude trying to cook again downstairs, I think."

"Don't be ridiculous."

"Maybe Otto's boiling something alive."

"That's possible."

"Want me to knock on his door and draw down on the consarned varmint?"

"Only in one of your novels, hon. I couldn't sleep. It's too hot in the bedroom. I'm gonna turn down the thermostat a notch."

"Okay. I'll open the hall door to get a little cool air."

Warner crossed the room to open the door.

When his fingers touched the brass doorknob, he drew back his hand. The knob was hot. No, only warm. He touched it again, leaving his hand on it this time. *What the hell?* . . .

"Alan," his wife said behind him.

"The doorknob's warm."

He pressed the flat of his hand to the door's wood surface. It, too, was warm.

"Alan, maybe you better not—"

But Warner, curious, had turned the knob and opened the door.

The fire was waiting for him.

Had him!

He turned and tried to run. But the fire was beyond him, behind him, had rushed into the apartment like a hot and roaring hurricane.

As the pain bent him over and his vision went, he saw the flames leap for the hem of his wife's nightgown.

"Alan!"

He tried to take a step toward her but the fire was everywhere and everything.

Stack and Rica could smell the smoke even on the other side of Manhattan. As they were halfway to the scene of the fire, the lighted windows in the upper floors of tall buildings faded, then became invisible. There was a dark pall over the city, blotting out the night sky and hanging low enough to sting the eyes and leave an unpleasant taste of ash on the tongue. When the unmarked reached the Upper East Side, its headlight beams were visible in the lowering haze.

The street was blocked off, and Stack and Rica had to show ID, then proceed on foot. They made their way through a maze of emergency vehicles. Hoses and feeder cords lay in a network on soaked and ice-glazed pavement. An FDNY vehicle was nearby, its aerial ladder disappearing in the haze only about three stories up. A pumper was parked next to the ladder truck. Was there actually a firefighter up on that ladder, directing water into the flames? Sirens howled like wolves as ambulances carried victims away. Strangely, there wasn't much shouting. By now, everyone was exhausted.

Beyond police barricades, people in heavy coats, some of them wearing house slippers, stood and stared vacant-eyed at the building they'd called home. A few of them were seated on the curb, sobbing or simply staring, being attended to by family or neighbors. A blond woman wearing nothing but a thin nightgown sat in a parked squad car, looking straight ahead, tears streaming down her cheeks and reflecting in the eerie red and blue roof-bar lights playing over the scene.

"Those people on the sidewalk," Rica said, "they remind me of those old films from World War Two when the German army rousted people from their homes in the Warsaw ghetto."

"Different kind of war," Stack said, "but war nonetheless." He could hardly believe what he was seeing. On their right were rows of formless shapes beneath blankets on the wet sidewalk. He knew they were corpses. There weren't enough body bags.

"Christ!" Rica said. She'd seen the blanketed forms, too. She crossed herself. It was the first time Stack had seen that, though he'd heard she was Catholic.

A tall form in boots and a rubber slicker strode toward them. He had on a firefighter's helmet and what looked like an inhalator slung around his neck. He got closer, removed the helmet, and used both sides of his wrist to wipe some of the soot off his face. Ernest Fagin. His eyes were haunted. He was breathing hard.

"What the fuck happened?" Stack asked.

"C'mon over here," Fagin said. "Gotta sit down."

They walked to the curb, between a parked squad car

and a sedan with a roof light and an FDNY plaque on its lowered sun visor. Fagin slumped down on the curb, not minding that it was wet and that water flowed over his booted toes toward a storm sewer.

"Fire on the fifty-seventh floor. It burned for a while before we were notified; then traffic held us up. Goddamn people don't move over for sirens anymore!"

"It looks like a modern building," Rica said, glancing in the direction of the still blazing fire that was a dim glow overhead in the haze.

"It is. That became a problem, especially with our slow response time. The building's vented for air-conditioning, and we didn't get the call soon enough to use our blitz tactics. The place is equipped with a sprinkler system, but it hadn't been checked for a while and didn't maintain pressure. The more water it sprayed, the weaker the pressure became, until finally it was a trickle. What it did was slow the fire, dampen everything, and increase the smoke."

"Are the elevators working?" Rica asked.

"Hell, no. In about a third of major high-rise fires, they fail to operate. Fire, heat or water damage cause electrical failures. This is one of that third. We got here, and the elevators shafts were like chimneys; we had to ascend by foot up the fire stairs, lugging most of our equipment on our backs."

"I thought the floors in these buildings were more or less sealed off from each other," Stack said. "Built with flame-retardant material."

"The building is classified as fire-resistive," Fagin said. "But that's not the same as nonflammable. Still, it might have been enough."

Rica squatted down next to Fagin. "Except for . . . ?"

"Tragedy number two," Fagin said, "after the sprinkler system failed. The butterfly valves in the air-conditioning shafts and ducts were supposed to close automatically if smoke was detected, or above a certain temperature. They didn't work. Maybe the wiring had burned through and shorted out, maybe this, maybe that. . . . Thing is, they didn't close, and the fire traveled up through the ductwork. The smoke traveled up *and* down. Most of our fatalities are from smoke inhalation."

Stack stared at him. "I didn't think smoke traveled down."

"These modern high-rises have tightly sealed windows and doors. You need keys to open the doors, and most of the windows don't open at all."

"So once the fire stairs and elevator shafts are full of smoke, people are trapped," Rica said.

"It's not only that," Fagin said glumly. "Like Stack said, smoke does rise. But once it reaches the top floor, it's got no way to go in these sealed buildings except to start spreading down." He glanced up at Stack. "You won't like what it's called: the Stack Effect. Because the variance in outside and inside temperatures of a sealed building cause differences in pressure, the smoke and heat are moved fast—up or down. The building becomes in effect a giant smoke stack. Imagine what happens when you cap a smokestack."

"Didn't people break out some of the windows?" Rica asked. "Give the smoke a place to go?"

"Sure," Fagin said. *"We* broke out some of the windows to get streams of water to the fire from high floors of adjacent buildings, trying to contain it. But you break windows and you create drafts and feed the fire oxygen. That's what fire lives on, oxygen." He glared upward fiercely as if at an enemy who'd defeated him. "As long as we can't get to it with water and foam, it burns until it runs out of oxygen and flammable material. Until most of the building is a shell."

"Is it too early to know how it started?" Stack asked.

"Yeah. But we have an idea what unit it started in. From the early calls. Up on the fifty-seventh floor. Belongs to someone named Kreiger."

Stack shook his head.

"Doesn't register," Rica said.

Fagin shifted his lanky body forward to get his feet centered beneath his weight. "Could be the work of your guy," Fagin told her, hauling himself to a standing position.

"I hope not," Rica said. "I hope some human being didn't cause this."

Fagin shook water from his helmet and placed it back on his head. "I better get back. I'll let you know more when I find out more."

Stack and Rica nodded to him, then stood and watched him negotiate the slippery, littered street. Back toward the fire.

Like a moth, Stack thought inanely. Or maybe not so inanely. Maybe there really was an analogy.

"Whaddya think?" Rica asked.

"I think we oughta get outta the way," Stack said.

As they walked around the police barricades on their way back to the unmarked, a frenetic redheaded woman was arguing with one of the uniforms, trying to get through. She would have been attractive if her face hadn't been screwed up with rage and fear, her hair wild from wind and her wrestling with the cop who was restraining her.

"I goddamn *live* there!" she screamed, trying to get at

the cop's eyes with long red fingernails. "My husband might be in there!"

"I got somebody checking the tenants list, ma'am." The cop was nifty with his hands, fending her off without hurting her. *Must be like fighting with an eagle,* Rica thought.

"Fuck the tenant's list! I'm a tenant! Kreiger! Find Kreiger on your damned list!"

Stack and Rica glanced at each other.

"There'll be a better time to talk with her," Stack said. "Fagin's information might not be correct." He hoped it wasn't. He felt like clutching the woman to him, hugging her tight, telling her how sorry he was for her.

That was probably how the cop felt, too, only he had to protect his eyes.

THIRTY-ONE

Fagin came by the precinct to listen to the 911 tape with Stack and Rica in O'Reilly's office:

"Near Second Avenue and East Fifty-first, the Belmire Tower, there's a fire on the fifty-seventh floor."

"Could you give me your—*hello! Hello!"*

But the caller had abruptly hung up.

O'Reilly ignored Stack and Rica and looked at Fagin. "Sounds like some asshole fartin' through a fan blade."

"Not much help, I guess," Fagin admitted.

"Lab might be able to bring something up," Stack said.

O'Reilly snorted. "Shit, I don't even know if it was a man or woman, the voice is so fuckin' disguised."

"Maybe the techs'll be able to tell," Rica suggested, though she knew it wasn't likely. Whoever had made the call—and she was sure it was the Torcher—knew how to disguise a voice. Hell, these days there were devices you could buy at an electronics store that would make you somebody else on the phone.

"Lab can do wonders," Stack said.

O'Reilly tossed a cheap ball point pen down on the desk hard enough that it bounced onto the floor. "Damn! I thought this was gonna lead to something."

Fagin looked at Stack, then over to O'Reilly. "Sorry. We

do what we can with what we have to work with." Back at Stack. Maybe a smile. Bureaucracy was bureaucracy, in the FDNY or NYPD. It was all the same. What it took to be in charge was sometimes quite different from what it took to do the job.

"Then of course we got this dis-fuckin'-aster!" O'Reilly said, punching a forefinger into the folded *Times* on his desk. "Thirty-two dead, over a hundred hospitalized, six in critical condition." He glowered at Fagin. "Why didn't you guys get there sooner? Hell, you had a goddamn phone call, maybe from the guy that set the fire."

In the corner of his vision Stack saw Fagin stiffen. Fagin's right hand with its long, piano player's fingers clenched into a white-knuckled fist.

Briefly Stack thought Fagin might throw a punch at O'Reilly and was ready to grab his arm, but the lanky arson investigator drew a deep breath and relaxed. "I explained to Detective Stack the problems we have with high-rise fires and response times."

"Like you explained it to the media vultures," O'Reilly said. "Still, we got all those people dead, and explaining won't bring them back to life." He wiped a hand straight down his face, pulling at flesh and momentarily making him look mournful.

"It's politics," Fagin said. "We need more of the right kind of equipment, better inspection, and building codes that take into account high-rise fires. We got a city here that keeps growing straight up. Fire fighting's gotta catch up with it."

"Speaking of politics," O'Reilly said, "this Leland Brand jack-off is killing us."

"He does want to spend money on high-rise fire prevention," Fagin said.

"Wants to be goddamn commissioner, mayor someday, is all. Meanwhile, he's slamming the police department for not catching this Torcher nightmare prick! He actually gets himself elected mayor, then see if the FDNY gets its money and shiny new play toys. What you'll get is what we get, and it'll be up your ass!"

Fagin sat back, not about to argue with what he knew was probably true.

"The pressure is on to catch this firebug sicko," O'Reilly said, "and Channel One asks us what goes on, we ain't got diddly-squat! Anybody got any ideas?"

"Larry Chips," Stack said.

O'Reilly looked at him in disbelief, working his eyebrows. "Chips again? I told you, this guy's not our firebug. What do we know about him that leads you to keep coming back to Chips as our prime suspect?"

"He's our only suspect. We know he's a firebug, and he's not in California, and he's probably still in the New York area."

"That's not enough."

"Doesn't matter," Stack said.

"Doesn't goddamn *matter?*"

"Give him to the media."

"Ah . . ." Another tug at slack flesh; another brief and mournful hound. Here was something worth a thought. "Like tossing meat to following wolves, eh?"

Stack pressed on. "Exactly. Let them chew on it while we do our work without them breathing down our necks. Relieve that pressure. There's an LA murder-one warrant out on Chips anyway. The heat might bring him in."

O'Reilly grunted. "Heat's something Chips understands all too well."

"Bastard deserves to be meat for the wolves," Rica said. Not that she particularly cared one way or the other about Chips. Doing her part for Stack, helping her man make his case. Her man someday.

Stack seemed to shrug without actually moving his shoulders. Neat. All in the attitude. "You wanted a suggestion."

"What I suggest," O'Reilly said, "is the whole lot of you clear outta my office and start doing your jobs." He stood up and walked to the window, then turned his back on them as they filed out, probably already figuring a way to make using Chips as a diversion for the media his own idea.

Outside O'Reilly's office, Fagin looked over at Stack and Rica. "What an asshole!"

"Temporary asshole, anyway," Rica said, wondering if it was true, if the cancer would ever allow them to see Vandervoort again in the office they'd just left. Savvy and soft-spoken Vandervoort, the former ferocious street cop who had survived and understood it all.

They moved aside and stood in a knot to let two plain-clothes detectives past where the file cabinets narrowed the hall. One of them had on cologne that reminded Rica of a Dumpster on a hot day.

"Let me know, will you," Fagin said, "if the lab brings up anything useful on the 911 tape?"

"Sure," Stack said, "but believe me, there isn't a chance in hell that tape will give us anything more. Whoever made that call knew what they were doing. I've worked with the lab before on phone tapes; the conversation's too brief and they've got nothing there to grab hold of anyway."

"That wasn't what you told—"

"He just said that to appease O'Reilly," Rica explained.

Fagin nodded and gave Stack a fresh look, thinking that over, along with the rest of what had gone on in O'Reilly's office. "You're something of a politician."

"A survivor," Stack said, not showing his anger unless you knew him well.

"Like in the fire department," Rica added.

Oh, sweet Jesus!

The Torcher almost squirmed in agony. Thirty-two dead! And more suffering. How the fuck had it happened? How had it gone so wrong? The 911 call. Even that precaution hadn't helped to contain the fire.

Over and over the flashbacks, reliving last night, step by step by step. The kitchen floor had been ceramic tile. The sprinkler system had been going full blast. Smoke would soon set off alarms in the hall, even if other tenants failed to smell it. So how had the fire spread? The towel that Kreiger had wrapped around his fat body?

The Torcher's mind tried to recall the precise pattern of the towel on the floor, whether it provided a path for the fire to follow to something else combustible. If there was a way to more fuel, the fire would find it. Fire could do that, *would* do that. Intelligence was in the fire, along with craftiness, maliciousness. A cruel friend in a cruel life, not to turn your back on.

The accelerant! When the umbrella was tossed, might some more accelerant have somehow spilled from the bottle onto the floor? More sustenance for the fire?

No, the bottle was empty and safely in its pocket. The bottle was always empty before the flames. Had been last night. Had been . . .

But there was no way to recreate last night. Not for sure.
Sweet Jesus!

Liquor didn't help. Booze didn't help. Pills didn't help.
The flashbacks kept coming, all day long, since the morning news.

Whose fault was this, really? Where did the blame actually lie? The Torcher's mind darted this way and that, explored, drew back, explored again, trying to find a way around the guilt, beyond it, trying to escape it. What was the sequence of events here? Who bore the guilt? Who *should* bear the guilt? The guilt that was like fire.

The answer was of course in the beginning. Always. To really understand, to affix blame with any certainty, you had to go back to the beginning. Always. To the spark. Always. Always the beginning.

One thing for sure—you couldn't place your trust in a 911 operator, or in the fire department. *Ahhh, God!* . . .

The detective, Stack! He was a goddamn grown-up, someone with judgment and conscience. The most dangerous kind of cop, a plodder with brains. Relentless bastard who would take it to the wall. Who would be cool and deadly in an emergency. But steady, steady . . . a man who always knew what to do and then did it. Next time maybe he should be the early warning system.

Leland Brand fired up an illegal sixty-dollar Cuban cigar, courtesy of a UN friend with diplomatic privileges, and stood on the balcony of his East Side apartment, surveying the city. His gaze slid from the Queensboro Bridge's ornate steel beauty to the UN Building, to the slanted roof of the Citigroup Building. Near the Citigroup skyscraper towered the Lipstick Building, one of his favorite architectural accomplishments. Damned thing looked just like a giant, oval-based cylindrical tube of lipstick some whore might have dropped there on the sidewalk and stepped on; then it somehow got vertical and grew. He found himself wondering how it would burn.

Brand often came out to the balcony with an expensive cigar and congratulated himself when things went right. And things had gone right. The fire that had destroyed the upper floors of the Belmire Tower and claimed—so far—thirty-two lives had been a terrible thing. He felt bad about it, maybe even heartsick sometimes. But it had been precisely what he'd warned about. If Brand had been Public Well-being commissioner or even mayor of New York, if proper precautions had been taken, if money had been spent on high-rise innovation and fire-fighting equipment, this tragedy might not have occurred. If Leland Brand became commissioner and then mayor, it was unlikely to occur again. And voters with short memories would be reminded of that fact. Almost any New Yorker, or tourist, might find him- or herself on an upper floor of a high-rise building. Helpless if smoke appeared, if flames appeared. Somebody in public life had to think for them. Think ahead.

Etta Daggett was right about thinking way ahead. Brand was glad now that he'd hired her; she figured to be the smartest and meanest dog in the fight, and she was on his side.

He studied the smoothly burning ember of his cigar and marveled at its quality. The ancient pull of the steady red glow, and beyond it the scattered lights of the city stretching for miles, for galaxies, gave him the momentary sensation that he could fly. And he sure as hell would fly—eventually right into the mayor's office. Etta Daggett would fly with him. They would fly in formation. *Now there was an image to bring a smile.*

He took a long drag on the cigar, inhaling slightly, then expelled a dense cloud of white smoke that shredded with the breeze and became part of the night. He held the cigar out over the balcony rail and flicked it with his thumb to displace the precarious cylinder of ash beyond the ember. The breeze snatched the gray particulate matter and sent it chasing wildly after the smoke.

Ashes to ashes, Brand thought, grinning. *An ill wind . . .* Clichés served politicians well. Common denominators of the common man. The voter.

He didn't feel the cold in the slightest.

Ashes to ashes . . .

THIRTY-TWO

June 2000

Ed Marks had worked the afternoon shift and was exhausted. He'd been attacked by a junkie near Times Square only an hour after he'd hit the street. Later, he'd done crowd control when the plays began to break in the theater district. Now his feet and legs felt numb after climbing four flights of creaking wooden steps to the walk-up apartment he and Amy and the twins had been forced to live in until they could find something better.

He locked the door behind him, turning the knob lock, keying the dead bolt, then fastening the new brass chain lock he'd bought at a going-out-of-business sale in the next block. He looked at the old wooden door. One kick and it would break off its hinges and fly open.

This wasn't the safest neighborhood, but he really wasn't afraid of a break-in. It would take an ambitious or desperate thief to take four flights of stairs up, then down to rob anyone who lived in one of these rat traps. All to victimize somebody who probably wouldn't have anything worth stealing.

After tossing his uniform cap on the sofa, then loosening his tie, he walked quietly to the bedroom door and peeked into the dimness.

Amy was a shadowed form on the bed, the sheets twisted and tossed aside so she could sleep in the summer heat the apartment's decrepit window air conditioner couldn't fend off. He could hear her soft breathing. Or was it one or both of the infant twins, Adie and Allie, sleeping in the wooden crib near the bed? Either way, Marks's family was peacefully resting, out of harm's way.

Since the birth of the twins, the young cop and father had gained a different perspective on life. The bad breaks didn't seem so tragic, once a man realized what was really important. What really mattered. For Ed Marks, what mattered were the three people in the next room.

He started over toward the sofa to switch off the table lamp Amy had left on for him, before going in to undress and lie down beside her. Then he swallowed the dry, acrid taste suddenly in his mouth, and realized he was thirsty.

A cold beer was what he needed, what he deserved, after all the crap he'd taken out on the street. The afternoon temperature in New York had been in the nineties, and it didn't seem to have cooled down much during the evening. It was the concrete, Marks's sergeant was fond of saying. All the concrete held the heat in the summer, turning the city into a giant kiln that took a long time to cool down. And that never cooled down all the way even at night during the dog days.

The enameled wood door to the kitchen was closed. Marks knew the latch didn't catch, and all he had to do to open the door was to push.

As soon as the flat of his palm touched the faded green door, he felt the heat.

Marks knew the rules, how you were never supposed to

open a door if it felt warm. There might be a fire, and you might give it a big gulp of oxygen, set up a cross draft. But the motion had already begun, his body leaning forward, his right leg extended, foot a few inches off the floor, to take a step into the kitchen. Weight had shifted. Momentum was in charge. He couldn't stop himself, and the door swung open.

Heat rushed him like a solid wall. There wasn't much smoke yet, most of it hugging the ceiling. But the heat felt as if it were baking his eyes. Flames were leaping from behind the antiquated electric stove and where the tablecloth—the table itself—was burning. Much of the dark smoke was rolling from a melted plastic light-switch plate on the wall near the stove. Probably the source of the fire, the electrical connection inside the wall.

Frightening though it was, the fire was confined to the kitchen. It wasn't life-threatening yet; there was plenty of time to get out of the apartment and the building. But Marks knew how quickly these things could spread. He saw the stack of unpacked cardboard boxes in a corner, his and Amy's coats and winter clothes, their marriage certificate and lease copy, a photo album of the twins, the certificate Marks received when he'd graduated from the academy—their lives.

Marks remembered a fire in Queens where he'd done crowd control, how he'd glanced into a body bag just before it was zipped closed and seen the burned corpse of a small woman or a child. Blackened flesh had baked away and curled on one side of the face so that all the teeth were visible. It was a smile that made nightmares.

Marks spun around and rushed into the bedroom. He gathered himself and took a deep breath. There was time.

Definitely there was time. *Don't show her panic. Don't make her afraid!*

He reached out and gently shook his wife's shoulder, fighting the impulse to scream at her. "Amy . . ." *Stay calm! I'm counting on you.* "Better wake up."

She stirred and raised her head from the pillow. "Ed? . . ."

"Take it easy," he said in what he hoped was a relaxed tone. "You've got to get up now. Fast."

"Huh? Now?"

He reached over to turn on the lamp by the bed. The switch rotated in his hand and clicked without result. The fire inside the walls must have gotten to some wiring, broken the circuit.

Amy sat up. "What's going on?" Plenty awake now.

"There's a fire in the kitchen. I want you to take the twins and get downstairs now. Move calmly, not too fast, just pick them up and carry them downstairs to the street. Remember, there's plenty of time."

"What are you—"

"I'm going in to phone the FDNY. Then I'm going to grab some stuff from the kitchen and follow you and the twins."

"Don't be crazy! Forget the stuff in the kitchen! Grab one of the girls and come with me. Now, Ed!"

One of the twins woke at the sound of her voice and started to cry.

Marks clutched his wife's shoulder and squeezed. "The fire's not a big one yet. Just do as I tell you, Amy. There isn't time to discuss it."

"Ed—"

"Damn it! Do it, Amy!"

She was on her feet immediately then, her mind made

up that he wasn't going to change *his* mind and there was danger in arguing. For both of them, and for the girls. Her babies. Nothing was going to harm her babies. Not bothering even to put on shoes or slippers, she snatched up the twins, both crying now, and held them tight against her milk-swollen breasts.

Marks followed her out of the bedroom and was standing picking up the phone, watching her leave, when it suddenly struck him with a force that almost doubled him over that he might never see her or the girls again.

At least the phone was still working. After calling in the fire, Marks hurried back into the kitchen. This time when he opened the door a hot rush of air whooshed past him and he saw that there was more smoke.

He held his hand over his mouth and nose and went to the stack of boxes, thanking God the fire hadn't yet reached them.

Quickly he got down the top box, tore open the flaps, and found the small metal box used to hold his and Amy's important papers. He set it aside, rummaged swiftly through the box, then tossed it behind him. The next box contained only clothes. The one beneath it more clothes, some shoes. Marks felt beneath the clothes and his fingers touched something rough, like cobbled leather. Or vinyl made to look and feel like leather. He tugged the object out and was pleased to see he'd found the photo album. Marriage photos, twins photos, the fire wouldn't get them.

The flames were hotter, and it was becoming more difficult to breathe. More smoke now, working its way down from the ceiling. Greasy, heavy-looking smoke.

Enough . . . enough . . . time to get out.

Marks snatched up the metal lockbox, tucked the album beneath his arm, and turned to leave.

Only to find that the boxes and some of the clothes he'd hurriedly tossed behind him were now blazing. And the floor itself, old sheet goods and ancient plywood and plank, was now dancing with flame and emitting thick black smoke.

The fire had taken advantage of him when he wasn't looking. Moving swiftly, finding the opportunity it needed. So what he'd read about it so many times was true: it was deceptive, seemed to have a mind of its own, was never to be trusted or taken for granted. The problem was, Marks hadn't realized just how true the warnings were. Fire could surprise you like a clever enemy, a retired fireman had told him one time in a bar near the precinct house. It *loved* to surprise you.

Marks swiveled his head one way, then the other, then turned his body in an entire circle. He swallowed hot and burning fear.

The fire had him surrounded.

Amy stood across the street from the burning building, still clutching the twins. The fire had been in the stairwell, and her face and bare arms were blackened with soot. Some of her hair was singed, and her left arm and shoulder were burned beneath the soot, but she ignored the pain. Almost as much as the burns, her neck hurt from staring up at the fourth-floor windows of the apartment. Behind the glass the rooms were alight as if all the lamps were glowing, but she saw no sign of her husband. Fire-fighting equipment was still arriving, sometimes accompanied by sirens so loud and piercing they made her wince. An ambulance passed her, almost close enough to run over her toes, but she seemed not to notice and didn't move back. Firefighters in helmets and long slickers were moving as dark figures on the periphery of her vision, darting, shouting to each other, paying out hoses and equipment. Now and then a powerful diesel engine roared as a ladder truck or pumper was maneuvered into position.

It was all a dream. It had to be. How could it be real?

Someone was next to her, saying something she couldn't understand. She realized he was wearing a cop's blues. *Ed?* She almost said his name aloud.

But it wasn't Ed. This man was about the same size and build but had blond hair sticking out from beneath his cap and had a mustache.

"You okay, ma'am?" the cop repeated, louder this time.

So he was real. The rest of it had to be real.

She stared at him for a moment, dazed, then nodded and looked back up where her apartment burned.

Amy wasn't religious, hadn't attended church in years, but that would all change if Ed lived. That was a silent, solemn promise she made as she prayed for her husband.

The curtains in the bedroom suddenly blazed and disappeared, and the window shattered from the heat, showering glass shards down on the sidewalk.

He would have to be out of the apartment by now, Amy thought. It was pointless to keep watching the windows. Instead she fixed her gaze on the building entrance with the same intensity she'd focused on the windows.

Almost immediately a figure emerged, and her heart almost exploded with hope.

But it was a fireman dragging out onto the sidewalk what

looked like the threadbare armchair that sat in the lobby. The chair was smoldering and leaving a trail of dark smoke.

"Holy Christ, look!"

It was the blond cop. He'd moved in front of Amy, blocking her view of the entrance. But he was staring upward and pointing.

Amy, along with others in the street and on the sidewalks, also looked.

A man—*Ed!*—was standing in the kitchen window of their apartment, waving his arms. He was in silhouette, backlit by a wavering orange glow.

"There's a guy up there!" the blond cop yelled to two nearby firemen. "Get a net! You guys got a fuckin' net? Tell me you got a fuckin' net!"

The two firemen stopped and stared up at Ed, then broke into a run toward where several pieces of emergency equipment were jammed up against the curb. One of them hurdled a thick hose draped over a police sawhorse, amazingly graceful considering his bulk.

"He's coming out," another fireman near the blond cop said. "The heat's driving him out." This one's voice was calm, almost resigned. It was the voice of a spectator and it turned Amy's heart to lead.

She heard herself gasp. Or was it a collective gasp from the crowd? Ed had raised the window all the way and was turned sideways. He threw a leg over the sill, shielding his eyes from the flames with a forearm, almost falling. He was facing in toward the kitchen now as he backed away from the heat and flames.

"You guys got a net?" the blond cop asked again in a voice that cracked like a teenager's. A voice that held no hope.

* * *

"Get a net set up!" Fagin yelled, but he knew there wasn't time for a net, just as there wasn't time to maneuver a ladder truck and send someone up to rescue the man. The poor guy backing out of the fourth-floor window would have to choose between burning or falling to his death. And choose soon.

Fagin didn't even look away to see how the futile efforts to obtain a net were going. He stared upward like everyone around him, watching the dark figure above back farther and farther out of the window. The man now had both legs out, then his hips, sliding across the sill on his stomach. Only his upper body remained inside and out of sight. A woman screamed as the doomed man lurched all the way out of the window and was hanging on to the sill by his hands.

Then he began to lower himself, hand over hand. Fagin swallowed. Did the man have a rope ladder? Anything? Was he one of the smart ones who kept a coiled rope beneath the windows of these walk-up fire traps? *Does the poor sunuva bitch have a chance?*

The man was slowly lowering himself on what looked like a dark length of rope. His clothes were smoldering, and he began moving his legs in a way Fagin had seen before.

He was giving in, losing strength, trying to fend off the moment.

The rope, or whatever it was, wasn't long enough. No more than three or four feet. The figure above inched downward, still grasping the very end of what had at least allowed him to escape the hell on the other side of the window. Only to face another hell to fall into.

The crowd began screaming for him to hang on, hang on, hang on . . . a chant. *Hang on!*

But he couldn't hang on. Or maybe whatever he was hanging onto burned through where it was anchored inside.

It always amazed Fagin how quickly a body could plunge from a high window. Life to death in brief seconds. He stared with horror and sorrow, his gaze following the limp and smoldering figure all the way down, hearing or imagining he heard the impact of soft flesh on hard concrete.

In the corner of his vision, he saw a woman collapse. A cop was nearby and rushed immediately to her aid, then bending over her motioned frantically for more help.

The woman was burned but not seriously. It took several minutes before the paramedics gave up and resigned themselves to the fact that the infants she'd been holding and had instinctively protected in her fall were dead. They'd died from smoke inhalation in her escape from the burning building.

Myra didn't sleep well for weeks after the fire. When it became obvious that the distraught Amy was going to have an almost impossible time coping with her grief, she offered her a job as file clerk at the agency.

Not that the agency needed a file clerk.

Myra needed to help Amy.

THIRTY-THREE

February 2002

Mirabella watched the headlights out the living room window as Chips turned her car into the driveway, how he deliberately fishtailed it a little in the snow that had collected near the curb. A funny kind of guy, but not unlike some others she'd known. He was cautious, even timid, but at the same time, *or maybe because of his timidity,* he wanted his little kicks—but safe kicks. Challenges, he would tell himself, pushing to validate himself as a man, tempting fate, but only after figuring all the odds. She hoped he wouldn't wreck her car.

His footfalls crunched on the gravel driveway as he made his way to the front porch. *Clomp! Clomp!* Stamping the snow off his shoes. She'd asked him please not to track it in.

When he came through the door he was grinning as if he'd just sneaked the last piece of chocolate. The way his eyes were, at first she thought he was drunk, but then she changed her mind. There was a slowness to the way his eyes moved, a drowsiness to them. It was the way he sometimes looked at her after sex.

She wondered if he was coming back from seeing

somebody else, and a warm flame of anger began to grow in her gut. She held no illusions, but she'd been unable to keep herself from making an emotional investment. She'd put some trust in Chips. Maybe she should have known better than to think he was different. She'd learned this hard lesson before.

And forgotten it before.

Now some of her growing anger was directed at herself. Asking for it, as her father had told her over and over. Just goddamn asking for it.

Chips had pushed the guilt and fear to the far edges of his mind, concentrating on the best part of the night, the reason for the night. He could do that, almost as if he were two people living in two different worlds. *Man of mystery,* he thought. *They should make a movie out of my life, star that guy James Woods even though he's a little older than I am. Maybe whazzisname . . . Jude Law. Too bad Newman's doing character roles these days. Frank Sinatra, long time ago. Christ, wouldn't that be typecasting!*

Now he told himself to keep a straight face, but he couldn't help grinning when he stomped the snow off his shoes, then went into the house and closed the door behind him.

He was still grinning as he stood taking Mirabella in with his narrowly focused eyes, the way she was standing with her weight on one leg, one hip thrust out, wearing her robe that was gaping at one pale bare thigh, as if she didn't know she was flashing him a go signal. He pushed the night's terror away again, everything that had happened except for the good parts. What the whole thing was, it was fuckin' exhilarating. *So what's not to grin about?*

"Why the big smile?" she asked. As if he could tell her. No, he didn't nearly trust her that much yet. Probably never would.

"I look at you," he told her, "and I feel lucky. That makes me smile." She knew he was bullshitting her, but that didn't matter. She'd convince herself. Chips knew women like Mirabella top to bottom. Knew them the way predators knew prey.

"Sure you feel lucky," she said, still obviously angry, the little parallel vertical lines above the bridge of her nose deeper than usual, the vein in the side of her neck throbbing. She had the thickest carotid artery, or whatever the hell it was, he'd ever seen on a woman. Like a damn fire hose. The way it pulsated during sex was a turn-on. He was getting a boner, the way he had driving here from the city thinking about her. Maybe she'd notice. Well, let her. Really get that vein pumping.

Chips took off his coat and tossed it in a heap on a chair, then slipped off his wet shoes and left them on the rug just inside the door. He turned on what he thought was his sexiest smile. "I guess I have to prove it's really you that makes me grin."

He moved toward her in his stocking feet, still with the high-wattage smile, and she backed away. Not fast enough as he rushed and had her by the waist, attempting to kiss her. She kept turning her head and trying to shove him away at the same time. Still pissed off at him, all right. He laughed and nuzzled the side of her neck, the vein, and pretended he was taking little bites out of her, using just his lips, making that sound he knew they liked. Tightening the pressure with his right arm, he drew her close and ground his pelvis into hers, letting her feel what he had for her.

She stopped struggling and he tried to kiss her on the mouth again. This time she only made a motion as if to turn away, and he had her, used his tongue. When they separated she still looked mad, so he kissed her again, which wasn't easy because he was faking a laugh. She couldn't help it and started to laugh with him.

"You're something else," he said, releasing her waist and moving his hands up to her shoulders. "You really and truly are."

She was looking up at him now, her eyes kind of dreamy. *Works every time,* he thought. Her weakness was that she wanted so much to believe in him. He didn't have to give her much to go on and she'd make the effort. *Work at it, baby.* He'd have her in bed and on her back in no time.

Chips pulled her to him again, being a little rough, this time kissing her for a long time, waiting until she'd almost but not quite had enough and then pulling back before she did. The way she was gazing up at him now, breathing hard with her tits rising and falling, she was plenty ripe for it.

Something else about her, though, like she was puzzled. She lowered her head, sniffed, and looked back up at him.

"You been smoking?"

"Not me," he said.

Rica stared down at the blackened corpse on the kitchen floor, thinking she should be getting used to this but wasn't. "This one's only on the second floor," she said.

But everything else fit. Well, almost everything. The

fire had been carefully and deliberately confined to the kitchen. The umbrella had been used to shield the burning body, then left at the scene. The body had been bound with cloth strips before being set on fire.

The only significant difference Rica could see was the lower-floor apartment.

This victim was another woman, name of Victoria Pike.

Stack and Rica had already talked to some of the neighbors. By their accounts, Pike had been a quiet woman and friendly enough. She'd even served on the building's co-op board until about a year ago, when for some reason she'd quit. Then she'd begun to keep more to herself, not smile or talk to people sometimes when they passed in the hall. Maybe something had happened to her about a year ago, some of the other tenants speculated.

"So now what?" Rica asked. "We gonna have to go back a year or more in the victim's life and see if she suffered some kinda trauma?"

"Could be," Stack said. He was sloshing through the puddles of black water left on the kitchen floor, not minding if some of it got on the leather of his thick-soled black shoes. "But let's learn a little more first. Maybe she had a more recent trauma that led to her last one." He glanced at his watch. "Burns oughta be here soon."

Burns was Ed Burnschmidt, the Mobile Response computer genius. Stack had called for him because in the kitchen, on a small built-in wood desk that was sheltered from the sprinkler system by an overhanging cabinet, was one of those dedicated computers, which was to say it was made expressly for sending and receiving e-mail. A small, oblong aqua-colored machine with a raised lid, it wasn't even hooked up to a printer or monitor other than its own narrow screen. Stack had seen the machine advertised on TV, aimed at people who were technophobes, like he was; the commercial showed a grandmother using the device to keep in touch with the family. Only Pike hadn't been a grandmother; she'd died in her forty-first year.

Despite the fire in the kitchen, the e-mail machine had been on and somehow stayed on while the FDNY had extinguished the fire. They'd had plenty of time, since they'd been notified again by phone, this time directly and not through 911, that a fire at the apartment's address was in progress.

Stack glanced over at the e-mail machine's glowing screen that showed nothing but some icons he wasn't sure he understood. Evidence. Maybe the Pike woman had been interrupted while sending or reading an e-mail. Or maybe she'd simply forgotten to switch off the machine. Stack wasn't completely comfortable around any kind of computer. He didn't fully understand the damned things. So when the techs were finished dusting this one for prints, he'd called for Burns. Electronic evidence. Not to be messed with by a ham-handed cop who felt more at home disassembling and cleaning a revolver.

"You want," Rica offered again, "I think I can figure out that computer easy and check the victim's e-mail."

"Be better if Burns was the one who testified about it in court," Stack said. "Expert witness and all."

"You're right," she said, and gave him a wicked wink. "My expertise lies in other, more sensitive areas."

Stack stared at her, then down at the corpse. "Jesus, Rica, show some respect."

"The dead don't know if I show them respect," she said. "You would."

* * *

Burns didn't arrive until after the body had been removed and everyone other than Stack and Rica had followed. He was a skinny little guy with jug ears and a bad haircut and looked about eighteen though Stack knew he was in his early thirties. He even had a case of acne, and malicious blue eyes as if he might be thinking up some adolescent prank. Burns was a wiseass who feared no one and got by with his attitude because he was the best at his work. Stack liked him but would never let him know it.

He nodded hello to Stack and Rica, then looked at the computer with unmistakable disdain.

"Christ, Stack! You mean you can't sit down and figure out this thing? It isn't even an honest-to-God grown-up computer."

"You're the expert," Stack reminded him.

"Okay. Next time call me if you need the push buttons set on your car radio."

"The only radio in my car gets police calls."

Burns gave him a look. "Somehow I believe you. This clean?" Nodding toward the e-mail machine.

Stack said it was, and Burns went over and didn't even bother to sit down at the kitchen desk. "Electricity must be off because of the fire. It's on backup battery power."

He worked a few keys and a log of e-mail messages appeared on the screen. "You want messages sent, or received?"

"Let's look at the sent ones first," Stack said. No sooner had he spoken than a different long list of e-mails winked onto the monitor. "These won't be deleted, will they?"

"Not to worry," Burns said.

He worked the keys again. Stack and Rica stood on either side of him, staring at the illuminated screen, and they began to read.

After about twenty minutes, everyone's back was sore, but every message sent or received by Victoria Pike during the past month had been read. Most were uninteresting family chitchat between Pike and her mother in Ohio. Some of the e-mails were gossipy, to and from a woman whose e-mail moniker was *peeps252*. Peeps's real name was Corlane, and the e-mails made it obvious that she worked with Victoria Pike at Juppie's Restaurant, only a few blocks away on West Forty-seventh. The interesting thing about those messages was that they mentioned somebody named Ned who might have been Pike's lover. It seemed Ned liked to feel up Victoria in public places when no one was looking. In line to get into theaters, he would often move close behind her and snake his hand beneath her coat. Victoria wondered if this was in any way normal behavior. Corlane said what's the difference? She'd been dating in New York for ten years and there was no normal out there. Normal in New York was if they didn't rape you, then chop and dice you with a machete.

"I kinda like peeps252," Rica said.

"I'm gonna log off now," Burns said, "before the battery goes. Everything'll be saved. If you want, I can disconnect the machine and bag the whole thing for evidence. No trouble at all, with the keyboard and monitor built right in."

"Thanks," Stack said, straightening all the way up and stretching his back. He thought he heard a couple of vertebrae crack.

"You oughta buy one of these machines," Burns said, yanking the plug from its dead socket, by the cord, just in case the crime scene techs hadn't thought to dust the plug. "Communicate more. Join the human race."

"I've seen enough of the human race. You get this thing bagged and in the trunk of your car. Then Rica and I will buy you a beer across the street before you go back to the precinct."

Burns smiled. "Human of you."

THIRTY-FOUR

Juppie's was JUPPIE'S JUMPIN' JOINT, according to the lettering on the sign over its door. But when Stack and Rica entered, they found themselves in a gloomy restaurant with half a dozen senior citizens seated at round tables with red-and-white checked tablecloths. A couple of tired-looking waitresses, plodding their way toward swinging doors that apparently led to the kitchen, glanced back at Stack and Rica, who were removing their coats and hanging them on a rack with coat hangers near the door. Convenient for coat thieves, Stack thought as he and Rica moved over to stand near the defaced HOSTESS WILL   EAT YOU sign.

"Somebody'll be right there," one of the waitresses called, before the two of them disappeared through wide swinging doors. Off to the left, Stack saw a dim bar occupied only by a morose-looking man seated on a stool and staring at a TV mounted up near the ceiling. His resigned isolation and the way he was dressed in black slacks and white shirt, a towel tucked in his belt, Stack figured him for the bartender coping with a slow night.

"Somebody at Juppie's has a sense of irony," Rica said.

A stout woman about forty, with wide, Slavic features and carefully coifed black hair, approached them hurriedly

in a whirl of strong perfume scent and a swish of volumi-
nous black jacket and skirt. She walked as if her feet hurt,
but her unwavering smile suggested she was used to the
pain and could put up with it. "Sorry for the wait. It's senior citizen night here, but that's okay despite what the
sign says. You're welcome."

I'll bet, Rica thought. "We didn't notice a senior citizen
sign."

"That's okay. Gonna be just the two of you?"

"We already had dinner," Stack lied. He turned his back
on the diners and unobtrusively showed the hostess his
shield. "What we'd like is to talk to one of your employees, a woman named Corlane."

The welcoming smile faded and the hostess turned pale
beneath her dark hair. Stack noticed her eyes momentarily
widen, imperceptibly unless you were watching closely for
it, before she got hold of herself. "I'm Corlane."

Something to hide, Stack thought. Most people had
something to hide, and it almost always showed when the
law introduced itself.

"Corlane Chadner," she quickly volunteered, showing
she was cooperative, an honest citizen.

"This isn't about you, Corlane," Stack said, making
friends. "Our only interest is in what you can tell us about
Victoria Pike." He smiled reassuringly. "Don't worry, dear.
We're very single-minded. Unless you've robbed a bank
recently, you have nothing to fear from us."

Corlane looked relieved. What was it? Stack wondered.
Outstanding traffic tickets? A previous drug conviction?
Maybe just a long-ago bad experience with a cop.

Corlane led them to one of the tables out of earshot of
the customers who retained sound hearing, and motioned

for them to sit down. When they were seated in uncomfortable bentwood chairs, she asked if they wanted some coffee. Both declined, and she didn't summon the waitress she was keeping in sight. Instead, she sighed and said, "So what's with Victoria?"

"Not *Vicky?*" Stack asked.

"Naw. She doesn't like being called anything but Victoria. That's one of the first things I learned about her when she started here last year."

"You were close friends?" Stack asked.

Corlane caught the past tense and blanched again in the dimness. "Something's happened to her, hasn't it? You said—"

"I'm afraid your friend is dead," Stack said. "I'm truly sorry, Corlane."

Corlane stared at Stack, then at Rica. Her eyes were tearing up. Genuine shock, Stack thought. She was wrestling hard with what she'd just learned. She licked her lips. Her broad brow wrinkled, and her surprisingly small hands knotted into fists. "That fucking Ned!"

"Why Ned?" Stack asked.

"You know about Ned?"

"Sure. A little. We'd like to know more."

"He bruised her up. She showed me. Until then I thought he was okay, maybe a little quirky. But when he turned physical I advised Victoria to dump him like dog shit. They don't change. Once they start knocking a woman around, it never gets any better."

"I've never known it to," Stack agreed.

"You've had a bad time like that?" Rica asked Corlane in a sympathetic voice.

"Long time ago. When I was slender and young and vulnerable." And very attractive, Stack figured.

"You looking for Ned?" Corlane asked. She sounded hopeful.

"Not really," Rica said.

Corlane looked confused.

"What made you think Victoria was murdered?" Stack asked. "We never mentioned it. Only that she was dead."

Corlane glared warily at him. "I wouldn't have been so cooperative if I knew you were gonna play games like some kinda TV cop."

"We're not playing games, Corlane. And please, try to understand we're only doing our job."

Corlane motioned for one of the waitresses to come to the table. "Have Eddie pour a Walker Red for me," Corlane said. "A double, straight up." Then she turned her attention back to Stack and Rica. "A couple of cops come here at my place of work and tell me one of my friends and fellow workers is dead. And after what I learned about Ned, who's always had a screw loose, what would you figure I'd think?"

"Exactly what you did think," Stack said. "We just needed it for the record."

Corlane frowned. "Is this conversation being recorded?"

"Heavens no!" Stack said, holding up both his hands as if that proved his denial. "But if you really distrust us that much, I'm saying that this is an illegal recording and anything that comes out of it is entrapment." Another smile. "Over and out."

Corlane sighed. "Okay . . . sorry. I guess I'm shook-up."

"Naturally," Stack said.

"So what happened to Victoria?"

"She died in a fire in her apartment."

"Ah, an accident!"

"Oh, no. Someone set the fire deliberately, I'm afraid. Set *her* on fire, actually. Even held an umbrella over Victoria so she'd burn for a while after the sprinkler system came on. People will burn that way, you know, like meat that catches fire in a frying pan." Stack brutally painting her a picture, trying to flick her even more off balance. In case she *was* hiding something significant.

"Jesus! . . ."

"I'm sorry, dear. I didn't mean to—"

"That's okay." Corlane swallowed hard and brushed his apologies away with a wave of her pale hand.

"I know it must be difficult," Stack said. "We should have broken it to you easier, I guess. We grow mental calluses in this job and sometimes forget ourselves."

"Still think it was Ned?" Rica asked, playing the mean cop. Insensitive, anyway. Those mental calluses.

Corlane took a deep breath, then shook her head. "Comes right down to it, I don't know." The waitress came with her drink, approaching the table tentatively, sensing something was wrong. Corlane thanked her and took a long pull of scotch before setting the glass on the table. "I guess, to tell you the truth, I can't imagine Ned doing something like that. He wasn't even to the stage where he was likely to cut skin or break bones, though he would have gotten there eventually. You know how it is; they work up to it over time. Ned and Victoria, the way they are together, *were,* he mighta got a little too rough with her and left a few bruises on her, like I said.

But to set her on fire and stand there and watch her burn . . . Naw, not our Ned."

Our Ned? "Too decent a guy?"

"Naw. To my way of thinking, he doesn't have the balls."

"Usually they don't," Stack said. "Bedroom badasses like Ned."

Corlane actually smiled at him, a cop talking her language. Ten minutes and Stack had her. Rica loved it.

"Victoria have any enemies you know of?" Stack asked. "Other than her love-hate thing with Ned."

Corlane didn't have to think about it more than a few seconds. "She was a sweet, lovable person. You'll see. Everybody who knew her will tell you the same. Even Ned, prick that he is."

"She was a waitress here, right?"

"Yeah. But you might say the job was beneath her station. She used to be a big-shot investment counselor, then got mixed up with booze and drugs and came down in the world. I might as well tell you about the substance abuse, 'cause you'll find it out anyway. But I'm also gonna tell you she went through rehab two years ago and she's been clean ever since. She told me that and I believe her, and I never saw her even smoke or take a drink since I've known her."

"She might have fallen off the wagon," Rica said.

"Naw. She was a convert and a true believer. You know the type. She *drove* the wagon."

"Okay," Stack said. "Anybody come in the restaurant lately and have words with her? Give her any kind of trouble? Even if it was just over burnt food?"

"All the food's burnt here. Honestly, Victoria was a sweetheart."

"Our Ned the prick got a last name?" Rica asked.

"Salerno. Ned Salerno."

"We're gonna want to talk with him. You know his address?"

"I can get if for you. But it won't make any difference."

"Why? He the kinda guy who might go underground?"

"That I don't know."

"So where do you think we might find him?" Stack asked.

"In the kitchen," Corlane said. "He's the chef."

Ned Salerno didn't keep a clean kitchen. The grill was littered with onion scraps and crumbs of burned ground beef. There was a slice of bread and some lettuce on the floor that had obviously been stepped on and ground in.

Ned was a medium-sized guy in his forties with a gut barely contained by a white T-shirt tucked into too-tight jeans. He had a head of wavy black hair and the face of an aging, petulant schoolboy. The only other person in the kitchen was a teenage kid stirring something pretending to be soup in a big steel pot. The kitchen was warm, and the kid had on a T-shirt like Ned's that showed lots of tattoos on his skinny arms. The tattoos featured artistically rendered knives, snakes, and writhing, tortured nude women, and didn't go with the kid's hair net.

When Stack and Rica identified themselves to Ned, the kid stopped stirring soup. Ned told him to take a break. The kid disappeared like a wisp through a door that must have led outside, because it let in an eddy of cold air as it opened and closed. The stirring of air moved the scent of the soup, which smelled pretty good but was still unidentifiable.

"So what's *this* all about?" Ned asked, wiping his hands on a towel. Whatever *this* was, he seemed already geared up to deny it. "I don't remember any parking tickets or walking outta someplace without paying."

"Any recollection of murder?" Stack asked.

That seemed to take Ned back a bit, but it might not have been genuine. Guys like Ned had been acting since they were weaned. "You saying I killed somebody?"

"Did you?"

Ned looked as if he might get really angry. Then he gave a cocky grin, shrugged, and shook his head, apparently deciding to take the philosophical line. Cops in his soup again. "I'm afraid I don't have time for this bullshit from my public servants. I got a busy kitchen here."

"Sure," Rica said. "Senior citizen night."

"It's something we do for the neighborhood," Ned said. "Charitable stuff. That's how you build a customer base. Besides, it makes us feel pretty good." He winked. "You know how it is . . . it's the right thing to do."

"Are you patronizing us?" Stack asked. "I wouldn't like it, Ned, if you were talking down to us."

Ned gave up half of the grin and sighed elaborately. "Okay, I'll play. Who'd I kill?"

"We say you killed somebody?" Stack asked.

"C'mon, now. Quit stringing me out. Am I gonna need a lawyer?"

"You can certainly call one any time," Rica said.

"Which ain't what I asked."

"Victoria Pike," Stack said in a flat voice.

Ned stared at him. "What about her?"

"You kill her?"

Ned's jaw dropped and he backed a step toward the hot grill. If he was acting, he had a modicum of talent.

"Victoria got popped?"

"Shot, you mean?" Stack asked.

"Yeah. You said murdered, so I just figured shot. Drive-by or some such shit. Happened to some guy last week right in her neighborhood."

"She was burned to death in an apartment fire."

"I thought you said murdered."

"We did."

Ned glared at Stack, ignoring Rica, letting them both know he was losing patience and they could no longer count on him to be nice. "You come into my kitchen, tell me my girlfriend's dead, give me a lotta crap. Okay, you told me what happened, now let me see if I can get it straight in my mind that my woman's dead. Quit playing word games with me."

"Games?" Stack asked.

"I said, do I need a lawyer? You didn't say yes or no, only told me I could call one, which I already fuckin' knew. Then you tell me about Victoria, jerk me around with that information. Games, you ask? Yeah, fuckin' games. Dumb cops' games. Know what I say now?"

This guy was working up a serious mad, Rica thought, glancing over at Stack, who was gazing calmly at Ned.

"What *do* you say now?" Stack asked mildly.

"I say get outta my fuckin' kitchen or I'm gonna call my lawyer. Victoria was murdered, you talk to me only if I got an attorney present. I know my rights. Now I said get outta—"

But Stack had him by the throat. Ned was staring at him, stunned. He instinctively took a swing at Stack, which Stack absently brushed away with his free hand. Neatly and quickly, Stack spun Ned around, had one arm bent behind him, and had shifted his grip so his big hand clutched the back of Ned's neck. Rica could see his fingertips digging deep into Ned's flesh.

Stack shoved Ned's head down and held it so his face was inches above the hot grill. He spoke to Ned in a gentle, almost crooning way. "This kitchen of yours isn't a church and you're not a priest. You're a smart-mouth little punk and a woman beater, and if you really want a murder charge hung on you, I can accommodate. We might want to talk to you some more, Ned, and if I hear of you misbehaving in any way with any woman, I'll come here and shove your head up your ass. You know your rights. I know what I can get away with. You want to file a complaint and start trading trouble, I'll trade. Maybe it'll be your last rights you'll hear. You got that, you miserable piece of shit?"

"Yessss!"

"Now here's our arrangement. You swear in this fucking church-kitchen of yours to cooperate with us in the future, minding your manners, or I fry the side of your face like cheap hamburger. You swear?"

"I swear!" Ned groaned, as his face edged closer to the sizzling grill.

"In a holy place like your kitchen," Stack said, as he released Ned's bent arm only to clamp his hand around it again, low near the wrist, "is what you swear sacred even if you don't place your hand on the holy grill?"

"It's sacred!" Ned's voice was hoarse with terror. *"Please! It's sacred!"*

Stack raised Ned's head, then shoved him halfway across the kitchen into a butcher-block table. Some of the pots and pans hanging above it clanged and clattered to the floor.

Ned managed to stay on his feet, bent over, rubbing the back of his neck and gaping at Stack. He started to say something, then changed his mind and clamped his lips together to keep the lower one from trembling.

"Somebody'll be around to chat with you some more about Victoria Pike," Stack said. "You gonna remember our agreement and your holy oath?"

Ned nodded, but Rica saw his eyes dart to where a six-inch paring knife lay next to a tangle of potato peelings on the table.

Stack picked up a chef's knife the size of a machete and tossed it over so it landed next to the paring knife, easily within Ned's reach if he wanted to pick up one of the weapons.

Stack waited, looking as if he might be thinking idle thoughts.

Ned kept his frightened gaze fixed on Stack and moved away from the table.

Stack grinned in a way that frightened Rica and shook his head. "You guys and your rights . . . C'mon, Rica."

Rica followed as he strode from the kitchen. He thanked Corlane politely; then he and Rica put on their coats and left the restaurant.

They'd walked half a block through the cold, fast, before they slowed down and Rica spoke. "Jesus, Stack! . . ."

"Don't worry about it," he said mildly. "Ned's not our firebug."

"Stack—"

"Put it out of your mind, dear."

Which, to Rica's way of thinking, meant she should put it someplace where she would never talk or think about it again.

Which she did. More or less.

After they emerged from the restaurant, the Torcher had to walk fast to keep them in sight. Detective Stack's face, when it had been in the light, was set and grim as death. His partner Erica looked stunned.

Something had happened in the restaurant. Maybe an argument. The woman was in love with Stack, and he was with her but didn't know it yet. She was a pushy bitch, Detective Erica Lopez. It could be that every now and then she went too far. She unnerved Stack in ways she didn't seem to suspect. It was easy to see that, watching them from a distance, enjoying objectivity, seeing facial expressions when one or the other was turned away. The Torcher was getting to know them, had learned to read their body language. Sometimes Detective Lopez's body language was too easy to read. It was her sexuality that was putting off Stack. Why? Was he involved with another woman? Maybe he was married and had five kids.

The media hadn't gone into the personal lives of either detective. Using alternative sources, the Torcher had learned something of each pursuer, but the information was more professional than personal. Their affair struggling to be born was interesting, even something to be envied, but to the Torcher it really didn't matter. Stack and his partner were on the wrong path; that was what mattered.

They bore watching, but they were on the wrong path and were safe if they stayed there.

For now.

THIRTY-FIVE

Myra juggled her brown paper bags from Blooming-dale's while she fished in her purse for her key, then unlocked her apartment door. She'd bought two expensive business suits after ruining two during the last week by getting ink on the jackets. Myra had taken to using fountain pens rather than ballpoints, expensive pens from Mont Blanc and Argaan. Their writing was so much more distinctive, unique calligraphy that put the brand of her personality on everything she signed, every memo she dashed off. Trouble was, it was taking her a while to get into using ink from a bottle again, working the little plungerlike devices she'd been given to fit into each pen instead of the cartridges. She didn't want to go to the cartridges and lose the experience of using a precision writing instrument in the classic manner, but—

Something was wrong!

Someone had been in her apartment.

She placed the paper sacks on the table near the door, careful to keep any crinkling sound to a minimum, then took a few silent steps on plush carpet and stood gazing around the living room. That someone had been here in her absence was more than just a feeling. But what was different? How did she know?

Everything was softly lighted from the lamps that she kept on a timer. And there was light from the opposite hall beyond the kitchen. Had she left a bathroom or bedroom light on? She thought back on it and couldn't be sure.

But it wasn't just that the light wasn't quite right. That didn't account for the knowledge and wariness deep in a primitive part of her mind. It was, more than anything, the air in the place. It wasn't the still, slightly stale air of an apartment that had been unoccupied all day and most of the evening. There was a subtle freshness, and the slightest movement, to the air, as if someone had stirred it in passing not long ago.

Deftly she slipped off her high-heeled shoes and padded silently in her nyloned feet toward the rear of the apartment. Her coat was unbuttoned, and at the lower periphery of her vision she was aware of her ruffled white blouse rising and falling with her rapid breathing.

It was when she was a few feet from the open bathroom door that there was a slight change of light. A pale shadow.

She wasn't alone in the apartment!

Someone or something in the bathroom had moved.

Myra knew she should turn and leave as silently as she'd made her way this far. But that might not be possible, the way her heart was pounding and her breath was trying to catch in her throat. Surely whoever was there could hear her loud struggle for oxygen.

And there was something else preventing her from sneaking away. Frightened though she might be, she was also angry. This was, damn it, *her* apartment!

She hadn't gotten this far in life by playing the shrinking violet. Or so she told herself as she reached to her left and picked up a heavy brass ballerina figurine from a marble-topped half-moon table.

She gripped the ballerina by her impossibly long legs, raised the heavy statuette above and slightly behind her head, then took a deep breath and stepped into the bathroom doorway.

Gasped!

Billy Watkins gasped and cut himself.

He was standing at the washbasin, shaving.

"Jesus, Myra! You surprised me!"

Myra lowered the ballerina and slumped against the door frame, able to breathe again.

"Sorry, Billy . . . I thought . . ."

"That I was an intruder?" He grinned through the layer of shaving cream still on half his face. "You were gonna take on a burglar with *that?*" He pointed one of her disposable blue plastic razors, dripping water, at the ballerina.

"I didn't look forward to it," she said.

"Don't you make any noise at all when you come in?"

She smiled at him. "Not when I think somebody might be searching through my personal things, deciding what he should leave me and what he should have."

"I'm glad I never decided to rob you," Billy said.

Myra giggled nervously.

Billy stared at her. "What's funny?"

"You look like the Phantom of the Opera whose mask has slipped."

Billy turned and looked at himself in the mirror, tanned handsome guy, shirtless and with a white mask over the left side of his face. The shaving cream had even gotten up on his temple as he jumped when he was surprised by Myra. He grinned at her in the mirror. "I guess I do at that.

If only I could sing, hey?" He raised his chin to examine the drop of blood just above his Adam's apple.

"I'm sorry I made you hurt yourself," Myra said.

"I won't bleed to death." He dabbed at the cut with a damp washcloth. "I was gonna surprise you, Myra." Still watching her in the mirror. "Turns out we surprised each other."

Myra studied his reflection in the mirror, the way steam was rising from the hot water in the basin and clouding the glass down around his tight, tanned stomach, how some of the shaving cream had dropped down among the golden hairs on his chest. "You can still surprise me, Billy."

He carefully put down the washcloth, blood up. "You want me to finish shaving?"

"I don't see the point," Myra said. "Come as you are."

Later, they lay together in her bed, sipping champagne and watching a classic replay of a Yankees–Red Sox game on ESPN. It was the one when Mike Mussina had come within one pitch of throwing a perfect game. Billy and Myra were both big Yankees fans. The Yankees were winners.

An SUV commercial came on between innings, and Billy scooted up so his back was against his wadded pillow and picked up the remote. "We can come back to the game. I seen this commercial about a thousand times and it gets on my nerves."

"Mine, too," Myra said. She didn't mention that she'd considered buying one of the SUVs, in white with a tan leather interior. Her Lexus was pushing three years old.

She noticed the shaving cream had almost completely evaporated from Billy's face. Intriguing.

Billy was like most men—not as interested in what was on TV as in what might be on. He aimed the remote and systematically worked through the channels down to one, the local news.

A fire was being covered. No surprise, Myra thought. Television news loved fire. It was such a wonderful visual; it had fascinated and held the gaze of human beings since before recorded time. There on the TV screen was an apartment building blazing away against the night. Billy had muted the sound, and after a few seconds closed caption lettering automatically appeared at the top of the screen, cutting off the upper part of the woman newscaster's hairdo that had lifted almost like a wig and was whipping in the wind. "*. . .Upper West Side, Brad. Neighbors have informed us that the burning apartment's tenant, Victoria or Vicky Pike, had just been switched to the day shift where she worked and was probably home earlier tonight, when the fire broke out, then promptly ripped through the second-floor co-op. As you can see behind me, firefighters struggled valiantly to control sheets of flame shooting . . .*"

Victoria Pike?

Myra suddenly recognized the burning building.

"Something wrong, Myra?"

She realized she'd sat up straight in bed and was staring at the screen.

"It's nothing," she said. "See if the ball game's back on. It makes me think of summer."

Billy obediently pressed a remote button and there were the Yankees and Red Sox again.

Myra settled back with her head propped on the pillow. She was watching the ball game but thinking about the fire. And about other fires. And about the pattern in the fires. It was obvious to her, but would the police notice the pattern?

"Myra?"

"Huh?"

"You okay? You look scared."

Scared? Well, she had plenty of reason, and there was nothing she could do about it. Not tonight, anyway. She smiled. "You're too perceptive, Billy."

He touched the tip of her nose. "I been told that."

She snuggled closer to him and watched the game into the ninth inning, when pitcher Mussina's perfect game was broken up by pinch hitter Carl Everett's soft single to left center.

"Ouch!" Billy said, watching the ball settle to the ground out of reach of the desperately charging Yankees outfielder. "I know it's gonna happen, but that hurts every time I see it."

Myra watched the disappointed Yankees pitcher's shoulders slump as he stoically observed the action in the outfield, then turned away, the magic suddenly gone.

One pitch away from perfection, Myra thought. The dejected young man on the pitcher's mound was learning what she'd come to understand long ago. There was a universal law: get close to perfection and somebody or something always messes it up. Always. Every time.

Somebody or something.

THIRTY-SIX

"Who was that?" Rica asked, as Stack hung up the phone.

"Laura. This is moving day for her. Into her new co-op. She called to give me her new phone number."

"I'm glad somebody's making progress," Rica said.

She and Stack were at Stack's desk, sorting through the murder file on Victoria Pike. They'd gotten about halfway through reviewing the preliminary autopsy report, and the results of interviews with Pike's neighbors. Ernest Fagin had phoned earlier and told them the accelerant mixture was the same as in the other Torcher murders, an important missing piece. Almost everything about the Pike murder fit neatly into the killer's pattern. Almost.

Stack had sat back and was absently sipping the cooling coffee he'd forgotten until a moment ago, when the phone rang again and Sergeant Redd told him he and Rica were wanted in O'Reilly's office.

"Probably wants to shower you with compliments," Redd said. "Make your morning."

"That's not the way he makes mornings," Stack said.

"He never mentioned what he wanted."

Stack thanked the sergeant and hung up the phone. Rica was looking at him expectantly.

"O'Reilly's office," he said.

"Shit! When?"

"A few seconds ago." Stack stood up, while Rica began assembling the material they'd spread all over the desk so they could take it with them. "Leave it," Stack said. "It'll only provide more ammunition for O'Reilly, make the meeting longer."

Rica grinned and put down the papers and file folders. She waited for Stack to wait for her to precede him down the hall to O'Reilly's office.

This morning, as was getting to be his habit, O'Reilly hurled his pen down on his desk to let them know he was pissed to the gills. Quite a dramatic gesture. Stack noticed it was a cheap plastic substitute pen rather than the expensive one he liked to show off. "When the fuck is this Torcher crap gonna end?" O'Reilly asked.

It took Stack and Rica a few seconds to realize it wasn't a rhetorical question.

"When we catch the killer," Stack said.

O'Reilly crossed his arms and puffed out his chest, rocking far back so he was glaring down at Stack even though they were both standing. George C. Scott in *Patton,* Stack thought. He could almost hear the distant trumpets.

"I won't even dignify that," O'Reilly said. He motioned for Stack and Rica to sit in the chairs angled in front of the desk, then sat down quickly himself so his ass met his chair cushion an instant before anyone else was seated. "We got business. What progress have you made on the Torcher thing?"

"From our partial review of the material we got this morning, it's apparent Victoria Pike is his latest victim."

"Apparent how?"

"Same circumstances—dead body in a co-op kitchen fire, body itself the fire's point of origin, same accelerant, same MO with the cloth bonds and the umbrella."

"Same kinda victim?" O'Reilly asked, looking slyly at Stack from half closed eyes.

A quiz, Stack thought. "Not exactly. This one was another woman. First L'Farceur, then Pike. The lab says the cloth used to bind her was black men's ties, but they don't provide much of a lead. We don't know the brand, and they're the cheap kind you can buy all over the place."

"Ah!" O'Reilly said. "What do you figure that means?"

"I don't figure yet. It's still too early. We haven't put together enough information."

"Ties are often used by sadists to tie up their victims," O'Reilly said. "They're convenient and don't leave marks. Not that marks would matter in this case."

"They're also easily explained if the police happen to stop you for some other reason," Stack said. "Easier than ropes or chains, anyway. Besides, we don't know for sure that ties were used to bind the other victims."

"That's the point. This victim was another woman, so our Torcher's getting more and more into the sadistic part of his sick fantasies. And don't rule out a sadist like this might also kill men for pleasure."

"That the victim's a woman could simply be coincidence," Rica said.

O'Reilly had produced his expensive pen from somewhere and was tapping it lightly on the desk. "Not much room for coincidence in police work."

"We'll find out if it means anything," Stack said. "Pike was female, but before she did some serious backsliding she was similar to the other victims all the same, including L'Farceur. She was a successful solid citizen, liked by neighbors and coworkers, even a past member of the co-op board where she lived."

"That pretty much describes me," O'Reilly said. "And those co-op board memberships are passed around. Most people don't wanna take the time or trouble to serve. What about Pike's occupation? Doesn't it strike you odd she was a waitress, while the other victims were stockbrokers, attorneys, gallery owners, retired CEOs, and the like?"

"It would," Stack said, "only Victoria Pike was a Wall Street stock analyst before that backsliding I mentioned. She got deep into drugs and the bottle and went from blue chip stocks to blue-plate specials."

"Still," O'Reilly said, "there's nothing wrong with being a waitress, but it's not exactly a six-figure income, right?"

"Not where I eat," Rica said.

"And there's still no getting around that L'Farceur and Pike were the only female Torcher victims. Also, this wasn't a high-rise fire. Pike lived on the second floor."

"That actually could be coincidental," Rica said, "especially when you figure a lot of buildings have shops and offices on the lower floors. Mathematically, most apartments are gonna be on high floors. And the taller the building, the greater the odds a victim's gonna live high in the air."

O'Reilly looked at her and shook his head. "Maybe you shoulda gone to work for an insurance company, or found a job handicapping race horses."

"It could all mean something," Stack admitted. But there was something else nudging at the edge of his mind, trying to gain entrance. Something—

"So you and Rica go find out what it means," O'Reilly said. "Get that fuckin' Leland Brand off our ass."

"I saw the morning paper," Stack said. "Nothing about Larry Chips. I thought we were gonna give Chips to the media wolves."

"I'm getting around to it in my own good time," O'Reilly said. "Wouldn't you say that's my decision?"

"Sure, but the pressure's mostly yours, too."

"Oh, don't bet on that one, Stack! If you don't feel the pressure—"

"What should we tell them?" Rica asked.

O'Reilly stared at her, momentarily derailed. "Huh?"

"The media wolves. If they corner us and ask if we got a suspect, what should we tell them?"

After making a steeple of his fingers—the guy had more neat moves than De Niro—O'Reilly smiled and said, "Give 'em fuckin' Larry Chips."

She nodded solemnly. Stack had to admire her.

O'Reilly stood up.

Stack and Rica glanced at each other and also stood. "That it?" Stack asked.

"No," O'Reilly said, "you bring me the goddamn Torcher, and that'll be *it!*"

In the hall outside the office, Rica said, "I guess that's what you'd call getting our asses reamed."

"Felt like *it,*" Stack said, walking slowly beside her. "Why do you suppose he hasn't fed Chips to the media yet?"

"Easy. Because it was your idea and not his."

Stack stopped walking and she stopped beside him, turned so they were looking squarely at each other. "You think so, Rica?"

"I said so, didn't I?"

"Why would he do that? It's still my idea and not his today. Putting it off wasn't reasonable."

"He's acting on emotion," Rica said.

"Fear for his career?"

"Jealousy."

Stack looked hard at her, trying to figure if she was kidding. "You're serious?"

"Sure. He thinks you're balling me and he resents it because he'd love to trade places with you and can't. He knows I won't let him."

"Rica, are you sure you know what you're saying?"

"Of course."

"How do you know this?"

"It would be obvious to any astute woman in my position."

Stack thought about that as they continued walking.

"Notice he didn't say anything else about you and me?" Rica said.

"I noticed," Stack said. "He knew he damn well better not."

"At least we escaped with some dignity."

"You bet," Stack said, and patted her on the rump.

Astounding her.

Back at the desk, he said, "Something occurred to me while we were in O'Reilly's office."

She smiled. "Apparently."

"Not that," Stack said. "At first I couldn't get hold of it, but now I have."

"I'd say," she told him, still smiling.

"Business, Rica."

"Monkey?"

"Police. Co-op. We need to go through all the Torcher files and make sure, but I think all the victims were previously, or at the time of death, members of their co-op boards."

Rica sat on the edge of the desk, in no way suggestive this time. She was all cop now. "I don't have to go through the files. You're right." She picked up Stack's cup and sipped some cold coffee. He didn't complain. "But I dunno, Stack. O'Reilly's also right about tenants taking turns serving on those co-op boards. In fact, most of the boards have rules saying you can serve only so long."

"True. Most of the time. But people like Danner and Kreiger know how to get around rules. And even if they're off the board, they might still have a lot of unofficial influence."

Rica chewed on her tongue for a moment and stared at Stack. "Where you going with this?"

"You ever been interviewed by a co-op board? Lots of people could be pissed off at co-op boards. They have too much power. Some of them run their buildings like little fiefdoms."

"But one killer with a mad-on over all those boards?"

"That's a problem," Stack admitted. "But there are all sorts of other possible motives involving co-op boards."

"Such as?"

"I don't know right now. But I might after we get the minutes of all those co-op board meetings in the buildings where victims burned to death, going back as far as we can, even if we have to subpoena them. There might be a motive buried somewhere in them. Maybe some guy kept getting kicked off co-op boards because he's a nutcase."

"Nutty enough to set people on fire?"

"Somebody's that nutty," Stack pointed out. "At least co-op board membership is a common denominator among the victims.

"So's having arms and legs. A dick was even enough until Bruni L'Farceur and Victoria Pike."

"Jesus, Rica!"

She stood up from the desk and smoothed her skirt. "Okay, Stack, maybe you've got something."

"*We've* got something," Stack corrected her. "You said *you've*."

Rica laughed. "Don't make too much of that, Stack."

"And you don't make too much of that pat on the posterior," he grumbled, getting back to shuffling the papers on his desk.

"What I think's really significant," Rica said, "is you're the only cop I ever heard say *fiefdom*."

"I figured you'd understand what it meant."

"I know . . . I know . . . Tell me, you ever said *fiefdom* to any other cop?"

Stack thought about it. "Not to any other living human being."

She winked at him.

Stack went that evening to Laura's new building, successfully avoiding co-op board members, and knocked on her apartment door.

Her blue eyes widened with surprise when she saw him, but her facial muscles gave nothing away. He was glad to see she was getting better at concealing her emotions. That would come in handy in her new independence. "Ben!"

"You recognized me," Stack said, immediately kicking himself for being sarcastic. "Sorry. I didn't mean to wise off, Laura. I just wanted to come by and see where you were living."

She smiled, suddenly making it 1983 again, herself a compact, sandy-haired young woman with freckles and an extra ration of sex appeal. The smile hit him like a punch in the stomach. She was his again, and life was theirs again.

"Come on in," she said, stepping back. "I haven't got the mess under control yet."

"You haven't had time yet," Stack said, following her into the apartment. It was small but clean and freshly painted, with what looked like new blue carpet. What used to be her chair at home was in a corner. What used to be his chair was nowhere in sight. Only a few other pieces of furniture were familiar, a coffee table, a lamp. There were still cardboard boxes stacked in a corner, and a vacuum cleaner stood near them like a sentinel on alert.

"You want something to drink, Ben?"

"No, Laura. No, thanks." He was trying not to feel possessive of her, protective, but he didn't like the thought of her living here by herself. Being with her still seemed to carry a responsibility. At the same time, he knew there was no going back to what they'd had before everything went sour.

"Want to see the kitchen?"

"No," he said, "I actually just came to see you, to make sure you were okay. I guess I missed you."

"You're going to have to get over that, Ben."

"I know. I'm scaling back. I can't be here long." He'd deliberately left his coat on, hadn't even unbuttoned it.

"I don't want to talk about old times," she said.

"Me either."

Especially about Robert, she'd meant. Neither of them had talked about Bobby for years, their three-month-old son who'd died of sudden infant death syndrome, so long ago. They had talked about him at first, when they both felt guilty, or thought the other might be guilty, of something, anything. It seemed there must be some responsibility. Three-month-old children didn't simply die that way, healthy and happy one hour, lifeless the next.

But they did die that way. And no one so far had been able to explain why adequately. It simply happened. And this time it had happened to Bobby, to them. No one was guilty, but could everyone involved feel blameless?

So they'd stopped talking about Bobby, placed the subject in the basements of their minds where they seldom ventured.

"I want to thank you again for what you did for me," Laura said. "I mean, with the co-op board. Speaking up for me."

"You're worth speaking up for." Maybe he shouldn't have phrased it that way. "It wasn't that much trouble." He glanced around, seeing nothing. "You gonna like it here?"

She nodded thoughtfully, as if seriously considering the question. "I think I will eventually. That's how it has to be."

"I guess so," he said. He shifted his weight to the other leg. "Well . . ." he said.

"Well . . ." she said back, again with the smile.

"I better get back, Laura." *Back to where? To my crummy, too-small apartment?*

She didn't ask him back to where. They told each other to take care of themselves, and Stack left. He thought about kissing her good-bye, a peck on the cheek, but decided against it.

He realized, walking down the hall, that he was clenching his fists. They hadn't talked about Bobby, and probably never would again. Probably no one would talk about Bobby ever again. But they both knew that in some strange way his death had been largely responsible for how they felt about each other. Then how they hadn't felt about each other. Stack didn't know how it could have been any other way.

Some things you didn't talk about because they were beyond words.

Some things you put away in the dark.

Some things grew in the dark.

Most of the co-op boards had willingly handed over their minutes. Two refused, only to have the minutes seized on court orders.

By the next afternoon, Stack and Rica were back at Stack's desk, poring over the reams of minutes.

"I never knew these boards had so many meetings," Rica said, rubbing her tired eyes with her knuckles. "And that the members talked such endless bullshit."

"Mostly what boards do," Stack said.

After a while, the work wasn't quite so tedious. They learned to skip over obviously irrelevant subjects, motions to discuss new rules for dog walkers, to change the trash pickup system, to name a panel to discuss revised rules and hours for the swimming pool or exercise room, motions to discuss panel findings, to discuss other motions. It had to turn you into slag, Rica thought, serving on one of these boards.

"I motion that we take a break from this," Rica said.

The phone rang.

Stack picked it up and wished he hadn't. It was O'Reilly.

"Heard the news?" O'Reilly asked.

"No. We got another fire?"

"Sort of. Leland Brand's been appointed City Department of Public Well-being commissioner. Not only that, he's made it official. He's forming what he calls an early bird campaign committee and he's in the hunt for mayor. You know what that means?"

"Higher taxes?"

"More pressure, Stack. Brand's already put in a call to the police commissioner, who put in a call to me."

"And now you've put in a call to me," Stack said. "Shit rolling downhill."

"It'll start rolling at us from every direction if you and Rica don't quit fuckin' around and make some progress on this case. The media's not gonna chew on Larry Chips forever." O'Reilly had finally tossed Chips to the wolves yesterday, timing it for the evening news.

"Chips is another guy feeling the pressure," Stack said.

"It doesn't matter, remember? He's not the Torcher. What he is, he's a diversion."

"Probably," Stack said. "But we can't rule him out entirely."

"Sure we can. He's a small-time pyromaniac who sets fires for clients who want insurance claims. Half businessman, half fruitcake. Only thing sets him apart is, he screwed up out in LA and shot somebody."

"Still—"

"Don't give me *still,* Stack. Give me the Torcher. You understand?"

"Sure," Stack said. He was getting tired of putting up with O'Reilly. The problem with establishing authority through intimidation was that intimidation wore off. And when it was gone, so was respect.

O'Reilly hung up without saying good-bye.

"Something important?" Rica asked, looking up from the minutes she was reading.

"O'Reilly."

"Oh. What did he want?"

"Wanted a date with you."

"I hope you told him I was busy."

"You'll be busy, all right," Stack said, and plopped down another stack of bound minutes in front of her.

Stack waited about fifteen minutes before getting up from his desk chair and wandering toward the lounge as if for a glass of water or some coffee.

Out of sight of Rica, he sat at an unoccupied desk and used the phone.

Corlane at Juppie's told him Ned Salerno had the day off. Stack had his home number in the file, but got it from Corlane.

Ned answered on the third ring.

"This is your new close friend Detective Stack," Stack said. "I hope I made enough of an impression that you remember me."

It took Ned about ten seconds to answer, and his voice

was high and tight. "I remember you. Why are you call-ing?"

"I like it, Ned, that you get right to the point."

"I'm in the middle of something," Ned said, getting a little more bold on the phone, the way they always did, separated as they were by distance. "Something real im-portant."

"All I wanted," Stack said, "was to ask you a question."

"Which is?"

"Do you ever wear a tie, Ned?"

Stack listened closely for something, anything, in Ned's voice.

"Tie? Yeah, sometimes I do. Why would you wanna know that?"

"How many ties you own, Ned?"

"I dunno. Well, yeah, I got about half a dozen. Two got stains on 'em and I don't wear either one anymore. Mostly I wear a red one I got. Then there's a dark blue one with some kinda design on it. I think that's about it."

"That's only four, Ned."

"Then I only got four. I remember now."

"You got any use for them other than dressing up?"

"Huh? Not that I can think of."

"If you're lying to me, Ned, you know what I'm gonna do with those ties?"

"I got an idea."

Stack hung up without saying good-bye, thinking how much he really disliked Ned Salerno.

THIRTY-SEVEN

Etta Daggett sat on the edge of the bed and neatly snorted a half line of cocaine off the smooth surface of Dani's hand mirror. It might be true for some people that coke was addictive, but that wasn't the case for Etta. She'd been using it almost a year now, and with no ill effects.

She lay back in bed next to Dani and pulled the sheet and thick comforter up beneath her chin. Then she waited awhile, listening to Dani's even breathing, watching shadows from the swaying curtains move back and forth across the ceiling like night clouds in some kind of planetarium show with rapid-time-lapse film. Etta always felt so relaxed after sex with Dani.

She'd been doing *that* since she'd started coming to New York five years ago. Dani wasn't her first and only girlfriend. There'd been a few adventures in college, but they could be categorized as youthful experimentation. Etta had been strictly with men for years before Dani.

A friend in Washington, DC, who for some reason must have seen something in Etta (or had she heard something long ago at Smith?), had told her to look up Dani. She hadn't given Etta a last name for Dani, only a phone number.

The first night in her hotel, Etta had nervously called

the number, and Dani had immediately put her at ease, using only the slightest innuendo to steer the conversation. Nothing was done in a rush. They'd met the next evening over coffee. Later, after going to a discreet club in the Village, they'd returned to Dani's nearby apartment and their relationship had begun. It was all so natural, the way events flowed in that direction. There had been some conversation about certain preconditions; then there had been no need for words. Etta still thought often about that night. Easily, knowledgeably, Dani had demonstrated to Etta layer by layer who and what she was, what she really wanted and needed.

Etta had never dreamed it could be this way between two women. Two people. Two of any species. She could tolerate pauses, but she wanted what she and Dani shared never to end.

There was no reason why it should end, as long as they respected each other's individuality and privacy outside the bedroom.

Dani, as far as Etta knew, had never revealed to their mutual Washington acquaintance that Etta had used the phone number. In Etta's business, it was almost universally understood that relationships like this were best kept very private. She was sure Dani realized that. They had to trust each other. And they did. Dani had never objected when Etta returned to her hotel bed rather than spend the night in the apartment. Etta had explained to her how in the political world appearances might be even more important than actuality. Etta's vulnerabilities were automatically those of her clients.

"You all right?" Dani asked beside Etta. She was a frail-looking blond woman who wasn't frail at all. When Etta didn't answer, Dani reached over and playfully tugged at Etta's right nipple with her thumb and forefinger. "Hey, you hear me?"

Etta lolled her head to the left and smiled at her. "I thought you were asleep, the way you were breathing."

Dani squinted, staring at her. "You into the shit again?"

"A little"

"Fine with me." Dani sat up, then nimbly rolled out of bed to stand and walk into the bathroom. Etta watched her shadowed nude form, the easy rhythm of her hard, lithe body. Dani had a dagger tattooed high on her right buttock. Shortly after they'd met, Etta had asked her what it meant. "I stabbed my husband to death," Dani had said.

Joking, Etta was sure. She had never asked again, but the dagger tattoo intrigued her all the more.

After a few minutes she heard the toilet flush; then Dani padded across the hardwood floor and got back into bed, under the covers with Etta. When Etta reached over to touch her, she found Dani's thigh dry and cold. "I don't see how you can get up and walk around nude like that without freezing to death," she said. "You keep the apartment so cold."

Dani didn't bother answering her. No surprise. Instead she said, "This new client you're shilling for, Leland Brand, what's he really like?"

Shop talk. Interesting, since Dani usually wasn't concerned with or involved in politics. Etta didn't know much about Dani's occupation, or how she spent her time. She'd told Etta she was an advanced software test pilot. Whatever that was. Now Dani was curious about Brand. "You a foreign spy?" Etta asked.

"Yes."

"Brand's like the rest of them, then. Ambitious, wrapped up in himself, blinder than most. I have to take him by the hand and lead him."

"Doesn't sound like you."

"You'd be surprised."

"No. This Brand gonna go somewhere, you think? Become president and take you with him to the White House?"

Etta heard herself giggle. "Why?"

"I always wanted to sleep in the White House. Answer the question."

"He'll become mayor of New York, after he gets voted in next election."

"Election's a long way off."

"Gotta plan ahead, in my game."

Dani turned toward her and kissed her on the forehead. "I know your game."

"Hmm. You certainly do. How come you're interested in Leland Brand?"

"I'm not. I'm interested in you. You *can* be naive in some ways, and I wanted to make sure you knew you weren't in Kansas anymore. And I wondered about how Brand's treating you."

"He's okay. He listens. Because deep down he knows that without me he couldn't find his ass with either hand. He's like a strong horse that needs coaxing and direction. He needs me. I remind him of that from time to time, though he doesn't realize it."

Dani smiled. "A whole other side of you."

"Does that surprise you?"

"Not at all."

Etta felt better than contented now, felt like teasing.

"You worried about me cause I'm surrounded every day by all that testosterone?"

"No," Dani said. "I'll show you why not." Her head disappeared beneath the covers.

Etta hadn't told quite all the truth to Dani about Leland Brand. She did owe some loyalty to her client. She hadn't told Dani that what was different about Brand, what she really liked in him as a client, was that after a few weeks with him she'd realized he had no moral convictions whatsoever. His ego and ambition were the most expansive she'd ever seen in a politician. He would do anything to realize those ambitions—*anything*.

It wasn't that these were rare qualities at all in politicians. It was that Brand had less conscience and more pit bull in him than even he knew. Etta was still learning how to draw it out. This boy had possibilities. He was an interesting challenge.

But not one she wanted to consider at the moment.

Dani often thought how astounded a smart cookie like Etta would be if she ever learned in the future what she didn't know now. But people like her seldom did eventually learn.

It wasn't that Dani wanted to take advantage of Etta; she would draw the line at hurting her in any way Etta didn't want to be hurt. One of the things Etta might be surprised about was how fond of her Dani actually was. Dani hoped that someday, if Etta ever found out how duplicitous her secret lover was, Etta would understand and forgive her. Dani knew that would be a lot to ask, so she was content to leave their relationship unchanged.

She'd never confided to Etta her real occupation. She had nothing to do with software or computers; she worked for a medical supplier. That was where she could obtain what she needed, then secretly put it in Etta's drugs or booze.

One of the characteristics Dani liked best in her lover was that she talked in her sleep. Sleeping soundly after a night of sex and treats laced with the proper medications, Etta could be extremely conversant. Awake, she was secretive about her life in politics. Asleep, she couldn't be more eager to share information.

During long, warm nights of pillow talk, like tonight promised to be, it was surprising what Dani could learn.

Some of the information she could sell.

THIRTY-EIGHT

Stack's phone roused him from sleep at—he squinted at the glowing red numerals on the clock radio—2:17 A.M. Lying on his stomach, he reached out with his right arm as if doing a swim stroke, miraculously found coiled wire, and reeled in the receiver.

"Stack? . . ."

It was Rica. "Um." He realized he'd been dreaming about her but he couldn't recall the dream. About her, though, and not Laura. It had been a while now since he'd dreamed of Laura. Stack rolled over onto his side, then worked his body parts so he was sitting up but slumped over.

"Stack?"

He managed to wriggle backward and sit up straighter. The wooden headboard was cool on his bare shoulders. What did Rica want? Had he gone too far at the precinct and encouraged her? Was this going to be an invitation to take a cab for a late-night ride to her apartment? Phone sex? God, he hoped not. He'd never understood why people . . .

"You awake, Stack?"

"Yeah, it's me. Yes, I'm awake." *Half awake, anyway. Probably couldn't even get a hard-on, if that's what she—*

"Listen, Stack. Ernest Fagin phoned. Said he just happened to dial my number before yours, so I told him I'd contact you. Another call came in a few minutes ago to the FDNY, a high-rise fire on East Sixty-fifth near First Avenue."

"I'm on my way," Stack said. He scooted sideways on the bed and stood up too fast, pressing the phone to his ear and still dizzy with sleep. Terrible taste in his mouth. "I'll swing by in the unmarked and pick you up."

"I'm close enough to this one, I'm gonna cab over to it. I can be there while you're still getting dressed."

Stack doubted it, but he didn't argue. "See you there." He hung up and said, "God!" Then he switched on the lamp and set a course for the bathroom.

And stopped in midstride when the phone rang again.

Rica calling back, he figured.

When he picked up the receiver and said hello, a familiar gravely voice said simply, "A high-rise fire on East Sixty-fifth off First Avenue. Hurry."

Hearing the voice momentarily froze Stack. "Wait! Hey, where—"

But the Torcher had hung up.

When Stack's skin stopped crawling, he took the caller's advice and hurried.

Ten minutes later, he was driving toward the East Side when he heard the sirens. They got louder as he drove. What the hell? he thought, and decided to join the chorus. The streets he was speeding along were almost deserted, but he placed the unmarked's light on the roof and switched on the car's siren. All that howling and warbling in the night, he thought, all closing in on the same point. Like a pack of wolves on the scent.

* * *

The Torcher stood across the street among the crowd
that had formed when tenants from the facing building
came down to view what was happening. Neighbors often
didn't know each other in Manhattan, even if they lived in
the same building and on the same floor. Certainly everyone didn't know everyone else in a large building, so no
one would pay particular attention to who under other circumstances would be a stranger.

Quite a sight, this fire, with flames leaping from the
windows of the twenty-first-floor apartment. But only that
apartment, the Torcher noticed with satisfaction.

This time the Torcher had decided to stay close and
make sure. This time precautions had worked: the care
taken to contain the fire in the kitchen, or at least the apartment, then the call to the fire department, then to Stack, to
be doubly safe. Mark Drucker lived alone; he was the only
one to die tonight. A plan gone right.

A cab stopped at the corner, near the police barricade,
and Detective Erica Lopez climbed out. The Torcher
moved back somewhat in the knot of spectators and
watched.

Odd that Stack, so respected and even feared in the
NYPD, hadn't come with Lopez, even after the phone call.
The Torcher rotated a wrist to peer at a gold watch. Well,
it was a bad time of night even for cops. Stack had probably been roused out of bed by the call, and decided he
wasn't coming. Nothing could be done tonight; it would
wait till morning and be more comprehensible then. They
worked long, hard hours, did cops. They didn't always
have the advantage or all the energy in the world. Stack

might simply have sent his partner to observe the fire and ascertain the facts. Seniority could be a wonderful thing. And a good thing for the Torcher, who unquestionably felt some relief that the venerable Stack hadn't appeared.

The flames were fascinating, but the Torcher ignored them and kept watching Lopez. Such a small, nimble woman. But she moved decisively, as if she was strong. Time at the gym, probably, to make up for her short stature. Most likely, despite changes in society, it was still a hard life, being a woman in the NYPD.

Lopez crossed the street, flashing her shield, carefully stepping over hoses and avoiding scattered equipment. She seemed to know she was out of her element and didn't want to get in the way. Water was streaming down the front of the building, and the street was wet from curb to curb. The boots of the firefighters, who were bustling back and forth in their dark slickers with the luminous horizontal yellow bands, were starting to kick up rooster tails of spray.

Lopez had stopped to talk to one of the firefighters, a tall, lanky man. He was wearing a slicker but his helmet was different from the others and his boots looked like ordinary black rubber galoshes. The Torcher remembered seeing him before and wondered about him. Was he a fire department bigwig? Some kind of cop? Someone else to fear?

There was Stack!

All of a sudden. The ally and nemesis. Standing across the street and facing away from the burning building, his gaze scanning the apartments opposite as if he were searching for someone looking back at him. He was wearing his too-long, bulky coat, like a biblical robe.

A stab of fright almost like panic sliced through the Torcher.

There was no reason to stay here now. Only the flames. Only the flames. But they were high and majestic, taunting the enemy because they'd done their work for the night. They were invincible. If they were extinguished here, they would reappear there. By match or coal or lightning or destiny. Invincible and forever.

The Torcher separated from the knot of onlookers and drifted to the side, then stepped into a narrow, dark gangway that ran between two brick buildings. It would take only a minute or so to cut through the gangway to the next block, to be well away from danger, from Stack.

Movement caught Stack's eye. Everyone on the other side of the street was staring transfixed at the darting and licking flames high above. It was almost as if they were paying homage to some ancient god. Their fascination and immobility was striking.

Except for one dark figure that moved.

When Stack looked more closely, it was gone.

Someone had slipped away from the hypnotized, stationary crowd on the sidewalk and disappeared. It took Stack only a second to realize the one way that was possible.

The dark mouth of the gangway.

He forgot about joining Rica and Fagin, and instead ran across the street, his shoes splashing water and getting his cuffs and socks wet.

He ran around a coiled fire hose and found himself aligned directly with the long gangway. There was a tall slab of faint light from the next block, like a crack leading to another world, and for only an instant, but an instant for sure, his gaze caught the silhouette of a dark running figure.

Stack felt adrenaline kick in like a massive injection. He ran faster. When he entered the darkness of the gangway, he slipped his right hand beneath his coat and drew his venerable Police Special from its holster.

He could hear his breath rasping loudly, the slap of his soles on concrete. Ahead there was a slight sound, a brief metallic clatter, as if a trash can had been brushed or its lid knocked off. Yet he could see nothing but—

There!

When Stack was more than halfway through the black gangway, he saw a figure pass like an illusion through the tall slash of dim light, dart around the corner, and turn right on the sidewalk in the next block. Someone was there, all right. He knew who it was, who it had to be!

Stack didn't have his two-way. Didn't matter anyway. Now he had to run faster than he'd ever run as a young man. He knew he could do it. He knew! His chest heaved and his legs were pumping hard beneath the heavy wool coat. His right thigh brushed something, maybe the same trash can his quarry had disturbed, and metal clanged.

Then he was through the gangway! Into the next block. Looked right. Just in time to see whoever he was chasing turn the corner at the intersection and head back toward the block where the fire was blazing.

Stack tucked in his chin and pulled deeper breaths. *Go ahead and run, you bastard!*

He ignored the ache in his lungs, the pain in his thighs, and ran faster toward the corner.

Skidded around it and almost fell.

He stood with his breath fogging in front of him.

No one was there when he'd made the turn. Not even a bum sleeping on a grate for warmth, an insomniac smoking a cigarette or walking a dog. Only the dark, cold street with a few parked cars.

He ran down to the next block and peered up the street to where the fire blazed a block away. Against the glare of the floodlights and the flames, it was impossible to be sure one of the moving, silhouetted figures wasn't the Torcher.

No, not that dumb!

Stack took a chance. He raced down the street to the next block.

It was a street almost narrow enough to be an alley, with a few cars parked along one side. Stack ran several yards up it and peered into the dimness ahead.

No sign of movement.

Then a faint, rhythmic sound. Footsteps?

He took a deep, gasping breath and broke into a run toward the sound, pretending there was someone there. Hoping!

To get so damned close! . . .

Movement! He saw it, he was sure!

He was sure he saw someone running toward the street one building over from where the fire was blazing in the next block.

At the intersection the street was barricaded by police sawhorses, but there was no cop around. Didn't need to be at this time of night. Early morning.

Stack angled around the barricade and tried to run even faster. He'd closed some of the distance between himself and the figure he was chasing. If he couldn't run as fast, he could damn well outlast his quarry, out-*will* him! He was gasping now instead of just breathing hard, and his legs ached and seemed to weigh twice what they should. His soles were making a different slapping sound as they struck the pavement, his shoes hitting heavily heel first, then flat.

It took him only a short time to know why the block was barricaded. The night breeze was carrying the smoke this way, causing a black haze to settle over the street. Stack was having a harder time breathing now. He was sucking in thick, acrid smoke rather than crisp night air.

The pain in his side was getting sharper as his oxygen was cut off. He stumbled and had to slow down.

For a moment the smoke cleared and he saw the dark figure he was pursuing only about ten yards in front of him, head down, staggering as he was but still running hard.

Stack tried to yell halt but couldn't find the breath. He raised his revolver to fire, then realized he couldn't. There was no way to know how far, or where, the bullet might travel if he missed, and he could no longer see the dark figure, only imagine where it must be.

He had to keep his head. *No target. No fuckin' target! Warning shot, anyway . . . Fuckin' regulations!*

He lowered the revolver and ran harder, harder . . . almost sobbing now as he fought to breathe. His eyes were burning, watering. He pushed himself on, feeling the tears tracking down his cheeks, feeling his legs going numb, hearing the gun drop to the pavement and fire as he lurched deeper and deeper into the lowering pall, into darkness.

The Torcher staggered like a drunk, weaving, face red and wet with tears, eyes squinted narrowly in order to see anything at all.

It seemed to take forever to reach the car and unlock the door, then collapse into the front seat on the passenger side.

Thank God it was so late! So dark!

Jesus, the pain! This had been so close! So goddamned close!

Never again! Never again come back and watch the flames! Never again!

Everything smelled like smoke, like death, like finality. It was inevitable, but not tonight . . . Not tonight . . .

The pain! . . .

So goddamned close!

"Stack? . . . Stack? . . . Stack? . . ."

He opened his eyes and saw figures looming over him, the night sky above and beyond them boasting a few stars. Then he realized something was covering his mouth and nose, and he shook his head from side to side, trying to shake whatever it was away so he could breathe. Someone pressed the thing harder so it covered the entire bottom half of his face. Others held him down. What the hell were they—

"Breathe, Stack! Please! Just relax and breathe!"

He took the advice and forced himself to stop struggling. Cautiously at first, he began drawing deep breaths. He knew now it was a respirator held to his face.

He tried to remember what had happened as he studied the figures above. It was Rica bending over him, he was sure, though it was too dim to see her features. Near her was someone in a firefighter's helmet; he was the one applying the respirator. Above them, standing where he was catching more light, was lanky Ernest Fagin.

Stack relaxed his body completely so they'd know he was okay and was finished resisting. He reached up slowly and deliberately and held the firefighter's wrist, coaxing the respirator mask away from his face.

He could breathe on his own! Cold, pure air. New York air he'd never again think of as polluted. He coughed violently, regained control, and sucked in some more of the sweetest air he had ever breathed.

"You okay, Stack?" Rica asked.

He looked around and realized he was about a hundred feet down the block from where he must have fallen. There was some smoke here, drifting high between him and the stars, but not nearly as much as when he'd been closer to where the building was burning in the next block. "What? . . ."

"The smoke got you," Fagin said. "Can you breathe okay now?"

"Yeah," Stack said. "I was chasing . . ."

"We figured," Rica said.

"My gun . . . I dropped it and I think it fired."

"It did," Rica said. "The sound of the shot's what brought us here. You killed a ninety-seven Chevy."

Stack raised himself up on his elbows.

"Lie back down," Fagin said. "We got an ambulance coming for you."

"No, no," Stack said. "I don't need an ambulance!"

"You don't know how much smoke you breathed in."

"I know I feel okay."

"Sure you do. But smoke inhalation's no joke. Tell him to lie down, Rica."

Rica studied Stack, then shook her head no. "I don't think so. It's gotta be up to him."

"Jesus!" Fagin said. "Macho cops. Even you, Rica. He's getting in an ambulance."

The fireman with the respirator stood up. Stack grabbed one of his legs and used it to pull himself to his knees, then managed to stand. Someone's hand on his elbow helped him. "Listen, I'm okay. Really."

"You don't know that for sure," Fagin said. "You might need medical treatment. At least some observation."

"No," Stack said. "I'm okay, damn it!"

"Stubborn fucker!"

"Listen, I can damn well do—"

"Listen yourself!" Fagin said.

"I'll take him to my place," Rica said.

"Fine, if your place is Roosevelt Hospital."

"I'll keep an eye on him and see he gets help if he runs into any problems. That's a promise."

"Doctor Rica! . . ."

"If he says he's okay, I think he really is."

Fagin used his forearm to wipe soot from his face and looked at Stack with a mixture of disgust and concern. "Her place. That okay with you, Stack?"

"Yeah, okay. Thanks, Ernest. Now get back to your fire where you belong."

"It's under control," Fagin said.

Rica handed Stack the Police Special and he slipped it back in its shoulder holster.

"So where's the car?" Rica asked.

He told her and they began walking unsteadily toward where the unmarked was parked, weaving a little, Stack leaning on Rica for support.

Then he realized Fagin would be watching, so he straightened up and walked on his own.

THIRTY-NINE

When Stack awoke, his head was nestled between Rica's bare breasts.

This is okay, he thought groggily, remembering last night. *Better than okay.*

Without moving, he let the gaze of his free eye roam around her bedroom and saw spare, lightly stained furniture he thought was Danish, white walls with only a few items hung on them, winter landscape prints to go with the Danish furniture. There were no drapes or curtains on the windows, only white, wooden horizontal slat blinds that were lowered and angled to keep the room dim. For privacy, Stack hoped. He remembered the floor being hardwood, cool on his bare feet until they came in contact with one of several woven throw rugs.

He swallowed. He could still taste ashes, still smell the acrid burnt stench that had hung in the air last night. His throat seemed okay, though. Not sore, as he suspected it would be.

"You okay?" Rica suddenly asked, her voice a little hoarse and sounding distant to Stack, who was listening with one ear.

"Yeah. How'd you know I was awake?"

"I felt you blink."

"Hmm." Stack turned his head slightly and kissed her between the breasts, then on each nipple.

"Glad I brought you home?" Rica asked.

"What do you think?"

"I think you're glad. Better than any old hospital. Besides, you weren't that badly hurt or anything, just breathed in a little smoke."

Stack pulled away from her and put on a mock hurt look. "I could use a bit more sympathy and understanding, now that I'm here."

"Did you get a look at him?"

Stack didn't have to ask whom she meant. "No. Just a glance at someone in the night, half the time concealed by smoke."

"Might not even have been the Torcher."

"It was him," Stack said. "He called me last night right after you did. To warn me about the fire."

"*What?* You're serious?"

"Serious."

"Same voice?"

"Without a doubt."

She was quiet. Thinking. "Making sure," she said, after a while.

"Uh-huh."

Rica ran her tongue over her lips, then used her fingertips to brush strands of hair off her forehead and out of her eyes. "There's what you'd expect in the burned-out apartment. The victim, Mark Drucker, was on the kitchen floor, looking like forgotten toast and bound with black cloth, same accelerant poured over him. No sprinkler system in the building, so no umbrella this time."

Stack worked himself away from her compact warm

body onto cool sheets and propped himself up on an elbow. "How?—"

"I was up earlier, made some phone calls."

"Earlier? What time is it?"

"Almost ten."

"Jesus!" He sat up. "C'mon."

"Where?"

"We got things to do. Then we'll add the co-op board minutes from last night's fire to our stack of material. See if we can get them without going to a judge. Then we've gotta get some uniforms talking to the neighbors, witnesses. Learn something about this Drucker guy—"

"Stack?"

"What?"

"Wanna go again?"

"It's a thought."

By that afternoon they had most of what they needed. The police and FDNY reports confirmed Drucker's death as another Torcher murder. And he fit the victim profile— a successful sort, fifty years old, divorced, a professor and teacher of Urban Analysis and Development at New York University. He'd been having a torrid love affair with one of the women in his Segmentation of Rich and Poor class, was well liked by most of his colleagues, served on various city development committees, and was a past member of his co-op board. Which board, whose members were stunned and saddened by Drucker's death, readily turned over the minutes of two years' worth of monthly meetings.

Stack and Rica had already listened to O'Reilly's expected harangue, toned down somewhat because O'Reilly himself was confounded and worn out by the Torcher murders and the crush of bureaucratic pressure from above. He'd expressed mild disappointment that Stack had discerned nothing new from the Torcher phone call, but only mild.

Most of the afternoon was spent poring over board minutes.

Finally Stack sat back and rubbed the nape of his neck, then extended his arms and stretched. He looked again at the reams of paper on his desk, then at Rica. "Here's something," he said. "Maybe."

Rica put down what she was reading, knuckled her eyes, and stared blearily across the desk at him.

Stack wondered why he'd never noticed how beautiful and vulnerable she looked when she was exhausted. He shook off the thought. "Notice how often the name Myra Raven comes up in these minutes?"

"Yeah. But what struck me isn't that it appears all that often, but that it appears somewhere in the minutes of just about every board."

It gave Stack a kind of pride he hadn't felt before when he realized she'd been half a step ahead of him.

"But that's not too surprising," Rica said. "She's a hotshot real estate agent, broker, whatever. Haven't you heard of the Myra Raven Group?"

"I seem to have," Stack said. "Lots of newspaper ads, right?"

"Right. She's got the most successful agency in town, so it's normal her name'd pop up at these board meetings."

"But how normal would it be," Stack asked, "for her agency to have bought or sold property in virtually every one of the co-ops where the fires occurred? I mean, how much property could her agency turn?"

Rica absently stroked her chin where Stack's shoulder had rubbed it that morning, almost smiled, then got her mind back on the job. "I see what you mean, Stack. But"—she shrugged—"it still might signify nothing."

"We oughta talk to her and make sure. Put her on our list, at least. If nothing else, she should be a good source of general information about New York co-ops."

"Agreed," Rica said. She clasped her hands together and leaned slightly forward, her voice lower. "Notice the way that prick Mathers has been looking at us most of the day?"

"The Beave? No."

"He knows something. Knows about us. I can tell."

"I wouldn't figure you'd care," Stack said.

"I don't, except we better not give O'Reilly any more ammunition. He's the kind of jerk that'd bring IA into it, or at least insist on knowing all the details himself."

"I don't recall seeing Mathers in your bedroom with us last night or this morning," Stack said. "So let him think whatever he wants. Let him tell O'Reilly whatever he wants."

"A *he said, we said* situation, huh?"

"Exactly."

Rica smiled. "You don't seem to have any regrets."

"I don't," Stack said. "In for a penny . . ."

Rica guessed that might be a compliment. Anyway, she'd known what *she* was getting into and also had no regrets. "Stack—"

The phone rang and he picked up.

Rica listened to his succession of yeses, nos, and uh-huhs; then he promised the caller he'd be somewhere at four o'clock, half an hour away.

When he hung up, he looked puzzled and interested at the same time. Rica knew the look, had seen it on Stack before, and on cats at the moment they became intrigued by mice.

"Gertrude Kreiger," he said. "Otto Kreiger's widow. From the Belmire Tower fire. She wants to talk to us. She wouldn't say about what over the phone."

"She say why not?"

"No, but I can guess. She doesn't trust us completely and thinks the conversation might be recorded. Doesn't trust the police. Can you imagine?"

"After last night," Rica said, "I can imagine all sorts of things. In fact, I can't stop imagining. You ever experience flashbacks after sex, Stack?"

"She's spooked," Stack said, staring somewhere beyond Rica's right shoulder.

"Me?"

"No. Gertrude Kreiger." He stood up from his desk chair and made sure his shirt was tucked in tight and there were no twists in his shoulder holster strap. "Let's go talk to her and find out why."

Chips had been so scared at first his bowels almost let loose. There he was on the news and in the papers. The old him, anyway. With his name right under the photo. He was suspected of being the Torcher. There was his picture right now on the TV, behind a cute blond news bunny looking serious and saying to call the phone number below if anyone had any information as to his whereabouts. Mirabella walked into the room and saw it.

"Is that *you?*" she asked, stopping cold in her tracks.

Chips was jumping around inside but kept it under control. He laughed. "Sure. I'm gonna set fire to this place soon as I finish my beer. Hell, Mirabella, the only thing I ever burned was a steak. It warms up outside, I'll buy us a barbecue grill and show you."

She tilted her head to the side and looked more closely at the TV. "That's something. That guy could be your twin brother, only with darker hair."

"You're saying that because he's got almost the same name."

"You're shittin' me!" She stared again at the TV. "My God! It does say he's Lawrence Chips. It *is* you!"

"C'mon, Mirabella. Look closer at that ugly dude. Shave off his beard and mustache and we wouldn't look anything alike. You just saw his picture there on the screen and your subconscious read the name even if you didn't."

She looked at the TV, at him, the TV, him. "But you're—"

"Anyway," he said, "I was named plain old Larry on my birth certificate. My mother never would've called me Lawrence. Sounds too successful."

"You oughta go to the police and explain about it," she said. "Somebody's liable to see you right after they see a picture of that Lawrence guy and turn you in." Was she really buying it? Chips wasn't sure. He knew she wanted to believe him, so she probably believed him enough for now. He'd have to keep working on her, reinforcing his story just in case she was wavering.

"I'll think about it," Chips said. "Or I could grow a

beard and mustache like his, dye my hair brown and comb it—*like I had it in California*—like his, and we wouldn't look nothing alike. Besides, my last name's not really Chips. It's Chiperella. I shortened it 'cause it sounded better. Your name really Mirabella?"

"Maureen," she admitted. "When I started as a dancer, I figured Mirabella was more exotic."

Chips grinned. "It is, baby, believe me." He got up from the sofa and went to her, hugged her tightly, glad to see she didn't try to pull away. "And you're exotic, erotic, all that stuff." He kissed her, feeling the hot wedge of her tongue playing over his lips like an eager flame. Maybe she didn't need more convincing, but she was going to get it.

It felt good to be putting one over on her. Putting one over on everyone. This being famous was dangerous, but he could see it would have its moments.

Chips felt better after he'd convinced Mirabella he wasn't the Torcher, and he relaxed somewhat. The truth was, he didn't look at all like his old photograph, older and clean shaven as he was now, and with his natural blond hair. The beard and long mustache were kind of dorky, he decided. He was better off without them, was Larry Chiperella.

But to be on the safe side, from then on whenever he left the house he made sure he wore a baseball cap and a pair of dark-framed glasses with clear lenses. The cap was a Yankees one with a cheap adjustable plastic strap in back so it fit any size. The glasses were display frames he'd pocketed in the optical department at Wal-Mart in a mall in New Jersey. He'd used a little nail clipper to snip the plastic cord that attached the price tag, then wore the glasses as he walked from the store.

When he left the mall and got to where he'd left Mirabella's old Neon parked, he slid in behind the steering wheel. The clear glasses he removed and slipped into his shirt pocket beneath his jacket. Then he put on the sunglasses he'd found in the glove compartment and always wore when he drove.

After leaving the mall, he crossed over into Manhattan and cruised around for a while, battling the stacked-up traffic they had in this city that no matter what anyone said was worse than out in LA.

As he tried to make a left onto Third Avenue, a city trash truck almost flattened him, unsettling his nerves. While he was thinking about that, trying to calm down, he pulled out just before a traffic light changed and a cab roared up within inches of the Neon and the driver blasted his horn. Chips jerked so violently at the sudden noise that the top of his head hit the little car's roof. The cab driver, who looked like some kind of Arab, glared at him, leaned his head out the cab's rolled down window, and shouted angrily at Chips in some foreign language.

Chips cranked down the Neon's window and raised a middle finger for the cabbie to see. "I remember what you did to the World Trade Center, you fucker!"

"My name's McGregor, you idiot!" the cabbie said with a thick Scottish brogue.

"Yeah, so's mine."

The cabbie studied him through narrowed dark eyes, then accelerated around the front of the Neon so the cab's tires screeched. The slush-splattered taxi sped away and barely made the light at the next intersection.

Somewhat mollified by how he'd managed the confrontation, Chips turned a corner. There was less traffic here. He pulled to the side and studied his tourist map a few minutes, then drove slowly past the address, the building he was looking for.

He circled the block and went past the building two more times, fixing the image in his mind, the surrounding neighborhood of shops and small eateries, the brownstones tucked away like bashful old maids between newer, taller buildings. The image was important. It gave him a sense of the whole thing and made strategizing much easier. Before breaking into any place, he had to know the neighborhood and the building from the outside, and he had to know the floor plan. That way you couldn't get tripped up by an unexpected sleeper in a bedroom, or a dog that was perfectly nice until you riled it just by being there. Some territorial thing a lot of pooches had.

One time when he didn't know there'd be a dog, this mangy little poodle thing, much ornerier than you'd expect and with jaws that didn't want to release their grip, had snarled and come at Chips from the shadows beneath a chair. Chips, prepared, had tossed a wad of uncooked ground beef to the dog.

The dog had wolfed down the beef in one gulp without slowing down and kept coming at him, then dug its teeth into the flesh at the back of his ankle. Teeth like needles. "Stop!" he'd yelled, frantically shaking his leg to try throwing the dog off. Damned thing thought it was a pit bull. "Halt! Sit! Stay! Lie down!"

The dog had been untrained and the scar was still there.

Since the dog episode, Chips always wanted an image fixed and clear in his mind before going in. He knew the unexpected happened, like ferocious five-pound poodles, like triple sevens in a slot machine. You had to be prepared for the bad, the good, anything. So he wanted an image and, if possible, a floor plan.

Together, they provided an escape route.

FORTY

Mirabella wondered if Chips thought she was stupid. How could she possibly believe him when he denied he was the Lawrence (Larry) Chips the newspapers and TV said was wanted for questioning in the Torcher killings? A different guy with the same name? Uh, sure! He was just *Larry* on his birth certificate, anyway, not *Lawrence*. And the old photo of the other Chips in the paper and on TV didn't even look much like him. Yeah, that all made sense—if you had no sense.

Was he kidding? Mirabella wondered. Did he really think that just because the Chips in the news photo had a brown hairdo, a beard, and a mustache, she wouldn't recognize him as the same man? The guy looked like her Chips dressed up for some kind of gag photo.

Question was, what was she going to do about it? She really didn't believe her Chips ever killed anybody. And his police record, assuming he was the same guy, suggested he was nonviolent. Mirabella had enough experience with the cops not to suggest Chips should get a lawyer and turn himself in, get the truth out there. Even though Chips wasn't the Torcher, he might be convicted. Then where would she be, having sheltered him all this time? She knew how that could turn out, the way the authorities could twist and mold everything until it fit their theory. First you had the truth by the tail; then all of a sudden it had you, and it wore a badge or a black robe.

Of course there was the off chance Chips was telling the truth, and he really *was* a different Larry Chips from the one pictured in the news. *When monkeys fly out of my ass.* Or that he was the same Larry Chips and really was the Torcher. *When monkeys fly out of his ass.* Or that he was the same Larry Chips but never burned anyone to death. *The most likely and easiest to believe.*

Either way, he was going to end up in the arms of the law instead of her arms.

So should she make the call? Turn him in? He was her man, and what was her loyalty worth? She should stand by him, like the song said.

But she didn't see herself as naive. There was, she had to admit, a slight chance he really was dangerous.

What should she do? She might be making a mistake doing nothing. On the other hand, if instead of standing by her man she turned him over to the cops, then they arrested somebody else for the Torcher murders, she'd hear that song all the rest of her life. It was a problem, all right.

Mirabella thought about it.

She drank a lot of tequila thinking about it.

She fell asleep thinking about it.

She wasn't good with hard decisions.

Gertrude Kreiger was a leggy and buxom thirtyish woman with fluffed red hair, a face etched by tragedy, and dark shadows beneath sad brown eyes. Stack couldn't help but think of a ravaged cheerleader. She was living temporarily in a vacant apartment three floors beneath the one where her husband had burned to death, and when she opened the door to Stack's knock she apologized to him and Rica for the lack of furniture.

She invited them to sit on the one sofa, but Stack refused twice at her urgings, so she finally nodded and smiled glumly at his male stubbornness. Her husband had been stubborn, Rica would bet. Gertrude looked like some kind of redheaded Barbie Doll zombie with credit cards for brains.

Gertrude sat in one corner of the sofa and Rica sat in the room's only other chair, a wooden kitchen job so uncomfortable it had to have been designed by one of those extreme religious orders that equated comfort with sin.

Stack the chivalrous remained standing, his coat unbuttoned, his hands in his pants pockets. "We're sorry for your loss," he said. "Is there anything we can do?" Rica knew he already knew that answer. Every cop did.

"I want you to catch whoever killed him," Gertrude Kreiger said.

Stack's line, Rica thought, keeping her silence.

"Take my word, dear, we're doing everything possible in every way."

"I do believe you," Gertrude said. She placed her hands together in prayer position and sat with them squeezed between her knees. Stack had seen rape victims assume that posture.

"You mentioned on the phone you might have something to tell us," he reminded her gently.

"I had my reservations about this, but I want to do anything I can to help catch Otto's murderer."

"Of course, of course . . ."

"And I feel a responsibility toward whoever else the maniac will set on fire like . . ." She bowed her head and clenched her eyes shut to an emotional storm that passed quickly. "I don't know what it'll mean for my husband's reputation—his memory. But you need to know about an envelope I found tucked beneath a copy of his will in our wall safe. It had my name on it, and inside was a safe deposit box key with a note telling me the contents of the box were mine. I was to go to the box, retrieve what was in it, then close the account and tell no one about it."

Rica watched Stack. Showing no particular curiosity, he shifted his weight, his hands still in his pockets. "And did you follow the directions, dear?"

"Of course. There was money in the box. Fifty thousand dollars, most of it in twenty-dollar bills."

"My goodness. Was there anything else in the box?" Stack asked, his expression unchanged. Rica looked on silently, really enjoying watching him work.

"Nothing," Gertrude said. "No note, no explanation of any kind. Nothing but the money."

"Where is it now?"

"In what's left of our—my apartment. In the wall safe."

"Do you have any idea where your husband might have obtained this money?"

"None. Or why he hid its existence from me until after his death." She stared hopefully up at Stack, tears in her eyes. "Do you think it had anything to do with Otto's murder?"

"Well, it might have," Stack said.

"Is it evidence? Must I turn it over to the police?"

"I suppose that would be a good idea," Stack said. "Temporarily, of course. As of now, it's simply money your husband wanted you to have and keep confidential, for what might have been his own good and perfectly legal reasons. Paper money seldom yields anything in the way of fingerprints or other physical evidence, but we should take a look at it, check to see if the serial numbers are recorded anywhere, that sort of thing. It will be in good hands, and we'll give you a receipt, of course."

"Yes," Gertrude said, "a receipt." She shook her head and her brow furrowed, as if it occurred to her that with her husband gone, she was in charge of her life and would have to become accustomed to business matters. "I just hope it helps in some way to catch whoever's doing these terrible murders."

"You've done the right thing," Rica said.

Gertrude looked over at her as if she'd forgotten Rica was there. "Yes, yes . . ." She stood up. "If you come with me to the apartment, I'll get it for you."

They left her temporary apartment and elevatored three floors up. On the floor that still smelled of smoke and death, Gertrude hesitated.

"I don't want to go in there," she said, actually backing away. "Not until the decorators are done."

Stack and Rica looked at each other.

"I do trust you, both of you," Gertrude said. "If I tell you where the safe is and give you the combination, will you go in and get the money? It's the only thing in the safe right now."

Stack lifted her right hand and patted it gently. "Of course, of course . . ."

Rica stayed out in the hall with Gertrude while Stack went into the burned co-op, then emerged a few minutes later carrying a bulky paper bag.

"We'll need to count it, dear," he said to Gertrude. "A procedural thing."

Gertrude said she understood, and they escorted her back to her temporary apartment, counted out fifty thousand dollars even, then thanked her again as Stack wrote out and signed a receipt.

"By the way," he said, as they were leaving, "did your husband ever mention a woman named Myra Raven?"

Gertrude stared at the floor while she thought. "No, I'm sure he didn't. But the name is vaguely familiar."

"She has one of the most successful real estate agencies in Manhattan," Stack said. "Maybe you saw her name in an ad."

"Yes, yes, that is where I saw it. The newspaper, or maybe on the subway."

The remark struck Rica as odd. Gertrude Kreiger didn't seem the type to spend much time riding subway trains. But then, the subway was a democratic form of transportation.

"What I was wondering," Stack said, "was if you and your late husband bought your apartment through her agency."

"No, we bought directly from the owner. Otto didn't like paying anyone a commission."

They thanked her again and left.

"Like Danner's twenty thousand in his safe," Rica said, tapping the bulky, folded paper sack tucked beneath Stack's right arm as they waited for an elevator.

"Maybe," Stack said. "Or maybe what's in this bag is money Otto didn't want his widow to have to pay taxes on. As we both know, there are plenty of possibilities, money being the root of our employment."

As they stepped out of the elevator at lobby level, a model-handsome man in his late thirties, with thick blond hair and a small, flesh-colored Band-Aid on his neck, was waiting to enter. He did a double take when he saw Rica, then smiled warmly at her.

Stack had waited for Rica to exit the elevator first, and as he stepped out he noticed the man pressed the button for the floor where Gertrude Kreiger grieved in her temporary home.

Myra sat at her desk and stared out at the darkening sky. One of her agents, a man she'd been having some doubts about, had brought in a contract from a major brokerage firm still searching for additional business space after the World Trade Center tragedy. It would be a complicated deal involving multiple lenders, but the commission profit would be immense. She knew that under normal circumstances her focus would be intense; with part of her mind on autopilot, she would be thinking with the other part only of solidifying the contract. But this evening, while outside her office door the Myra Raven Group was closing down around her until tomorrow, she wasn't thinking about real estate at all. She was worried.

Her gaze followed the distant lights of a plane flying well beyond the city, and she wondered what it would be like to be aboard and traveling almost at the speed of sound away from her problems.

She watched the plane until it disappeared.

Billy Watkins. She wanted to see Billy.

As she was turning around in her swivel chair to reach

for the desk phone, there was a soft knock and her office door opened about a foot.

Amy Marks stuck her head in. She looked nervous.

"Come in, Amy. What is it?"

Amy entered and held out a white letter-size envelope. "I just got around to opening the afternoon mail delivery," she said. "This was in it." She approached the desk so Myra could reach the envelope. "It wasn't marked personal," she added. "And I wouldn't have read it if there'd been a name."

"That's all right, Amy." It was company procedure for Amy to open mail addressed only to the agency, then see that the contents went to the appropriate parties. Myra looked at the envelope that had been neatly slit at the top by Amy's letter opener. There was no name typed above the agency address.

But Myra's name was on the folded typed note inside:

For Myra Raven:
Unto the fire and death all things are pure.

The note was unsigned.

Myra tried not to show her concern as she refolded the brief note and slid it back in its envelope. "Sort of cryptic, isn't it?"

"Sort of scary," Amy said. "What with the Torcher murders and all, maybe you should call the police. They might be able to trace whoever sent it. They can bring out fingerprints from paper, maybe even identify the typewriter."

"If they could find the typewriter," Myra said. One thing she knew was that she couldn't turn the note over to the police. "I don't think this note is all that serious. It isn't exactly threatening."

"I'd call it threatening. I'd call it downright creepy."

"Has anyone else seen the note?"

"No. As soon as I saw it was personal and for you, I brought it right to you. I didn't show or mention it to anyone else." She absently adjusted the plain gold wedding band she still wore. "You really oughta consider calling the police."

Myra looked down at the envelope now lying in the center of her desk. "You might be right. I'll think on it. Meanwhile, don't mention to anyone else about the matter."

"Of course not," Amy said. She stood awkwardly for a moment. "Is there anything else?"

Myra smiled at her. "No. And thanks for bringing this directly to me. You did the right thing, Amy. As usual."

Alone again in her office, Myra read and reread the note. Someone was playing with her mind. Warning her? Setting a trap for her? She couldn't be sure. But the note must mean *something*.

She was still uneasy as she left the office, elevatored down to the garage, and drove her SUV through wet and sometimes icy streets to her co-op.

When she'd been home only a few minutes, she realized someone had been in her apartment in her absence.

More angry and curious than anything else, she explored and decided that nothing was missing, but many things, from furniture to the smallest items, seemed to have been moved slightly. So odd. It wasn't even as if a search had been conducted. More as if someone had taken a hurried inventory.

Why would anyone do that? Because they planned on returning later? Did whoever it was know she couldn't call attention to herself with the police?

Myra crossed her arms, cupping her elbows in her palms, and stared across the room and out the window into the cold night above Central Park.

Standing in what she knew with her Realtor's eye was the geometric center of her high and violated home, with its expensive furnishings intact, she felt terribly alone.

And for the first time since reading the note in her office, her uneasiness became raw fear.

It was late, and Stack and Rica were about to leave the precinct house, when the call came in.

When Stack picked up the phone on his desk, Sergeant Redd told him there was another call on the Torcher murders. Not unusual. The police were inundated with calls. Not only did hundreds of people have deliberately misleading or otherwise useless information about the Torcher to feed to the police, but, perversely, dozens of people pretended to *be* the Torcher. "Their fifteen minutes of flame," the Beave had once remarked. Only some of the calls did Sergeant Redd take seriously enough to patch through to Stack or Rica.

"What is it about this one?" Stack asked the desk sergeant.

Redd knew what he meant. "It's the fresh angle. And something in her voice."

And something in your gut, Stack thought. "Put her on," he said. Then: "Detective Stack here."

"Hello?" A woman's voice, throaty and nervous.

"This is Detective Stack," Stack repeated patiently in a neutral tone. Sometimes this job was like being a radio call-in show host. "I understand you have some information to convey."

"Yes. About the Torcher."

"And what would that be, ma'am?" He deliberately hadn't asked her name. There was a pause. Stack liked that. She was reconsidering, screwing up her determination to forge ahead and tell her tale. Making sure she really wanted to do this. "I guess it's what you'd call a tip." Her voice was steady now; she'd turned the corner. "If you want to find the Torcher, I suggest you look in the mayor's office."

Fresh angle indeed. "The mayor of New York?" Drawing her on. Keeping her talking.

"Of course New York!"

"His office?"

"Yes. Among his aides."

"Oh? And which of his aides would that be?"

"You're the police. You should be able to figure that out. If I give you a name, it might be too obvious where you got the information. That might be harmful to me."

"What's your connection with this person?"

"I'd rather not say."

"You do understand that before we can act on this, we need to establish credibility."

"That's up to you. I only wanted to make sure you have the information."

"We get dozens of calls a day like this," Stack said.

"I'd be surprised if you didn't."

"Would it be possible for you to elaborate on your information just a bit more?"

"No."

Clamming up. Losing her. "I only need something from

you that makes your call more credible than most of the others. Is that too much to ask?"

Silence. Had she walked away? Left a phone off the hook somewhere?

"May I ask your name, ma'am?"

"Ask anything you damn well please. I don't have to answer."

"Well, I suppose you're right about that, dear. But I do need—"

He was interrupted by a click, then a loudly buzzing dial tone that sounded like an angry wasp. She'd abruptly hung up the phone.

Stack replaced the receiver on his desk phone. "Anything?" Rica asked.

"A woman suggesting we look in the mayor's office for the Torcher."

"He'll be hiding beneath the desk?"

"I don't think she meant it precisely that way."

Rica finished buttoning her coat to leave. "Another nutcase."

"Probably. But she didn't exactly sound like one."

"Lots of them don't." She raised her chin high and flung one end of her long red muffler about her neck so that it dangled down the back of her coat.

"Well, it probably was another crank call," Stack said. "But it's one to put in the hopper."

"With all the others."

Hundreds of them.

The phone jangled again.

Sergeant Redd: "The call came from a pay phone down in the Village."

Stack thanked him, then reached for his own coat.

* * *

After hanging up, Dani walked quickly away from the phone, her head bowed, her fists jammed deep in her coat pockets. For all she knew, the cops had traced the call and a police car was already on the way. That was why she'd kept the conversation short.

She was glad she'd made the call. She'd done the right thing, she told herself. No second-guessing.

A cold wind kicked up and propelled litter along the sidewalk, causing a dancing sheet of newspaper to snag for a moment on the instep of her left boot.

Dani crossed Bedford and hurried along Christopher Street toward Bleecker, thinking back on the phone conversation. What, really, might she have told Detective Stack that would mean anything and prompt police action? She really didn't know anything substantive. It was all gleaned from her conversations with Etta, and during most of them Etta had been talking in a drug-induced haze or in her sleep. Fragmented, fanciful statements that might be fact or dream.

Dani sensed strongly that Etta was in danger. She worried about her. Feared for her. She was surprised by how intensely she cared.

Rica was tired enough that when she entered her apartment the first thing she thought about was dropping into bed and letting herself go unconscious.

Then she noticed the desk by the window. Something maybe only a cop would have noticed. Rica always, *al-*

ways, closed drawers all the way after opening them. Some kind of anal thing, she'd once been told. Well, maybe.

But one of her desk drawers was open perhaps a quarter of an inch. The drawer where she kept her notes on the Torcher case.

Before going to the desk, she glanced around.

Everything seemed okay, undisturbed. Except for that lamp shade that was slightly crooked, as if somebody might have brushed it. She might have brushed it herself on the way out and not realized it.

Rica wasn't the sort to stand and agonize. She did a quick walk-through of the apartment, which didn't take long, considering the size of the place. She encountered no monsters, and nothing else seemed to have been disturbed.

She went back into the living room and examined the desk.

The contents of the drawer had definitely been disturbed. Her notes were at a slightly different angle to the sides of the drawer, and she was sure a paper clip had been lying on top of them.

Stack! He must have come in and looked at her case notes. Checking on her, in their new intimacy. What was hers was his.

Screw that!

Then it occurred to her that he didn't have a key. She smiled. That would be no problem for an experienced cop like Stack.

Stack, all right. Something to know about him. Maybe he'd say something about it to her. She'd wait for that. See what happened.

Then she told herself to ease up, she was thinking and acting out of exhaustion. There was probably a reasonable explanation for the drawer business, and she was the one being paranoid. Stack might only have wanted to refresh his memory about some aspect of the case, so he'd dropped by when she wasn't home and done just that. They were sleeping together, so why shouldn't he feel free to take that liberty? There was no real reason to believe he'd be checking on her work.

She made extra sure the door was locked, then staggered toward the bedroom already beginning to undress.

Lying in bed, she thought about what had happened. Maybe she was unused to intimacy and that was why she was making too much of a small thing. It could happen when you lived alone, lived for your work. It could happen. Especially when you were so tired and not thinking straight. . . .

By the time she fell asleep, she was no longer mad at Stack.

No longer uneasy.

No longer on guard.

FORTY-ONE

The next afternoon, Chips dropped Mirabella off at work, and at the last moment, just before she closed the car door behind her, told her he'd be seeing somebody in the city about a consultant's job and would spend the night there. He'd be home sometime the next morning, and she wasn't to worry about him.

But she was worrying already, he could tell.

Consultant's job! Does he think I'm brain-dead? "Listen, Chips, why don't you just tell me—"

"I'll explain later," he said, glancing behind him. "I can't stay parked here, baby. I hate spending the night away from you. It's business."

"But what kind of—"

"Baby, I gotta go." An angry horn blast behind the Neon made Mirabella jerk. Good. "See, I'm holding up traffic parking here. I'm a navigational hazard."

"But, Chips—"

"Tomorrow morning, baby." He blew her a kiss. The driver behind him gave the horn two long blasts this time.

"Blow it out your . . ." Mirabella was shouting at the driver, as Chips pulled the Neon back out into traffic and drove away. There was no doubt she was upset.

Chips was breathing kind of fast, but he felt okay about this. You could trust any woman only so far, even a dumb one like Mirabella. When he got back to the house in New Jersey, he'd pack his suitcase and put it in the car with what he'd need for the job. Maybe drive the Neon to Philadelphia and leave it in the airport parking garage, then buy a ticket to Boise. He knew somebody in Boise, and the law would never think of looking for a guy like Chips in a place like Boise, was his reasoning. Though he'd never been to Boise.

"We'd like to speak with you," Rica said to Myra Raven. She'd been sitting at Stack's desk and working the phone most of the afternoon, when at 4:10 P.M. she was finally able to get through to the real estate maven. Myra Raven, according to the receptionist, had been in a meeting all afternoon. Rica would bet that if the receptionist had a wooden nose, it would be about the size of a two-by-four.

"Speak with *me?* The police? About what?"

Rica picked up something in the woman's voice. *Why do I think you've been avoiding this conversation?* "It's just a routine matter concerning the Torcher murders. We thought you'd be the logical person to ask some general questions regarding New York real estate."

"Me? But, why?"

Rica put a deliberate chuckle in her voice. "Well, I guess it's just because yours is the most successful real estate agency in town, and everybody else we've asked about the subject recommended we talk with you." Another chuckle, like the ones in Stack's repertoire. "You're what we in police work call an expert."

"As in expert witness?"

"Oh, I don't think it would go that far. It's just that if we knew more about New York real estate, the investigation might go easier. Your chance to perform a public service, I guess. We'll hardly trouble you. We'll come to you, and I promise we won't take up much of your time."

"Well . . ."

"It could be great publicity for your company. Unless of course you wanted to keep our conversation confidential." *You don't have a reason to refuse, lady. Unless you want to attract suspicion.*

Myra Raven said nothing. Neither did Rica. She knew when not to talk.

After a long pause, Myra's defeated voice came over the line. "I would insist on confidentiality. For business reasons."

"You would know best about that," Rica said, with a huge grin. "We can be at your office in fifteen minutes, get it over with."

"Today, you mean?"

"It happens I'm on a cell phone, and we're only a few blocks away from you."

A sigh like water from a tap came over the phone. "All right. Anything to help the police stop these ghastly fires. Not only are they tragic in human terms, they're terrible for business."

"I can imagine," Rica said. "See you soon." She hung up the phone before Myra Raven could change her mind, then looked up at Stack, who'd been standing next to his desk listening to the conversation.

"Bullshit like magic," he said with a smile.

"I learned from a master."

"We'll use the light and siren for a while," he said. "Maybe we can make it in less than fifteen minutes. If she's got something to be nervous about, it's all the better if we're a little late and she has to wait."

At that moment in New Jersey, Larry Chips was hefting his suitcase into the backseat of the Neon. There would be room in the trunk, but he didn't want his clothes to pick up any of the accelerant scent.

He shut the Neon's door and went into the garage. On the workbench were five leak-proof containers that were ice bags of the type used by hospitals to relieve swelling and headaches. They were pliable plastic encased in rubberized blue felt. Once full and attached with duct tape to his inner thighs, his waist, and the small of his back, they would conform to the shape of his body and draw no attention beneath his knee-length coat. Though they were plastic, it would take a long time for the accelerant to cause enough of a chemical reaction for them to leak. Chips had been using them for years, using phony ID if he had to in order to buy them from medical supply stores; they were ideal for his purpose.

Using a metal oil-change funnel, he carefully transferred the contents of most of the orange juice bottles into the ice bags. As an afterthought, he filled two more of the plastic bags to put in his coat's generous side pockets. He didn't spill a drop.

When he was finished, he arranged the swollen ice bags on the workbench and stepped back. He was satisfied with his preparations, still relaxed, though soon he'd be on edge in the way he enjoyed.

There was only one ice bag left over. He carried it with him into the house, then went to the kitchen and got some ice from the refrigerator. It wasn't the kind of refrigerator that supplied crushed ice, so he had to dump a couple of trays in the sink and break up the cubes using an ice pick. Scratched the hell out of the sink, but what did he care? He'd stuff some ice in the plastic bag, add water, then sit on the sofa with the bag over his eyes and forehead, taking it easy and going over in his mind his plans for the evening. He could unwind completely that way, wait for the edge, and the cold bag would help him relax and at the same time keep him from drifting off to sleep.

It felt good, knowing he was leaving New York tonight. He'd done enough here, shown himself to too many people. Though that old photo the cops and media were flashing around no longer looked much like him, there was still a chance some sharp citizen would recognize him, then phone *America's Most Wanted* or some such shit. He remembered an old guy, name of Ernie, who was so afraid of being on one of those TV shows he couldn't even watch football, thinking there might be a network commercial—

Enough ice. He turned on the cold side of the tap and held the ice bag beneath the spigot. Good. Still not a drop spilled. A challenge met. That meant his luck would hold tonight. He began screwing the bag's white plastic cap back on.

"Chips."

He spun around, feeling cold water splosh over the webbing between his thumb and forefinger.

Mirabella was standing in the kitchen doorway. "Jesus, baby! You scared the hell out of me. I thought you were at work."

A funny look in her eye. Not exactly anger. Not exactly fear. "You got a headache, Chips?"

"Matter of fact I do. I was gonna turn on some music, lay back on the couch, and try to relax with this ice bag on my head." Keeping his voice casual. "How come you came home? You're feeling okay, aren't you?"

"I didn't feel right about the way we left each other, you saying you wouldn't be home this evening. All night, you were gonna be gone. But here it is evening, and you're home."

"I came to pick up some things; then I'm gonna drive back into the city."

"You can't do any of that if you're laying on the sofa with an ice bag on your head."

"I didn't plan on getting a headache." He made himself grin. "Hey, why the interrogation?"

"I got to thinking about a lot of things, Chips. About us."

He nodded. "I think about us all the time."

"I saw your suitcase in the car, Chips." She moved farther into the kitchen now, maybe starting to get really mad, hurt. "I saw the garage door was open and went inside. There are more ice bags on the workbench. I unscrewed the cap on one to see what was inside." Another step toward him. "I'm not stupid, Chips. I know who you really are. You're the Torcher. I just want you to—"

Jesus! Where'd the ice pick come from? How'd it get back in my hand?

It was as if the ice pick had a mind and mission of its own, as if it were pulling Chip's hand rather than him pushing it into Mirabella low between her breasts, then up into her heart, almost lifting her off the kitchen floor. She made only a slight sound, a funny little *"Uhnn!"* Then she fell back and down, sliding off the ice pick.

Chips had always heard that once you killed, it was easier each time. He guessed now that was true. He even tried to feel remorse but couldn't. His mind, bent on self-preservation, was too busy racing ahead to explore the new terrain of his life.

In a way, Mirabella was now a problem solved. A problem he hadn't asked for. So why should he feel guilty? The truth was, any second she mighta gotten a wild hair up her ass and called the law down on him. At least Chips knew now where she was, what she was doing. On the kitchen floor, doing nothing. Guilt? Piss on it. Why should he feel guilt?

What did bother him, what was kind of eerie, was the look on Mirabella's face when the ice pick went in. Not really surprised. It was if she'd been expecting something like what happened. Like it was why she'd come back home.

Chips understood women. He knew she *had* come back just so she could catch him in a lie, so he'd have to show her he loved her enough not to kill her. That was what she wanted, but not what she really expected. She got what she expected. She put him in a position where he didn't have any choice.

He stared down at her body where she'd rolled onto her side against the cabinets under the sink. Her skirt was up around her thighs, twisted tight. One red high-heeled shoe was off except right at the toes. *Fuckin' loser! What else could I do?*

He dumped the ice and water from the plastic bag into the sink, then carried the bag out to the garage.

When he came back, the bag was full. He carried it into the kitchen and glanced again at Mirabella's body. *Worthless bitch!* He was still so mad at her, at what she'd done to him, that he felt like kicking her. He actually drew back his right foot, then stopped.

What good would it do?

What would it change?

FORTY-TWO

The interview with Myra Raven might have gone better.

"What do you think?" Rica asked, as Stack maneuvered the unmarked through heavy midtown traffic.

"Myra's a tough number. And smart."

"She was playing dumb," Rica said.

Stack steered around a florist's delivery van parked with its flashers blinking and turned a corner, then had to brake again and join a new line of stalled traffic. Rica watched his set features in the reflection of oncoming headlights. She knew his mind was working relentlessly behind that Mount Rushmore exterior. *Give the man time to think.*

After another two blocks of stop and go, she finally said, "So how do you see it?"

"We keep Myra in mind," Stack said.

"That's all? Keep her in mind?"

"No," Stack said, "that's not all. We go over those co-op board minutes again, the ones where she was mentioned. We talk to her employees, see if we can get one of her salespeople to—"

The radio crackled and a patched-through call came in on the detectives' band. Rica recognized Mathers's voice. "Stack, we just got a squeal on a homicide in an electronics store around Fifty-sixth and Lex. You and Rica will be interested."

"We're near there now," Stack said, and punched the accelerator.

Officer Dennis Blainer was a sixteen-year veteran of the NYPD. He sat on a big Samsonite suitcase on display near the door, thinking about how it had all happened. And what it might mean to him.

Rattling doorknobs. That was how it started. That was how a lot of things started, when you were walking a beat. You rattled doorknobs, making sure a property was secure. That was what beat patrol was all about. It was boring most of the time, almost *all* the time, strolling from one shop door to the next, gripping cold metal with your gloved hand, giving a doorknob a quick turn or pressing a swinging door to make sure it was locked.

Automatic, almost hypnotic, was the act of walking a beat in this part of the city.

Until one of the doorknobs turned.

So the owner or manager forgot to lock up when he left. It's happened before.

Without opening the glass door, Blainer peered through it into the shop's dark interior. He saw nothing but shadows and stillness. *Place might as well be a photograph.*

He was about to turn away when a dull gleam caught his eye, like something had moved and reflected what little light there was. It had been real. He was positive.

Blainer felt his heart jump. He backed away, out of sight of anyone who migʰt be inside. Then he used his two-way to call for backup, drew his gun from its holster, and kicked up his courage to enter the store.

It was one of several electronics stores in the area, the kind that sold luggage, plastic Statues of Liberty and Empire State Buildings, and umbrellas. But mostly its profit came from cameras, watches, cell phones, stereos, and various handheld electronic devices for everything from reading novels to surfing the Internet.

Blainer had been around. He knew enough to reach up and use his cupped hand to silence any bell that might be above the door. Only there was no bell. Instead there was an electric eye somewhere that sounded a brief but loud electronic beep. Blainer immediately chastised himself. *What the fuck did you expect, in an electronics store?*

He stood still just inside the doorway, listening to his breathing and the distant whisper of traffic, not knowing one from the other. Then he heard something else, a slight scraping sound, coming from the back of the store. As if someone had bumped into something and moved it on a concrete floor.

His limbs stiffened by fear, he made himself get away from the doorway so he wouldn't be such an inviting target. Part of him wanted to slide over a few feet, then slip back out the door and get as far away from the place as he could. But that was impossible. That wasn't his job.

Slowly he made his way toward the faint sound. Whoever might be there would make it out the back way soon—if there was a back way. He didn't like himself for it, but he found himself hoping there was another way out.

There was only silence as Blainer edged through almost total darkness toward a doorway with a heavy curtain pulled across it. The entrance to the storage room, no doubt.

That was when he smelled the fumes. Something like gasoline.

He didn't hear any backup coming, but he knew that with a possible burglary-in-progress they'd be driving without lights or sirens. They might be close. Might even be out there.

He moved toward the doorway and felt for hinges but found none. So the door, now missing, had opened away from his side. Which meant the wall switch should be just around the corner from where he was standing. If he found and flipped that switch, he'd be standing in darkness, and whoever might be back in the storeroom would be illuminated.

A plan. A fuckin' plan . . .

Blainer held his breath as he slowly snaked his arm around in the darkness, felt rough plaster, then the smooth plastic of a switch plate. A toggle switch. His heart started a wild hammering but his mind was calm. It was almost as if he were standing off to one side watching what was happening here.

Freeze! I always wanted to yell Freeze!

He flipped the switch up, then kept his silhouette slim as possible as he hugged the side of the doorway and aimed his 9mm into the storeroom, peering over the barrel where the curtain was pushed away.

"Freeze, you bastard!"

Holy shit! He was looking at a guy on the floor with his head in a pool of blood. Then, suddenly, he was aware of someone else in the storeroom, looking at *him!*

In an instant Blainer saw the trapped, frightened expression on the man's face, the gun in his hand. The guy was . . . Yeah, Chips! That Larry Chips everybody was so hot on finding!

The gun in the man's hand rose and flame leaped from its barrel.

The bullet nicked the door frame, then Blainer's shoulder, sending him backward to a sitting position on the floor. The blast of the shot seemed to slow time. Blainer ignored the ringing in his ears and looked around. There was his gun, lying by his right leg. He was reaching for it when Chips burst from behind the storeroom curtain, tearing it off its moorings, and dashed past him.

Real time again! The curtain had landed on Blainer. He hurled it away from his face, found his gun, and got off a shot at Chips just as he was yanking open the street door and actually leaping outside. Heard Chips yelp. He knew he'd hit him!

When Blainer tried to stand up and give chase, he put his weight on his right arm, and the pain went through it like a lightning strike and dropped him back down. For a moment he thought he might have been shot a second time.

He lay writhing and cursing, then tried again, more slowly and carefully, to get to his feet.

He managed, but he knew it was way too late. Unless he'd hit Chips where it would slow him down, he'd be blocks away and gaining speed.

Blainer staggered to a display of big suitcases in the middle of the shop and sat down on one, bending over and holding his shoulder just below where it was bleeding. He was afraid to touch the actual wound.

He heard a faint metallic squeal outside and the *shuu-*

ush of rubber on concrete. A car pulling rapidly to the curb.

A stolid figure appeared in the doorway, off to the side, gun drawn. Blainer recognized the dark clothing, the paraphernalia dangling from the figure's belt, the uniform cap. He caught the glint of a badge. Backup had arrived.

"It's clear," Blainer said. "C'mon in."

The patrol car cop played a narrow flashlight beam over Blainer, then stepped inside and found a light to turn on.

"Smells like gas in here," he said. A young guy, stocky and with only dark bristle between his cap and ears, looking not at all afraid. *"O-leen,* I mean."

"Better not touch anything else," Blainer said. "There's a homicide victim on the floor in back. Dead, I mean."

"The owner?"

"That'd be my guess."

"How 'bout the perp?"

"Alive but long gone. Maybe with a bullet in him."

The cop saw for the first time that Blainer's shoulder was bleeding. "I'll call for the paramedics," he said. "Then I'll notify Homicide, get the yellow tape, and establish a crime scene."

It already is a crime scene, unless you plan on committing another one. But Blainer didn't voice his thoughts. Young cops!

EMT got there five minutes after the first homicide detectives, and were about to load Blainer into an ambulance, when a big guy walked up and asked if it would be okay if they talked for a minute or two before the drive to the hospital. Blainer knew who the guy was: Stack. He'd heard about Stack. Everybody had heard. Blainer had already been told the shoulder wound wasn't serious, so he waved away the paramedics with his good arm and told Stack what had happened.

"Any doubt in your mind it was Chips?" Stack asked, when Blainer was finished.

"None whatsoever. I read the bulletins, studied the picture that's been all over the news. Like the bulletin says, he'd shaved off his facial hair from how it was in the photo. And he was wearing a blue baseball cap. Yankees, I think. Fuckin' shame."

"You sure you winged him?"

"Had to have. I heard him give out a yell, and I think there was a hitch in his gait."

"You sure about the hitch?"

"No. Sure about the yell, though." The female detective with Stack—Rica, he'd called her—had gone inside the store. Sexy little bundle with a great rack. Blainer was glad he could think of such matters; it meant he couldn't be hurt bad, didn't it? Now she was back.

"There's a fair amount of blood just inside the door," she said. "Chips might have been hit solid."

Stack clutched Blainer's good shoulder and gave it an approving squeeze, then nodded to the waiting paramedics.

"The place smells like gasoline inside," Rica said. "There was accelerant splashed all over the storeroom, especially on the dead man's clothes. Chips was about to set the place on fire."

"Yeah," Stack said, watching the red and white ambulance carrying Blainer make a U-turn, then head down Lexington with its lights flashing. "It's what he does, sets fires."

"And shoots people," Rica said, remembering the LA homicide warrant.

"And shoots people," Stack agreed.

Etta and Dani sat across from each other in a dim booth near the back of Shebob's in the Village. Etta was sipping a daiquiri and Dani was working on a Heineken dark. Etta was worried. Dani had phoned and suggested they meet here tonight, hinting there was something they needed to discuss. This, Etta had thought, hanging up the phone, was the way affairs ended.

It was much too warm in Shebob's, and Etta didn't really feel like drinking. What she wanted to do was leave and walk the short distance to Dani's apartment.

"I guess there's a reason you wanted to meet here instead of at your place," she said apprehensively to Dani.

Dani smiled at her. "Are you afraid of the reason?"

"Yes. Should I be?"

"I'm the one who's afraid, Etta."

"You?"

"I'm afraid for you. That something's going to happen to you."

Etta was mystified. "What would happen to me?"

"I don't know, exactly." Dani reached across the table and squeezed her hand.

Dani's hand was cold from gripping the glass of beer. Etta didn't like the way this was going. "But what do you want me to do? How can I reassure you?"

"By quitting your job. Resigning as Leland Brand's advisor."

Etta was astounded. This she hadn't expected. "You

think something bad might happen to me in my work? But why?"

That was one Dani couldn't answer. If Etta knew she'd called the police on the basis of pillow talk Etta hadn't even been aware of, that would be the end for the two of them together. Time to be assertive, which always worked with Etta. "I can't and won't tell you. But let me put it this way, I am telling you to quit."

"Brand won't make it without me," Etta said.

"Maybe that's the idea."

"Whatever you might think about him," Etta said, "it really doesn't matter. Politics is nothing more than power finding its comparative levels. Inside that structure are good people and bad people, but the end result is always the same. The good people just suffer more and find different rationalizations to get to the same point. It doesn't make any difference in the long run if I'm working for a saint or for somebody like Leland Brand."

"That's a cynical point of view."

"I'm in a cynical business. I didn't make it that way."

"I don't care about any of that. Quit the bastard, Etta." Etta began gnawing her lower lip, trying to understand this unexpected development. Then she had to ask. "Or? . . ."

Dani tossed back the rest of her beer and looked hard at her. "You work it out."

Five minutes later they were walking together through the cold night, toward Dani's apartment.

FORTY-THREE

Myra had been trembling when the cops left her yesterday afternoon. The cold lump of dread in her stomach had stayed with her the rest of the evening, and all day today. She hadn't been treated with such disrespect for years. Wasn't used to it, didn't deserve it, didn't like it.

The female detective, that goddamned Rica Lopez, had misled her on the phone. From the moment Amy had shown the two detectives into her office—Lopez looking more like a Latin sexpot than a cop, Stack like some kind of shopworn movie hero who should be playing straight-arrow Harrison Ford roles—Myra knew it was going to be bad. She hadn't imagined just how bad.

After only a few general questions about New York real estate, there'd been a subtle but definite shift in the conversation. Everything Stack asked seemed to have a double meaning, and one Myra grasped seconds after it was too late. He was so reassuring, maturely handsome and polite, and seemed so innately kind, that the answers seemed to slip from her before she could weigh them. Lopez would stay out of it except to make a remark now and then that would keep Myra off balance. Then Stack would refer to Myra as "dear" and close in like a shark. They had a hell of an act, those two.

Myra had been prepared to lie in answer to direct questions, but direct questions hadn't been asked. Conversationally, between questions, Stack let it be known obliquely that there was a pattern to the murders, and Myra might be part of it. They'd given her a chance to tell them about the pattern herself, to incriminate herself. Of course she hadn't. She couldn't. But not to answer or mention the pattern of the murders was taking a chance. If they did see the entire design, knew what she must know, why would she not acknowledge that such a design existed? What could be motivating her other than guilt?

She'd thought staying late at the office this evening, losing herself in her work, would help. But it hadn't. All day her nerves had been getting progressively more raw. That grinding-away process had continued into the evening.

As she entered her apartment, she tossed her purse down on the table by the door, then strode to the credenza and started to mix a martini. Then she changed her mind and poured herself a straight single malt scotch.

After downing the drink, she felt slightly better. Calmer, anyway, but still devastated, as if she were being torn down brick by brick, pound of flesh by pound of flesh. She kicked off her high-heeled shoes, the left one so hard it bounced off a wall and left a mark like a dark comma.

The sudden action, along with the drink, temporarily lowered the pressure on her. She'd been angry and depressed, in a mindless funk far too long. That wasn't her. Not her at all.

Myra knew her mind was working better now; she could think her way through this, do what was necessary. She'd been doing that almost all her life, so why not this time?

She strode into the bedroom and changed into jeans, a bulky gray cable-knit sweater, and jogging shoes. Then she walked into the bathroom to apply a cool washcloth to her forehead with one hand while she used the other to brush her teeth. The milk glass tumbler she used to rinse out her mouth was on the left of the washbasin's marble vanity rather than the right, but she failed to notice.

She replaced her toothbrush in its holder, then patted her forehead and set the cool washcloth aside, feeling at least somewhat renewed.

One more scotch, despite the minty aftertaste of the toothpaste, so her nerves grew steadier while her mind still functioned. She sat on the living room sofa and sipped from a Waterford on-the-rocks glass while she gazed out the wide window at the lighted city. Here was where Myra did her best thinking, where she accepted reality and mapped her strategies in the war of life. Everything was coming to a head, that was for sure. She had to act. Myra was no fool. She knew they might be watching her, waiting for her to make the next move. Even so, after contemplating the future, weighing the risks, she simply had to act.

She glanced at the mantel clock. Still early enough. Tonight. There was no reason to wait. It might be ruinous to wait. Why not tonight?

Her building had a seldom-used side door anyone staking it out might not know about. Dressed as she would be, in her jeans, with a dark navy jacket and knit watch cap, even if they happened to see her leave, they might not recognize her. She wouldn't be wearing anything that could be described as a disguise, but at a distance she'd look unlike her usual self, and she wouldn't act in any way furtive. It was possible that she might slip past unnoticed if they were watching the building.

She set the half-empty glass aside, then stood up and went to the closet for her coat and hat. After putting them on, she decided gloves would be a good idea. Black leather dress gloves.

Before leaving the apartment, she checked her image in the mirror. Middle-aged, trendy woman, lean and with some angles, harshly attractive in dark colors. Smart, cocky, determined. *What I am,* she told herself. *What I am.*

She keyed the dead bolt when she left, locking in the demons of uncertainty and pessimism. Myra was out in the world and taking action. Doing something.

It felt good to be doing something, even if it might be wrong.

From across the street, the Torcher watched Myra Raven round the corner of the building and hurry away down the sidewalk. A silver lighter clicked, flame appeared, then quickly disappeared. *Click!* Again. *Click!* Myra probably hadn't yet missed the lighter, and if she had, too bad. She didn't really deserve it, anyway. And it didn't make any difference now.

How could Myra Raven think she wouldn't be noticed, with her lean build even in her bulky coat, her almost masculine walk that bespoke authority? Like a marathon runner's stride, every motion of every part of her body on the line of her direction, no wasted or hindering sideways movement. There was a deceptive speed to that purposeful, rhythmic walk. Myra Raven would get where she was going faster than she knew.

Click!

The Torcher emerged from the shadowed doorway and followed.

The terror had grown in Myra. Stack and the bitch Rica wouldn't stop with their one interview. They hadn't been satisfied, that was for damn sure. They underestimated Myra if they thought she hadn't seen through them. They'd never stop, neither one of them, ever.

She should never have left proof, she thought, as she shivered in the cold and hurried from the subway stop toward her office building. There was no way to retain proof without also keeping records. Myra had to have records, had to know what transgressions had been committed so that if pressed in the future she could defend herself with facts. A precaution.

One that had turned into potential evidence in a criminal trial. Dates and times and names and payments that were all cash transactions. They would coincide with other information. They would lead to more questions, if not by the law, then by the media. Myra knew she was something of a celebrity in New York, even though it was true she'd paid for the advertisements that made her so. Day after day there was her name in the media, there was her photograph every weekend in the real estate section of the Sunday *Times*. Her success, who she was, would make her a story, and a big one.

More questions and answers, more information about Myra, further and further into the past, wider and wider into the more immediate. It wouldn't simply be the questions about illegal cash transactions and real estate deals.

Those questions would lead only to the destruction of the Myra Raven Group. The other questions would lead to Myra Ravinski, and to the destruction of Myra Raven.

Myra reached her building and thought of sneaking into the garage, using her key to elevator up to her office floor and maybe not be noticed. But that would be a mistake. Why should she sneak? That was the way they wanted her to think and act, as if she were guilty of something. She used the number code on an outside keypad to activate the intercom and buzzer.

When Barry, the night watchman, appeared on the other side of the glass doors, he squinted at her, then recognized her and smiled.

He came through the inside doors, then crossed the tile foyer and unlocked the door alongside the row of frozen revolving doors.

Barry was a large Hispanic man with a mane of white hair and a beautiful smile. He'd once mentioned to Myra that he had eight grandchildren. "Miz Raven! You forget something?"

"Again," she said, smiling apologetically. Though in truth she hadn't returned to the building for a forgotten item in months. *An anomaly. The police search for those and use them to good advantage.* "And I got restless and thought I might catch up on some paperwork," she added.

"You ought to get you one of those little computers 'bout the size of your hand, do your paperwork on that at home. Technology."

Cover that earlier lie to Barry. The police will be checking. "I already have one of those, Barry. That's what I forgot." *Tangled webs, tangled webs . . .*

"See," Barry said, pressing the elevator's UP button for

her, "they need some kinda reminder technology to prevent that."

Less than five minutes later, Myra entered the Myra Raven Group offices and switched on the lights. She didn't even bother removing her coat before striding directly to her office.

The lights there had come on with the outer lights, so she crossed to her big desk, clear of paperwork and clutter, clear of almost everything but a phone, a leather-edged desk pad, and success, and stooped down alongside it. The scent of lightly oiled, expensive wood was somehow reassuring. She felt beneath the desk, tripped a tiny lever, and with a barely audible click the entire end panel popped out just far enough for her to grip its back edge. She swung the panel wide to reveal the secret and fireproof safe where she kept the records she wanted no one but herself to see.

It took only a few seconds to work the safe's simple combination and open the insulated steel door.

Myra gasped and felt a chill run through her as she tried to comprehend what she was seeing. What it might mean.

The safe was empty. The records had been removed.

There was a whispering sound behind her, like a faint breeze through dark summer leaves. Childhood secrets. Damp basements. *Someone breathing!*

Myra realized someone was standing behind her and tried to turn and straighten up at the same time. Pain exploded brilliant and cold in the back of her skull, then shattered into icy needles throughout her body. She couldn't be sure if she'd managed to stand up very far, only that now she was sinking. Losing consciousness but not terror.

Control! She struggled to keep control, to stay aware. To *be*.

Somewhat surprised, she found herself kneeling. She tried to open her mouth to protest but couldn't unclench her teeth, might have heard, or herself made, some kind of muffled, wounded animal sound.

Something struck her again, this time lower, on the back of the neck. *Different pain. Numbing pain.* She knew there was no point in fighting unconsciousness now; she welcomed it. *Don't hit me again! Please!* Myra Ravinski silently pleaded. *It really isn't necessary . . .*

The last thing she saw as the side of her face slammed unfeelingly into the floor was a folded umbrella leaning in a corner.

Not her umbrella.

Oh, God! . . .

It was almost midnight. Stack and Rica had spent much of last night and most of today putting together what was known about the electronics store murder and Chips's escape after he and Blainer had exchanged shots. Aran Ahib had been the victim's name. Forty-two years old, married with two children. His wife had already driven in this morning from New Jersey and identified him.

If heat had been on Chips before, it was twice as intense now. His name and photo were everywhere, his capture top priority in every cop's mind. He was probably the Torcher. He'd killed a man, then was preparing to burn him to death along with the building where the crime occurred. He'd shot at and wounded a cop in making his escape.

Only Stack, who'd earlier pushed for Chips to be designated the prime suspect, was becoming less sure, now that everyone else seemed convinced Chips was the Torcher.

"You sure we still wanna go over more of those Myra Raven co-op board minutes?" Rica asked. She was getting tired. The hunt was on for Chips as their firebug.

"You think we should be concentrating on Larry Chips?"

Rica wondered why Stack didn't look tired. "Sure. Isn't everyone else?"

He leaned back and looked at her. It was different, she thought, the way he looked at her now, since—

"None of the other Torcher victims had been shot," Stack pointed out. "This fire was going to be in a place of business. The victim lived in New Jersey. And I'll bet that tomorrow the lab tells us the accelerant isn't the same as in the other Torcher murders."

"I've thought of all that," Rica said. "But Chips is what we've got, and he is a fleeing homicide suspect. It's not like running the bastard to ground would be wasted effort, even if he isn't the Torcher."

Stack propped his feet with their clunky black shoes up on the desk and grinned at her. "Rica . . ."

She sighed. "I know. . . ." Getting used to their new relationship, giving him an uneasy, appraising look as if she were somebody who'd just sealed the deal on a high-mileage used car. "Ever consider Italian loafers?" she asked.

"This a political correctness trap?"

"No. You know. The shoes. Loafers with pointed toes, maybe tassels."

"Uh-uh. Never seriously considered them. You gonna try to make me over, Rica?"

"Over and over again."

"Hmmm."

She smiled and shook her head, then walked over to the file cabinets for the co-op board minutes. She gave her hips an extra swish, knowing he was watching. Used the bending motion to reach the lower steel drawer to good advantage, stretching the skirt fabric of her tight red business suit.

"You wear red a lot," he said.

She stood up with a bundle of files and stared innocently at him, knowing he saw through her. "You don't like red?"

"It isn't that. The expression 'plainclothes' means—"

Stack's desk phone jangled. Still looking at her, he lifted the receiver. "Stack." His gaze remained locked with hers. "Yeah. Yeah." Something changed in his eyes. They were no longer seeing her. "Okay. Sounds like it. Got it. Thanks." He hung up the phone. "There's been another high-rise fire, and we've got another body."

"Chips again, you think?" She placed the file folders on the desk.

"I don't know." He recited the address of the fire.

"The Myra Raven Group."

"A smaller group now," he said.

FORTY-FOUR

The fire had been neatly contained, and there was the black, half-folded umbrella propped against the desk.

"Shame about the desk," the ME said. "It was a beauty."

An odd thing for him to say, Stack thought, considering a woman had died here. He glanced around. "Where's the body?"

"At Roosevelt," the ME said. "EMT just left with her. I was called here because the first officers on the scene assumed the victim was dead. She sure looked dead and will probably be dead by tomorrow. Second-and third-degree burns over most of her body."

"Can she speak?"

"Get serious," said the ME. "She suffered head injuries also. Looks like somebody bludgeoned her, then bound her with black ties before setting fire to her." He looked over at the discarded umbrella. "The night security guard must have scared your firebug away; then the sprinkler system did its job well enough to keep the victim alive until he got to a fire extinguisher."

"Is there a chance she'll be able to talk—"

"Before she dies? No. I doubt if she'll regain consciousness. Her stopping breathing is just a formality. You might as well look on this one as a homicide."

Stack thanked the ME and looked around at the charred office and soaked, burned carpet. At what appeared to be the remains of a leather coat and a few strands of black cloth, where Myra must have lain while she burned.

Men's ties. Stack wondered if O'Reilly was right and the ties were linked to sadomasochism—ties were a convenient way to bind without much bruising, and could be purchased without embarrassment or undue attention. It was difficult to believe eroticism wasn't somehow involved. Serial killers were usually psychosexually driven.

Stack swallowed a terrible taste and tried not to inhale too deeply the sweet burnt scent of roasted human flesh. The smell, even the taste of these fires, wasn't something you got used to. It was more like something that built and built until you couldn't stand it any longer. Stack was beginning to understand the vegetarian point of view.

"I guess Myra's no longer a suspect," Rica said sadly. "If she ever really was."

Stack glanced over at her. "Isn't she?"

"Don't play cryptic with me, Stack. If you didn't have stamina and a big—"

"Rica!"

One of the techs bustling around the office looked at Stack and grinned in a way Stack didn't like. If this guy—

"You see the desk?" the tech asked.

What is it with this desk? Stack turned and looked.

"Near where the victim was," the tech said.

Now Stack saw what he meant. So did Rica. She and Stack slogged across the mushy carpet together and looked at the way the desk's end panel protruded a few inches. Stack poked a ballpoint pen behind the panel, then swung it out.

"My, my," Rica said.

The door of the shallow steel safe that had been concealed in the desk was also slightly open. Standing aside, using the pen again, Stack slowly opened the steel door all the way.

The safe was empty. Which meant its contents were probably the reason Myra Raven was murdered. If Myra wasn't the Torcher, she was in the case up to her eyeballs. If she still had eyeballs.

Stack and Rica looked at each other.

"You still tired?" Stack asked.

"Somehow I'm not," she told him.

She knew he didn't have romance in mind.

In a back booth of the bar at the Edmundton Hotel in Manhattan, Milton Fedders was working on his fourth bourbon and water of the evening. Nobody paid much attention to him, another slightly overweight, middle-aged businessman in a rumpled off-the-rack suit, a tie loosened as if he'd had a rough day and had worked late and was choking to death on his fate. Or maybe he was a road warrior sales type and had struck out on a critical deal, and now the flight back to the home office would be a glum one. Clean shaven, thinning gray hair, weak chin, nothing unusual or impressive about Milton Fedders. No way to look inside his mind at the raw, pulsing pain.

Aran was dead. That hadn't been part of the plan when Fedders hired Chips. It sure as hell hadn't. Without lifting his elbow from the table, Fedders raised his glass and took a long sip of his diluted drink. Nothing should have gone wrong. Nothing could have!

But it had. Now Aran was gone, and his wife Zel was a widow, and the kids . . . Jesus, the kids!

Chips had been so positive. He'd been recommended by a reliable source on the West Coast, had come even more highly recommended by a previous client. And meeting Chips had reassured Fedders. Chips had done this dozens of times, he'd told Fedders. Nothing ever went wrong, because it was so simple, because he had the cooperation of the owner, because he was a pro who took pride in his work. Fedders believed him.

Chips had obviously believed Fedders when Fedders told him his business partner and part owner of the electronics store knew about the arrangement but wanted to stay out of it as much as possible. Fedders had lied some more, said he wanted to protect Aran because he was a nervous kind of guy who didn't like this kind of thing, burning down the business for the insurance payout, even if there was a guarantee no one would be hurt.

The truth was that Fedders had floated the idea past Aran only once, and Aran had been horrified by the mere thought of it. Fedders had gone on to assure Aran he'd only been joking, musing out loud. An honest and sweetly naive man, had been Aran. Surely he'd thought the matter was settled, that they were going to continue grossing less than they owed while loan interest ate their business, then put them on the street with their pockets turned inside out.

So Fedders went ahead anyway and hired Chips, figuring that even if Aran might—even *would*—suspect he, Fedders, had something to do with the convenient and profitable fire, he would never ask Fedders about it and risk confrontation and learning what he didn't want to know.

It should have gone smoothly. Fedders and Aran should both be in a position now to cash the insurance settlement check, pay off the business debt, and have money left over.

But now Aran was dead. Fedders was despondent. And Chips was wounded and would probably be caught soon. According to the police, Chips was the Torcher. That meant the law would never stop searching for him until he was found. Then, if Chips survived the inevitable confrontation, he would surely talk and bargain for a better position in the legal system, try to save his own life. Everything would be known.

Not that it mattered now. What really mattered was Aran, and Zel, and the kids. Fedders might be a lot of things, but he'd never seen himself as a murderer. But now he was one. Chips had made him one.

Then Fedders remembered the cop who'd been shot. He, Milton Fedders, was responsible for that shooting, too. They came down hard on people involved in cop shootings. And who could tell from the newspaper or TV how badly somebody was wounded? If the cop should die . . . Two deaths. Fedders would be a multiple murderer.

Fedders actually moaned, then glanced about to make sure he hadn't attracted anyone's attention. The bartender, a large black man wearing a red vest, remained standing behind the bar, talking to the loudmouthed guy who'd proclaimed he was from Detroit. The well-dressed couple near the door were still in the booth up front, near the archway into the lobby, interested only in each other and out of earshot anyway. Nobody seemed even to know Fedders was there. Fedders the murderer. Aran . . .

Whenever he made himself stop thinking about Aran, he couldn't keep his mind off what was in his suit coat's right pocket. It was almost like premonition, like fate at work, when he'd agreed to take in the 9mm Ruger hand-gun as partial payment for a display model Sony CD player. It was almost as if Fedders, or the down-and-out-looking man who'd brought the Ruger in with an improbable story about finding it in a trash can, had some-how sensed he might have a use for the gun. Milton Fedders, who hadn't shot a gun in years and didn't even like guns, who thought they were dangerous to whoever owned them, who had no use for guns.

He had a use for this gun now. It would be after this drink, maybe some of another. He'd know when it was time. When Milton Fedders, murderer of Aran Ahib and seducer of Zel Ahib, would be ready to go out to his car and use the gun on himself.

"They've got this bastard now," Leland Brand said to Etta. "It's only a matter of time before they take him alive or dead." There wasn't much doubt in his mind it would be dead. That was what Brand wanted, for the Torcher, Larry Chips, to die. Finality. Voters loved closure. "It's going our way, Etta. We can do as you suggested, make clear that my involvement, my prompt action and the pressure I applied to the police, led to the end of the Torcher fires."

Etta had been standing at the closed glass doors to the balcony, staring out at the cold, brightly lighted city.

Behind her, Brand said, "You mentioned there was something you needed to tell me, Etta."

She stood very still for a moment, gathering her thoughts, her words. Making sure her mind was made up. To gain something, you often had to give up something of lesser value. It required intestinal fortitude, and afterward, if you were smart, you never looked back. That was what she'd told most of her clients. It was true for everyone at one time or another. Now it was true for her. The thing about a fork in life's road was that you kept moving as it approached. You had to choose or you crashed.

Finally she turned around to face Brand.

"The former chief of police is one of your likely future competitors for office of mayor," she said. "I think we can link him to the funds that disappeared from the board of education five years ago. It's not a solid connection, but it's enough. Whether it's true or not, once we tie that can to his tail, he's out of the race."

Brand grinned. "You do think ahead, Etta. A long way."

She smiled. "That's why you pay me, Leland. A lot."

It was with renewed enthusiasm that Stack and Rica tackled the co-op board meeting minutes, along with their growing file on Myra Raven and her real estate agency. They were back at Stack's desk, Stack in his desk chair, Rica in a padded chair she'd rolled in from another office cubicle.

They weren't sure exactly what they were searching for regarding Myra Raven, but both suspected it would be found by scrutinizing the board meeting minutes and cross-checking them with information about Myra or the Myra Raven Group.

Stack and Rica had settled down for a long night's work, fueled by a fresh pot of coffee and sheer determination. This was the phase of the investigation that would require almost infinite patience. They were sure they'd found the haystack; now it was only a matter of locating the needle.

"It would have been nice," Rica said, "if you'd found something in my notes that would have broken the case."

"Yeah," Stack said absently, then glanced up at her. "What are you talking about?"

"You let yourself into my apartment and looked over my case notes. It's okay. You got a right, and not just because we're partners. Cop partners."

Stack was starting to feel a chill. "Are you saying somebody was in your apartment going through your desk?"

"Of course that's what I'm saying. You—"

"Not me, Rica. Don't go back there. You're coming home with me. Don't go home tonight."

Now it was Rica who felt a shiver pass through her. "That bastard was actually in my place, handling my things . . ."

"It looks that way."

"We'll find him," she said, more angry now than frightened. She picked up a handful of minutes from the desk. "Even if I have to sit here all night and grow to this goddamn chair."

Stack watched her, afraid for her. Caring about somebody too much again. *Vulnerable again.*

He wasn't quite sure how he felt about that.

Less than an hour passed before Rica suddenly sat straighter, then stood up and carried a file folder out to one of the desks with a computer on it. Stack had caught from the corner of his eye what she was doing, knew she thought she might have something pertinent. But that had been the case with both of them before, and each time, further checking revealed some explanation or undercut whatever lead they thought they might have found.

Stack paused in his work and watched as Rica peered at the glowing monitor and played the computer keys with her left hand, using her right to nudge the mouse this way and that on its Dilbert pad that proclaimed technology was no place for wimps.

Suddenly all movement ceased, even the almost imperceptible dance of her dark irises as they explored the screen's contents. She said, "Holy Christ!"

"You got something?" Stack asked, unnecessarily.

She turned and stared at him with an expression he'd seen on her face only a few times before, during sex.

"I've got everything," she said.

FORTY-FIVE

October 2001

Amy Marks had never gotten over the death of her husband and infant twin daughters. After the first six months, the grief was less a sharp blade in her stomach than a dull ache, but it remained. She'd emerged from clinical depression but continued to take a cocktail of prescription drugs daily. No longer did she attend her cognitive therapy group sessions, but that was her decision and not her analyst's. It was also her decision to stop going to her analyst last year, when she enrolled at the Montrose Real Estate Academy, where she was taking courses that would allow her to pass her state exam and become a sales agent.

Myra Raven had been wonderful since the death of Ed and the twins. She'd provided another apartment for Amy to stay in, found an MD to treat her in conjunction with a psychologist, and picked up all her medical bills. She'd even paid for Ed's funeral. Amy was aware that part of Myra's motive was guilt, that she felt largely responsible for what had happened that night when Ed and the twins died. After all, if the contract for the co-op Amy and Ed thought they'd purchased had gone through, the destruction by fire of their family wouldn't have occurred.

Amy had been in hell for months after the fire; then her pain became such that she simply surrendered to it, let it carry her into a numbness that would have left her as dead as Ed and the twins if Myra hadn't given her a make-work job as file clerk at the agency. The job gave Amy a routine as well as an income, a simple responsibility she could fulfill despite the weight of her grief.

When the other file clerk quit to be married, Amy's job was expanded. She had to be even more responsible and self-disciplined; a mistake now might be costly to the agency and more difficult to rectify. The effort had been good for her, made her feel useful for the first time since the fire. It helped give her the strength to look into the future and enroll at Montrose.

But the night of the fire was always with her, the flames, the cold, sure knowledge of death, the sight of Ed clinging to life high in the air, her own screams, over and over, changing nothing. At times she could feel the almost weightless forms of the twins in her arms, clutched tightly to her, silent and unmoving while she embraced death as if she were nurturing it. Somewhere in her mind, the night, the pain, played almost constantly in her thoughts, in her dreams, darkening like a gray tinting agent each of her days. The only thing that helped, finally, was to lose herself in her studies at Montrose, learn more and more about the business she found herself in.

And the more she learned, the more she wondered about the aborted deal that had deflected her family from the co-op they'd tried to purchase, and placed them in the firetrap walk-up that led to death. When she secretly used a company computer to do an archives search and examine the incomplete transaction, she was surprised to find no record of it. Odd, considering how tightly controlled and easy to track the flow of cash was in the agency. Money had been deposited for a down payment, returned, and the unit was eventually sold by another real estate agency, but under its Myra Raven Group listing.

Maybe not so odd, Amy decided, after mulling it over. She was studying sales, not accounting, so how would she know? It wouldn't do to ask bookkeeping about it, where they might think she was questioning their competence. Or to ask Myra, who'd warned her more than once it was destructive for her to continue dwelling on the past, on Ed and the twins. So Amy remained silent, following what was probably good advice, and picked at mental scabs as little as possible.

About a week later, she'd entered Myra's office without knocking, to drop off the afternoon's mail. A surprised Myra shifted a hip and thigh to one side, against her desk, and gave Amy a look that was unmistakably furtive and hostile before quickly regaining her composure. She also gave Amy a long lecture about the sanctity of her private office and the necessity of knocking.

Chastised, Amy listened quietly and patiently, only later deciding she was sure of what she'd noticed as Myra leaned her weight against the desk. Amy had heard a faint but distinct metallic click. Like the snicking of a well-oiled latch.

It took her four mornings of coming to work early, then finding a way to sneak into the building on Sundays to spend two secret afternoons in Myra's office, to discover the source of the metallic click, and of Myra's furtiveness and momentary hostility the day of the interruption: The trick panel on the side of the cherry-wood desk, and the gleaming steel safe concealed inside.

Of course the safe was locked, and a search of the office for the written combination was futile. But Amy knew every combination was written down somewhere, or it was linked to someone's numerical identity so it would be almost impossible to forget.

She became obsessed with getting into the safe, and at her desk and on the subway and in her bed before sleep, would try to figure out what numbers Myra would choose for the combination. Whenever she had the opportunity she'd try the numbers on the safe. Myra's birth date in various combinations. The agency's address, Myra's home address, phone number . . . all in various sequences.

Finally, in a company four-color brochure, she came across the founding date of the Myra Raven Group, kept scrambling the numbers in different sequences, and the safe opened.

What was inside changed everything.

Over the next week, whenever she found the opportunity to be alone and unobserved in Myra's office, Amy absorbed it all. There were the names and addresses of influential co-op board members who accepted payoff money in return for approving Myra's clients for residency to the exclusion of other applicants. There were the dates and amounts paid. And lots of detailed notes. The safe held a secret record of how the agency had become the most successful in the city. No wonder Myra wanted the contents to remain secret; they were her insurance policy against the threats of her coconspirators, and incriminating enough to put her in prison.

One of the names was of particular interest to Amy:

Hugh Danner. His address was in the Ardmont Arms, where Ed and Amy had been rejected as residents.

Amy stared at the name and address, and read accompanying notes giving details of how the money she and Ed had passed through Myra's hands went to Danner, and how Danner had double-crossed Myra, cast the deciding vote for the board to reject Amy and Ed, and kept their money.

How Hugh Danner had killed Amy's family.

Seated cross-legged on the carpet in Myra's office, staring at the papers before her on the floor, Amy felt all the grief return to her as if it had been circling in time, a dark bird of prey glimpsed only now and then in dreams, patiently winging and waiting and gaining strength before descending on her again.

Its sharp beak found her mortal core and tore at it, releasing her rage.

FORTY-SIX

March 2002

"When I noticed the name Amy Marks on the Myra Raven Group employee list, it all came together," Rica said, still seated at the computer just beyond where Stack sat at his desk.

"The Ardmont Arms co-op board minutes," Stack said, already ahead of her. "Hugh Danner argued and voted against Amy and her husband Ed's application for residency." He was standing now, adrenaline chasing away any semblance of fatigue. "Danner's was the decisive vote. Amy's husband, Ed, was a cop, right?" He realized the back of his hand had knocked his coffee cup from his desk. That was okay. Not much coffee left in it and it hadn't broken. He ignored the cup lying where it had clinked against a wall.

"Yeah, the one who died in that fire, remember?"

Stack remembered, the news of the apartment fire, the deaths of infant children as well as their father. Like most cops, he'd given generously to a benefit fund. "There was something about that fire . . ."

"I've got the report here in the computer. Ed Marks was trapped by the fire. He removed his tie and knotted one end to a radiator so the other end dangled out a fourth-floor kitchen window, hoping if he used the tie to lower himself before dropping, the fall might not prove fatal. But the length of the tie wasn't enough. And Amy Marks watched it all, holding a dead infant daughter under each arm."

"Holy Christ! Isn't that the kind of thing you try not to think about!"

"But if you're Amy Marks, you think about it anyway."

"Every minute, one way or the other, somewhere in your mind, whether you know it or not."

"Ed Marks wouldn't have survived his burn wounds anyway," Rica said. "In fact, he might have been dead before he hit the ground."

"Burned to death . . ." Stack leaned back and propped himself, half seated, against the edge of the desk with his arms crossed. "Black ties were used to bind the Torcher victims. Black ties are part of an NYPD patrolman's uniform." He straightened up and moved toward his desk chair to sit back down, then found that he couldn't. Tension almost hummed in him. He could sense the culmination of the investigation, the hunt, the way a carnivore smelled blood. "Amy must have blamed the co-op board residency rejection by Danner for the destruction of her family in a firetrap walk-up. So in her grief she avenged their deaths."

"Way I see it," Rica agreed. "Then Amy found the contents of Myra's concealed safe, learned through Myra's records that there were other Hugh Danners out there, other co-op board members taking illegal payoffs and rejecting perfectly qualified applicants."

"And she couldn't stop avenging the burning to death of her family."

"Seems to fit," Rica said, "but are we sure about that last part?" For the first time she was feeling some doubt. Niggling, but there. "One murder, yeah. But all the others? . . ."

"I'm sure," Stack said. "The kitchen fires, the symbolic black ties . . . These are the kinds of homicides that set patterns that have to be acted on. Fire and revenge . . . They can both become addictive, increasingly compulsive."

"Like with a psychosexual serial killer? I don't know, Stack . . ."

"Ask an arsonist," he said. "He'll tell you what fire can do, how it can spread in unexpected ways."

Now Rica stood up from where she'd been sitting at the computer. "I guess we have to do that."

She still wasn't as positive as Stack about Amy Marks, but she'd learned to believe in him. And there was one thing they agreed on and couldn't escape.

It was time to visit Officer Marks's widow.

They were halfway there when O'Reilly's rasping voice broke in on the detectives' band on the unmarked's radio. "What's your ten-ten, Stack?"

Stack gave their location: "Driving south on Second Avenue, near Sixty-third."

He watched the traffic ahead, taillights reflecting like bloodstains on a street now glistening in a fine mist.

"Keep traveling the way you're going," O'Reilly said. He gave Stack and Rica a lower Manhattan address and told them to proceed there.

Stack had put up with about enough of O'Reilly. This wasn't the time to indulge him in his misconceptions. "I don't think it's such a—"

"Larry Chips is trapped in an apartment at that address. We're about to go in and get him."

"We?"

"NYPD and FBI. They got the building surrounded and are about ready to move. We need for somebody from MR to be there."

For the career, Stack thought. O'Reilly's career. The wipers, on intermittent, thu-thunked to clear the windshield. Stack figured let the FBI have Chips. They were up to their ears in the case anyway. Interstate flight, insurance fraud. "We got another strong possibility to look into, sir. We're on our way there now."

"Like hell your are!" O'Reilly said. "This is the goddamn Torcher we're talking about!"

Stack and Rica looked at each other.

"Amy can wait," Rica said softly. There was a time to dig in their heels, but this wasn't it. "Let's take the call."

Stack flashed a stubborn glare her way.

Men! Some gender! Stack in particular.

"We don't want it to be Amy, anyway," she said, working hard to keep Stack out of trouble. Something he wasn't used to. "Maybe that asshole O'Reilly's right."

"What?" came the voice over the radio. "What the fuck was that? What'd Rica say?"

Stack realized he'd depressed the mike button early. He left it that way. "Something about you being right. We're proceeding to the scene."

He held the mike button down for a few more seconds so O'Reilly would hear the siren kick in. If Chips was the

Torcher, Mobile Response would have a share of the collar. Under O'Reilly's command. The visit with Ed Marks's widow would have to wait.

Compromise.

Stack thought it left a bad taste.

Sorrow and rage and fear were like a corrosive chemical mix in Amy. She couldn't eat or sleep or even straighten up completely from the pain that was like fire. She'd thought there would be some relief when finally it was over, but it hadn't turned out that way. She knew now that it was over.

She stood up from where she was hunched in the corner of the sofa and trudged into the bedroom. From a closet shelf she got down a shoe box and opened it.

Inside was the one thing that somehow had survived the fire that took her family—Ed's gun. She unwrapped it from the oily rag that preserved it and held it cradled in both hands, then sat on the edge of the bed and stared at it. There was something oddly comforting in its sleek metallic efficiency, the scent of finely machined steel and light oil.

Finally she stood up and went to her dresser. She opened the top, flat drawer and looked at the assortment of objects it held: a comb, a small jewelry box that contained earrings, a watch that had been a gift from Ed and no longer worked, a stack of photographs from years ago before their marriage, a box of bullets.

Amy placed the gun in the drawer next to the bullets, then slid the drawer closed and went to the closet, where she returned the shoe box to the shelf.

With a backward glance at the closed dresser drawer, she walked slowly into the living room and sat down.

Stood up.

Began to pace.

Sleep was out of the question, but she was exhausted and wanted to sit.

Yet she couldn't sit. She couldn't be still. She could only pace, only walk. The fear, the sorrow, the rage, wouldn't let her be still. The pain that was like fire.

At first it looked as if the building where Chips was supposed to be holed up, a brick walk-up off First Avenue, was unoccupied. But it wasn't. As Stack drove the unmarked slowly past the decaying structure, he and Rica saw lights glowing beyond the tattered curtains or yellowed shades in some of the windows. Stack had killed the siren a few minutes after O'Reilly was off the radio; then a few blocks from the building he'd switched off the cherry light and brought it back inside the car. If Chips happened to be looking out a window, the car wouldn't arouse his suspicion.

Stack rounded the corner at the end of the block, and there were the troops. Half a dozen cruisers and some Ford Taurus unmarkeds. Stack knew the Tauruses were FBI. There was a SWAT team van parked farther down the block. Half a dozen dark, bulky figures stood nearby.

"We've been waiting for you," a tall man in a black topcoat said, when Stack and Rica climbed out of the unmarked. Flashing ID, he introduced himself as Special-Agent-in-Charge Matt Perriman. Stack would have known he was FBI even without the credentials.

After Perriman had glanced at Stack's and Rica's shields, he said, "I give the signal, and we close the block on both ends and move in on the building behind the SWAT team."

"You sure Chips is in there?"

"We got it from an informer who's been gold so far."

Stack wasn't going to ask any more questions. He understood the necessity of keeping faith with a reliable informer. Perriman wasn't going to reveal anything more, and Stack didn't blame him.

"Chips is in Two-C, end unit south, second floor."

"Away from the street," Stack said.

"We've got the back of the building covered," Perriman told him. He glanced at his wristwatch. "You wanna lead the way?"

Stack was surprised. "No agency rivalry bullshit?"

Perriman smiled slightly. "No time for it these days. The collar seems to be important to your boss. Me, I just want this piece of crap off the streets."

"We'll do it together," Stack said, "now that you guys are on the side of the angels again."

"Hell of a way to get there," Perriman said. He turned away and ducked his head the way some people did when speaking into a two-way. Then he turned back and said to Stack, "Wanna tell your men to take up their stations?"

Not really a question, Stack thought, looking at the agent's grim features. He nodded to Rica, who hurried toward the parked cruisers. Within seconds, two of the cruisers sped away with no sound louder than the swish of tires, then turned the corner to the block behind the building.

When Stack looked back, he saw that the bulky dark figures of the SWAT team were gone.

Perriman glanced again at his watch. "Okay, we'll walk down the street casually, then we'll go in the front, behind the SWAT guys. We'll follow them to the apartment and they'll go in hard. We'll enter right behind them."

Stack and Rica both nodded, and with Perriman set off down the dark, wet sidewalk. What scarce late-night traffic there had been on the street had now ceased, as Stack was sure had happened on the next block. He hoped Chips wouldn't realize it had suddenly gone quiet outside.

They entered the old building's gloomy vestibule. Stack caught a strong ammonia scent of stale urine but didn't have long to notice. The SWAT detail was waiting. They detached themselves from the walls like deep shadows coming to life, then took the stairs silently, led by two men carrying a three- or four-foot-long battering ram slung between them on straps.

There was no hesitation. Stack and Rica followed Perriman and the bulky shadows along the second-floor hall to 2C. Some of the shadows moved to the side and paused, but the two with the battering ram picked up speed, and the tubular ram swung forward, backward, forward as they strode. It was like a dance done in practiced rhythm to music only they could hear.

Their timing was perfect. The ram struck the apartment's old door with maximum force, splintering it and knocking it completely off its hinges. The SWAT members darted in, guns at the ready.

Stack and Rica exchanged a glance, damned impressed. Like Perriman, they also had their guns out.

Perriman seemed to count silently to about three, then

gave a hand signal and led the way through the door. Stack pushed in front of Rica, irritating her because she knew he was trying to protect her, and they actually charged over the unhinged, splintered door into the apartment.

Silence, stillness, dimness . . . on the edge of the edge . . .

"Clear!" a deep voice shouted.

There was a rushing sound of collective released breath.

The SWAT members in the cramped living room lowered their weapons. Perriman, Stack, and Rica holstered theirs.

Someone switched on the lights.

The place was a mess, with a bare minimum of flea-market furniture, a TV with the screen broken out, some yellowed newspapers and Spanish-language porn magazines scattered over the floor. Stack noticed it smelled like urine in here, too.

And something else.

A SWAT guy in a dark baseball cap with a gold insignia on it appeared in a doorway and motioned for Perriman, Stack, and Rica to enter what turned out to be the bedroom.

Larry Chips was lying on his back on the bed, his legs straight, his feet together, his hands folded peacefully low on his chest, as if he'd assumed the coffin position to make it easy for the mortician. There was a large and messy exit wound in his stomach just below his sternum.

Blainer's bullet had found its target, all right.

"Oh, Christ!" Rica said. Looking at Chips's corpse, the way it was laid out, had reminded her of something.

Stack stared at her. It wasn't like her to gag at the sight of a dead man. Not after what they'd seen lately. "You okay, Rica?"

"The funeral!" Rica said. "Little Eden Wilson's funeral! Amy was there. It didn't ring a bell when we saw her briefly at the Myra Raven Group office, but I'm sure I remember her being there."

"What's this about?" Perriman asked.

"We're not positive," Stack said. "Another lead that probably won't pan out."

He was even more sure than when they'd left the precinct house to visit Amy Marks.

There were voices and footsteps out in the hall and in the living room. The news media had been appropriately notified and had arrived in force and fury.

"No farther," said a cop outside the bedroom. "Nobody goes any farther than this right now. We'll have a statement in a minute."

Rica saw that the blood around the wound, on Chips's shirt and on the sagging mattress, was dark and crusted. Almost black. One of the SWAT guys, following protocol, rested fingertips on Chips's neck just below the ear to feel for a pulse, and Chips's head lolled to the side. Rigor mortis had come and gone.

Rica didn't have to be told Chips had been dead for quite a while. That he must have been already dead when Myra Raven was set on fire. She knew Stack didn't have to be told, either.

There was no doubt now of the truth neither of them wanted to believe.

FORTY-SEVEN

Stack and Rica were silent during the drive across town. They both understood that everything meaningful on the subject had been said. Stack had considered bringing along Perriman and the FBI, the SWAT members and the media hounds. But he knew what that would mean, and Amy Marks was a cop's widow and deserved a chance. Ed Marks was owed something. And Amy was owed something for the loss of her husband and children. The news media, Internal Affairs, a civil review board, might not agree, but Stack saw it as his call and that was the way he'd made it.

He'd voiced none of this reasoning to Rica. There was no need.

Amy Marks lived in a modest but well-kept apartment building on West Eighty-fourth Street. It had a stone fa-cade, green canvas awnings above the ground-floor windows, and wasn't the sort of place that would feature a doorman. Stone planters that held what looked like long-ignored dead mums flanked the entrance. Lights were glowing behind about half the windows.

Stack parked the unmarked a few buildings down the street in a loading zone. He didn't flip down the visor sign identifying it as an NYPD vehicle; it was always possible that Amy was out, would walk past the car on the way home and notice the lowered visor, then turn around and walk fast in the other direction.

Stack and Rica passed no one as they strode back to the building through the cold night, then entered the small outer lobby. It was cold in there, too. Chipped and cracked gray marble ran halfway up the walls. Near the door was some graffiti in black spray paint, recently and ineffectively altered to read BOOK YOU.

There was no way to get farther into the building without using the intercom and being buzzed through. The intercom buttons were beneath rows of brass mail slots, and Stack saw that *A. Marks* lived in 8D, on the top floor. He scanned along the mail slots and was about to press the button for the super when the street door opened behind them and a woman with a baby stroller struggled to enter.

Stack hurried to hold the heavy door open for her, while Rica picked up one of several paper sacks the woman had dropped. Rica noticed the bag contained a loaf of bread and a package of hot dog rolls. Stack was about to compliment the woman on the cuteness of her child, when he saw that the stroller contained only two stuffed grocery sacks from D'Agastino's. He was prepared to show his shield and allay her suspicions so they could gain further entrance, but the woman smiled her thanks to both of them, then asked no questions as they followed her into the main lobby and entered the elevator with her. People should be more careful.

They all exchanged polite smiles again as she got out at three. Stack held the elevator door for her to make sure it wouldn't close as she dragged the heavily laden stroller out.

"Nice woman," Rica said inanely, not knowing why. Nerves?

Stack said nothing.

He and Rica rode alone the rest of the way to the top floor. Rica could feel her heart thumping; her body knew something her mind hadn't quite caught up with. No time to think about it now.

The elevator door slid open, and she and Stack stepped out and walked down the hall to 8D. Stack knocked on the door softly but persistently.

Nothing happened for about a minute; then Rica heard the floor creak slightly on the other side of the door. The light changed in the tiny round glass peephole. They were being observed.

When the light in the peephole changed again, both Stack and Rica expected it was because Amy had stepped back to open the door.

But the door didn't open. There was no more sound from inside.

Rica looked over at Stack and whispered, "She knows what we look like."

That would be true, Stack figured. Not only had she seen them at the Myra Raven Group offices, but their photographs had been on TV and in the papers. Amy was the widow of a cop; she would have been curious about whoever had her case, whoever was stalking her. Possibly she'd been watching them for weeks. As she had been the night of the fire on East Fifty-ninth, when Stack had chased and almost caught her.

He knocked again, louder, this time stepping to the side and motioning for Rica to do the same.

No answer. But Amy was in there. She had to be.

Only one way now.

Stack drew his gun from its shoulder holster. Waited for

Rica to get hers out. She nodded to him. He stepped quickly square to the door and kicked it hard with the sole of his right shoe, just below the doorknob. It splintered away from the frame, sending hardware clattering across the floor. Even before the door could bounce off the wall, Stack and Rica were inside.

No one.

Only a small, neatly furnished living room, unoccupied and with no place to hide. Blue sofa. Wood shelving with books and TV. A table with a lamp glowing. Framed Monet exhibit print on the wall.

But cold. Drafty.

Motioning for Rica to stay behind him, Stack slid along a wall to a doorway, then gripping his heavy revolver with both hands, moved quickly into the apartment's tiny L kitchen.

It was immediately clear why the apartment was cold. The window near the stove was wide open, one sheer curtain swaying, the other pressed by the night breeze to the window frame.

"Fire escape!" Rica said behind Stack.

He went to the window, then carefully peered outside. There was an iron fire escape, all right. He raised a leg and went out over the sill, into the night, pausing to see if he could pick up sound or vibration in the steel made by someone descending.

Nothing.

He moved to the rail and leaned out so he could look straight down.

There was no one on the fire escape.

Eight floors, though. Would Amy have had time to make it all the way to the ground?

When he turned to go back inside, he saw the narrow black steel ladder attached to the brick wall behind him. The fire escape extended to the roof.

As Stack began climbing the ladder, he could see Rica's hand, then leg and hip emerge from the window below. She was coming out to join him.

When he reached roof level, he slowly raised his head to peer over the tile-edged parapet. Rica was right behind him, her left hand near the heel of his right shoe on a cold iron rung.

She heard him say, "Amy Marks. You don't have to do that, dear." Moving his bulk slowly above her, he climbed the rest of the way onto the roof.

Rica followed, faster, almost scurrying. She had to know what was going on up there.

Amy Marks was standing at the far edge of the roof. She was barefoot and wearing a simple white blouse and a full blue skirt. Stack was about twenty feet away, facing her. Something about Amy's skirt, Rica thought, then realized it was the darkness and drape of the material. It was soaked, along with the white blouse that clung to her torso so that her small breasts and dark nipples were visible.

Rica moved slowly and smoothly to stand beside Stack. Amy's face in the soft reflected light was all downturned mouth and wide, anguished eyes. Like a mask. As the breeze shifted, a faint scent came to Rica. She recognized it and understood the wetness of Amy's skirt and blouse.

Amy had soaked her clothing with the accelerant she used to set her fires.

"You don't want to do anything rash, dear," Stack said gently. "We truly do understand. We're cops, like your loving husband was, and we want to help you, is all. You've nothing to fear from us."

"If you come closer," she said, "I'm going to jump."

"That will solve nothing. But you know that, don't you?"

"It's the only way to solve everything."

He decided to give her something to think about, a hint of absolution. "Myra Raven is still alive." *For a few more hours.*

"I'm not surprised. In fact, I'm glad. I didn't want to kill her, but she was starting to suspect me, I'm sure. Even after I gave her a threatening note I pretended came in the office mail. So I waited for her and followed her to the agency, hit her on the head, tied her up, then set her on fire. The night security guard phoned up to her office and kept asking over the answering machine for her to pick up, is there something wrong? I couldn't say anything to him. He knew me, knew my voice, and he would have known I sneaked into the building. I thought he might be on his cell phone, on the way up in the elevator."

"He was," Stack said. "He found her soon enough to save her life."

"That's good. Myra's a fine person. She did right by me."

"I don't think you know how near you are to the edge of the roof, dear," Stack told her in a concerned tone. A kind uncle. "I think you had best move a few steps toward us."

Instead Amy slipped her hand into her skirt pocket.

Rica tensed to raise her gun and fire. Knew Stack was ready, too. Had to be.

Not yet . . . not yet . . . be sure . . . it's forever . . .

Amy drew from the pocket a small object. Not a gun.

When she gripped it tightly in her fist and crooked her thumb over it, there was no doubt it was a cigarette lighter.

"I told you, don't come closer!" There was a note of pleading in her voice now.

But Stack did edge closer, drifting to the side at the same time, drawing Rica along as if by magnetism, hoping Amy wouldn't notice as he tried to soothe her with his words. "The plain truth is, we really do understand. Once a cop, or a cop's wife, it's that way always. We're all in the same family, dear, and when one of our own is in trouble, by God, we help our own. And now we want to help you. And we can, I swear to you."

Rica saw the change in Amy's expression. She no longer seemed trapped and terrified. Now the mask was serene. Rica knew what it meant. There were two ways down from the roof, and Amy had chosen one.

Spark, then flame appeared in Amy's hand that held the lighter, and she stared at the tiny orange-red dance with a kind of wonder, as if she'd just discovered fire.

"Amy!"

Stack had time to call her name only once before the flame jumped to her skirt and blouse, grew, and then greedily wrapped itself around her and consumed her as she whirled and leaped from the roof. One pale arm extended languidly, as if reaching for the moon, and the brilliance fell from sight.

Neither Stack nor Rica moved to look down.

Instead Rica glanced at Stack and saw the tears in his eyes, the clenching of his jaw and quiver of his lower lip. It was something she didn't like seeing.

Rica holstered her 9mm and crossed herself.

Stack was looking over at her now, smiling down at her

with an ineffable sadness. "Ah, the good Catholic again."
He reached out and softly touched her shoulder.

"It comes and goes," she said.

FORTY-EIGHT

July 2002

The wedding was small and nondenominational because the priest had explained to Rica that in the eyes of the church she was still married to her first husband. It made sense to Rica, and she knew there was no way around it, but she didn't much mind.

A chaplain from the Two-seven precinct performed the service. Mathers and Fagin were there, along with Sergeant Redd and the rest of the Eight-oh and Mobile Response. Rica actually sent an invitation to Myra Raven, who would have been there, but she was still hospitalized and undergoing skin grafts. The two women had gotten to know each other when Myra, herself under indictment, gave evidence that resulted in the indictment of the surviving co-op board extortionists. Myra's amazed doctors said she was a fighter the likes of which they'd never seen, a survivor who used adversity for fuel. She'd lost sight in one eye and would be permanently disfigured, but she would live and stand trial for real estate fraud. Stack figured she'd find a way to be acquitted, then maybe sue the prosecutor and win.

After the wedding there was a reception in an American

Legion hall, because Rica thought the best wedding receptions she'd ever been to were in American Legion halls. It sure wasn't ritzy, but it was just fine. It felt right. Rica felt married.

This time, she knew, it would take.

She and Stack went to Cancun for their honeymoon and had a great time. They stayed at a nice hotel, swam, had sex, ate a lot of shrimp. Neither of them got sick from the water. A success.

They had extended leave after their week in Cancun, so as soon as they got back to New York they started looking for somewhere to live that was roomier than either of their apartments. Since neither of them was particular, it didn't take long to find a place. Since neither of them had much in the way of possessions, it didn't take a lot of time or effort to move. They'd chosen an apartment on the Upper West Side. One on the third floor with a view of some treetops out the main bedroom window. They paid rent. Neither of them wanted to buy. It was too uncertain a world.

Stack thought it was too uncertain for them to have children.

Rica thought maybe it wasn't.

When they returned to their jobs, NYPD policy kicked in. Husbands and wives didn't work as partners, so Rica was transferred to Brooklyn South Homicide. Stack seemed okay with the arrangement, and Rica didn't mind.

It was all family.

More Books From Your Favorite Thriller Authors

More Nail-Biting Suspense From Your Favorite Thriller Authors